Praise for
House on Fire

"Evocative writing and wholly realized characters complement a multifaceted tale that's both harrowing and profound."

—*Kirkus Reviews*

"Bonnie Kistler captures the madness of losing a child with profound understanding in *House on Fire*. My anxiety rose with each page as I swung with the characters from hope to rage, and back again as I followed this family through the shattering aftereffects of a drunk-driving accident, but somehow Kistler manages to hold the reader's exploding heart safe as this gut-wrenching story unfolds. I lived inside this novel with every word."

—Randy Susan Meyers, bestselling author of
The Widow of Wall Street

"A nuanced and compelling story of a family in crisis. Kistler handles a tragedy and the questions that swirl around it with a depth that will take your breath away and have you asking yourself—what would I do? Outstanding!"

—Liz Fenton & Lisa Steinke, bestselling authors of
The Good Widow and *Girls' Night Out*

"Kistler has a clear mastery of the legal drama but also a deft touch with complicated family dynamics and the tightening noose of a trauma that refuses all efforts at a cut-and-dry solution."

—CrimeReads

"Relatable and thought-provoking . . . Readers who enjoyed Ian McEwan's *The Children Act* (2014) and especially Emily Giffin's *All We Ever Wanted* (2018) should be guided toward this absorbing read, which deftly examines the meaning and strength of family bonds and forgiveness. Kistler is a promising new voice in the legal-mystery world."

—*Booklist*

"Intensely emotional and instantly gripping, Bonnie Kistler's *House on Fire* is a masterfully written saga of family drama in the vein of Celeste Ng, Liane Moriarty, and Sally Hepworth . . . [Kistler] has a knack for putting life on the page, and the book is full of these tautly written and achingly relatable interactions . . . an instantly compelling and compulsively readable novel."

—Bookreporter.com

House on Fire

A Novel

BONNIE KISTLER

ATRIA PAPERBACK

New York   London   Toronto   Sydney   New Delhi

An Imprint of Simon & Schuster, Inc.
1230 Avenue of the Americas
New York, NY 10020

First Atria Paperback edition December 2019

ATRIA PAPERBACK and colophon are trademarks of Simon & Schuster, Inc.

For information about special discounts for bulk purchases, please contact Simon & Schuster Special Sales at 1-866-506-1949 or business@simonandschuster.com.

The Simon & Schuster Speakers Bureau can bring authors to your live event. For more information, or to book an event, contact the Simon & Schuster Speakers Bureau at 1-866-248-3049 or visit our website at www.simonspeakers.com.

Interior design by Alexis Minieri

Manufactured in the United States of America

1 3 5 7 9 10 8 6 4 2

Library of Congress Cataloging-in-Publication Data
Names: MacDougal, Bonnie, author.
Title: House on fire : a novel / Bonnie Kistler.
Description: First Atria Books hardcover edition. | New York : Atria Books, 2019.
Identifiers: LCCN 2018016333 (print) | LCCN 2018019931 (ebook) | ISBN 9781501198700 (eBook) | ISBN 9781501198687 (hardcover) | ISBN 9781501198694 (pbk.)
Subjects: LCSH: Domestic fiction. | GSAFD: Suspense fiction.
Classification: LCC PS3563.A2917 (ebook) | LCC PS3563.A2917 H68 2019 (print) | DDC 813/.54—dc23
LC record available at https://lccn.loc.gov/2018016333

ISBN 978-1-5011-9868-7
ISBN 978-1-5011-9869-4 (pbk)
ISBN 978-1-5011-9870-0 (ebook)

For my daughters

A liar's house is on fire, but no one believes him.

—Turkish proverb

"I prefer his lie to your truth," said the king to the vizier. "Your truth came from a heart bent upon mischief. His lie came from a good heart, and good has come of it."

—Sheikh Sa'Di Shirazi, *The Good Lie*

. . . to tell the truth, the whole truth and nothing but the truth.

—Testimonial oath sworn by witnesses in U.S. courts

Chapter One

A half hour before midnight the greatest day of Kip Conley's life came to an end.

The *day* would have ended regardless. It was the *greatest* part he expected to go on forever. That afternoon he got into his top-choice school; in thirty minutes he'd be eighteen and legal to do anything he wanted in the world except drink and run for Congress; meanwhile, the beer was flowing at Atwood's party and some excellent weed was circulating; and finally, the girl currently wriggling on his lap was glowing a steady green light at every intersection of her plush, pliable body.

"This is the greatest day of my life!" he shouted, and the girl preened, imagining herself to be the cause. The party was in full Tilt-A-Whirl swing throughout the Atwoods' well-appointed suburban home. Music streamed into the Jambox and funneled out through the family room to blast through the entire first floor and up both staircases. In the front hall, the overflow crowd wheezed in and out of the flanking rooms like the bellows on an anesthesia machine.

The better part of St. Alban High's senior class was there—not numerically but qualitatively, at least in the eyes of the people in attendance. They all got into someplace that week, and they were all in the mood to celebrate. They pogo-sticked to the beat, bottles to mouth and shoulder to sweaty shoulder. Taylor Swift was shaking it off on the Jambox, and the kids were shaking it off, too. Shaking off the weeks of mailbox-watching, the months of vocab drills and personal statement essays, the years of trying to shape themselves into every college's dream candidate. *Shake It Off. Shake It Off.* That song was every high school's anthem in the spring of 2015, and the same party was playing out in every affluent neighborhood across the country, everywhere there were seniors with acceptance letters and at least one set of parents out of town.

When the song ended, Ryan Atwood vaulted onto his mother's granite-topped kitchen island and muted the Jambox. "Here's to us!" he screamed with a bottle raised to his classmates. "And to bigger and better parties next year!"

The crowd roared its endorsement. Someone switched the music back on and the dancing resumed, but Atwood switched it off again and stopped all movement like a game of freeze tag. "But here's what I want to know," he yelled. "How the fuck did Conley get into Duke?"

Everyone laughed, no one louder than Kip. He leaned back, ready to revel in his roast.

"I mean, okay," Atwood said. "Maybe he had the scores, but what else? Sports? His only contribution to the soccer team was running the betting pool. Theater? He almost got kicked out of the drama club, remember? When he ad-libbed those new lines for Hamlet so he wouldn't be such a pussy? Community work? Volunteer activities? Zilch.

"So no good deeds but plenty of bad. There was that DUI on New Year's Eve. He lost his driver's license over that. But guess how he got here tonight?"

"He drove!" the chorus cheered and hooted.

"Then there was his arrest last year for retail theft."

"Hey, that was only catch-and-release," Kip protested. He was still laughing. There were times he could enjoy his bad-boy reputation, and this was one of them. A joint finally made it his way, and he took a hit and passed it on to the girl with a heavy-lidded grin.

"He has the thickest disciplinary file in the history of St. Alban High."

"Only because I submitted a twenty-page rebuttal to every allegation."

"Dude. You put a goat on the gymnasium roof."

"Ah," Kip said, basking. "Good times."

His classmates remembered it that way, too, and laughed their appreciation. "Well, whatever," Atwood said. "Here's to you, Conley. Congrats and all that shit."

Kip grabbed his empty off the end table and held it up in a salute, and Atwood thumbed the music back on and the dancing resumed.

The greatest thing about the greatest day of his life was that it would only get greater from here. In an hour or so, he'd pull the girl into an empty bedroom, and after she staggered downstairs and found a ride home, he'd flop over and fall asleep, and in the morning he'd wake up sober and sated, both feet firmly on the launch pad and ready for blastoff. Out of Podunk, Virginia, and off into the great wide world beyond. He'd rocket his way through college and grad school, do a couple years on Wall Street, a couple more in a think tank, then onward into politics. He felt like he'd scaled a mountain today, and from up here he could see the path ahead so clearly, a ribbon of all his bright promise unspooling before him.

But at 11:30 p.m., the best day of his life turned into his worst.

"Who's that?" the girl said, squirming upright on his lap.

He followed her line of sight across the room to a head of penny-bright curls bobbing through the herbal haze. His fourteen-year-old stepsister was pushing her way through the crowd and scanning their faces with desperate, darting eyes. She was too young for this party and not the type to crash. There was only one explanation for her presence here. "Oh, shit." He groaned and scrambled to his feet.

Chrissy turned her search in the other direction, and he followed, tracking the beacon of her hair through the kitchen to the front hall. She was wearing a rain slicker and barn boots over her pajamas and reflective cyclist cuffs wrapped around her calves. That gave him a particle of relief. If she rode her bike over here, it meant his father wasn't waiting—seething—in the driveway. He reached around a pair of grinding classmates to grab her by the shoulder.

She whirled. "Kip!"

"They're back?"

"On their way. Mom called from the road."

"Shit." He was supposed to have two more days of this furlough. "Why didn't you call?"

"I did!"

"Oh." He'd attributed the vibration in his lap to something else.

"There's still time, though. We can beat them home." She tugged on his sleeve. "Come on, hurry!"

He grabbed his jacket and raced her out the door.

Peter Conley was the kind of man who couldn't be a passenger. If he was in a vehicle, he had to be the one driving it. It took some time for Leigh to adjust to that. Her father wasn't that way, and neither was Ted. But she'd come to view this as one of the perks of her second marriage. She learned to use the time to work, or on rainy nights like tonight, to lean back and let the rhythmic swish of the wipers lull her to sleep.

But Peter liked to listen to the news as he drove, and tonight the news was too awful to sleep through. Another school shooting here. Another terrorist attack there. This wasn't the note she wanted to end their anniversary trip on. It was already bad enough they were leaving the resort two days early. They'd just clinked their champagne flutes in an anniversary toast—("The best five years of my life," he said. "Here's to fifty more," she said because love was greedy that way)—when the phone rang in her clutch. Parents of teenagers couldn't ignore phone calls, especially when they've left them home alone for the first time. But it wasn't the kids. It was Richard Lowry, calling from New York with the referral of a new client who could only meet Saturday morning. Could she be there?

Leigh couldn't ignore that either, not when her billings were down and tuitions were up. But this was their big anniversary getaway, and she'd worked so hard to make it perfect. As a matrimonial lawyer, not to mention a happily remarried divorcée, she knew that the secret to marital success was to work at it. Prioritize it. Treat your marriage as Job One. Two-thirds of all second marriages ended in divorce, but she was determined to beat those odds. She hated to let her work disrupt her efforts.

But Peter didn't mind. That afternoon Kip had called with the thrilling news about Duke, and Peter was happy to get home to celebrate. The kids would be asleep by the time they got in, but he was planning to take them out for a big diner breakfast in the morning.

The rain would end overnight, the radio told them. Sunny and high of sixty-five tomorrow. But then the broadcast looped back to the school shooting in Missouri, and Leigh couldn't take it anymore. "Want me to drive for a while?"

Peter shook his head. "I'm fine."

"You sure?" She trailed her fingertips along the length of his forearm. "I mean, you must be *exhausted*."

He laughed and gave her hand a squeeze. His golf game had been rained out at the resort, along with Leigh's trail ride and the mountain hike they'd planned. Instead, they had stayed in, dined on room service, and had as much sex as any couple approaching fifty could hope for. Not since their honeymoon had they been able to make love under a roof that didn't also shelter a houseful of sharp-eared adolescents. But now the kids were old enough to be on their own for a few days, long enough for Leigh and Peter to get away and throw off all their restraints. It was thrilling, albeit a little shocking sometimes, to hear what animal noises still lurked inside each other's skin.

"Oh!" she said as the memory struck. "We forgot to listen to the kids' mixtape."

"Mixtape?" Peter teased. "What year is this? 1985?"

"Hey, keep up, Grandpa. That's what the digital version is called, too. All the cool kids say it."

"Says the lady who still uses an iPod."

She laughed as she rooted in her bag. Chrissy had tucked Leigh's old iPod in there on their way out the door Wednesday night. *We downloaded some road songs for your road trip*, she said while Kip pretended to hide a smirk behind her.

Peter ceded the radio, and the first song began. After a few bars, Leigh recognized the intro to "Highway to Hell." "Ha-ha. Very funny," she said. But it wasn't the AC/DC original, and when the vocals came in, she realized it wasn't even a cover. "It's the kids!" she hooted and turned up the volume. She could make out all five voices on the track: the twins' booming basses, Kip veering from a theatrical tenor into a beatboxing rap, and there was Chrissy's strong clear soprano rising above the fray with Mia's whispery little voice piping in below. Leigh and Peter looked at each other and burst out laughing. The kids must have borrowed a karaoke machine, last month when Zack and Dylan were home on spring break, during a weekend when Peter had Mia so all five kids were together. A dozen songs followed—"King of the Road," "Life in the Fast Lane," "Get Outta My Dreams, Get Into My Car"—and Leigh laughed till she cried. "I can't believe they did this!"

Peter shook his head fondly. "What a goofball that kid is."

Leigh smiled. She could also see Kip's mad genius behind this stunt, but she knew it would have taken Chrissy's special powers to get everyone on board. Chrissy was the glue who held this family together. She loved everyone and everyone loved her, so almost by default they had to love one another.

The final song on the mix wasn't karaoke. It was just the kids singing, a cappella, "We Are Family," and that was when Leigh cried for real. Six years ago she felt like a dried husk—forty years old and suddenly single and financially strapped with three children to raise on her own. And now here she was, married to this good man, mother and stepmother to this amazing bunch of kids. Theirs was the most successfully blended family she'd ever encountered, in life or in work. Remarriage was the triumph of hope over experience, so the cynical saying went, but theirs really was a triumph, of luck and love and looking forward instead of back. *Blessed* wasn't exactly a word in her vocabulary, but there was no denying that some kind of fortune had smiled upon them and the new life they'd built together.

Her phone rang in her bag as the mixtape ended. It was after midnight, she couldn't imagine who— She shot Peter a questioning look as she pulled out her phone, and at the same moment, his rang, too. He answered it through the radio speaker as she pressed the answer button on hers.

"Mom!" Chrissy cried in her ear as Kip's "Um—Dad?" came out of the dashboard speaker.

Peter braked and pulled off to the shoulder of the highway, and they stared at each other as they received the same news in their separate calls. It seemed the kids weren't safe at home after all. They were at the police station.

Chapter Two

Peter was an easygoing man. He didn't fly off the handle or punch walls or smash furniture. Even when things went very wrong in his business—subcontractor no-shows, delivery delays, interest rate spikes—his anger was more of the slow burn variety. But slow burns could get pretty hot, and Peter's was searing by the time they reached the St. Alban police station. "How can somebody so smart be so goddam stupid?" he yelled.

Leigh knew how. Kip had been working so hard these last months, years really, perfecting his GPA, racking up his AP scores, acing the SATs—hours and hours cracking the books every day and somehow still expected to present the profile of a well-rounded, athletic, community-engaged young man. And he did it, he got into his dream school, and he must have felt like the top of his head was going to come off if he didn't do something stupid tonight. But she held her tongue. She'd learned to defer to Peter where his son was concerned. He needed to be in the driver's seat there, too.

St. Alban was a small town, barely more than a village, and most of its government functions were handled at the county level in Arwen. But it had its own small police department, headquartered on a tree-lined road in an old brick house that had been repurposed into the town administration building. The parking lot was nearly empty. Two police cruisers were out front, three cars in employee parking, and no one at all in Visitor Parking until they pulled in.

Chrissy was right inside the front door, hunched on a hard-slat bench in the corridor, her skin white as ash under the fluorescent ceiling panels. She jumped up and flew into her mother's arms. "Sweetie, are you all right?" Leigh held her back and ran her eyes up and down her slight frame. She was nearly as tall as Leigh but still pipe cleaner–thin. "Did you get hurt anywhere?"

"I'm fine. Mom, don't be mad at Kip!"

"I'm not—"

"Don't let Pete be mad, please!"

Peter was already ahead of them down the corridor, speaking in a low, tight voice to a uniformed officer. Another uniformed officer was at a desk in the bullpen behind them, peering at a screen and pecking with two fingers on the keyboard. Somewhere a printer whined, and a faint rumble of voices came from behind a closed door. Otherwise the building appeared to be deserted.

"Maybe you can help us out here," the man was saying to Peter when Leigh caught up. "Your son's not cooperating."

The officer was middle-aged, paunchy, with a broad, genial face. He looked like one of the dads Peter used to coach softball with, or one of his more reliable subcontractors, somebody he would have liked under different circumstances. But he was bristling at him now. "What do you mean, not cooperating?"

"He won't tell us where he got the alcohol."

"He was drunk?"

Leigh winced. Kip hadn't mentioned that in his phone call.

The cop shrugged. "He measured point-oh-five-five on the blood alcohol. But remember, it's zero tolerance under twenty-one, and he failed the field sobriety besides."

Peter's jaw clenched.

"Here's the thing," the cop said. "If there's an underage beer party in progress in our town tonight, we need to know where it is." He glanced at Chrissy, where she clung to Leigh's side. "We haven't questioned the young lady yet.

We were waiting for a parent to arrive, since she's a minor." He rapped on a door and turned the knob, and the voice inside stopped rumbling.

"Wait." Peter's tone was sharp. "You questioned my son without a parent present?"

Inside the room Kip sat staring a hole into the battered laminate surface of a small conference table. Across from him was another uniformed officer, this one a young woman with a stern mouth and her hair pulled back in a tight bun like a ballerina. She looked up peevishly at the interruption.

Kip didn't look up. He was a handsome boy, Leigh thought—of course he was; he looked like his dad—but where Peter's looks were a little rough around the edges, Kip's were buffed to a fine polish. If *GQ* put out a high school edition, he could have been its cover boy. He didn't look very polished now, though. His dark hair was usually gelled to perfection, but now it hung limp in a damp tangle over his narrow, flushed face. He wasn't as tall as Peter or as beefy as the twins, and he looked even smaller now as he slouched low in his chair.

"Mr. and Mrs. Conley are here, Officer Mateo," the softball-coach cop said. "Why don't you take the young lady and her mother across the hall, and I'll continue here with the boy and his father."

Ballerina Bun nodded and pushed back from the table.

"No, wait." Peter's voice swelled too loud in the tiny room. "What's the idea here? You had no right to question my son before I got here. And you drew his blood, too?"

"Okay, calm down, Mr. Conley—"

"Dad—" Kip began.

"Peter—"

"He's a minor, for God's sake! What kind of operation are you running here?"

"Dad—"

"Okay, Mr. Conley, I'm asking you to lower your voice."

"Our lawyer's on the way. Let's see what she has to say about your tactics."

"Dad!"

"What?!" Peter roared, wheeling on him.

Kip ducked his head. "I'm not," he mumbled.

"Not what?"

"A minor. It's tomorrow, Dad. I'm eighteen."

Leigh put her hand over her mouth. In all the excitement about Duke, they'd forgotten there was also Kip's birthday to celebrate. Despite the gift-wrapped set of golf clubs hidden in the attic, despite their Sunday night dinner reservations complete with cake and a kazoo band—despite all that, they'd forgotten that Saturday was his actual birthday. He was officially eighteen now, and the police had every right to question him on his own.

"Listen, come on," Softball Coach said. "Mr. Conley, have a seat and we'll talk this over. Diane, why don't you take the ladies—?" He pointed to the door, and Ballerina held out one stiff arm to herd Leigh and Chrissy into the corridor.

Another woman was swinging through the front door of the building. She was an imposing figure, tall and black, wearing stilettos and a thigh-high spangled dress under a chinchilla shrug. She spotted Leigh and headed her way in long-legged strides.

"Shelby!" Leigh reached up to embrace her. "Thank you so much for coming."

The taller woman turned to the ballerina cop. "Shelby Randolph, counsel for Christopher Conley." Her voice was refined, but her tone was a rough, demanding bark. "Where is my client? In here?" She brushed past the female officer. "Hi there, doll face," she whispered to Chrissy as she opened the door to the interview room.

"Hi, Aunt Shelby," Chrissy whispered back.

"End of interview," Shelby announced to the room. "Step outside, Sergeant." She looked back over her shoulder at Leigh. "I assume you're acting as counsel for your daughter?"

"Uh, yes." The formality of *your daughter* put Leigh on alert. "Yes, that's right."

"I suggest you advise her not to answer any questions at this time."

"Yes, right, of course."

Softball Coach came out of the interview room with his eyebrows raised at his colleague, who threw up her hands and walked away.

Leigh put her arm around her daughter and drew her back to the slatted bench in the corridor. Chrissy sat down beside her with her hands folded. She'd painted each of her nails a different color of polish. It looked like she'd emptied a bag of Skittles in her lap. Feel the rainbow, her fingertips said, but her face said something else.

"You sure you're all right, honey? Maybe we should go to the hospital and get you checked out."

"We barely hit that tree. Really, I'm fine."

She laid her cheek against Leigh's shoulder, and Leigh gave her a squeeze. She cherished each of her children, and she adored her stepchildren, too, but Chrissy always shined a special light. Her little fairy child, she used to call her. There was something magical about her from the moment she burst into the world with her startling cap of red ringlets. The color had faded a bit since then and she'd probably be a pale strawberry blonde by the time she was grown. But the magic would always be there, in her lively eyes and her quick smile and her heart as big as a house. And a good solid head on her shoulders, too. Even though Kip was nominally in charge this week, it was Chrissy they counted on to be the responsible one. Kip's lack of responsibility was in full evidence tonight.

"Aunt Shelby is so awesome," Chrissy said.

"She sure is."

"Was she like this in law school, too?"

"Always."

"I think she must have been at a party tonight."

"Hmm. I think so." Leigh looked closely at her daughter. "And I think Kip was, too?"

Chrissy looked up with a flood of tears in her eyes. "I'm sorry, Mom. I didn't want him to get into trouble."

"Where was it?"

"Ryan Atwood's house."

"He drove there, and you—what?—rode your bike over there to warn him?"

Chrissy nodded.

"In your pajamas. Five miles in the rain."

"I know, I'm sorry! I just thought—"

"Oh, honey." Leigh kissed the top of her curls. "You can't rescue people from their own bad decisions. This is Kip's problem, not yours."

"But, Mom, it really wasn't his fault! I mean, that dog ran out right in front of us. There was nothing we could do!"

"Honey." Leigh put a finger under Chrissy's chin and tilted up her pale face. "He went to a party we didn't know about. He drove the truck without permission and on a suspended license. And if all that wasn't bad enough, he drove after drinking. It *is* his fault, and Peter has every right to be angry. And you should have stayed out of it."

Tears swam in Chrissy's eyes. She hated there to be any kind of discord in their household. Leigh's divorce from Ted was louder and messier than it should have been, and ever since, all Chrissy wanted in the world was for everyone to please get along. "But we're a family, right?" she pleaded. "We look out for each other."

Leigh gazed at her fairy child. At home they had a pair of barn cats she'd dubbed Goodness and Mercy for the way they seemed to follow her all the days of her life. The same words came to her now. Goodness and mercy. "Yes, we do," she said finally. "But this is between Kip and his dad, okay? We have to stay out of it."

Working the room, Shelby called it, whether she was trying a jury case or negotiating a plea bargain or holding a press conference on the courthouse steps. Three rooms were in play tonight, and over the next hour, she worked all of them, stalking on her stilettos between the interview room where Peter and Kip remained sequestered, the bullpen where the officers huddled over their Styrofoam coffee cups, and the lobby where she gently shook Chrissy awake to ask her two questions. The first one Chrissy answered without hesitation. The party was at Ryan Atwood's, and she recited the address, too. Her loyalty was to Kip, not his friends, and if this was the cooperation the police were looking for, she was happy to supply it. But she couldn't answer Shelby's second question. She had no idea what time it was when they swerved off the road.

"If it was before midnight?" Leigh said. "Would that help? If he was still a juvenile?"

Shelby gave a noncommittal shrug and returned to the interview room. Soon after the third officer rose out of the bullpen, squared his hat on his head, and left the building, stopping only to confirm the Atwoods' address with Leigh.

Another thirty minutes passed before Shelby emerged again, but this time she had Peter and Kip in tow. Leigh caught Kip as he passed and pulled him into a hug. He was stiff in her arms, but he dropped his head briefly to her shoulder. "I'm sorry, Leigh," he mumbled.

"Don't worry," she whispered. "It'll be all right."

"Let's talk outside, shall we?" Shelby said and strode ahead of them through the door.

The rain had stopped, and the night air smelled of wet grass and crushed forsythia blossoms. Peter clicked the Volvo open, and Kip dove into the backseat. So did Chrissy. Only one other car remained in Visitor Parking, a red Corvette with a handsome young man lounging behind the wheel. Shelby flashed a hand at him—five more minutes—before she turned to Leigh. "Here's the deal. They got him on the BAC, so he's going to plead to baby DUI."

Baby DUI was the colloquial term for the zero tolerance law, the same one Kip broke last January. Adult DUI required a blood alcohol content of 0.08 percent, but for drivers under twenty-one, 0.02 percent was enough.

"But," she continued, "he won't be charged with reckless driving or driving impaired with a juvenile passenger or any of the other dozen add-ons they could have charged him with if he were an adult."

Leigh let out her breath. "So it did happen before midnight."

"Who knows? The neighbor's nine-one-one call came in at 12:06 a.m. How long did it take him to stumble out of bed and turn on the lights and pick up the phone? Could have been five minutes, could have been ten. But it's close enough that they're not going to bother piling on charges only to see them end up in juvenile court. Subject to the prosecutor's review on Monday." Shelby smirked at Leigh. "You remember him? Commonwealth's Attorney Boyd Harrison?"

"Oh." Leigh remembered him only too well. He was a little martinet of a man, a stickler for rules and schedules who tried to impose the same military-style discipline on his family as he did on his office staff.

"Don't worry," Shelby said. "He won't have any clue that defendant Christopher Conley and passenger Christine Porter have any connection to Attorney Leigh Huyett."

"What's this?" Peter's gaze snapped between them. "Who's Harrison to you?"

"Didn't she ever tell you?" Shelby said. "Leigh represented his wife in their divorce. And really took him to the cleaners."

Leigh pursed her lips. "It was a fair and equitable settlement."

"And he's holding a grudge?"

She shrugged. They always seemed to, no matter how fair the settlement.

"It doesn't matter," Shelby said. "The name Huyett doesn't appear anywhere in the police report. Unless you think Harrison's been keeping tabs on you all these years—"

"Of course not."

"Then there's nothing to worry about. He'll rubber-stamp the cop's recommendation, and your boy'll get another one-year suspension of his driver's license plus a five-hundred-dollar fine."

"As opposed to—?"

"Same suspension, bigger fine, plus up to a year in jail."

"Oh, God," Leigh said as Peter clenched his jaw and looked away.

"Try not to worry." Shelby opened the passenger door of the Corvette. "Even Hardass Harrison isn't going to throw the book at a nice white boy. But I'll touch base on Monday and let you know for sure." She swung her long legs into the car and leaned over to receive the young man's kiss before she pulled the door shut.

Peter didn't speak for a full five minutes. No one did, and the tension was so tight inside the car it was almost a relief when he finally lit into Kip. How could he be so stupid. There goes his summer internship, and what if this gets back to Duke, he could lose his place, his scholarship for sure. And after the last time, he promised, he *promised*.

Chrissy sniffled through his tirade from her corner of the backseat, but when Peter yelled that Kip couldn't ever be trusted again, her sob finally broke out. "Stop! Stop it!" she cried. "Don't yell at him! It wasn't his fault!"

"Shut up! You idiot!" Kip hissed.

"Hey!" Leigh snapped. Her soft spot for Kip only went so deep. She wouldn't allow him to take this out on Chrissy.

"Sorry," Kip muttered, and that was the last word anyone spoke as they drove on over the dark and empty roads.

Hampshire County was technically part of the Washington metro area, but there was still a lot of open country in this part of Northern Virginia. Patches of woods lined the narrow roads, and acres of rolling pastures lay behind post-and-board fences. These were the vestiges of old plantations and gentleman farms where rich people used to dress up in nineteenth-century clothes and ride to the hounds and pretend it was a sport instead of a costume party. Some of those old estates still blanketed these hillsides; the rest had been carved up into subdivisions where more ordinary people slept between their long commutes in and out of the District. Leigh grew up in one of the earliest of those subdivisions and later became one of those commuters, willing to endure two hours in the car every day, and sometimes even more, all for the sake of a little taste of country life at either end of it.

Hollow Road was the five-mile stretch of blacktop where Peter's truck would still be foundering in the ditch. It wasn't a through road to anywhere: it cut in off the highway at one end and cut back in again a few miles later, so there was no reason for anyone to drive it unless they lived there, or like Peter and his crew, worked there. Or unless, like Kip, they were hoping to avoid the police patrols out on the highway. It ran along a twisting creek, and all the houses on that side of the road had a little bridge at the end of the driveway, like moat crossings to a castle. On the other side of the road sprawled some old farms and estates, including the site of Peter's current construction project—a custom home three stories tall perched at the top of a hill. Hollow House, Leigh had dubbed it, and its empty frame loomed darkly as they drove past.

Peter drove silently through another mile of darkness until Kip mumbled from the backseat, "Up there on the left."

As the truck took shape in the shine of the headlights, Leigh felt a rush of relief. It wasn't overturned or smashed up or wrapped around the proverbial tree. It was upright on all four wheels in the ditch and only nosing up against the tree trunk, like a horse nuzzling for a sugar cube. Fifty feet away was a driveway that ran over one of those little moat bridges. The house was dark now, but it was probably where the neighbor lived who had called 911.

Peter parked and jabbed a finger at Kip over the seat back. "You. With me."

Their doors swung open at the same time, and Leigh got out, too, to circle around to the driver's side of the car. Peter caught her as they passed in the headlights. "Sorry about this," he muttered.

She pressed her cheek against his chest. "It'll be all right," she said. "Don't worry."

"You go on home and go to bed. This may take a while."

"I should wait here. What if you get stuck?"

"Hey, if there's anything a builder knows, it's how to drive through mud. Go on home. Chrissy needs to get to bed. You, too. You have that meeting tomorrow."

She nodded and stretched up to kiss him. His lips were tight against hers, and when she tilted her head back, his eyes were still grim in the glare of the headlights. "Peter. It'll be okay. This is only a bump in the road, right?"

He chuffed a laugh and kissed her again, harder, even though the kids were watching, Chrissy from the backseat of the car, and Kip from the cab of the truck. "I love you," he said.

She smiled. "Always and everywhere."

They headed their separate ways, she to the car and he to the truck, she to her child and he to his.

Chapter Three

Pete Conley kept a file open and running in his head, like lines of computer text scrolling through the background screen of his thoughts. All his worries, digitized. A punch list of everything he needed to take care of and everything that would go wrong if he didn't. Deadlines to meet, bills to pay, permits to get, inspections to pass.

Early Saturday morning he woke to some new entries lighting up the screen. How much was Leigh's friend going to charge for her services last night? What if Duke found out about this? Did they do criminal background checks after the acceptance letters went out? For sure the state would, which probably meant Kip would lose his summer internship with the governor's office.

Other, deeper worries scrolled on the back screen. Was this just teenaged hijinks, or did his son really have a drinking problem? This was twice now, and those were only the times he got caught. Pete's father was an alcoholic—at least that was the term they used to explain away the years of unemployment and abuse before he finally took off. Some people thought there was a gene for that, and while Pete was never more than a beer-a-day kind of guy, it could have skipped a generation and landed on Kip.

But as tempting as it was to blame the old man for this, what if it was more nurture than nature? Because then it would be Pete's fault.

Like most divorced fathers, he carried a lot of guilt for moving out on his kids. Not that he had much choice—Gary was practically waiting in the driveway with his suitcases to move in—but it was hard on them. Both of them, but especially a boy on the edge of puberty. The bad behavior started immediately—he was acting out at school, talking back at home, and waging enough open warfare against Gary that Karen finally gave up and let Pete have primary custody. For the next year it was only the two of them in a two-room apartment, eating pizza and watching sports and playing video games. Not a bad life for a twelve-year-old, but at the end of the year, Pete moved him again, into Leigh's house. He had to change schools twice in two years, and this time he even had to change his name. It was too confusing to have both a Chris and a Chrissy under one roof, so his little-boy nickname was resurrected and he was Kip again.

In the space of only two years the boy went from a basic nuclear family of two parents/two kids, to bachelor life with a single dad, to this current chaotic mash-up of two stepparents and two different sets of step-siblings, not to mention the step-grandparents and step-aunts and -uncles and -cousins. And somehow he was expected to get along with all of them. Which was kind of unfair, Pete had to admit, considering what started this whole thing was that none of the original parents could get along with each other.

Another worry glowed on his digital screen, and it was the one lying beside him with her auburn hair fanned out on the pillow. Nothing like this had ever happened to Leigh or anyone in her family. She was an Ivy League–educated lawyer, well brought up by good and loving parents who took her to church and bought her a horse and taught her to write thank-you notes. While Pete worked construction, paid room and board to his mother from the time he was sixteen, and ended six years of night school four credits shy of a degree in architecture. There was no question he was punching above his weight when he married her, even if she refused to acknowledge it. *That's what blended means*, she insisted. *We're all the same now*. He didn't believe that for a minute, but at least he hoped she might raise him up. Not that he'd drag her down.

The screen was scrolling too fast for him to get back to sleep. He slipped from their bed and dressed in the dark and took the back stairs down to the kitchen. This was the remodel project that first brought him here. It was a big, heart-of-the-home room with all the trendy finishes and fixtures, but lots of cozy touches, too, like the raised hearth fireplace and the window seat tucked between the bookcases. The house was originally an old Foursquare, a tenant farmhouse to a long-gone estate, but over the decades it had been extensively expanded and remodeled. Clapboard siding was changed to fieldstone and stucco, the tin roof replaced with cedar shakes, an addition built out the back and wings tacked on either side. The result was this crazy patchwork of a house. Pete made over the front facade a few years ago so the outside looked right, but inside nothing quite lined up. The vaulted ceiling in the front hall led to a couple of boxy, low-ceilinged parlors, down two steps to a vaulted family room and up two different staircases to the bedrooms. The layout was so confusing that Kip was always making the wrong turn when they first moved in. Little Lost Boy, Zack and Dylan used to tease him until Leigh made them stop.

The most recent addition was this one, housing the new kitchen downstairs and the master suite up. The idea was Ted's, but he took off even before the footings were poured and left Leigh to manage on her own from there, with both the financing and the design. She turned out quick rough sketches of what she wanted, and Pete did his best to build it for her. He was already falling for her by then, this beautiful brave woman getting on with her life, working hard all week and laughing and playing with her kids all weekend. He never would have guessed she was hurting if he hadn't walked in on her crying one day. It was a mortifying moment for both of them, except it was also the moment that changed everything in their relationship.

Shepherd jumped down off the window seat and wriggled a good morning, and Pete filled his bowls and scratched behind his ears while he gobbled and slurped his breakfast. He was a border collie they got as a pup early in their marriage—an *ours* to go with the *yours* and *mine*. Pete started a pot of coffee and went outside, and Shep abandoned his half-devoured breakfast to trot along after him to the little two-stall barn at the back of the property. Inside were Romeo, Chrissy's big dark bay, and Licorice, her old black pony. Licorice was supposed to be Mia's now, but his little girl was still too scared of horses to even venture into the barn.

The horses nickered and sighed and buzzed their lips as he came in, and he gave them grain and water and turned them out into the pasture before he mucked out their stalls. These were Chrissy's morning chores, but she'd had a late night last night and he wanted her to sleep in. Not that she wasn't in trouble, too. She had no business riding her bike out on those dark, rainy roads. She could have gotten sideswiped in the dark, or snatched by some pervert. And no matter how good her intentions were, her rescue mission only made the situation worse. It turned out Kip was planning to spend the night at his friend's house. If Chrissy hadn't gone to warn him, there would have been no accident and no arrest. He'd still be in a shitload of trouble, but only with his father—not with the whole goddam Commonwealth of Virginia.

Back inside, the coffee was done, and Pete poured one to go and headed out to the truck. The front bumper was dented, and he scowled at it a minute before he wrenched his door open. Shep vaulted in around him and took his seat at shotgun as usual. Anytime a vehicle left their driveway, the dog insisted on being in it. Border collies were bred to perform a single job—keep the flock together no matter what—and Shep seemed agitated when his human flock scattered every morning. Riding along was his best hope of getting everyone back together at the end of the day.

The radio switched on with the engine. The headlines this morning were the same as last night's: the terrorist attack in Kenya and the school shooting in Missouri. Both events were already indexed and added to Pete's digital screen of things to worry about. *You don't have to keep watch on the whole world,* Leigh liked to tease him, but he kind of felt like he did. It was his job to keep this family safe.

That lesson had been permanently tattooed on him back when he was a new father and the Beltway Sniper was on his rampage in the Washington Metro area, picking off random targets at gas stations and parking lots from a distant hilltop perch. Karen had just miscarried their second child and was even more fearful than usual, and for the three weeks of the siege she refused to exit the house, leaving Pete to do the grocery shopping and drive

Kip to and from preschool every day. He remembered peering through the windshield as he drove, scanning the surrounding summits for any glint of light that might be the reflection off a gun barrel. He remembered how careful he was to shield Kip with his own body as he lifted him in and out of the car and the tremendous relief he felt after he'd safely delivered him into school. They caught the guy, finally—two guys, as it turned out—but Pete never really got over it. That sense of danger looming in on his family—it never went away, and neither did the imperative that he be alert for it and ward it off however he could. That would always be Job One for Pete.

The broadcast had more on the shooter in Missouri. A disaffected youth, they called him. Pete had his own disaffected youth to worry about today. He had no idea how to punish an eighteen-year-old. Theoretically the kid was an adult now, though what a joke that was. He had no more sense than a twelve-year-old. A good talking-to wasn't going to do the job. They'd talked and talked after he was arrested on New Year's, and Kip promised it would never happen again. Yet here they were. Grounding wouldn't work either. He'd been de facto grounded ever since his license was lifted in January, and look how well that went. If there was anything else on the menu of disciplinary measures for so-called adults, Pete didn't know what it was.

He turned onto Hollow Road, and as he drove past the scene of last night's crime, a yellow dog came streaking down the driveway to warn him off. It yapped furiously until Pete was past the property line, then it barked a final self-satisfied woof—*showed you!*—and trotted back to the house. He wondered if that was the same dog that made Kip drive off the road last night. Which was another thing that made him fume. Kip knew he shouldn't swerve to avoid anything smaller than a deer. Pete drummed that lesson into all three boys when he taught them to drive. They might feel sad if the squirrel died, he told them, but their parents would feel a hell of a lot worse if they ended up in a wheelchair. The boys all understood and accepted the rule. Chrissy was the only one who ever argued the point. *There must be some way where nobody gets hurts*, she insisted during their off-road lessons. It was lucky they had two more years before he had to worry about her softhearted driving on real roads. Kip, though—he said he got it, but it looked like he lied about that, too. He took a swerve on a dark, rain-slick road and ended up in that ditch, and it was a miracle neither of them got hurt.

It was five miles from home to the job site, and another two minutes brought him there. *Hollow House*, Leigh called it, but it wasn't going to be hollow much longer. The roofing was nearly complete, and as soon as the place was dried in, the electrical and HVAC subs could get in there and run the wiring and ductwork. Finally. The winter weather had put them a month behind schedule, which meant the Millers' progress payments were also a month behind. Money was always tight in this business; lately it was starting to squeeze hard.

Pete was paying the crew overtime to work on Saturdays, but they weren't due until eight, so he was surprised to see a car in the driveway, and even more surprised when he saw it was Drew Miller's silver Porsche. He pulled alongside. The driveway wasn't a driveway yet, only a rough-graded road spread with a little gravel to keep the mud down. None too successfully after last night's rain. The Porsche was mud-splattered up to its door handles.

Drew was nowhere in sight, but Yana was there, perched on the hood of the car and wearing her perpetually unfocused gaze. "Morning," Pete called as he swung out of the truck and Shepherd jumped out after him. "What brings you here today?"

Yana shrugged her bony shoulders. She was a strange-looking woman, tall and too thin and with eyes so far apart he was reminded of a rabbit or some other creature of prey. A "swanling," Leigh called her, because with one turn of her head, one trick of the light, Yana went from ugly duckling to beautiful swan. She was Drew Miller's Russian bride, but not of the mail-order variety. She was a famous fashion model, which Drew never missed an opportunity to mention. *My wife, she used to be a super-model,* was the way he introduced her. Or *I stole her off the runway.* She was twenty years younger and acquired only recently. Miller ran a hedge fund, and according to the newspapers he was having a run of incredible good fortune. *Midas Miller,* Leigh called him, or sometimes simply *King.*

"Drew inside?"

Yana lifted her narrow chin, and he followed her line of sight all the way up the three stories of the house. There was Miller, a chubby fifty-year-old balancing himself on the highest peak of the roof.

"Jesus!" Pete sprinted around to the back of the building with Shep at his heels. An extension ladder rested against the eave of the lower roof, and another reached from there to the upper roof. "Drew!" he hollered. "Come on down. It's not safe up there." He scrambled up the ladder with his digital screen lighting up with new alarms over liability and insurance coverage. Miller was sitting with his legs splayed over the peak and a pair of binoculars at his face. "Drew, you need to get down. The roofers wear spikes when they're up there." Miller was wearing a pair of slick-soled Italian loafers.

"Hold on a minute. Lemme get some focus here."

He was aiming the binoculars at the neighboring property, a grand old estate that changed hands shortly after he bought this lot. The new owner promptly erected a ten-foot wall around the entire property and a pair of enormous steel gates at the entrance. The Hermitage was the snarky name Kip coined for the place, which Leigh found so clever that she'd adopted the term, too, and with the same pretentious pronunciation. *Hermit-taaj*. But Pete didn't do snark. Nothing wrong with a man enjoying his privacy, he said.

"Who are these fuckers?" Miller snarled. "Where do they get off building that wall?"

Lately he was obsessed with trying to learn the identity of his neighbor-to-be. He paid his lawyer to dig through the property records, but all they showed was a chain of holding companies, the final one chartered in the Caymans. He stopped repeatedly at the gates, but no one ever answered the buzzer on the security panel. Pete was on-site seven days a week, but he had no better intelligence. The place was pretty well secluded even from this rooftop vantage, especially now that the trees were in leaf and formed a dense green canopy over the property.

Miller lowered the binoculars with a scowl. "Well, if I can't see into their place, they sure as hell won't see into mine. I want a ten-foot wall, too. Or, no, make it twelve, all the way around."

"Can't do it, Drew. The zoning doesn't allow anything higher than six."

"Then how the fuck did they get theirs?"

Pete explained that there'd been a temporary lapse in the zoning code, and the owners must have hurried in and gotten their permit before the code was reinstated.

"What, like they got a team of lawyers standing by, waiting for loopholes to open? Who the fuck are these people?"

"They like their privacy, that's all. Which means they won't disturb yours."

Miller wasn't placated. He cursed and snapped the whole time Pete was steering him down the ladders, and when he landed with a wobble at the bottom, he let out a string of obscenities. "This isn't over," he vowed.

One more line of text scrolled down Pete's screen of worries: Miller might try to back out of the contract altogether. He didn't know if he could get away with it, but one thing he knew for sure. His business would be ruined if he did.

Yana was still perched on the hood of the car, and as Drew stomped to the driver's side and slammed his door she unfolded her flamingo legs and got into the passenger seat without a word.

Chapter Four

Leigh dressed that morning in her standard first-meeting-with-a-client ensemble—dark suit and pearls—and started down to the kitchen with her heels clicking sharply on the back stairs. But halfway down she slipped out of the heels and turned back and crept down the hall to the children's rooms. It was silly, of course they'd be in their beds, but still she pressed an ear against Chrissy's door until she heard the slow, steady rhythm of her sleep-breathing. Then she stole across the hall and did the same at Kip's door. No sleep-breathing there, but she could hear the quick, steady rhythm of his fingers tapping on a keypad. Not asleep, but at least where he was supposed to be. Both of them, safe in their own rooms.

Downstairs in the kitchen she found a fresh pot of coffee and a note from Peter. *Gone to the site.* Obviously there would be no big breakfast celebration today. But he signed it with a string of *x*'s and *o*'s that gave her hope that his good mood would return. Maybe she could switch their dinner reservations to tonight. A noisy restaurant, a sparkly cake, a kazoo band—surely that would help ease the tension. On Monday they'd hear from Shelby that baby DUI would be the only charge and the tension would be gone for good.

She left her own note, reminding the kids of her meeting, and headed for the garage. The radio came on with the engine, still tuned to one of

Peter's news channels. She switched to a music station and backed out into
the morning sunshine.

And instantly slammed on the brakes as a girl sprang up behind
the car.

Leigh's heart clutched. "Jenna!" Recognizing the girl only barely tem-
pered her fright. She jumped out of the car. "Jenna! What are you doing?
I could've run over you!"

The girl's hands went defiantly to her hips. Her own car was behind
her in the driveway, and like Leigh's, the engine was running and the door
flung open. She was barely dressed, wearing only a jacket over her pajamas. The jacket didn't close and the pajama top didn't meet up with the
pajama bottom, exposing six inches of swollen belly. "You need to get me
a restraining order," she shouted. "Like, today!"

"Okay, now let's calm down." Leigh put an arm around her shoulders—
not her standard behavior with clients, but this one was the daughter of
an old friend, and she'd known her since infancy. "Take a deep breath and
tell me what happened."

"He's stalking me, that's what!" Jenna shook her off, wild-eyed. "I
knew he would, and last night he was there, lurking right outside my
window!"

"Hunter?" Such behavior wasn't unheard of in divorcing husbands,
but Leigh couldn't quite picture the tech billionaire crawling through his
in-laws' rhododendrons.

"Him or one of his goons."

"You didn't see him, then."

Jenna tossed her head, but her mouth was trembling. "I heard him!
Or more like, I felt him." Below the too-short pajama top, her navel pro-
truded like a pop-up timer announcing the turkey was done. The baby
wasn't done yet, though. She was only five months along. "It was like this
disturbance out there, you know? Like electricity buzzing through the air.
He gives it off, that vibe. I used to feel it all the time whenever he was
close. I used to think it was exciting, you know? But now? It's like this evil
force in the universe. It totally freaked me out! You need to get the judge
to issue a restraining order. Today!"

Leigh tried again to put a soothing arm around her. Jenna wasn't always this high-strung, and it was tempting to blame the pregnancy hormones for the transformation, but that was Hunter Beck's excuse (*We had the perfect marriage*, he told the judge, *until the hormones made her crazy*), so Leigh was more inclined to blame Hunter. "Did you call the police?"

Jenna shook her off again. "What's the use? They won't believe me. Even my own parents don't believe me!"

Her parents lived on Hollow Road, a half mile from Peter's job site, on a farm they operated as a nonprofit retirement facility for aging horses. Jenna grew up there, a pretty girl who'd enjoyed all the conventional successes in school—cheerleader, homecoming queen, sorority president. After college she went to New York and took a low-level job in a high-tech company where she made the conventional mistake of sleeping with her boss. A rite of passage, some would say, that would have left her older, wiser, and working somewhere else—except that her boss then made the unconventional move of marrying her. Less than a year later she was here, half-dressed and hysterical in Leigh's driveway.

"I understand," Leigh said. "But we need to prove he was there. There has to be some actual violence or threat of violence before you can get a protective order."

"But the judge likes me. I know he does! He took my side on every one of Hunter's stupid motions."

After she fled their marriage, Beck filed a bizarre, grandstanding lawsuit demanding the right to attend all of her prenatal checks, access to the obstetrical records, and regular visitation with his unborn child so it could hear his voice in utero. Leigh got the case dismissed—not because the judge liked Jenna better, but only because the law was clear that a woman's body was her own and a father had no rights until the child was actually born.

But Hunter Beck wasn't a typical father. He was a man unaccustomed to hearing the word *no*, and he would never accept defeat. He held a press conference on the courthouse steps decrying the court's undermining of the sacred bond between father and child. His wife would return to him, he assured the reporters; their marriage would be fine. All he wanted in the meantime were the same rights that every other expectant father enjoyed. The judge's ruling meant this precious time would be lost to him forever. He filed an appeal, too, which was even more grandstanding: by the time the upper court heard the case, the baby would be born and a whole new set of rules would apply.

"It wouldn't necessarily be the same judge," Leigh said. "And no matter who it is, he can't issue a protective order unless there's been violence or a threat of violence."

For a moment Jenna stared blankly. Then her wild eyes squeezed shut, her lovely complexion erupted in mottled red patches, and she shrieked, "By then it's already too late!" and burst into furious tears.

"Jenna, honey—"

A third vehicle rattled into the driveway, and Leigh was relieved to see the Dietrichs' old farm truck. Carrie jumped down from behind the wheel, a faded blonde with a hard-muscled body clad in denim from collar to cuff. "Jenna, my God, look at you!" she said, charging up to her daughter. "Not even dressed and bothering Leigh at this hour!" She took the girl by the arm as her husband, Fred, climbed out the other side of the truck cab. "Come on now, let's get you home before you catch cold. Out here in this damp with practically nothing on."

Jenna flailed for a bit but there was no vigor in it, and she didn't resist as her parents hoisted her into their truck. Carrie looked at Leigh and mouthed *Sorry* as Fred headed for Jenna's car. He was a stoop-shouldered man in glasses and a gray cardigan, a gentle soul Leigh always thought, but he was scowling ferociously now. "You didn't hear anything?" she asked him.

He shook his head. "No footprints either. With all that rain yesterday, there'd have to be some kind of tracks." His mouth pulled tight. "That son of a bitch did some number on her. I don't know what."

Nobody did. Leigh had questioned Jenna about physical abuse or any other fault grounds that would have allowed her to file for divorce without waiting out the year's separation, but Jenna refused to answer. "Try not to worry," Leigh said to Fred. "She'll be herself again when this is all over."

He sank behind the wheel of Jenna's car. "You know the worst of it?

We were thrilled when they got married. It was like our girl won the lottery. Like she was crowned Miss America." He looked up at Leigh with bleak eyes. "Some parents we turned out to be."

"No, Fred—"

He shook off her attempt to reassure him and slammed the door and followed his broken family as they clattered down the road.

Leigh's meeting this morning was in an odd venue—the Saks Fifth Avenue store in Tysons Galleria—and at an odd time, since the mall wouldn't be open for another hour. Nevertheless, a well-dressed young woman was waiting outside the main entrance to greet her as she pulled up. "Leigh Huyett?" she asked through the car window. ASHLEY GREGG, her name tag read, PERSONAL SHOPPING CONSULTANT. She placed a parking permit on the dash and pointed Leigh into a towaway zone next to the entrance. She used a security card to unlock the door and led the way through a cool array of glass-encased cosmetics and perfumes until they reached a private elevator at the back.

Upstairs Leigh followed her past racks of beautiful clothes and around headless mannequins draped in exquisite fabrics and finally into a room lined with three-way mirrors and furnished with divans upholstered in a pale mauve silk. It was the designer wear salon, a place Leigh had only ever dreamed of visiting. A silver tea service gleamed on a glass-topped table next to a plate of berry-studded biscotti. "Please help yourself," the young woman said as she took her leave. "The sheikha should be here shortly."

Sheikha? Leigh's eyes opened wide in twelve different mirrors around the room. Richard Lowry hadn't mentioned that when he called with the referral. He said only that she was the wife of a wealthy Middle Easterner. He received the referral from a solicitor in London who was relaying it from his correspondent counsel in Dubai. Richard received many such referrals—he was internationally known as the dean of U.S. matrimonial law—but divorces were intensely local affairs, which meant he usually served as a kind of switching station to refer the matter out again. When he learned of the Washington locus for this case, he thought of Leigh. He remembered a journal article she'd written a few years ago dealing with the intersection of religious law with U.S. divorce law—specifically whether the Jewish ketubah and the Islamic *mahr* could be viewed as enforceable prenuptial agreements. That would be the key issue in this case, he told her. That article contained the sum and substance of Leigh's knowledge of Islamic matrimonial customs, but she was intrigued by this new case. A wealthy client combined with challenging legal issues was at the top of every lawyer's wish list.

Her phone beeped as she opened her briefcase, and she frowned when she saw Kip's name glowing on the screen. She knew why he was calling—to lobby for her support in this fracas with his father. He'd make her the first stop on his comeback tour. Loosen her up with his patented Kip Conley charm, and let her do all the heavy lifting with his dad. Leigh had a real soft spot for Kip—he was smart and lively and she loved how he made her laugh—but he could be manipulative. Christopher Con Man, she called him whenever she caught him running another scam. She often joked that he was either headed for two terms in the White House or one long term in the penitentiary. But this was no joke. She mustn't let him manipulate her into taking sides against Peter. She turned the phone off and put it away.

She took out the checklist she'd developed for initial client interviews in cases like this. Matrimonial law was all she'd done for most of her career, though not by choice. She started her career as a litigator with dreams of trying the big corporate cases: IBM, Microsoft, Pennzoil versus Texaco. But when her first baby turned out to be twins, she quickly got mommy-tracked at the firm. The big cases were all-consuming, and the wise old men who ran the management committee didn't believe she could handle them and motherhood, too. They shunted her off to the family law department, and she didn't have the energy to fight back, which probably meant the old men were right after all. She made the best of it, though. Earned a pretty good living and built a pretty good reputation. Good enough at least to land her this referral today.

The door to the salon opened, and a Middle Eastern man in a dark suit entered and swiftly surveyed the room. He looked like a Secret Service agent except without the sunglasses and coiled wire at his ear. He stepped back with a bow, and into the room swept a figure swathed in black silk from head to foot. Nothing of her was visible but her eyes behind a gauze-veiled slit in her niqab. She murmured something to the man, and he backed out of the room and closed the door.

Leigh rose to her feet. "Good morning."

The woman didn't speak as she glided across the floor to the mirrors and slowly began to remove her wrappings. They came off in a spiral, a whisper of tissue-soft silk that drifted slowly to her feet. Underneath was a stylish figure wearing a St. John suit in a bright coral pink. She turned, a beautiful woman on the bright side of forty with a chic layered haircut and eyes like black coffee. "I must apologize for the cloak-and-dagger," she said. At the word *cloak*, she cast a look down at her abaya where it lay puddled on the floor.

"How do you do—sheikha?" Leigh said uncertainly. "I'm Leigh Huyett."

"Please. You must call me Devra." The woman set what looked like a genuine Birkin bag on the floor beside the divan and sat down with an elegant cross of her legs. She nodded for Leigh to sit as well. "You come highly recommended. I'm told you specialize in divorce cases?"

"Yes. Are you contemplating divorce?"

"Every moment of every day."

She pronounced the words like a death sentence. Leigh had represented a lot of distraught wives and a lot of angry, vindictive wives, too, but there was something peculiarly desolate in the sheikha's tone.

"How may I help?"

The woman poured herself a cup of tea and took a delicate sip. "I wish to understand what my rights would be should I seek a divorce in your American courts. Whether it is even possible for me to seek a divorce."

"So long as you meet the residency requirements, of course it's possible."

"In my home country, it is not. Under sharia law, I have no right to divorce my husband absent his consent."

"Which you don't believe he would grant?"

The woman let out a mirthless laugh. "Never."

"May I ask how long you've been living in this country?"

"A little more than one year."

"I would have thought much longer. Your accent is flawless." Leigh would have guessed that most highborn Middle Easterners had English accents, but the sheikha's was distinctly American.

"My mother was an American. Which makes me an American, too, I suppose. But I never lived here until my husband brought us over last year."

Leigh picked up her intake form. "May I have your address?"

"No."

Her head came up. "Excuse me?"

"I'm afraid I cannot disclose my address at this time. Or, indeed, my true name. I do apologize for the secrecy, but there are—circumstances."

"Sheikha—Devra—you do understand our discussions here today are confidential? Even if you decide not to retain me, I can't disclose anything you tell me."

Devra shook her head. "In our next meeting perhaps."

Leigh couldn't proceed on this basis. She couldn't advise this woman of her rights until she knew where she lived, because each jurisdiction's laws were different, and she couldn't represent her at all until she knew her name. Whenever she took on a new client, she had to first confirm there was no conflict of interest with any other client her firm represented, and the only way to do it was to run the full legal name through their database.

"In that case." She slid her useless checklist back in her briefcase.

"Oh, but—"

"We'll discuss these matters on a hypothetical basis, shall we?"

The sheikha sank back against the divan cushions. "Thank you, yes."

"I practice in the courts of Virginia, Maryland, and the District of Columbia. May I assume you reside in one of those three jurisdictions?"

"You may."

Leigh briefly summarized the grounds for divorce under Virginia and Maryland law: no-fault if the parties were separated for at least one year; otherwise the petitioning spouse had to prove one of the enumerated fault grounds. The District of Columbia was strictly no-fault, but the spouses had to be separated for at least six months, or separated from bed and board for at least one year.

"What does this mean? Separated from bed and board?"

"Living under the same roof but not as a married couple. Essentially, not having sexual relations."

"I see. This is true also in Maryland and Virginia?"

"No, there you must be physically living apart for a year before seeking a no-fault divorce."

"And if this is not possible?"

Leigh cocked her head. "You're still living with your husband?"

Devra nodded.

"Well, if he won't leave, then you should. If money's the problem," Leigh added, "we can petition for a temporary support order."

"That is not the problem."

"If there are children to consider—"

"There are none."

She was at a loss. "You wish to divorce him but not to leave him?"

"Of course I wish to leave him. But he would never allow it. You must understand. In my country, in our culture, a wife cannot leave her husband, not without his consent."

"But you're in America now. Things are different here."

Devra sighed. "One does not live in a country. One lives in a marriage and a household and a culture." She folded her hands. "And so you are telling me divorce is not possible for me in my circumstances."

"Not in the District," Leigh said. "Not unless you can prove you're not living as husband and wife. But it is possible to divorce in Maryland or Virginia, even in the absence of separation, if you can prove one of the enumerated fault grounds."

"Which are?"

Leigh ticked them off. Desertion. Felony conviction. Cruelty. Adultery.

Devra leaned forward at the last point. "Defined as?"

"Sexual relations with someone other than his spouse."

"What does *spouse* mean?"

"A husband or wife," Leigh answered slowly, as if speaking to a child. Then she realized. "Oh! Are you asking about plural marriage? Only the first spouse qualifies as the spouse. Sexual relations with any subsequent partner would constitute adultery."

"Even if the subsequent marriages were lawful in our home country?"

"Even so."

"Even if they were sanctified by Allah?"

"In this country, divorce is a civil matter only. Religion is irrelevant."

Devra shook her head. "I confess, I cannot comprehend such a thing. In my country, law and faith are one and the same." She paused. "And it presents a further difficulty. If your courts will not burden me with the requirements of sharia law in seeking a divorce, then I assume I must likewise forfeit the benefits I would have received under sharia law?"

"You're referring to the *mahr*?"

"Yes. Specifically, the deferred part of the *mahr*, the *mu'akhkar*. This is the sum agreed upon at the time of our marriage to be paid to me in the event of divorce. How can I hope to receive that money if sharia law is not enforced?"

This was the subject of Leigh's article, so she could answer with some confidence. "Courts in this country have ordered payment of the *mahr* without treading into questions of religion, by treating it the same as any nonreligious prenuptial agreement. It simply has to meet the statutory requirements for an enforceable prenup. Namely, that the agreement be in writing and entered into voluntarily, after a full and fair disclosure of assets."

Devra seemed stunned. "So it is actually possible your court would grant me a divorce over my husband's objection, and at the same time compel him to pay me the *mu'akhkar*?"

"Certainly it's possible."

"Well." She sat back with a dazed look in her deep dark eyes. "My mother told me things were different in America, but I never . . ." Her voice trailed off. She was silent for a long moment before she forced a smile at Leigh. "You've given me a great deal to reflect upon. May I ask that we meet again in a few weeks to discuss these matters further?"

"Yes, I'd be happy to."

She pressed a button on the end table beside her. "Someone will contact your office with the particulars."

A brisk knock sounded on the door, and it swung open to admit a rolling rack of clothes steered by the personal shopper.

"And now if you will excuse me," Devra whispered with a glance at the bodyguard standing at attention outside the salon. "I must spend enough money to convince my husband I've been shopping this morning." She raised her voice. "So you recommend the Versace?"

"Ye—es." Leigh faltered only slightly. "Yes, I think that would suit you best."

"Very well. I thank you."

The bodyguard escorted Leigh to the elevator and glowered at her until the doors closed. On the ground floor, she hurried through the empty store, and as soon as she cleared the front door, she took out her phone and powered it up. She couldn't wait to get home to tell the kids about this encounter. Chrissy was studying the Middle East in her World Cultures class this term and was fascinated by it. She'd be thrilled to hear about her mother's meeting with a real live sheikha. While Kip would get on the internet and figure out in five minutes exactly who this woman was.

She slid into the car as her phone glowed to life. Six calls had piled up since she turned it off. Three from Kip, two from Peter. And the last one from the hospital.

Chapter Five

P ete swerved into the parking lot and squealed to a stop at the ER entrance and tore inside to the reception kiosk. But he was already too late, and they sent him to Admissions, but Admissions wouldn't tell him anything except how to fill out the paperwork. When that was done they sent him to the surgical floor, but the elevator wouldn't come no matter how hard he punched the up button, and he finally gave up and ran to the stairwell and galloped up four flights and down a couple of halls until at last he burst panting into the room.

Kip didn't look up at Pete's arrival. He was staring at his hands, cradling his phone like a bird with a broken wing. His mouth trembled when he spoke. "They made me turn it off. I never got through to Leigh."

"I reached her. She's on her way."

"I was googling these words. *Cerebral aneurysm. Subarachnoid hemorrhage.* I don't know what they mean. I'm not even sure I'm spelling them right. They made me turn off my phone before I could figure anything out."

Pete stared, too, not at the phone but at Kip's fingers. The tips were still smudged black with the ink residue from last night's fingerprinting. "Where's the doctor?"

"I don't know. They won't tell me anything."

Pete went back out in the hall and did another circuit of the floor until he came to a glass-walled room with a row of doors along the back wall. He thought it might be the nurses' station but there was no reception desk and no one inside the cube was looking outward. They were all looking at screens and talking on phones.

A phone was hooked on the wall next to Pete. He picked it up and it rang automatically. A woman answered, though no one in the glass cube looked his way.

"I'm looking for Dr. Rowan, I think it is?"

"He's in surgery."

"With Christine Porter?"

"What's your name?"

"Pete Conley. I'm her stepfather."

There was a pause. "I have a note here that the mother is en route."

"My wife, yes."

"Have a seat in the waiting room until she arrives."

The phone went dead in his hand, and still he couldn't tell which nurse he'd spoken to. He hung it back on the hook and returned to the lounge down the hall. It was decorated in prints and plaids in shades of red and yellow, homespun and cheery, the kind of room often adorned with uplifting proverbs in framed needlepoint. These walls were blank.

Kip had given up trying to stare his phone back to life. Now he was staring at the braided rag rug on the floor, elbows on his knees and his chin on his chest. Pete sat down beside him on the nubby plaid sofa. "Tell me again what happened."

Kip told it in a halting whisper. How Chrissy shuffled into the kitchen that morning and slumped down at the table. She moaned she didn't feel good. There was something off about her eyes. Like they didn't match. One was the usual blue, but the other was black—the pupil was completely dilated. And then—then it was like one side of her face melted off her skull, and her mouth opened up and she vomited all over the table. Kip ran for some paper towels, and by the time he got back—seconds, it was only seconds—she was on the floor, convulsing. "I—I turned her on her side so she wouldn't choke, you know? But I couldn't get her to come to, even after the seizures stopped. I tried calling you, and Leigh, then I called nine-one-one."

Pete scrubbed a hand over his face. "Did she ever wake up?"

Kip shook his head. "They took her for some kind of scan, and one of the ER doctors came out and said it showed a subarachnoid hemorrhage and asked if she'd ever been diagnosed with a cerebral aneurysm."

"Never." Leigh would have wrapped her in lamb's wool for the rest of her life if she had.

"Or if she ever had a head injury."

What child hadn't? They'd had each of the boys to the ER one time or another with a suspected concussion, and Chrissy played sports as hard as they did. She rode horses, too, which meant she'd had her share of hard falls, not to mention crashes into stable walls every time a horse took a sudden sidestep.

"It could be congenital." Kip's halting whisper picked up speed, and his next words came out in a rapid-fire stutter. "Google said these things—these aneurysms, whatever—are also caused by old age or drugs or infections. But she's not old and she doesn't do drugs and what kind of infection do they mean? It's gotta be something more than bronchitis, right? So it's either congenital or a head injury."

"She never showed any symptoms."

"He said they go undiagnosed until they rupture and bleed. Then he said they couldn't wait for a parent and they had to go in now and clip it. Dad—" His voice broke on the word. "—I think he meant into her brain."

"Yeah, buddy, I think so." Absently Pete patted him on the knee.

"They'll have to shave her head."

"Yeah."

"Man, she's gonna hate that so much."

The elevator chimed again out in the corridor, and this time it was followed by the sound of footsteps that Pete instantly recognized as Leigh's. It was the sharp strike of her high heels in a building full of soft soles, and the brisk rhythm of those heels on the hard floor, like the pace of a horse running at a controlled trot. Control was what he heard in her footsteps, and it was a relief to hear it in her voice, too, when she addressed someone down the hall in her clear, strong, lawyerly tone.

He jumped up and ran down the hall to join her, but she was already out of sight. He turned a slow revolution in the empty corridor. "Leigh?" he called.

She didn't answer. She must have been out of earshot, too. Someone must have escorted her to the doctor. He trotted back to the glass cube and picked up the phone again. It felt like the intercom in a prison visiting room. "Hey," he said to the faceless voice that answered. "My wife just arrived. Did you take her back to see Dr. Rowan?"

"Dr. Rowan's in surgery."

"Okay, where did you take her? My wife. I want to join her."

"Your name, please?"

He went through them all again. Pete Conley. Leigh Huyett. Christine Porter. One family with three different surnames. There was a reason why couples used to pick one and stick it on all their kids, and at that moment he was willing to become Pete Huyett Porter if it would get him past that glass partition to wherever Leigh and Chrissy were.

"Have a seat in the waiting room. Someone will be with you."

Shortly. She forgot to tack on *shortly* at the end of that sentence.

He returned to the lounge. The TV was on now, and Kip was dispiritedly clicking through the channels with the volume turned low. He passed through the cable news stations and some Saturday morning cartoons and a couple infomercials until he finally stopped on the History Channel and turned up the volume.

"What's this?" Pete said.

"I saw it already. It's about the Crusades."

Kip was writing his final AP History paper on the Christian Crusades, about some pope back in the Dark Ages who basically incited all of Europe to march to Jerusalem and conquer the infidels.

"Hey, what was that phrase?" Pete asked as the narrator droned on. "That Latin war cry you wrote about?"

"*Deus Vult?*"

"Right. What's that mean again?"

"It is the will of God."

Right. The will of God. Pete had a sort of reflexive belief in God, much like his belief in, say, Neptune. He had no reason to doubt the planet's existence, not when other people seemed so sure, but he couldn't personally verify it, and it didn't have much to do with his actual life. The same was true of God. He never thought of God as watching him or listening to him and certainly not exerting his will over him. So what did it mean to say something was the will of God? In the Dark Ages it meant a command that had to be actively obeyed. Take up arms and march east. But today it meant only a passive resignation. *It's out of our hands. There's nothing we can do. It's the will of God.*

There was no way it could be God's will that Chrissy sustain any kind of brain damage, but Pete had to accept it was out of his hands. There was nothing he could do for her now.

It was afternoon before the crisp rat-a-tat of Leigh's heels sounded from the far end of the corridor. Pete looked at his watch as he got to his feet. It was more than three hours since they took Chrissy to surgery. They must be done now, the artery was clipped, and Leigh was coming to tell them that everything was going to be okay.

The brisk rhythm of her footsteps faltered. There was the clatter of a stumble, then a machine-gun burst of quick running steps. Then a sound that came not from her feet but from the bottom of her throat. A sound that in five years he never once heard her make.

Chapter Six

Afterward there was a luncheon at the house. Pete made all the arrangements, for that and everything else over the past three days, but now he had nothing to do. He wandered through each crowded room, looking for a forgotten detail or one more fire to put out. The caterers had the bar and buffet covered, and Leigh's longtime assistant Polly was answering the door. A cop was directing traffic at the corner, and two young guys from Pete's crew were valet-parking the visitors' cars in the meadow. Pete had nothing left to do but find a place to position himself. Suddenly that seemed the hardest task of all.

More than three hundred people came through the door that afternoon. Family, friends, neighbors, business associates. Leigh's parents, up from Florida and sitting silent and pale beneath their leathery tans. Leigh's friends came in three sets: her lawyer friends, her horse friends, and her mom friends. Her law partners made a big showing, along with a couple of judges and some of her clients. A few of Ted's friends were there, and his colleagues from his stockbroker days, before he chucked it all to sail the seven seas. Most of the neighbors dropped by to pay their respects, and some of them stayed all afternoon—the Markhams from next door, the Dietrichs with their pregnant daughter. And the house was full of middle schoolers: Chrissy's school had declared a half day and sent two activity-busloads of her classmates.

Polly was supposed to be there as a guest, but she didn't know how to stop working, and she spent all afternoon on her feet, opening the door for each new arrival and steering the guests like an usher at a wedding. Friends of the father? Ted was at the bar in the dining room, and she showed them the way. Friends of the mother? She waved at Leigh in the wing chair by the fireplace in the living room. Friends of the brothers? She pointed to Zack and Dylan standing like statues behind their mother, each with a hand on one of her shoulders. They were big hulking boys, and standing together like that, they looked like the defensive line they used to be part of back in high school football. But they were red-eyed and shell-shocked and drowning too deep in their own grief to be of any help to Leigh.

That role fell to Shelby Randolph, who sat perched on the ottoman at Leigh's feet. She was the real defensive line today, sheltering Leigh from hysterical teenaged girls and maladroit well-wishers, fending off anyone who tried to do more than offer a brief word of condolence. If any guest dared even to sniffle in front of Leigh, Shelby hustled them away like the Secret Service frog-marching a protester out of a presidential town meeting. She ran interference with Ted, and with Pete, too, for that matter. Twenty-five years of friendship trumped five years of marriage.

Pete couldn't have taken care of Leigh these last three days anyway. He had airport runs to make and trains to meet. Hotel rooms to reserve for anyone who didn't insist on staying at the house. Beds to strip and sheets and towels to change. A casket to choose, the cemetery plot to buy, and a headstone to order. The menu to approve. The music for the organist to play. The photos to select for the slide show that was playing in a loop on the big TV in the family room. Chrissy through the years, growing from just-born all the way up to last week. Where she would remain forever, frozen in time.

Now all the chores and errands were done, and there was nothing left for him to do, and no role for him to play either. Ted was the bereaved father here today, not Pete. No matter that Pete was the one who ate breakfast and dinner with Chrissy every day for the past five years. Who picked her up from her after-school activities and coached her softball team and coaxed a smile from her after her first middle school breakup. Still, he understood his lack of standing. If anything ever happened to Kip or Mia, the last thing he'd want would be Gary sitting front and center in the mourner's bench. That would be Pete's place, just as it was Ted's place today.

Ted's mourner's bench was a chair next to the bar, where he sat slopping whiskey from a tumbler while he wept out loud with maudlin memories of his sweet little girl. She was little by default in his memories, considering he moved out when she was seven. And not only out of the house—he left the whole goddam country. It took Pete two days to locate him at a marina in Bermuda, and he barely managed to book him a flight that would get him here in time for the funeral. But he made it. Chrissy would have wanted her whole family there, and Pete made sure she got it.

Pete had no family there. When he phoned his mother with the news, she said, "Oh, what a shame. Kristen, was it?" She didn't think of Chrissy as her grandchild; she made her excuses and sent a card. He asked Karen to bring Mia—she adored her big stepsister; *Where's Chrissy?* was the first thing she said when she arrived every other weekend—but Gary decreed that ten was too young for funerals, and he and Karen came without her. Kip was around somewhere, but he'd been doing his disappearing act ever since they got home from the hospital on Saturday. Even Shepherd was gone, penned up in the barn with the horses.

Pete threaded his way through the crowd into the living room and squatted beside Leigh's chair. "Anything I can get you, sweetheart?"

Her clouded eyes wandered his way. The sedatives her doctor prescribed were supposed to be low-dose, but they dulled her into a high haze. It was like somebody had dropped a veil over her head, and she looked out through layers of filmy gauze. "I'm fine," she whispered.

"Okay," he said. She didn't react as he kissed her. He got to his feet and circled behind the twins and clapped them each on the shoulder. "You doing okay, guys?"

They looked like their father, big and blond. Two years of college pizza and beer had softened them around the middle, too, like Ted. Zack started to answer before he choked up and ducked his head. With a loud sniff,

Dylan nodded in the direction of the bar. "Pete, somebody's gotta cut Dad off."

Zack found his voice to chime in. "Yeah. Before he starts singing or something."

By somebody, they meant Pete, but it wasn't his place to close the bar to their father. "It'll be over soon," he told them.

He spotted Karen and Gary standing alone on the far side of the living room. They didn't know anyone there, and Karen was getting that fearful look she often wore in a room full of strangers. He ought to go rescue her, even if it meant talking to Gary. He started to head that way when Gary buttonholed another passing guest and introduced himself as Dr. March. "It's like a balloon bulging out of an artery," Pete heard him say. "These things can go undetected for years until, bam, they rupture. Then they bleed out into the brain and it's all over." Gary was a dentist. He knew more about abscesses than aneurysms.

Pete did an abrupt about-face. He looked around for Kip but he was still AWOL. Probably hiding out in his room. Pete headed for the stairs. Time to flush him out.

Polly was still in the front hall. She'd been cornered by the Dietrich girl, who was speaking in a strained, too-loud voice. "I'm just going to disappear, that's what. He can't stalk me if he can't find me."

"Now let's think about that, dear." Polly was the secret weapon in the arsenal of Leigh's practice. She was like everyone's favorite grandmother, wise and soothing. "You don't want to be on your own with a baby coming. You'll want your mother and father on hand."

"They're no help to me. Not where Hunter's concerned."

"Excuse me," Pete said and cut around them to the stairs.

The buzz of the crowd faded as he reached the second floor. He turned right, past the old master bedroom, now fitted out for Mia, then climbed another half-flight of stairs. Three doors opened off the landing, and two of them stood open, to Kip's room and the twins', but he wasn't in either one.

The third door was closed. Pete hesitated before he swung it open, but that room was empty, too. The bed was made and the books and homework put away and the clothes picked up off the floor, but signs of life were still everywhere. The life of a girl teetering between childhood and young womanhood. Her Breyer horse collection arrayed on a shelf above the complete works of William Shakespeare and a year's back issues of *Seventeen*. The One Direction posters on the wall and the blue ribbons tacked to the bulletin board beside flyers for Habitat for Humanity and Doctors Without Borders. A rainbow of nail polish bottles lined up on her dresser next to a framed photo of the family, the one taken in front of the tree last Christmas. Pete picked up the photo and gazed at the grouping. He and Leigh stood smiling with their arms around each other's waists, the twins were taking a knee on either side, and Chrissy sat front and center with her arms flung around Kip and Mia and a thousand-watt smile spread over her face.

He clasped the frame to his chest and sank down on her pink-ribboned bedspread. The door to the closet stood open and he could see the heaps of sneakers and loafers on the floor and the jumble of dresses and shirts crammed on the rod. Leigh loved to buy Chrissy new clothes, loved it far more than buying clothes for herself. She delighted in her daughter's burgeoning beauty, and every time they got home from the mall, she had Chrissy give them a fashion show of each new ensemble. She'd sit down with Pete at the kitchen table and Chrissy would duck into the pantry with her shopping bags and come out giggling to prance and twirl with the tags still attached and fluttering like tails on a kite. Then the two of them would gallop upstairs and rummage through her closet to see what else might go with what. They'd be up there laughing for an hour after every shopping spree while Pete sat in the kitchen, grinning at all the ruckus.

He put his face in his hands as the echo of their laughter rippled away. It struck him for the first time: he'd never hear that sound again. Chrissy's laughter, gone forever, and he couldn't imagine life in this house without it. Or her. He might never hear the sound of Leigh's laughter again either. Not that laugh anyway, the one that bubbled out of her, a spring of pure delight. Chrissy was the heart and soul of Leigh's life, and Pete didn't know how she'd ever be the same again. His wonderful, lighthearted, wisecracking wife might be gone for good.

The voices of the crowd droned on downstairs as he got up and closed the door to Chrissy's closet. The clouds had been hanging heavy in the sky all day, and now the windowpanes were streaked with rain. He looked out through the glass. A drizzle was falling on the bluestone patio down below, and there was Kip, outside, hunkered on a chaise. Hiding out, as he'd suspected. No better than Pete, but he shouldn't be doing it in the rain. He headed downstairs to drag him inside.

Polly was talking to someone in a rain-splattered hat at the front door. It was the traffic cop, which meant another fire to put out. "I got this, Polly," Pete said. Until he saw that there were two officers at the door, and neither one was the traffic cop. He stopped short. "Is there a problem?"

Polly turned to him, eyes wide, and it was then that he registered who the officers were. They were the two cops from the police station Friday night.

"Mr. Conley," the man said. Softball Coach, Leigh had called him, though Pete learned that night his name was Hooper. "Is your son at home?"

"Sure. What's this about?"

The woman stepped up. Ballerina Bun, Leigh had named her, though she was actually Officer Mateo. "We have a warrant for the arrest of Christopher Conley."

"What?" Pete said, a little too loudly as Polly backed away. "What do you mean? He was already arrested. You released him."

Mateo held up a crisp sheaf of papers. "These are new charges."

"I'm sorry, Mr. Conley." Hooper glanced uneasily at the throng of guests spilling into the foyer. "I know the timing is—unfortunate."

Shelby charged into the hall with a glass of wine in her hand. "Let me see that," she snapped and thrust her glass at Officer Mateo as she snatched the warrant from her.

"What new charges?" Pete said.

Mateo scowled at the glass in her hand. "Manslaughter."

"What!"

"Vehicular," Shelby said, flipping through the pages.

"A Class Five felony." Mateo put the glass down on the hall table, clumsily, and it tipped over and spilled out a pool of red wine.

"We had a deal." Shelby looked up accusingly. "You agreed he was a juvenile."

"Subject to the prosecutor's review. And that was before somebody died."

"Let me guess. Harrison? And I guess the timing was his idea, too, to cause the most possible pain to the family. It's not bad enough they lost their daughter."

Pete wasn't following. "Wait. Are you talking about Chrissy? She had an aneurysm."

Mateo thrust out her chin. "Sustained in the accident that night, the doctors say."

"No. That can't be—"

"Mr. Conley." Hooper spoke in a low voice. "Is your son on the premises?"

"Here," Gary called, and he came into the foyer pushing Kip ahead of him.

The low buzz of the crowd swelled louder. Someone must have overheard what was happening and spread the word. A nervous clamor filled the house, and Pete could feel the heat of a couple dozen bodies pressing in behind him.

Kip stood blinking in the glare of the hall chandelier, his suit coat splotched with rain and his hair plastered to his skull. The cops each took him by an arm. "Christopher Conley, you are under arrest—" Mateo began.

"No, wait," Pete said. "This is a mistake."

They pulled Kip's arms behind his back. "—for driving under the influence of alcohol—"

"Dad?" Kip's voice cracked on the word.

"It's okay. Don't worry. We'll get this straightened out." Pete reached for him, but the cops pushed him aside as they snapped the handcuffs over the boy's wrists.

"—for driving recklessly or in a manner so as to endanger the life of another—"

"Kip, don't say a word," Shelby said as the cops pushed him to the door. "Not one word."

"—causing the death of Christine Victoria Porter."

A sudden silence sliced through the hum and hiss of the funeral guests. The crowd parted in two waves as Leigh wobbled into the foyer. She stood swaying, with her fingers twisted in her pearls and her eyes unfocused behind the veil of the sedatives. Her gaze wandered around the room and skittered past Kip where he stood with his head bowed. The only sound in the house was the rhythmic drip of the spilled wine from the hall table onto the floor.

"Peter?" she said, blinking hard.

"Leigh." He reached for her while one hand still stretched back toward Kip. His child was being arrested for killing hers, and he didn't know where to go or what to do. "It's a mistake. I'll take care of this."

"You have the right to remain silent—" Mateo pushed Kip out the door.

"Which he invokes. Right now," Shelby said.

Leigh's fingers wound tighter in her necklace.

"Anything you say can and will be used against you—"

Pete followed as far as the porch. Kip stumbled on the front walk, and the cops hoisted him upright and held him between them as they strode to the patrol car. "Hold on a minute," Pete yelled. "You're making a mistake!"

From behind him came a sound like artillery fire. He whipped around. Leigh's necklace had snapped, and a hundred pearls were spraying out from her throat. They hit the stone tiles like shotgun pellets and scattered through the pool of red wine still seeping across the floor.

Chapter Seven

That afternoon Kip was transported to the Hampshire County Adult Detention Center in Arwen to be held overnight pending a bond hearing before the magistrate in the morning.

That night Pete lay awake with the deadweight of Leigh in his arms and those strange words boomeranging through his head. *Transported* sounded like Kip was in chains on a ship bound for Australia. *Detention* was innocuous enough on its own—an hour after-school writing *I will not disrupt class again* a hundred times on the board. Nothing Kip hadn't experienced before. But put the word *Adult* in front of it and it turned into Pete's worst nightmare. His kid was in an adult jail, full of actual adult criminals.

The next morning Shelby Randolph met him on the courthouse steps and strode inside ahead of him in slender high heels and a suit as crisp as new money. There was a security checkpoint to navigate like at the airport, and down the corridor beyond it, two heavy wooden doors to the magistrate's courtroom. Other lawyers and family members were milling around in the pew-like rows of spectator benches.

"Sit here," Shelby said, steering Pete to a spot in the first row behind the railing. She swung through the gate and crossed the aisle to speak to a harried-looking woman who stood shuffling files at one of the two lawyer tables. The woman didn't look up from her files, only listened for a minute and shook her head.

A girl in flip-flops barreled into Pete's row with three small children in tow. The children wore flip-flops, too, and their feet looked red and raw with cold. The court reporter was setting up his equipment at the foot of the magistrate's throne-like bench, and another functionary was beside him, flipping through her own towering stack of files. Two of the children next to Pete started to scrap with each other. "Cut that out," their mother hissed. "Or I swear to God, I'm leaving your asses here."

Shelby slipped into the seat beside Pete as a door opened at the front of the courtroom. The magistrate emerged to take the bench, and the first case was called. A lawyer popped up from his pew like a jack-in-a-box and hip-checked through the swinging gate to take his place at the defense table. Pete dug his nails in his palms at the sight of the first prisoner to be led out in manacles—a young tough with a fat lip and a shiner starting over his right eye who still managed to look like the other guy got the worst of it. Assault was the charge, bail was set, and he was led out again, all in the space of two or three minutes.

The next prisoner was led out. "Daddy, daddy!" the children cried. The charge was unpaid child support, and the man didn't glance at his family on his way in or out of the courtroom.

Finally Kip's case was called. "Christopher Conley," the functionary mumbled, and Pete leaned forward on the bench as Shelby rose to the defense table. The door opened and Kip was steered into the courtroom with his wrists manacled in front of him. His head came up as he cleared the door, and his eyes darted wildly until they landed on Shelby first then on to Pete behind her. He walked in a strange shuffling gait that made Pete wonder if his legs were shackled, too. But when he came closer, he saw why: His shoelaces were gone and his shoes were flapping loose on his feet. His belt must have been taken, too. His pants sagged low on his narrow hips.

Pete tried to muster an encouraging smile, but before he could pull it off, Kip turned his back to stand at attention beside Shelby. His suit coat was striped with deep vertical creases. He must have wadded it up for a pillow in his cell last night. It was his first real suit. Leigh had taken him shopping for it last fall to wear for his interview with the governor and next for his graduation. Now he'd worn it twice in between: for his sister's funeral, and for his own bond hearing.

The clerk read the charges in a flat voice. Operating a motor vehicle after illegally consuming alcohol. Operating a motor vehicle after his license was revoked. Driving recklessly or at a speed or in a manner so as to endanger the life, limb, or property of any person. Driving recklessly and without a valid operator's license resulting in the death of another. Driving under the influence of alcohol and causing the death of another. Involuntary manslaughter.

Manslaughter. That was another word that boomeranged senselessly inside Pete's head. Chrissy wasn't a man, she was a girl. *Girlslaughter,* they should call it, except that Kip hadn't slaughtered her. He hadn't done anything to her. She'd died of a ruptured aneurysm that could have been sleeping inside her brain her whole life.

The magistrate wasn't there to hear about any of that. He wasn't there to consider evidence or decide guilt. He had only one function, and that was to set the terms of Kip's release. The female prosecutor rattled off some buzzwords. Second offense. Very serious charges. Potentially facing a long period of incarceration. Extreme flight risk. Shelby had a swift return for every lob. Christopher was a straight-A student. He'd been selected for a very prestigious internship with the governor's office this summer. His father was a custom builder with projects throughout the county. His stepmother was an attorney who'd lived her whole life in Hampshire County. It was an upstanding family with deep roots in the community.

"You headed to college this fall, young man?" the magistrate cut in. He was ancient, with deep hanging jowls like one of those dogs with the smashed-in faces.

Kip cleared his throat. "Yes, sir."

"Out of state?"

"Yes, sir."

Barely, Pete thought. Duke was only five hours away. He could drive there and back, overnight if necessary, to deliver Kip to his court appearances.

"Then we'd better give you some incentive to come back and grace us with your presence. Bail set at one hundred thousand dollars. Cash or bond."

Those words boomeranged even more wildly. Pete had to put the figure up on his digital screen before he could believe he had the right number of zeroes. Kip whipped around with a look of pure panic in his eyes, and Pete tried to give him another encouraging smile, but he could feel his lips stretch into a rictal grimace as the boy was led away again. Who had one hundred thousand dollars *cash*?

Nobody, Shelby explained as she led him out of the courthouse. Hence, the bail bondsman. She had to get back to her office for a meeting, so Pete was left on his own to stumble his way through the bonding process. It was late morning by the time it was done and another hour after that before Kip was released.

Pete grabbed him by the arm as he came through the metal door. "Are you okay?" He looked him over, up and down. His shoelaces were tied, his pants were belted, but there was something wrong with his eyes. They couldn't meet Pete's.

"I'm fine. Dad, the bail—"

"Don't worry about it."

"But how—"

"You're sure you're okay? I mean, you want to see a doctor or anything?"

Kip flushed. "Nobody touched me, all right?"

Pete realized his thumb was digging into the boy's bicep, and he let go and gave the spot an apologetic rub. "You want to get something to eat?"

"I just want to go home."

The rain had finally ended, and the sun was sparkling on the bright white blossoms of the Bradford pears that flanked the walkway to the parking lot. Kip usually called shotgun and sprinted ahead to claim his prize, but today there were no other contenders. He trudged to the Volvo and slumped down low in the passenger seat.

"Shelby said to call as soon as you got out." Pete punched her office number into his phone, and he was pulling out of the lot as her voice came over the dashboard speaker.

"Okay, first things first," she said. "Kip, you understand everything you tell me is confidential, right?"

"Right."

"Including from your father. If you don't wish him to be included in our communications, we can talk later."

"Now's fine."

"I need a verbal waiver of confidentiality."

"Yeah, I waive it." Kip cut a quick glance sideways. "But not for my mom, okay?"

Pete shot him a look. "Hey—"

"She'll only fall to pieces and repeat everything to Gary. I can't deal with that, okay?"

All true, but Pete knew how he'd feel if Kip cut him out this way. "She's your mother."

Kip set his jaw. "It's my decision, though, right?"

"That's right," Shelby said. "The privilege is yours to invoke. And you can change your mind anytime, about your mom or your dad. Just let me know."

"Okay."

"On that subject, have you spoken to anyone about your case? The cops in the car, the guards in the jail, and the other detainees in the cells?"

"No. None of them."

"You're sure? If anyone's going to claim a jailhouse confession, I need to know now."

Kip stared out the window at the passing countryside, where white board fences dipped and rose with the roll of the hills. "I didn't open my mouth once."

"Good. Now let's talk about what happens next."

It played like a canned speech from there, Criminal Procedure for Dummies. The first appearance would come in a week or two—apparently today didn't count—and the charges would be formally read and Kip would enter his plea. Next up was the preliminary hearing, where the government had to lay out enough of its case for the judge to agree that there was probable cause for the arrest and bind it over to the grand jury. The grand jury would then deliver the formal indictment and a trial date would be set.

"How long will all this take?" Pete asked, thinking, *How much will all this cost?*

"Many months, which is why I wanted to talk to you right away. We could try to fast-track this by waiving the preliminaries and ask for a trial date this summer so Kip can get this behind him before he leaves for college. So let's all think about that option soonish, okay?"

They reached the highway, and Pete had to turn up the volume to hear her over the whipping of the wind and the whining roar of the tires on the asphalt. Winter wheat stood in bright green swaths on either side of the roadway, and the limbs of weeping cherries hung heavy under their bloom.

"Even without a preliminary hearing, we can guess what the government's case consists of. The DUI is probably unassailable, but causation is wide open. It's the Commonwealth's burden, remember, so they have to present evidence that the accident was the direct proximate cause of the death."

The death. Pete wondered if that was the way all criminal lawyers talked. Like the death in question hadn't happened to any person in particular. It was just some abstract concept floating in space. The image came to him, of Chrissy, weightless and whirling in the void, and he had to close his eyes for a second, it hurt so bad.

"There're two prongs to causation in this case," Shelby was saying. "First, it had to be your intoxication and/or reckless driving that caused the truck to leave the road."

"It was a dog," Kip said. "A dog and a wet road."

"Exactly. If a sober and safe driver would have ended up in that ditch, too, then Chrissy's death wasn't causally connected to the alcohol you consumed. Pete, we may want to hire an accident reconstructionist on that point. Bookmark that, okay? The second prong of causation is that the accident had to cause the injury. I recommend we hire a neurologist to testify that the aneurysm could have been congenital or brought on by some previous injury."

"Wait, back up a minute," Pete shouted at the dash. "How'd the hospital even know there *was* an accident?" That was something else that had bounced around his brain all night.

Static buzzed through the silence over the line. There was silence in the car, too, until Kip said, "I told them."

"What?" Pete turned to stare at him. "Why?"

"They asked me about any head injuries she might've had. So I told them."

"You never told us," he said as Shelby said, "Told them what, exactly?"

"She said she was fine. I didn't think—"

Shelby spoke over him. "Kip, what did you tell them?"

He sucked in a breath to answer. "When we went off the road, we were airborne for a second. The truck kind of bounced across the ditch before we hit the tree. She might have hit her head then."

"But she had her seat belt on," Pete said. The boys sometimes neglected to buckle up, but never Chrissy.

Kip shrugged. "So did I, but I still bounced."

"What did you tell the doctors?" Shelby said again. "She did hit her head, or she might have?"

"I don't remember."

"Did you *see* her hit her head?" Pete asked

"The only thing that matters is what he told the doctors," Shelby said.

But Pete repeated, "Kip, did you see her hit her head?"

"No. But she was kind of rubbing it afterward, and I asked if she was all right, and she said she was fine." He turned a desperate look on Pete. "I swear she said she was fine."

"We'll interview the ER docs and find out what they think you told them. My guess is they won't remember anything. So, okay, I've got some experts in mind. I'll shoot you their CVs and we'll discuss."

They drove past the intersection with Rose Lane. A new brick Colonial stood on the corner behind eighty thousand dollars' worth of landscaping. It was one of the few spec houses Pete had ever built, and it represented more than a year of his life from start to finish. Typically he built custom houses, but this location was so prime he took a chance and bought the lot and built the house on his own dime—or the bank's, at least. It took longer to sell than he'd calculated, but it was under contract now and scheduled to close in a couple weeks. He'd been expecting to clear more than a hundred thousand at closing. Except now he wouldn't, because he'd just put up the property as collateral for the bail bond. Now the cash would go to the bondsman at closing, and Pete wouldn't see a penny of it until this was all over.

Shelby was still talking strategy. She wanted to send her investigator out to interview some of the other kids from the party, witnesses who might testify to Kip's sober demeanor that night. He probably couldn't beat the DUI, but they should try to head off any implication he was behaving in a wanton or reckless manner. She wanted names.

"They won't help," Kip said.

"Why not?"

"The party got raided that night. Everybody's in trouble now. Because of me."

"Shoot me their names anyway. My investigator can be very persuasive. I'll send him out to talk to the neighbor, too, the one who called nine-one-one. And, Pete, I'm going to need some up-front money for the experts. I can wait for my fee, but they won't. So factor that into your budget."

His budget. Like this was something he knew was coming and tucked a little money aside for. A rainy day fund, in case his son was ever arrested for killing his stepdaughter.

"Any questions?"

"Yeah." Pete cleared his throat. "These charges—they're all adult crimes, right? But what if it happened before midnight? What if he was still seventeen?"

"Right. Well, here's the thing. Where the offense is a felony, anyone fourteen or older can be transferred out of juvenile court. The fact that Kip was only minutes away from adulthood, if not there already, would almost certainly get him kicked upstairs to circuit court."

Pete stopped a minute to take that in. "Okay, but if they're calling him an adult, shouldn't he have to be adult-level drunk? His blood alcohol was only point-oh-five-five."

"Good question. But vehicular homicide has two alternative prongs. The first one is BAC of point oh eight or higher. The second is simply driving while under the influence of alcohol. That one's not as scientific. All competent evidence can be considered. Erratic driving. Boisterous behavior. Failing the field sobriety test, which is what the arresting officer will say."

"I didn't!" Kip said. "I passed her stupid tests just fine."

Pete shot him a glare. It was probably that attitude right there that made the cop haul him in for the blood test.

"With no other witnesses," Shelby said, "it'll be pretty hard to dispute what she says."

No other witnesses, Pete thought with a stab. Because the only one who could back him up was the one he stood accused of killing. "What if he's convicted? What then?"

"Worst case? Ten years. But let's not get ahead of ourselves. Most prosecutors don't pursue vehicular homicide cases when they're intrafamily. Maybe Harrison only wanted the headline in today's paper and tomorrow he'll settle for probation and a fine. We have to wait and see how it all shakes out. Let's circle back tomorrow, okay? Meanwhile, get some sleep and don't talk to anybody about the case."

Ten years. Pete felt a whiteout of panic as the call ended. Almost four thousand nights to spend the way he spent last night, with terror gnawing a hole through his gut. The light turned red at the shopping center intersection ahead, and as he braked to a stop, he peered up through the tinted glass of the windshield, scanning the rooftops of the stores and the hilltops beyond them. He almost longed for the days when a sniper was the only threat to his family. When he could protect his kid simply by shielding him with his own body. He had no idea how to shield him from this.

Chapter Eight

Waking was when it was worst. The little white pills wore off during the night, and Leigh rose up out of sleep on a buoyant senselessness. Feeling normal. Facing an ordinary day in her ordinary, happy life. For thirty seconds she floated there on a raft of contentment before the *Oh no* crashed over her. The realization that Chrissy was dead. It was like a tsunami, the way it knocked the breath from her body and left her drowning in grief again.

It was unnatural for a parent to lose a child, people said. Unthinkable. But when she was awake it was all she could think about. Her magic child was gone. She'd never see her face again or hear her tinkling laugh or feel her skinny arms in a hug. The last time she saw her was at her bedroom door Friday night. The last thing she said to her was *We'll talk about this in the morning.* But she never talked to her again. She never saw her again. Not in the hospital and not in the funeral home either. She wasn't Chrissy anymore, they told her. Her head was shaved. Her scalp was stitched. *You don't want to see,* they said, but they were wrong. How could she not want to see her own child? When she tried to push past them, they told her not to torture herself this way. As if this pain were something she was inflicting on herself.

It was too much, to have to lose her over and over again, every time she stirred from sleep, to have her heart gouged out again every single time. It would be better never to sleep, and better still never to wake.

The mattress dipped during the night, and for one foggy moment she thought it was Ted come back to her bed, and she kicked off and cast herself away from his touch. It was only later in the night when the currents of sleep bumped her up against him that she realized it was Peter, and she grabbed on and clung to him like a lifeboat. He wrapped his arms around her and whispered words to her, but, no, she couldn't listen. She couldn't wake to that pain again, and so she pushed herself back down, deep into the numbing waters of sleep.

She didn't feel the mattress rise again in the morning. She never heard him leave her.

It was afternoon before sunlight slipped through the cracks of her eyelids, and there was the pain, lurking in the corner of her consciousness with its glowing red eyes, waiting for her to wake so it could lunge at her again. She barely had time to cower before its great yawing jaws opened wide to swallow her whole. Blindly she groped along the nightstand, knocked her knuckles against the lamp and a half-empty glass of water and scrabbled her fingers through a snowdrift of used tissues, but she couldn't feel the prescription bottle.

She forced her eyes open. Bright afternoon light stabbed her retinas; her mouth tasted of cotton; her throat felt like steel wool. Noises reverberated through the house and in her head. A car door slamming in the driveway, Shep barking in the kitchen, drawers sliding open and crashing shut in the twins' room, footsteps pounding on the stairs. Shouts in fragmented conversations. Zack's flight, Dylan's train schedule, did you see my phone, is there anything to eat.

The last sound she ever heard from her daughter: the soft snuffles of her sleep-breathing. Through a closed door. While an artery was bursting in her brain. While Leigh hurried off to meet a new client.

The pain crashed over her again, and again she reached for the prescription bottle and when her fingers met only air, she raised up on an elbow to look. There it was, rolling on the floor. She slid off the bed and landed on hands and knees on the rug and peered through the amber plastic. The bottle was empty. She flattened on her belly to search for any spilled pills under the bed. It was dark there, and so alluring. Like a cave or a cocoon. How nice it would be to crawl in under there. *Like a return to the womb,* she thought.

A tap on the door. Her mother's voice. "Darling, the airport limo's here. We have to go now." Another tap. "Leigh, darling?"

She needed to get up. She needed to go to her parents. If it was unthinkable to lose a child, it was even more unthinkable to lose a grandchild, and they loved Chrissy beyond all measure. *I look at that precious girl,* her mother once confided, *and I know my time on earth has counted for something.* They were facing their own mortality in these last years of their lives—this was a loss they might never recover from. They needed Leigh now more than they ever had. She had to get up right now and hug them good-bye and tell them how much she loved them. Her boys needed her, too, and poor little Mia. They were all grieving, too. And Peter—Peter!— whose heart must be aching. The heart that he'd pledged to her care. She needed to get up and tend to them. All of them.

She didn't move. She lay silent and still on the floor until her mother's heavy sigh sounded through the door. "We'll call you tonight, dear."

Leigh closed her eyes and escaped into sleep again.

Another set of noises bombarded her ears. Shouts, ugly words, a slamming door. She reached for a pillow to clamp over her head, but she was on the floor and the pillows were up on the bed. She hooked a hand on the edge of the mattress and hauled herself up. More shouts, strangled cries that ricocheted like bullets from the children's wing. Some kind of argument was going on, she understood that much. Over the years she'd broken up a lot of tussles and scrapes among the children, and she had a routine. Pull them apart, send them to neutral corners, deliver a quick scolding about respect and communication, *Now, calm down and apologize.* She wouldn't listen to accusations or assign blame. She didn't care who started it. All that mattered was that the fight end, now. She made them say the words. *I'm sorry.* Then, *I forgive you.* She must have done it a thousand times over the last twenty years. She needed to stand up and do it now.

Something caught her eye. There, on the nightstand, another bottle of pills. She grabbed it like a lifeline and downed two and fell headlong into bed.

Later. Peter was in the room, and she tried to wake for him but the drugs were holding on too tight. Her eyelids weighed a hundred pounds each, and her ears were submerged in an underwater tank. He was telling her something, but the words came to her in aquatic garbles. He moved through the room in starts and stutters like a poorly spliced videotape, quick jerky cuts from the closet, to the bath, to the chest of drawers. The volume faded in and out as he spoke. Something about the bail hearing. Expert witnesses. The words tripped an alarm. This was important. She needed to wake up and listen. But the alarm was in another room, on another floor, and it grew fainter and fainter until it faded into silence.

She couldn't wake even when the twins tiptoed in to say good-bye. She felt their kisses on her cheek, and her eyelids fluttered and her fingers twitched with the effort to pull herself awake. But it was no use. They were already gone.

Pete hollered for the twins to get a move on, and they galloped out to the driveway and wrestled over the shotgun seat but ended up losing to Shepherd, who darted between them to claim it. They grumbled into the backseat, and Pete headed out like the family chauffeur.

An unfamiliar silence descended, and they were halfway to Dulles before there was anything but the sound of four males breathing a little too heavily inside the car. It was Zack who finally spoke and only after a dry round of throat clearing. "Um, we talked to Mia this morning."

Pete gave a guilty start. "Yeah?" He'd been putting that off. He didn't know how to tell her about this, any of this, especially over the phone.

"Skyped," Dylan clarified.

"How'd she look?" He'd been meaning to go and see her, every day he meant to, but there was never any time.

"Scared," Zack said.

"Lost."

Pete glanced up at the mirror. They were big burly college men but looked just as scared and lost as his ten-year-old. "Yeah," he said.

"We wanted her to know the schedule doesn't change. Every other Sunday at two, same as always."

The twins started it when they first went away to school. During Mia's visitation weekends—Pete had her every other weekend plus dinner every Wednesday night—they'd set up a three-way Skype call. Chrissy logged on, with Mia squeezed in the chair beside her and Kip's head looming in and out of camera range over theirs, while in split screens on the monitor, the twins grinned and mugged from two different time zones. For twenty or thirty minutes twice a month, the five of them bantered about nothing while their parents eavesdropped with big stupid smiles on their faces.

"She might need help logging on, though," Dylan said.

"Right," Pete said. Because Chrissy wouldn't be there to do it. "Thanks, guys. I'm sure that means a lot to her."

The first stop was Dulles for Zack's flight to Austin. Shep barked indignantly at his departure at the terminal while Pete went through the curbside litany of reminders: call on arrival, be good, be careful, and please don't break any bones because he was counting on his help this summer. "Yeah, yeah," Zack said with a big bear hug while Pete pressed a couple hundred dollars into the boy's hand.

It was what he always did, slip them some traveling money, but his bank balance was scrolling rapidly through his mind as he drove on to Union Station for Dylan's train to New York. He was going to have to make some steep austerity cuts. Ten thousand dollars was the 10 percent premium for the bail bond, and it was gone forever, no matter what happened. If Kip was cleared, even if the charges were dropped tomorrow, the bondsman still got to keep his 10 percent. Then there were the expert witness fees, not to mention Shelby's. *We'll talk about that later*, she'd said, but he didn't hold out much hope for a discount. She had a law firm to answer to, the same as Leigh.

They reached the drop-off circle at the train station, but Dylan didn't get out. "Hey, Pete?" He hesitated, his hand on the door handle. "There's something I have to tell you."

Chapter Nine

Leigh woke and rode out another tidal wave: Chrissy was dead, she was still dead and she'd always be dead. This was the world she was going to wake to every day for the rest of her life. World without Chrissy. Amen.

The world without. There was a world beyond this bed, this room, and as the fog of sleep began to lift, her awareness of that world began slowly to sharpen. She forced her eyes open. It was nearly as dark in the bedroom as it had been inside her head. She rolled over to squint at the alarm clock on Peter's nightstand. It was almost seven. By now her parents would be back on the ground in Florida. Zack would be in the air and Dylan on the train or maybe already off it, and she'd never said good-bye to any of them. She'd slept the day away.

Soon it would be the week. For four days, almost five, all she'd done was sleep. Her family needed her and she wallowed in sleep when she should have been with them. It was her duty to be strong for them. She'd never shirked it before and she mustn't now. They had to find some way to get through this, all of them, but she knew it had to start with her.

She staggered into the bathroom. The shower was too cold then too hot but she forced herself to stand in it and held her face toward the full jet-force of the spray. Strands of memory began to rise, loose tan-

Pete braced himself. Failing grades or he got some girl pregnant. Those were the worries he and Leigh most often had about these two.

"It's about Kip. Zack and me—we kind of roughed him up."

"What?"

Pete's tone held nothing but surprise, but Dylan winced like he'd been chewed out. "I know, I'm sorry. It was only heat of the moment, you know? But I feel bad about it now. I mean, I know it was an accident. It could've been me or Zack behind the wheel as easy as Kip."

"How rough?"

"A couple punches to the gut. One to the face."

"Jeez, Dylan."

"I know. I feel terrible now. But we were just hanging out in our room thinking about Chrissy, then Kip walked in, and we took one look at each other and jumped him."

Their secret twin communication. It wasn't the first time they brought out the worst in each other.

"Would you tell him I'm sorry?"

"Ought to come from you, don't you think?"

Dylan sighed. "Yeah, I hear you."

Pete got out and hoisted his bag from the trunk and peeled off another couple hundred dollars at the curb. "Thanks for telling me," he said when Dylan hugged him good-bye.

"We're gonna get through this, right, Pete?"

"If we can keep the punches to a minimum? You bet."

He wondered. All the way home he wondered. What if his son was actually convicted of killing Leigh's daughter? How well would they be blended then? *Their* son, *their* daughter, Leigh always said, but what now?

Shep jumped into the backseat and gave one last plaintive bark out the rear window as they left the District. He still seemed agitated at how he'd lost track of Chrissy. For four days he'd been nosing into every corner and cranny in the house, trying to pick up her scent. He leaped back into the front seat, and Pete hooked an arm around him and ruffled the fur on his chest. "I know, buddy," he said. "I know."

gled threads of everything that had happened in the past five days, and slowly they began to knit themselves together. Events came back to her. The surgery, the funeral, the luncheon. People—a slide show of the faces of friends and strangers. The words they spoke that she must have heard even when she couldn't respond. It was all coming back to her, and a list started to form in her mind of all the things she must do. Phone calls to make, thank-you notes to write.

But there was something else— Something else was struggling to climb up into her consciousness. It slid and scrabbled against the slippery slope of her memory, but finally an axe struck and held and the memory vaulted to the summit.

Kip.

He'd been arrested. He spent the night in jail and the morning in court, and he must be more terrified than he'd ever been in his life.

She shut off the shower and yanked on a robe and hurried down the hall. His door was open, and his computer screen glowed a blue light from the desk to the bed where he lay with his eyes closed and a pair of headphones on. Not asleep, though; one foot was moving in rhythm to whatever music was being piped into his ears. Her eyes misted as she stared at him, and the blue light bled into the shadows of his body. Slowly his dark hair blurred into copper curls, and suddenly it was Chrissy lying there, it was Chrissy's foot tapping, and Leigh gasped out loud.

Kip's head jerked at the sound, and the image dissolved in a puff of smoke.

Drugs. It was only the drugs. She took a steadying breath. "Want some company?"

His foot went still. He shifted over a few inches, and she came in and perched on the edge of the mattress. Across the room his suit coat was draped over the desk chair. He was wearing sweatpants now and a rumpled T-shirt, and she could see the tension in the clench of his fingers.

"Can you tell me about it?"

He tugged off the headphones but didn't answer, and the only sound was the music trickling tinny and faint through the speakers. It wasn't his usual percussive rap music. It was something more melodic, sad and eerie, like an Appalachian ballad. One night in jail and he was a country music fan.

He fumbled for the mute button. "Leigh, I—I don't know what to say."

"You don't have to talk about it if you don't want. I know it must have been awful."

"No, I—I mean about—Chrissy."

"Oh." Now she didn't know what to say. It was an accident. It was nobody's fault. It was a terrible loss for all of them, Kip as much as anyone. More than anyone, perhaps, except for Leigh herself. He never meant to hurt her. He never would. "It was an accident," she said finally, out loud.

"I'm sorry."

"Shh." She reached out and brushed his hair off his forehead. For a moment he didn't move, then his breath trembled out of him and he rolled up against her and hid his face against the folds of her robe.

"Kip, I'm here. You can tell me."

When he finally spoke, his words came out in a muffled choke. "It was a hundred thousand dollars."

"What?"

"The bail. We can't afford that."

"You let us worry about that." She wondered how Peter had managed it.

"We can't afford Shelby either, and all these expert witnesses she's talking about."

"You don't need to worry about that either. You don't need to worry about anything, okay? We're all here for you, you know that, right? Your dad and mom and me. Even Gary."

"The Gang of Four," he mumbled. That was the name he coined for his aggregated parents and stepparents. Imagine, she thought, a thirteen-year-old plucking a term out of Chinese history to describe his newly re-constituted family. He was always something special, this boy.

"That's right." She put her arms around him. "The whole Gang of Four."

By the time Peter got home, she was dressed and waiting at the kitchen table with a cup of tea. Shepherd burst inside first, and she gave him a quick pat as she rose and went to Peter. He pulled her close and nuzzled her hair, and when she turned her face up, he kissed her, gently.

She searched his face as they parted. He looked exhausted, and for the first time she realized: all those hours and days she was sleeping, he probably wasn't. The toll showed in the sags under his eyes, but his mouth was smiling as he held her back in the circle of his arms. "It's good to see you up," he said.

"Peter, the bail—"

"Taken care of."

"But the collateral—"

"Rose Lane."

"Oh, no." That was supposed to be his next big payday; he'd been counting on it for months.

"It's fine," he said and kissed her again.

She knew to let it go. "Are you hungry? I could fix something."

"Let's just forage. We must have enough leftovers to feed an army."

She opened the refrigerator while he got out the plates. "Boys make their connections okay?"

"Yep. They promised to call when they get in."

"They won't, though. They'll text. I never hear their voices when they're gone. It's like their vocal cords don't stretch beyond the house."

He laughed.

Half of a spiral-sliced ham sat in the refrigerator alongside some kind of green bean salad. "Sandwiches okay?" she asked.

He didn't answer, but a second later he was behind her with his arms around her. "I love you," he murmured into her ear.

"Me, too." She tried out a smile. "Always and everywhere."

He hollered for Kip while she spread the salad and sandwich fixings out on the kitchen table. She poured a glass of milk for Kip and opened a beer for Peter. No alcohol for her, though, not with the narcotics still paddling dopily through her bloodstream.

Kip came into the kitchen. "You okay?" Peter caught him by the arm, and he nodded and ducked into his chair.

The kitchen table was square with two chairs pulled up on either side. They dragged in extras on Mia's weekends or when the twins were home, and when all the children were home, they ate in the dining room. But for everyday meals they ate here, two on one side of the table and two on the other. Peter pulled out her chair and gave her knee a reassuring squeeze as he sat down beside her.

It wasn't until she looked across the table at Kip that she saw the livid burst of blood under the skin along his right cheekbone. "Oh, no!" She jumped up. "Did the cops do this to you?"

"No." Kip flinched as she grabbed his face and turned it to the light.

"One of the prisoners?"

He shook his head free. "I just tripped."

"Oh. Well." She stood back with her hands on her hips. "That's going to bruise. Hold on." She grabbed a clean dish towel and filled it with ice cubes from the refrigerator dispenser and tied it in a knot. How many times had she done this over the years? She didn't know why she never bothered to invest ten dollars in a real ice bag. No, she did know. Because it would be too much of an admission that her children were going to get hurt. That they were breakable. She handed the homemade ice pack to Kip. "Here. Hold this on it."

He placed it gingerly against his face, and they all busied themselves with passing dishes and assembling their sandwiches. It felt almost peaceful for a few minutes, breaking bread together in silence. But Leigh knew she had to ask about the charges and discuss what came next. They had to start planning how to deal with this. It was what families did when an outside threat loomed. They closed ranks and worked together to shield themselves from it. If anyone else had been in the truck with Kip that night, if anyone else had died, Leigh would be leading the strategy sessions by now. She'd be heading up the Kip Conley Defense Committee. If it was anyone else but Chrissy.

"Leigh," Peter said softly.

She looked up with a start.

"You need to eat something."

"Oh." She made herself smile as she picked up her fork. "I am. See?"

Kip was picking at his meal, too, half-slumped over his plate with his elbow on the table and the ice pack holding up his head.

"You call your mom?" Peter said.

"Not yet."

"Come on. That's the deal. You have to keep her in the loop."

"I know! I will. I just—" He put down the ice pack and sat up straight. "I need to tell you something first." His eyes shifted to Leigh. "Both of you. About what really happened."

Leigh felt suddenly weak.

Peter squinted at him. "What d'you mean, *really*?"

"Chrissy rode over to Ryan's to get me, and she put her bike in the back—"

"Yeah, we know. You already—"

"Then she got in the truck. Behind the wheel."

Peter's chair squealed against the floor as he pushed back hard from the table. "What?"

"She insisted on driving. She said zero tolerance and all that. She was afraid the cops would stop me and I'd get slammed. I said no, but I couldn't get her to shove over, and it was late and I finally said okay you can drive if you go the long way on Hollow Road." The words tripped and stumbled out of Kip's mouth. "She did fine until that dog ran out in front of us. She jerked the wheel too hard, and the road was wet and she lost control. We went in the ditch and she couldn't get out of the mud, so I got out and made her slide over. But before I could get us out of there, the cop pulled up. I didn't want Chrissy to get in trouble for driving without a license, not when she was only trying to keep me out of trouble. So I said to her, I was driving, okay? So that was the story we went with. But it was just a story. Chrissy was driving. Not me. I'm—sorry."

His voice trailed off at the end, and Leigh put her head in her hands and sighed. Here he was, at it again. Christopher Con Man, working another scam. And after she had such hopes that they could have a peaceful evening and try to work through this together. Now Peter was going to take his head off for pulling this kind of stunt, lying about something like this with Chrissy dead in the ground.

Peter's breath came out in a loud exhalation, too, but it wasn't a sigh—it sounded more like a rush of relief. "Kip!" Suddenly he was lit up. "This is—this is huge. Why didn't you say something? You should have told me."

"I was afraid it would look like I was making it up to save my own skin."

Leigh got to her feet. That was exactly what it looked like. She understood that he was scared and desperate, but blaming Chrissy? Peter needed to nip this in the bud. Send Kip to his room with an *I'll deal with you later*. But suddenly hope was blooming across Peter's face. He was so desperate to find a way out that he couldn't see that it was obviously a lie. Chrissy didn't drive. It was only a game when Peter let her take the wheel out in the fields. She was only fourteen. It was ridiculous to think she'd muscled her way past Kip into the driver's seat.

"Come on. We need to call Shelby," Peter said, and he pulled Kip up out of his chair and after him down the hall.

Leigh sighed again. Now they were going to drag Shelby into this travesty. She trailed after them through the length of the house to the den. Peter was bent over the desk, scrolling through the directory on the speakerphone in search of Shelby's number. "Here we go," he said and pressed the button.

Shelby would be livid. She didn't receive business calls on her personal line. If she picked up at all, it would only be because she saw Leigh's name on her caller ID. She'd be furious when she discovered it was Kip spinning this lie.

The beeps sounded through the speaker as the call connected. "Peter, wait," Leigh said.

"What?"

She glanced over at Kip where he stood in the corner, clutching his elbows. "Can we talk about this first? Before we take it outside the family?"

Peter gave her a quizzical look as Shelby's silky voice entered the room. "Leigh?"

"No, it's Pete. And Kip. He has something important to tell you."

"Go ahead."

Kip took a breath. "I wasn't driving," he said. He didn't look at Leigh. "Chrissy was."

Leigh looked at the ceiling as he told it all again. His delivery was smoother this time. His rehearsal in the kitchen must have helped. Peter watched him and gave him little encouraging nods as he spoke. He didn't look at Leigh again.

The line was silent when Kip finished. The quiet before the storm, Leigh was sure of it. Shelby was about to explode with anger. How dare you? she'd say. How dare you defile the memory of that sweet girl? What kind of coward are you, not to take responsibility for your own actions?

"Okay," Shelby said. "Let's talk about how we prove it."

What? Leigh blinked at the phone on the desk.

"Did anyone see you drive away from the party?"

Kip hesitated. "No, I don't think so."

Of course not, Leigh thought. It would be his word against nobody's.

"But there was a witness on the road," he said suddenly. "This dude stopped to ask if we were all right. He looked like a priest or something, with one of those collars, you know? The black shirt with the white patch at the neck? He must've seen it was Chrissy behind the wheel. When he called down to us, I was getting out of the passenger side and walking around to her door."

"Good. That's good," Shelby said as Peter gave a vigorous nod at the phone.

"Except he never mentioned a witness before," Leigh spoke up.

The mark on Kip's cheek flamed red from across the room. "'Cause before I didn't want anyone to know Chrissy was driving."

"She never mentioned it either. Neither of you did, despite the fact that a witness might have helped prove it happened before midnight. That was our biggest concern that night, remember?"

Peter stared at her across the desk, but Kip wouldn't look at her at all. "My biggest concern that night was keeping Chrissy out of trouble."

"This priest," Shelby said. "Did you get his name or his plates?" She was jumping right in with questions designed to locate the witness, as if Leigh hadn't just established there wasn't one.

Kip shook his head. "He barely stopped. He sort of halfway got out and shouted were we okay. And I asked Chrissy, and she said she was fine. I told him yes, and he got back in and drove away."

"What kind of car?"

"I don't know."

"Sedan, coupe, SUV, what?"

"I'm not sure."

Peter jumped in. "Four doors or two?"

"Four, I guess. It was kinda big."

"What color?" Shelby asked.

"Black, I think. Or some dark color. Green or navy."

Or deep purple or gunmetal gray. Leigh could understand why Peter wanted to believe him, but not Shelby. She was the most cynical person Leigh knew. She built her whole career on the principle that all of her clients were lying all of the time. "Shelby," she said in a calm, lawyer-to-lawyer voice. "You know what the prosecutor will do with this. Kip never mentioned a witness or another vehicle the night he was arrested or for four days thereafter. It wasn't until he spent a night in jail that he came forward with this new version. The prosecutor will rip him apart on those facts."

"Of course," Shelby said. "Which is why we need a corroborating witness. So let's get out there and find this priest. Sound like a plan?"

"Yes," Kip said quickly.

"Come in to the office tomorrow, and we'll sit down with my investigator and figure out how to locate this guy. What time's good for you?"

"Any time," Pete said with a nod at Kip. "The sooner the better."

"Let's say nine o'clock."

They were still saying their good-byes as Leigh left the room and went back to the kitchen. Their three plates sat barely touched, and the homemade ice pack was weeping across the surface of the table at the fourth place. Chrissy's place. Leigh grabbed up the towel and ice in both hands and carried it dripping across the floor to the sink, then went back to the table with handfuls of paper towels to mop up. The water had already pooled to the edge of the table and was trickling in steady plops onto the seat of Chrissy's chair. She wiped it down furiously and dropped to her knees to wipe the floor, too. Shep was under the table, as always during mealtime, and he licked her hands as she scrubbed the floor.

She got up and scraped her plate into the garbage and was rinsing it off at the sink when Peter came in and sat down at the table. "Is Kip coming back to dinner?" she asked without turning.

"No, he's gone up to his room."

"He didn't finish his sandwich."

"He thinks you don't believe him."

She shut the faucet off. "And you do."

"Yeah, I think I do. I mean, it all makes sense."

She turned then and leaned back with the edge of the granite counter cutting into her spine. "How? Tell me."

"Because I taught him better than to swerve for an animal. He knows that's dangerous. But Chrissy, she argued the point with me every time I took her out. So I can see her doing it. I can see her grabbing the keys from him, too. She was all about SADD and don't drink and drive, remember? She wouldn't go over there to rescue him only to have him drive home drunk."

"Except he wasn't drunk, not at point-oh-five-five. She's seen enough of her father to know what drunk really looks like. And he could have swerved reflexively no matter what you drilled into him. For a dog? I think even you might have swerved. Oh, Peter." She reached for another dish towel and wiped her hands. "Isn't this all just wishful thinking? You want to believe it."

"I want him to get off." He studied the label on his beer bottle. "Don't you?"

"Of course I do. But not if it takes a lie."

"I guess that's where we differ." He got to his feet. "I want him to get off no matter what."

He headed into the family room with his beer, and a minute later she heard the TV switch on. Now there were two plates of almost untouched food left on the table, and she picked them up and scraped them both into the garbage.

Chapter Ten

Shelby Randolph's office was on I Street a few blocks from Leigh's office on K Street. Both law firms were big and prestigious with hundreds of lawyers representing Fortune 500 companies, and both women were partners in their respective firms. But the similarities ended there. Leigh was something called a service lawyer, which Pete understood to mean one who handled the peripheral needs of the corporate clients brought in by the powerhouse partners—drafting wills for CEOs, procuring visas for the imported talent, and in her case, handling their divorces. Whereas Shelby was *the* powerhouse lawyer at her firm. Her specialty was white-collar crime, and she had a long roster of government-contractor clients she defended in billion-dollar fraud cases. She didn't represent teenagers in DUI cases even when the DUI led to a homicide charge. Pete knew she was doing this strictly as a favor for the family of her oldest friend.

But Kip was treated the same as any other client when they arrived at her office in the morning. Shelby's assistant met them in reception and led them through corridors of steel and glass and abstract art to a corner conference room with floor-to-ceiling windows overlooking Lafayette Square and offering a glimpse of the White House through the trees. Soon another woman came in, pushing a cart laden with minipastries and a full coffee service. And finally Shelby swept into the room in a strangely dramatic black dress with one white sleeve.

A retinue of three other people funneled in behind her. She made the introductions. Frank Nobbin was her chief investigator, a retired police detective from Baltimore. Elliott Sousa was something she called a social media coordinator. And finally there was her paralegal, Britta, a young woman who silently took notes for the duration of their meeting.

There were some papers to sign first, a retainer agreement, a revocable waiver of confidentiality so Pete could be present. Then Frank Nobbin took over. He was a crusty old black guy with a gray brush mustache that gave him a permanent frown. He questioned Kip about every detail of last Friday night while Shelby sat back and watched Kip stammer through his answers. It was like pulling teeth, but Nobbin finally got him to give up the names of a dozen kids at the party, including a girl Pete never heard of who was more or less Kip's date for the night. He also got him to identify every variety of refreshment on offer. Kip remembered a couple bottles of tequila and vodka circulating through the party but was adamant that he had only two beers.

"What d'you weigh?" Nobbin eyeballed. "One-forty, fifty?"

Kip flushed. He hadn't filled out yet, and he was self-conscious about it. "About that."

"Still. Oughta take more than two beers to register point-oh-five-five."

He shrugged. "So the lab made a mistake."

Shelby said, "We'll look into that," but Pete could tell from the glance she exchanged with her investigator that there was no realistic hope of beating the machine.

Nobbin homed in on the roadside witness next, and Kip repeated what he had said last night. A man stopped to ask if they were all right and drove on when Kip answered that they were. He remembered that he was dressed all in black except for that patch of white at his collar, which made him think he was a priest.

"Age?"

"I don't know. Middle?"

"Tall, short, skinny, fat?"

"Tall, I think. Not fat."

"His hair. Was it dark or light, long or short?"

Kip looked by turns helpless and pissed off at Nobbin's interrogation. "I don't know. I mean, it was dark and I only saw him for a second. I was more focused on getting the truck out of there, you know?"

Pete felt by turns frustrated and reassured by Kip's response. If he were lying about the witness, surely he'd do better than this?

Nobbin moved on. He opened a folder stuffed full of photos of what looked like every make and model of big, four-door vehicles available across the country. "Thumb through these," he said, "and pick out whatever looks like what the priest was driving."

"I'm not really a car guy," Kip said with a hangdog glance at his father. Pete would have been able to identify the make of every vehicle in the folder and come pretty close on the model year and equipment package, too. But Kip didn't get that gene. Anything between a Volkswagen and a Cadillac Escalade was the same generic *car* to him, and after only a few minutes he gave up looking.

"It's only a four- or five-mile stretch of road," Pete said. "There can't be more than a hundred cars traveling it a day and practically none at night. This priest has to be somebody who lives on Hollow Road or was visiting somebody who lives there. Can't we just put a notice in the local paper or something?"

"We're doing that," Shelby said. "And Frank and his team are going to do door-to-doors at every house along that road."

"Hey, I can do that. I'm there every day."

"No." Shelby and Frank said it nearly in unison and with a surprising forcefulness. "You mustn't talk to any potential witness," she said. "It could taint their testimony."

"What, like I'm gonna bribe somebody or something?"

"Avoid the appearance. It's best practice. Meanwhile." She turned to the other man in the room. "Elliott?"

He was a young guy wearing glasses and a skinny tie who handled social media for the firm's marketing department and occasionally provided investigative services, too. He'd already launched a search for the priest on three different internet platforms. First he set up a Facebook page with photos of the truck and the scene of the accident along with photos of Chrissy and Kip, and put out a call for anyone who witnessed the event to contact Shelby Randolph. He told Kip to share the page and get all his friends and family to share it, too. He also created a few different Twitter hashtags and sent out tweets every twelve hours with the same call, and he posted the same photos on Instagram. Some of Chrissy's classmates had already created a Facebook page in her honor, and he basically hijacked it and posted the photos there, too, along with an emotional plea for the witness to honor Chrissy's memory by coming forward and reporting what he saw. Kip should share and retweet all of it, Elliott said, and Pete and Leigh should signal-boost, too.

Pete nodded and made a note to ask Kip later what that meant.

Back to Frank Nobbin. It was likely that the priest had a church in the vicinity, he said. He'd run them all down and get photos of every clergyman and put together an array. He'd shoot the file to Kip in a day or two, and he should study each photo and see if he could pick out the witness he saw on the road that night.

That was it. Meeting over.

St. Alban High School was a flat-roofed sprawl of brick buildings surrounded by the bright green turf of five different playing fields. Pete parked in front of the main lobby entrance and went in with Kip to tender his excuse to the attendance office. But before he could get away, the principal tapped on the glass partition and beckoned for them to come in his office.

"Uh." Kip shifted from foot to foot. "I got physics."

"Go on," Pete said. "I'll take this. Hey," he added as Kip started down the hall. "You'll catch a ride home?"

"Yeah, with Brad. Like always."

Pete pushed through the door of the administrative suite as the elderly secretary rose from behind her desk. "Oh, Pete." She held her hands out to him. "We're all so sorry for your loss. What a terrible tragedy."

"Thank you, Patty. I appreciate it." That he was on a first-name basis with the principal's secretary was testament to the fact that he'd been summoned there way too often. Mostly for disciplinary infractions of the backfired prank variety, but Kip had been caught cutting classes, too, and the only thing that saved him from more serious penalties was that he was acing all those classes.

"Please give my condolences to Leigh."

"I will. Thank you."

The principal was waiting at his office door to usher him inside. He had a florid face and a belly that oozed over his belt like soft-serve ice cream over the rim of the cone. Dr. Dairy Queen, Kip called him. Pete hoped there wasn't a gay slur buried in the nickname.

"Mr. Conley."

"Dr. Fulton." No first-name basis in here.

Another round of condolences followed before the principal got down to business. He'd read about Kip's arrest in yesterday's newspaper and wanted a status update on the proceedings.

"Sorry," Pete said. "Our lawyer said not to discuss the case with anyone."

"Oh, of course. But you can understand that not only are we concerned for Christopher, but we also need to plan for certain eventualities."

Pete didn't understand at all. "What eventualities?"

"Well, for one thing, Christopher's on track to finish second in his class, which would ordinarily make him salutatorian at commencement. But under the circumstances."

For one surprised second Pete let himself bask. His son, going to Duke and speaking at his graduation. Who would have guessed the Conleys could come this far? Except they hadn't, yet. "I don't understand," he said. "If he earned it."

"Oh, of course, but we have to consider the reception he might receive. We wouldn't want him to be made to feel uncomfortable. With these charges hanging over him."

Pete tried to picture it. A stadium full of friends and family falling suddenly silent as Kip took the lectern. Probably waiting for him to deliver some kind of cautionary tale—*Don't drink and drive, kids; look what hap-*

pened to me—like the man with no jaw who came around once a year to talk to them about the dangers of smoking. Except that Kip wasn't drunk and maybe he wasn't even driving. "We expect the charges to be dismissed long before graduation," Pete said. "He has a complete defense."

"Oh?" Dr. Fulton raised an eyebrow.

"He wasn't the one driving," Pete heard himself say. He wasn't sure where that came from. He wanted to believe it, and now it looked like he'd gone and committed himself to it.

"Well." The principal's belly shifted as he settled back in surprise. "That would change things, wouldn't it? In that case suppose we table this for a few weeks?"

"Yeah." Pete got up to go. "Let's do that."

His phone rang as he headed for his truck. It was Kip, speaking in a whisper that told Pete he was probably ducking under his desk to make the call. "Can you pick me up after school?"

"What happened to your ride with Brad?"

"Fell through. Can you pick me up at three?"

It was already close to noon. Pete needed to get some work done before the entire day was gone. He swung into the cab and started the engine. "Sorry, champ. You'll have to take the bus."

Kip groaned, as if he couldn't imagine a worse fate. A kid who'd already spent a night in adult jail.

"Suck it up," Pete said and backed out of the lot.

Chapter Eleven

Peter was gone by the time Leigh woke that morning—Kip, too—and the house was eerily quiet. She couldn't remember a time when she was ever in the house alone. When the kids were at school, she was at work, and when they were out playing sports or performing in musicals or competing in horse shows, she was there with them, cheering them on. When they were at home, they were all together. It was why the house had always felt too small and why she'd agreed to Ted's elaborate expansion plans—because it was always bursting at the seams with the children and their friends galloping up and down the stairs and slamming in and out of doors. It was a house full of music and laughter and TVs blaring. Now, though, it seemed vast and empty. And quiet. As quiet as a tomb.

Even Shepherd was quiet when he jumped down from the window seat in the kitchen and wagged a greeting. "At least you're still here," she said, but he'd already had his breakfast and wanted only to go outside.

She let him out and wandered alone through the labyrinth of rooms, from the kitchen, where Kip dropped his bombshell last night, all the way to the den, where Shelby declined to defuse it. The three of them were together now, plotting a strategy. The truth would come out eventually, when Kip's manufactured witness failed to materialize, but meanwhile Peter was spending all his money and hope on a lie, and there was nothing she could do to spare him either one.

The house was so quiet she could almost hear her thoughts ricochet through the empty rooms. She should try to eat something, she knew. There was nothing in the refrigerator but funeral leftovers, but in the freezer was a bag of the chicken nuggets Chrissy liked to snack on. *Don't forget the barbecue sauce*, she'd holler whenever anyone left on a grocery run. Leigh shook a few nuggets out on a baking pan and put them in the oven.

A shower might help, she thought, and she went up the back stairs to her room. But instead of turning into the master bath, she drifted down the hall, past the guest room and up the half-flight of stairs to the children's wing. Chrissy's door stood closed, and she cracked it open. It was so quiet inside, and dark, too, with the blinds drawn. Chrissy never closed them. She always liked to wake to the sunshine. Leigh closed the door behind her, and the vast and empty house shrank to this little twelve-by-twelve-foot room. The darkness was strangely inviting. It felt like crawling into a cave when she pulled back the comforter and slipped into the bed.

Someone had changed the sheets, but when Leigh pressed her face into the comforter, she could still breathe in the sweet scent of strawberry shampoo in the fabric, and here and there the salty tang of the popcorn Chrissy liked to munch while she read in bed. During a single week when she was ten, she read the entire Harry Potter series in this bed. *Mom*, she wailed whenever she came up for air, *I wanna go to witch school!*

Leigh lay there and watched the slatted shadows of the blinds drift across the wall and ceiling as the sun moved into the afternoon. She knew she needed to pull herself together. She mustn't let this—development—come between her and Peter. She had to hold tight to what was left of her family. Peter and Kip and Leigh. The three of them plus Mia every other weekend. Everyone who was hers was gone.

No, no, that kind of thinking would undo everything she'd worked for these past five years. Her children were his and his were hers. Not even that. They were all theirs.

But Chrissy had been hers. Peter might have loved her, he did love her, but she was Leigh's magical child, Leigh's alone, and no one else's grief could ever begin to rival her own.

It was a shameful thought, and she quashed it as fast as she could.

She should at least get up and check her office email. She'd never gone a single day before without checking in with the office, whether on vacation, on her honeymoon, even when her babies were born. Now she'd gone—how many days? She didn't even know.

Or care. She wished she could take back all the tens of thousands of hours she'd spent at work and spend them with Chrissy instead. The old adage came to mind: no one on his deathbed ever regrets that he didn't spend more time at the office. The same was true when it was a loved one's deathbed. All those years she could have been home with her child instead of out practicing family law. What irony there. Leaving her family so she could help other families. And that wasn't even what she did. What she really did was help families to self-destruct. Her specialty: lawyer-assisted immolation.

That was the thought she went to sleep on.

A piercing shriek jolted her awake. She flailed out of the comforter and flung herself to her feet as the screech sounded again. It took a dazed moment to recognize the smoke alarm, and another to remember the chicken nuggets she'd left in the oven. She raced downstairs into a kitchen already thick with smoke. The nuggets had turned to charcoal briquettes, burned to cinders and still smoldering. She hurled them into the sink, and when she turned on the tap, a cloud of white steam hissed up.

She opened the doors and windows and switched on the exhaust fan and covered her ears until the shrill whistle of the alarm finally died. No lunch for her after all, and no shower either, but she should at least do one of the things she'd planned. She sat down at her laptop at the kitchen desk. Her inbox was overflowing with emails, but her assistant Polly had gone through them and sorted them into folders. The biggest folder was labeled CONDOLENCES, and Leigh left it unopened. Another was labeled FIRM BUSI-NESS, and she skipped that, too. Another folder contained messages from Polly herself, summarizing the snail mail and telephone messages.

Leigh scrolled through them dully. Hunter Beck's lawyer called; he wanted Leigh to join him in requesting an accelerated briefing and argument schedule on his client's appeal. *No, thank you,* she replied. Not only because she wasn't ready to work yet, but also because Beck's demand for access to his wife's uterus would be moot by the time the court heard the case on a nonaccelerated schedule. None of the other messages looked urgent. Some were merely sales calls. Solicitations for journal subscriptions. A life insurance offer.

She jumped when the doorbell rang. It was a sound that was always followed by pounding footsteps and a holler of *I'll get it.* A hundred pounds soaking wet and Chrissy thundered like a herd of elephants on the stairs. *Don't run,* Leigh would scold. *You'll slip and break your neck.*

You'll bounce and break your brain.

She got up and looked out the kitchen window. A little red car was in the driveway. A Mini Cooper, she thought, though she didn't know anyone who drove one. The bell rang again, and quickly she finger-combed her hair and went down the hall to answer it.

A young woman stood on the front porch smartly turned out in a belted trench dress and holding a designer attaché case. "Mrs. Leigh Huyett?"

"Yes. Can I help you?" The visitor was too well dressed to be a political canvasser or a Jehovah's Witness.

"My name is Emily Whitman. I'm sorry to disturb you." Her wheat-blond ponytail swung through the air like a scimitar as she stooped to lift a package wrapped in a shroud of green tissue paper. "The sheikha asked me to deliver this to you."

"The sheikha—? Devra?" Leigh said, stupidly, as if she knew more than one.

"Yes, ma'am. May I?" She swept around Leigh and carefully placed the package on the hall table before she stripped away the tissue paper to reveal an enormous floral arrangement.

"Oh." Leigh stood stunned. It wasn't the usual white lilies and pink roses that had flooded the house this week. This was a mix of exotic blossoms in rich, saturated shades of fuchsia, coral, and crimson. "They're lovely," she said. "She shouldn't have."

"She only wishes she could do more." The young woman stepped back

and clasped her hands together at waist level like a finishing school gradu-
ate. "The sheikha was devastated when she learned of your terrible loss.
Coming so soon after her own, it hit her particularly hard."

"Her own—?"

"It's been only three months since the sheikh passed away."

Leigh stared at her. *The sheikh—?* "I'm sorry—you're saying Devra's
husband is dead?"

"She didn't tell you." The young woman sighed. "I'm afraid she's still
so distraught that sometimes she denies the fact of his death even to herself. It was so sudden. A heart attack," she added in a confidential whisper.

Leigh could understand denial, but seeking divorce from a dead man
seemed more like derangement. She couldn't believe it. "Ms.—Whitman,
is it?"

"Please. Call me Emily. I was the sheikh's personal assistant, and I'm
staying on to help the sheikha adjust to her new life."

"Emily. I'd like to call and thank her in person. Is there a number
where I can reach her?"

"Of course. It's on the card." She turned to the door. "Again I apologize for disturbing you. You have my deepest condolences as well."

Shepherd squeezed in the front door as the young woman stepped
out. Leigh watched her swing gracefully into her little red car and back out
of the driveway before she shut the door and turned to the flowers. They
were exquisite, and it was such a kind gesture, considering they'd met only
once. But it was all so bizarre, Devra's detailed probing about the procedure for divorcing a husband who was already dead.

A card was stapled to the tissue wrapping. A business card. EMILY
WHITMAN, it read, ASSISTANT TO SHEIKH MAZIN AL-KHAZRATI, followed
by two lines of Arabic characters. Below that was a phone number with a
202 area code. Washington. On the back was a note written in an elegant
script: *I cannot begin to fathom the depth and breadth of your pain. I beg of
you, do not hasten your mourning, least of all on my account. My sorrows are
but dust compared to yours.*

I'm sorry, no rush, take your time seemed to be the distilled message, but
the Old World turn of phrase made it so much more moving. It reminded

her of the archaic language of the Bible verses she learned as a child. The cadence of those old refrains. *Verily I say unto thee* and *He restoreth my soul.* Language that had long since passed from everyday speech and seemed to carry so much more meaning for it. *Surely goodness and mercy shall follow me all the days of my life. World without end. Amen.*

World without Chrissy.

She went back to the kitchen and closed the door and windows and lingered a moment at the window overlooking the garden. Finches swooped into the feeder and pecked futilely before they took flight again. The tube was empty. It was Leigh's job to refill it, the songbirds fed heavily this time of year, she should go out and do it now. But she didn't. She looked out at the spring bulbs pushing up through the earth, and the late afternoon sunshine sparkling on the new green leaves of the trees. She could see Licorice in the pasture rubbing his flank against a fencepost like he was scratching an itch. He was still shedding his heavy winter coat. Both horses were. Chrissy had planned to clip them over the weekend.

For a moment she couldn't breathe. Her lungs felt paralyzed, her limbs frozen, as the oxygen wisped from her brain, and she thought: *This must be how it feels to die.* But it lasted only a few seconds before she choked on a sob and the air rushed back in, wet and ragged. She needed to turn it off, shut it down, all these springtime images of new life and rebirth outside the window. She needed to flee upstairs and dive deep into the burrow of Chrissy's bed.

But as she spun from the window, something caught her eye. The top fence rail beside Licorice was down, and Romeo was nowhere in sight.

This happened every few months. Romeo got loose and went wandering in search of the neighbors' garden delicacies. The pasture had a good fence, but with the top rail down he could easily jump the bottom two. Chrissy had a theory that Licorice was the culprit: he head-butted the rail to knock it free from its slot in the post, then stood back and egged Romeo on like a little boy trying to get his brother in trouble. Every time Romeo got loose, it was Licorice she scolded.

Leigh ran to the kitchen and slid her feet into her shoes and burst outside. Romeo wasn't in the pasture or the barn, and she grabbed a lead line and went hunting for him. The Markhams' house on the corner was Romeo's most likely destination. Their apple trees weren't in fruit now, but he probably had fond memories of gorging himself there last fall. She jogged down the road past swaths of sunny yellow daffodils, and when she rounded the corner, there stood Romeo with all four feet braced. There stood Kip, too, hanging on Romeo's halter with his own feet braced, tugging hard as he tried and failed to get him to move.

Leigh gave a sharp whistle and Romeo's head came up. So did Kip's. He dropped the halter and backed away, and she ran down the road and snapped the lead line on Romeo's halter. Kip bent to pick up his backpack from the ground. "He wouldn't budge."

"So I noticed." She clucked her tongue and started back, and Romeo followed in an easy amble beside her. Kip trailed behind, and Leigh stopped and waited for him to fall into step on the other side of Romeo. She glanced at him over the horse's withers. Seventy degrees and sunny and he wore the hood up on his sweatshirt like some kind of ghetto gangster. "You took the bus home?" He hadn't ridden the school bus for years; he always managed to finagle a ride from someone.

"Yeah."

"How did it go in school today?"

"Fine."

He wasn't normally a monosyllabic grunter like most teenaged boys. Normally he would spin out at least five minutes of entertaining conversation about the day's headlines. She glanced at him again. The bruise on his cheekbone was green going to purple.

"Good," she said. Normally she would have followed up with questions about last week's calculus exam, and was Ryan's father back from Tokyo, and how were things going with Ava? But today none of those questions would come to her.

Romeo's head dipped up and down between them as they walked toward home. "Kip," she began. "I know this is a terrible situation for you. I know you must be scared."

His Adam's apple bobbed in his throat as he pretended to study the blossoms on the Markhams' trees.

"But you've got one of the finest criminal defense lawyers in the country, and we're all going to help you get through this. You know that, right? We're going to do everything we can for you."

"Okay."

"But I need you to do something for me."

His eyes shifted to her.

"I need you to take back what you said. About Chrissy driving."

He looked away.

"*Recant* is the word lawyers use. Which tells you right there how commonly it comes up. That there's even a word for it. It doesn't have to be a big deal. Just say you made a mistake. It's not like you signed a sworn statement or anything. There's no question of perjury. Just tell your dad and Shelby the truth."

"I did. I am."

She sighed. "You know what I do when I cross-examine a witness who's changed his story? It's what every lawyer does. You confront them with their prior statement, then get them to admit they're telling a different story today. Then you hit them with the zinger. So were you lying then or are you lying now?"

"I already admitted I was lying before."

"And so was Chrissy, you're saying. You want us to believe she was lying, too."

"No. I mean, she didn't want to. I had to—"

He broke off. They'd reached the driveway, and he peeled off to the back door as Romeo picked up his pace to the barn. "Kip, wait a minute." She struggled to hold the horse back. "Could you help me fix the fence?"

He turned around, and maybe it was a trick of the light, or the shadow cast by his hoodie, but suddenly his straight dark hair turned to copper curls and his scowl became a grin and it was Chrissy standing there, shimmering in the sun like a desert mirage. She glowed, she sparkled, she was as three-dimensional as a holograph, and as real as a dream.

"I have homework," he muttered.

The image dissolved into ash. It was only Kip standing there in Chrissy's place.

Chapter Twelve

Pete met with the loan committee on Monday and wrenched a three-month extension out of them on his upcoming balloon payment. But nothing ever came free, especially where banks were concerned, and it was going to cost him an extra point. A steep price to pay, but three months meant he could push this worry onto the back burner and leave the front one open for more pressing concerns.

Like Hollow Road. Drew Miller was withholding this month's progress payment on the house, and Pete didn't have much ground for arguing otherwise given their lack of progress. He needed to hire more men, but he couldn't afford it. In six weeks the twins would be home from school, and they'd provide some good cheap labor, but until then he had to run a pretty lean crew. The only thing he could do was light a fire under his guys, get as much work out of them as he could.

But he felt like lighting a bomb under them when he pulled up the drive and found half of them not working at all. They were standing in a circle staring at a stack of lumber. Miller's Porsche was there, too, and that was another distraction they didn't need. His wife, the swanling, was perched on the hood as usual, filing her nails. "What's going on?" Pete asked her as he swung out of the truck.

Yana rolled her gamine eyes. "Drew ees show off new toy. Go and zee."

King Midas was in the center of the circle of men. Some kind of game console was on the stack of lumber, and he had his phone in one hand and was working the joystick with the other. All the men were craning their necks to watch the screen on his phone.

"Hey," Pete said as he came up.

The guys gave a guilty start and scattered, leaving Miller alone with his toy and a shit-eating grin on his face. "Check it out," he said.

Pete leaned over for a look at his phone. It didn't look like any video game he'd ever seen. Instead of a battle scene, an image of leafy green foliage covered the screen. "I don't get it."

"It's a vision quadcopter. Cost me fourteen hundred dollars. But look at that image. GPS-stabilized, baby."

Pete looked at the screen again, then the joystick. "Wait a minute." He could hear a buzzing overhead, like the sound of a hummingbird hovering by his ear. He looked up. "Are you telling me you launched a camera drone? You sent a camera drone over the neighbor's wall?"

"Free airspace, my friend. I got every right."

"Helluva wrong foot to get off on with your new neighbors."

"Yeah? Well, they started it when they put up that fucking wall. Hold on." Miller bobbled the phone in his right hand as he tried to maneuver the joystick with his left. "Let me fly in under those trees there and see what they're hiding."

Pete walked away, shaking his head in disgust. He started this business because he wanted to build exceptional homes with quality craftsmanship. He never set out to work for assholes, but that was where he ended up. Leigh, too. Some people might think they were rich, Leigh with her big-time law practice and Pete with his own business, but the truth was they were both servants to the real rich. He built their houses, she got them their divorces. The same was true of Ted, who drove their boats, and Gary, who whitened their teeth.

Kip was supposed to be the one who broke out of the family mold. He was going to be his own man. People were going to bow and scrape to him. That was the dream, right?

Still could happen, Pete tried to tell himself as he headed inside. In fact this ordeal could be the thing that kept him from turning into one of those rich assholes. If he got past it.

The HVAC crew was on-site today. He found them on the second story with the prints for the ductwork rolled out on the floor, and they all got down on their haunches to go over them. They were going to have to deviate from the plan in the master bedroom, since the Millers had ordered a last-minute change to the ceiling—vaulted instead of coffered—which was going to cut into the space available for the ducts. They needed to come up with some kind of work-around, but the HVAC crew was out of ideas, and for the moment, so was Pete. "I'll work on this tonight," he told the team.

He was hauling himself to his feet when a clamor erupted outside, a crash followed by a stream of obscenities. He ran to the window in time to see Midas hurl the drone control console to the ground. "Fourteen fucking hundred dollars," he screamed, while the swanling clapped a hand over her mouth to hold in her giggles.

Pete stopped for some Chinese takeout on the way home. Leigh hadn't had much of an appetite for anything he brought home all week, but she was a big fan of sweet-and-sour—*just like me*, she liked to tease—and he hoped the shrimp would tempt her.

He came in the kitchen and stopped short. The air was full of the aroma of roasting chicken, and Leigh was at the island, tied up in an apron and chopping a green pepper. "Oh, no," she said at the sight of the takeout bag in his hand. "I should have called."

"No problem." He sniffed the air appreciatively. "This'll keep." He opened the refrigerator and stowed the Chinese inside, then, hands free, came around the island and gave her a backward hug.

She leaned back into his arms. "How was your day?"

"Good. Great. No problems. Yours?"

She smiled over her shoulder. "Fine." The lively look wasn't quite back in her eyes, but the smile was enough to make up for it. More than enough. She had a beautiful smile. She could light up a room, and this one seemed brighter than it had for days.

He went upstairs to shower and change. On his way back down he popped his head in Kip's room. He was at his desk on the computer, the same as any other day, except today a clergyman beamed from the screen. Kip had been clicking through minister mug shots for days.

"Any luck?"

He shook his head.

"How about the car?"

"No."

"Well, don't worry. We'll find him." It had been a week already and still no response to the newspaper ads or any of the internet postings. Pete clapped both hands on Kip's shoulders. The boy's muscles felt like sailor's knots, and he gave them a brisk rubdown. "School okay today?"

"Fine." Kip clicked through to another photo, this one of a cherubic-looking man with a bristle of curly white sideburns.

Pete hesitated. "Coming down for dinner?"

"I'll grab something later."

It was a week since he'd joined them at the dinner table. Once Pete wouldn't have tolerated that. It was one of the rules of their household that the whole family sit down for dinner together. But the tension between Leigh and Kip was building more and more every day, and Pete was afraid it might blow if he tried to force him to the table tonight. Besides, it would be nice to have an evening alone with Leigh while her happy mood lasted. "Yeah, okay," he said finally. "There's sweet-and-sour shrimp in the fridge, and there'll be some leftover chicken, too."

Kip shrugged. "Hey, Dad?" He pushed back from his computer. "Can I talk to you a minute?"

That sounded ominous. Pete took a seat on the foot of the bed. The walls of the room were covered with posters, but not the usual sports heroes or bikini babes like the ones plastered over the twins' room. Kip's posters were world maps at various points in time. Geopolitical history was his big interest. *Because I'm plotting world domination*, he used to say, rubbing his hands with an evil *mwah-ha-ha* laugh. "What's up?"

"I was wondering if I could go to Mom's."

"Sure. When? This weekend?"

"For good. Till I leave for Richmond for the summer."

Pete stared at him. "What are you talking about? You have two more months of school."

"I was thinking Mom could drive me?"

"Ninety miles each way? Come on. What's this about?"

Kip looked past him to one of the wall maps, the one with all the 'stans in Central Asia that Pete had never learned. Kip could recite them all. "I just think things would be better if I lived somewhere else."

"Better with Leigh, you mean."

"She hates me, Dad."

"Don't be stupid."

"She can't even look at me."

"She just needs time."

"It's been over a week already. What she needs is space. From me."

"That's not true. But regardless, your mom can't spend three or four hours every day running you back and forth to school. And I doubt you want to live with Gary that long either."

Kip's shoulders rose and fell. "Maybe I could rent a place somewhere around here—"

"We can't afford that. Not right now."

"Someplace cheap."

"There are no cheap apartments in Hampshire County." Pete got to his feet. "Look, I know things are a little tense, but it'll blow over soon." He tapped Kip's computer screen. "Real soon if we find this priest. You concentrate on that."

After dinner they took their coffees to the family room and settled side by side on the sofa with their legs stretched out together on the ottoman. This was their nightly routine and always the best part of the day for Pete. But it was the first night they'd done it since Chrissy died, and it felt new to him and a little fragile. He reached for the remote and looked uncertainly at the TV. He didn't know the drill for grieving. Was it better to sit in silence and remember Chrissy, or to plunge back into their normal routine and try to forget her?

They'd built such a good life together, he and Leigh, and all he wanted was to get back to it. But that life included Chrissy—depended on Chrissy—and he knew they'd never get back to it. Not without their sparkling girl. The only hope was to try to build a new life out of the ashes of the old one. He didn't know how. But he was a builder. It was his job to figure it out.

After a moment he clicked on CNN, and when Leigh did as she always did and picked up a book, he relaxed a little and settled in to watch the news.

The broadcast cycled through the business report, the sports update, the latest news from the Middle East. Leigh never glanced at the screen. She seldom did, that much was normal, but tonight she never turned a page either. She was only staring at her book. He knew he'd made a mistake, it was too soon to be normal, and he was about to switch off the TV and find something else to do when a report came on that made her put the book down and sit up straight.

It was an update on the school shooting in Missouri last week. One of the victims had been in intensive care since the incident, and today she died. That brought the total fatalities to twelve, four boys and six girls. The segment concluded with a slide show of their school portraits, ten middle schoolers with fresh-scrubbed faces and broad smiles against a blue studio background.

Pete glanced over at Leigh as the shining faces flipped across the screen. Her own face was frozen. She stared at the TV like she could see through it and a thousand yards beyond.

He hurried to turn it off. "Let's see what's on the DVR," he said, and scrolled through the list of their recordings until he landed on a sitcom they usually enjoyed.

Leigh sat stiffly. But about halfway in, an unexpected punch line, delivered deadpan, tore a startled laugh out of her. A week ago he thought he'd never hear that laugh again, and the light tinkling ring sounded so good to his ears that he hooked an arm around her and pulled her in closer. She tucked her legs up and put her head in his lap, and he stroked her hair while they watched that show and two more stacked up behind it on the DVR. He could feel her muscles relax and her body go limp against his. He wondered if they should sleep where they were tonight. He'd have a stiff neck in the morning, but that was better than waking her to go to bed. She always woke with such a bleak horrible look on her face.

But she wasn't asleep. "The horses!" She bolted upright. "I forgot to bring them in!"

"Shit." That was Chrissy's evening chore, and they still hadn't developed a new routine to work around it. "I'll go." He pushed to his feet. "You go on up to bed."

It was unseasonably warm outside, the kind of hot spring night that all but guaranteed a violent thunderstorm tomorrow. His mind scrolled through the work plan for Hollow Road as he headed out into the pasture and snagged the horses by their halters. The masons were due tomorrow to start on the fieldstone facade, but he could bring them inside if he had to and have them finish pointing up the fireplace in the library.

He led the horses into their stalls and as he fed and watered them, he wondered if they should sell them. It didn't look like Mia would ever get over her fear of horses, and Leigh never rode anymore. *Nature tells you when it's time to quit,* she liked to joke. *It's when you don't look good in breeches anymore.* Pete didn't know what she was talking about: she still looked damn good to him.

She was already asleep by the time he climbed up the stairs to bed, and he was careful not to disturb her as he slipped in under the covers on his side. But as soon as he settled in, she rolled up tight against him, and he felt the wonderful shock of her skin against his. She wasn't asleep, and she wasn't wearing a nightgown either. She pressed up close, and he felt the even better shock of her hand sliding around his waist and slipping in under his shorts.

He rolled over and found her lips in the dark. He would have settled for this, the taste of her tongue, the soft heat of her mouth. But her fingers kept on stroking him as they kissed. "You sure?" he whispered.

She took his hand and placed it over her breast. Her skin felt so soft under his fingers, her breasts so full and supple. Five years in and he still regarded her body as a gift, something to be unwrapped and marveled at and consumed with gratitude. He wriggled out of his shorts and dropped his mouth to her other breast and gently sucked and stroked her nipples. He still wasn't sure how ready she was for this. He needed to take it slow, slower than his usual athletic approach to sex. But this time, for the first time, Leigh was the one who grew impatient. She almost had a growl in her throat as she opened her legs and pulled him down between them.

He'd been afraid he might lose her to her grief forever, but here she was, back again, full of life and lust. She hooked her heels behind his knees and rose up to meet him. "Oh, ye-ess," she moaned, and it almost undid him. He had to tune out the sharp little pants in his ear and the glorious slip and slide of her skin against his. He summoned up the least arousing image he could think of, and of course, Hollow Road popped into his head. He froze it there on the screen and thought of nothing but tomorrow's work plan, holding back until he heard the familiar gasp that would tell him he could finish.

There. It sounded a little different in his ear, but he was already thrusting to the end before he realized: it wasn't a gasp he heard, it was a sob. "Oh, God, babe—" But it was too late.

"I'm sorry!" she cried as he collapsed on her. "I'm so sorry!"

His chest heaved as he flopped on his back. "No," he panted. "It's me who's sorry. It was too soon. I shouldn't have—"

"No, I wanted it! It's only—" Another sob choked off her words.

"What?" He pulled her into his arms. "Sweetheart, tell me."

"I want her back!" The words tore out of her like something ripped inside her body. "I want her back!"

"I know," he whispered. "I do, too."

"I want her back! I want her back!"

"I know. I know."

He tried to hold her but she wrenched free and rolled over and sobbed the same words into her pillow, over and over again. Helplessly he stroked her back until her shoulders finally stopped shaking.

He pretended to sleep after that, and so did she. He heard her get up during the night and gulp down some pills, and sometime later she drifted off. He must have slept, too, at some point, because he jerked awake when the alarm chimed at six. He rolled one way to slam it silent and Leigh rolled the other way and got out of bed. She pulled on her robe but sank down again on the edge of the mattress with her back to him.

"Leigh?"

"Peter, I'm so sorry about last night."

"It was my fault. I shouldn't—"

"No." Her shoulders sagged. "It's mine. I can't— I'm just not coping."

He rolled toward her and reached to rub her back. "No one would expect you to."

"I hear her voice. I think she's calling me, but when I go look, she's not there. I thought it must be the drugs, these hallucinations, I thought it would wear off, but it won't. I see her out of the corner of my eye, and when I spin around, she's not there. Or I see her and she dissolves and it's Kip who's there, and I'm sorry—I'm so sorry!—but it's like a fresh wound every time. It's tearing me apart."

His hand stilled on her spine. "Seeing Kip, you mean."

"I don't blame him. I swear I don't. I know it wasn't his fault. I would've swerved for that dog, too."

"Then what?"

"Then why won't he tell the truth about it?"

Pete rolled to his back.

"You believe him, I know it, and I understand why. I wish I could, too. But I can't. And I don't know how we go on living like this."

"It won't be forever," he said. "One way or the other, the truth's gonna come out. We just need to get through this next little while, okay?"

"Peter." She took a deep breath and stood up to face him, and he was shocked at how drawn her face looked. She usually woke up looking as good as she did when she went to sleep. It made him wonder if she'd lain awake while he slept instead of the other way around as he'd thought. "Peter, I think I should go stay with Shelby for a while."

"What?" The word hissed in his throat.

"I can't be here anymore. In this house."

Shelby had an apartment in a luxury building on Logan Circle. Pete had never been there, but he imagined it as a glamorous art deco penthouse straight out of a 1930s movie musical. It was easy to picture Shelby on a set like that, sweeping down a dramatic helical staircase into a party of gyrating revelers. But he couldn't picture Leigh in the scene at all. She'd be in the guest room, trying to read with her hands over her ears.

"This is your home. You belong here."

"But I can't be here. Not—"

She put her hand to her mouth and didn't say anything more, and in the silence, a stuttering burst of rap music came from the far end of the house. Kip's alarm had gone off.

Pete got to his feet. All night the idea played like a bad dream in his head, but now in almost-daylight it seemed the only solution. Kip wanted to leave, and apparently Leigh wanted the same thing. "No. You stay here," he said as he stepped into his shorts. "We'll crash at the job site for a while."

"We?"

"Well, he can't live by himself."

"He is eighteen."

"You think that means he's grown up?" He went to the dresser and pulled out a clean T-shirt. "The twins are twenty. You think they're grown up? Is that what you thought when you called Zack's professor last month?"

"No—"

"I left him once before when he needed me. I won't do it again, not while he's going through the worst experience of his life."

The pipes whined in the wall as Kip turned on the shower at the other end of the house.

"But—oh, for heaven's sake, Peter! You can't live in a half-built house. It doesn't even have plumbing."

"It won't hurt us to camp out for a while." He pulled the T-shirt over his head and opened another drawer for a button-down flannel. "Actually it'll kill two birds. I'm at the point where I usually hire nighttime security. With me and Kip staying there, I can save that money. Win win."

"Win win," she repeated dully.

"No, I didn't mean—"

"I know you didn't." She came up to him and slipped her hands inside his shirt, and he pulled her head to his shoulder and pressed his face in her sweet-smelling hair. They stood together for a long moment, rocking slightly, like a boat on a swell.

"I don't want you to leave."

"It won't be forever," he said. "Just till we get through this. And I'll stop by here every day. How's that? You'll hardly notice I'm gone." She felt as limp as a ragdoll in his arms, but he knew she had a spine of steel. This was the woman who'd built an addition on her house while her marriage was crumbling and stayed cheerful and resolute through it all. "We're gonna get through this."

Chapter Thirteen

The storm blew in that afternoon. Black clouds scuttled across the sky, and the wind kicked up so ferociously that the American flag in front of the high school lashed and cracked like a snapped cable. It was after five by then, and Kip was sulking on the curb like the last kid picked for the team. "Come on, hurry it up," Pete shouted out the window. The wind was whipping at their camping gear where it lay exposed in the back of the truck, and Pete had to race the rain all the way back to Hollow Road.

He pulled up the drive and parked next to the garage. The siding and stonework weren't up yet, and the wind slipped in under the sheets of Tyvek wrap on the walls and swelled them out like a bullfrog's throat. "Let's get this inside before the rain breaks," he shouted, and they grabbed armfuls of duffels and sleeping bags and ran to the back door.

The wind was inside the house, too, whistling in through the window openings on one side and whooshing out the other. All the rooms were framed in, but they weren't drywalled or paneled yet, and the sightlines were clear for a hundred feet from one end of the house to the other.

They ran out for a second load, and the rain broke only seconds after they made it back inside. The drops beat a rhythm like a chorus line of tap dancers on the copper roof over the back door. "A week ago we couldn't have done this," Pete said as he squatted to begin the unpacking. "Good thing the place is dried in now."

Kip looked around with a scowl. "Yeah. Awesome."

"We got electric in as far as the box, so we can run some cords from there for lamps or whatever. Our laptops."

"Super."

"There's only rough-in plumbing, but we got a hose connected out back we can use to wash up. And of course we got the Johnny on the Spot." Pete grinned up. "All the comforts of home, right?"

Kip didn't answer. He had his phone out and was frowning at the screen.

"Bad news?"

"No news at all. I can't get a frigging signal."

That was one of the words Leigh wouldn't tolerate from the boys. *We all know what you're really saying,* she'd scold them. But Leigh wasn't here.

"Must be the weather," Pete said. "We usually get pretty good cell service here."

Kip held the phone aloft and went off on a circuit of all the ground-floor rooms. Pete decided to set up their cots in the center hall where they could sleep well away from the window openings. By the time Kip circled back, he was rolling out their sleeping bags.

"Uh, how many bedrooms in this house?"

"Six."

"Any chance I could snag one of them?"

"The stairs aren't in. You get up in the night, you'd fall through and break your neck."

"So I won't get up."

"It's not safe."

"Come *on.*" Kip moaned.

Pete was slow to understand. They always shared a tent on their camp-outs and motel rooms on their travels. But it occurred to him that those trips were all prepuberty. "Sleep anywhere you want," he said finally. "As long as it's on this floor."

Kip dragged his cot into the library at the far end of the house and set it up on the other side of the fireplace. The stonework there was the only solid mass in a house full of open stud walls, and Pete wouldn't be able to see him or probably even hear him back there.

Stay within sight and sound. The words surfaced suddenly in his memory. That was his constant refrain back when Kip was little and prone to wandering off at the park or the beach or the campground. *Stay within sight and sound.* He couldn't remember when he stopped saying it. After he married Leigh probably. He wondered if he stopped saying it too soon. If he'd kept a closer watch and a tighter rein these last couple years, if he hadn't left him and Chrissy home alone, none of this would have happened. They'd be home together right now, all four of them.

It won't be forever, he'd told Leigh. The truth would come out one way or another, and they'd put all this behind them. But she wasn't going to welcome Kip back with open arms if it turned out he was lying. She might not even welcome Pete back, the man who picked his kid over her and all for a lie.

Kip was roaming the skeletal rooms again, still searching for a signal on his phone. By the time construction was completed, the house would be equipped with state-of-the-art Wi-Fi, but until then the 4G network was the only link to the outside world, and Kip was starting to look panicky as he scaled the ladder to the second floor.

Pete moved into the dining room and climbed a stepladder to hang a pair of trouble lights from the ceiling joists. He ran the cords out the window and went outside to plug them into the box on the exterior wall of the garage. The rain was pelting hard by then, and the wind was gusting so furiously he had to put his shoulder into it to get the back door to latch shut. A couple sawhorses stood in the kitchen, and he dragged them to the dining room and balanced a sheet of plywood over them.

"Check it out," he said when Kip clattered down the ladder and came into the room. "Dining table and desk all rolled into one."

"Hey. Over at the Hermitage?"

His stupid joke name for the neighboring estate. Pete remembered how Leigh laughed when he first came out with it. She was always egging him on that way. Pete felt like a third wheel sometimes when the two of them got going, riffing on this or that, playing their witty word games. He pulled a wooden crate across the floor. "And these'll make do for our chairs."

"Somebody's over there."

"What?" He dragged another crate into place at the table.

"I saw a light on."

"What are you talking about? You can't see over the wall from here." The table wobbled, and he dropped to the floor to slide a shim under one of the sawhorse legs.

"The way the wind's blowing the trees? From the third floor? I could see straight in."

He climbed to his feet. "Well, don't say anything to Miller, okay? He's already got the heebies about that place."

"Like I ever even talk to the dude."

"Hey, I left the pizza in the truck." He tossed him the keys. "Run out and get it, would you?"

The rain was still coming down hard after they polished off the pizza. Pete craned his head out of every window to check how bad the gutters were overflowing while Kip walked another loop through the house with his phone held high. "Got it!" he yelled excitedly from the bump-out for the breakfast room at the back of the house. Like he wasn't facing trial and living in exile. Cell service, a full belly, and a room of his own were all it took to make Kip happy.

As for Pete, this was usually his happiest time of day, home on the sofa with Leigh, the kids popping in and out of the family room, everyone under one roof. He didn't know what to do with himself here, alone under this roof.

Work. That was the only thing he knew. He took note of some spots along the foundation outside where the rain was puddling too deep—they'd need to do some regrading there—then took a flashlight and did a room-by-room inspection of the whole house and made a list of items that needed to be fixed or done over or worked around. By the time he reached the top floor he'd filled three pages of his notebook. Tomorrow his foreman was going to regret that Pete was living here as much as Pete regretted it tonight.

He went to the double window on the gable end, the one Kip must have hung out of to spy on the place next door. There was no way he could have seen anything inside those walls. The trees formed an opaque green-black umbrella over all the buildings and grounds.

He took out his phone and held it to the window, and when all the bars lit up, he pressed HOME.

"Hey," he said when she answered. "Are you getting much rain over there?"

"Yes. It's really blowing hard. I had to bring the horses in already."

"I might've left a window open in the family room—"

"I closed it."

"Oh, okay." He paused. "How's everything else?"

"Okay. How's everything over there?"

"Fine. All the comforts of home." He winced as he said it. He was only repeating what he'd said to Kip an hour ago, but this time it sounded wrong. Like a rebuke, or a challenge. "Uh, listen, with the way this storm is brewing tonight—"

"No, of course. You shouldn't go out on these roads. Stay in. Stay dry."

"I'll see you tomorrow, though, all right?"

"Absolutely."

"I love you."

"Always and everywhere."

He pushed END CALL and sat back on the sill with a sigh. Always and everywhere. It was what she liked to say, to him and the kids both. It meant unconditional, she told him, and all-encompassing. But he had to wonder. Did *always* mean even now? Did *everywhere* include Hollow Road?

A gust of wind slapped a sheet of rain against his back and drenched him from collar to waist. He got up and shook himself like a dog, and as he did, a flicker of movement caught his eye. The security cameras mounted on the wall surrounding the Hermitage were doing their regular rotating sweeps. The wall was built of cinder blocks and faced with red brick to match the manor house, and it was topped with a little pitched roof shingled in cedar shakes to conceal the strand of electrified wire that wrapped around the entire perimeter. The only break in the wall was where the drive cut in from Hollow Road at the bottom of the hill, and that was blocked by solid steel gates that were always closed.

"Hey, listen," he said when he climbed the ladder back down to the ground floor.

"Yeah?" Kip was doing his homework at the makeshift desk, typing up some notes while his head swiveled from phone to laptop.

"Just in case. Stay out of sight and sound of those people next door, okay?"

"Yeah, whatever," he said and kept on typing.

Chapter Fourteen

Leigh remembered stories of long-ago pioneer women who were driven mad by the howling winds that swept across the wild empty plains of the frontier. She'd spent most of her life in the gentle rolling hills of Northern Virginia and couldn't imagine what it must be like, living in that kind of geographic desolation, battered by those relentless prairie winds.

But she knew what the desolation of her own house felt like, and the incessant whining of the dog had to come in a close second to the wind. Shepherd was driving her insane with his agitated rounds through the house as he sniffed out the corners of every room and reared up at every window to press his nose and paws to the glass. Whining for his family to gather into the fold.

She thought it was awful when Ted left, but at least then the house was full of people. The kids and all of their friends were there, and all of Leigh's, too. Her girlfriends were united in their outrage at Ted, and Leigh spent some of the most boisterous evenings of her life those first few months, drinking wine and trash-talking about men with Peter Pan syndrome. Her mornings were full of company, too, since the new kitchen was under way by then and the construction crew arrived early every day. And her days would begin with her handsome builder knocking on the door to go over the work plan and lingering for a cup of coffee and a little conversation.

Now the house was empty. Hollow House was her stupid joke name for Peter's latest job, but this was the house that was truly hollow. Gutted, as if a fire swept through and incinerated everything they'd built here. The fire was sparked by Kip, but who fanned the ember into flames? No one but Leigh. It might be Peter's decision to leave, but it was her fault. It was the worst sin a stepparent could commit. She made him choose between her and his son.

She felt a thud in her belly like a rock dropped down an empty well when she watched them pack up and go. She was responsible—she'd said the wrong thing, she flicked a domino and all the others had to fall—but it wasn't at all what she'd intended. She certainly didn't want Peter to leave, and not even Kip. She wanted to be the one to go, because then she would be the one to come back. When the day came that she could look at Kip and not see Chrissy, she would come back and they would be here waiting for her. But now it was all turned around. Now it was Peter's decision when to come back. Or whether.

The second Peter suggested moving to Hollow House, she should have said *No. Don't go. I'll try harder. We'll get through this.* But all she'd said was *I don't want you to leave.* She may have even said *I don't want* you *to leave.* No wonder he left.

She wandered through the empty rooms of the first floor. The kitchen still stank of smoke and ash, a lingering reminder of the chicken she'd cremated, and she fled upstairs to escape it. Their bedroom was their sanctuary, she always thought, but now it looked like a place hastily evacuated in the path of a wildfire. Peter's closet door stood open, his dresser drawers gaped empty, the bed was still unmade after three days.

She closed the door on that room and wandered, inevitably, to the children's wing. Kip's door stood open, and she closed it. Chrissy's door was closed, and she opened it and stood on the threshold, gazing in at the space her child had occupied most on this earth. Where she'd left her deepest mark. Now it was all that remained. It was a dinosaur's footprint, fossilized in the rock.

She sat down on the narrow bed and smoothed over the fabric of the comforter. Grosgrain ribbons were stitched into a frame around the edges, and she ran a nail across their corrugated surface. Then her fingers touched something else—a spiraled filament, gossamer-fine—and she plucked it up and held it to the light. It was a hair. A single red-gold hair.

Every night after her bath Chrissy would run down in her pajamas and sit on a stool at Leigh's feet to get her hair combed out. She smelled of soap and strawberries, and her firm young back melted into a soft puddle of flannel as she pressed against her mother's knees. Leigh worked out the tangles, and when she was done she plunged all ten fingers in until a perfect little corkscrew twisted around each one. When she let go, the curls sprang out all over Chrissy's head. Like a nimbus.

She cupped the single hair in the palm of her hand to hold in the memory, and when she lay back and wrapped the comforter around her it was like she was spinning her own cocoon.

He'd stop by every day, he'd said, and though they hadn't discussed exactly when, dinner was the most likely time. Mornings were when everyone rushed about and scattered. Evenings were when they slowed down and came together. So she forced herself out of bed that first day and made a salad and put on a pot of water for pasta. But the storm blew in that afternoon and he didn't come. He was right not to—they'd already lost too much to wet roads in this family. They talked on the phone instead, but she was so terrified of saying the wrong thing again that she barely talked at all. The pot boiled dry before she remembered to turn off the burner.

The next day she marinated a pair of lamb chops and made a fresh salad. She was upstairs doing her hair when she heard Peter's truck in the driveway, and she ran down to find him in the kitchen, on his haunches, ruffling Shepherd's fur and accepting his slurping licks all over his face. He stood up to kiss her, and she felt the wet scrape of his beard against her cheek. He hadn't shaved and his face was covered with heavy black stubble.

"Would you like a drink before dinner?" she asked. "I only have to grill the lamb chops and we'll be ready to eat."

Peter looked at the table, already nicely set. Then his eyes slid toward the front window.

The realization hit her like a sledgehammer. "Kip's outside?"

"I'm sorry, babe. He wouldn't come in."

She'd made another terrible mistake. Setting only two places on the table, marinating only two lamb chops. There was no way Peter wouldn't take this as a slap in the face.

"Shall I see what I can pack up out of the fridge for you?"

He shrugged. "Don't bother. We'll hit a drive-thru."

"Oh. Wait a minute." She went to the desk built into the kitchen cabinetry. Mission Control, she'd described it to Peter when they were designing the space. It was where they kept the bills and the message board and Leigh's laptop and a little file box, which she flipped open now. "We have some coupons here." She started to sort through them but finally gave up and thrust the whole handful at him. "Some of them might be expired, though."

"Okay." He stuffed them in his shirt pocket, then didn't seem to know what to do. Neither did she. They stood six feet apart in the middle of the kitchen and shifted from one foot to the other with their arms folded awkwardly. "I guess I should be—" he began.

"Okay." She turned her face slightly when he stepped in to kiss her, enough to avoid the worst of his beard-scrape.

He stepped back stiffly. "I guess I'll see you tomorrow?"

"Good night." She felt foolish after she said it. It was still broad daylight outside. But after he left, she went back upstairs and into Chrissy's bed again.

He didn't come the next night, even though she dressed and waited and watched for him. He called instead, at seven, and she flew down the hall to answer the phone in the bedroom. But when she saw PETE'S CELL on the display, her hand froze. He wouldn't be calling except to say he wasn't coming, and she didn't know what to say in return. *That's okay?* Or *Please come!* No, she wouldn't muster anything but banalities. She could only talk of weather and food and coupons.

Three rings, then four, then voicemail cut it off, and she lost her chance. He'd be worried about why she didn't answer. She needed to call him back, and she tried to think what to say. *I love you, always and everywhere,* that much she could do. *I miss you.* But what next? The fear that she would say the wrong thing again was paralyzing.

She picked up the phone, and when a rapid beeping told her a voicemail was waiting, she dialed in.

Hey, sorry, he said. *I got held up on the job today. We had a couple snafus, and it took me a while to straighten things out. So I'm running too late to stop by. But I'll see you tomorrow, okay?*

Carefully, she hung up the phone. There were times in her practice when emotions ran too high and she couldn't trust herself to phrase her position correctly over the telephone or in person. Whenever that happened she managed the situation by cutting off voice contact with opposing counsel—sometimes even with her own client—and communicating only in writing. Whether in emails or letters or fifty-page briefs, she could control the dialogue so much better in writing.

She got out her cell phone and typed out a text. *Sorry I missed your call—* No, she wasn't sorry, not when he was the one who should apologize. She backspaced to delete that text and typed another. *No need to stop by. I'm fine. You?*

She pushed SEND the way she would have said *Over* on a walkie-talkie. It was his turn now. She sat down to wait for his reply on the edge of their bed. It was still unmade, and she could smell him in the sheets. She could smell the musk of their last failed lovemaking.

It was twenty minutes before the phone burbled with an incoming message. *OK.* That was all.

Over and out.

A week passed, and nobody came to visit. All her old friends seemed to have drifted away. She must have been too wrapped up in Peter these last five years to tend to her friendship fires. She'd missed too many book group meetings and coffee dates and wine-and-cheese gatherings. She'd been too content in her little circle of two and her bigger circle of seven. Or perhaps nobody came or called because they didn't think she needed them to. That was the trouble with a lifetime spent always striving to project an image of competence and self-sufficiency. *Oh, don't be silly, no need, I've got it covered.* Eventually people took her at her word.

Though maybe the reason nobody came or called was because nobody knew what to say to the crazy bitter bereaved lady. There wasn't even a name for what Leigh was now. If she lost her husband, she'd be a widow. Her parents, an orphan. But what did you call a mother who lost her child? There was no word for what she was. It was unthinkable and thus unnameable.

Shelby checked in now and then, but those calls were brief and unhelpful. They used to tell each other everything, no topic was ever off-limits, but now Shelby cut her short. *You know I can't talk to you about that*, she said whenever Leigh asked about the case or the quest for the mythical priest. Shelby was supposed to be her best friend, but apparently she changed her loyalties as often as her Agent Provocateur lingerie. Kip was her client now, and Peter was paying her hefty fees.

Leigh couldn't steel herself to call her office, but she stayed in touch with Polly by email, enough to juggle her calendar and postpone hearings or palm her work off on colleagues. Enough to track her phone messages and persuade herself nothing was so urgent that she'd have to poke her head out of her shell and pick up the phone. One day Polly flagged a message with a question mark: *Someone named Ashley Gregg called. She said you'd know what it's about.* But she didn't, she didn't even recognize the name, and she didn't call back.

The twins called every day, separately, in actual, live-voice telephone calls that would have thrilled her once. She would have pressed them for every detail of their classes and hoped for a few sanitized details of their social lives or just free-floated on the husky boy-man timbre of their voices. But now their conversations were full of false starts and awkward silences. They were trying hard to be dutiful sons to her, she knew that, but they were swimming in their own grief, and she couldn't make it worse by confiding how much pain she was in, or God forbid, by crying. It was her job to buck them up, though her attempts were feeble. Their calls inevitably trailed off into wisps of words. "So . . . ," and "I guess I should . . . ," and "Yeah, I guess."

One day she answered the phone and heard both their voices on a rare three-way call that obviously took some coordination. Their tones were different, too, with none of the meandering somnolence of their earlier calls. "We just heard," Zack said abruptly.

"What?"

"Everything," Dylan said.

"Is it true?"

"What?"

"Any of it."

She took the phone into Chrissy's room and stretched out on the bed as they explained. It seemed they'd been having actual, live-voice conversations with Peter, too, and today it came out that he and Kip were living at Hollow House and they badgered him until he explained why.

"What did he say?"

They didn't answer. They had other things on their minds. "Is it true, what Kip's saying?"

"Well—" She pulled the comforter up to her chest. "It's true that he's saying it."

"Do you believe it?"

"What do you think?"

"He's lying," Zack said.

"I don't know," Dylan said.

Zack was always the more impetuous of the two. He went with gut instincts while Dylan liked to think things through more carefully. The difference made them a good duo. They acted as a check on each other and usually ended up someplace in the middle. Leigh waited to hear where they'd end up this time.

"Pete believes him," Dylan said.

Zack snorted. "What choice does he have?"

"But think about it. If Kip was wasted, there's no way she'd let him drive."

"He wasn't wasted," Leigh put in.

"But if she *thought* he was. You know what that party must have looked like to Chrissy."

"Like Animal House or something." Zack's tone was grudging.

"Right."

The two of them fell silent, and Leigh held her breath as she waited for them to complete their silent deliberations and render their verdict. But when Zack spoke again, he had a grin in his voice. "Hey, remember spring break, how she took the course over by that church?"

Leigh was caught off guard by this turn in the conversation. Did Chrissy ride a steeplechase in March? Maybe, but she couldn't recall that the course ran anywhere near a church, and she certainly didn't remember that the twins were among the spectators.

"Oh, man, she was something. Tearing around those cones like Mario Andretti."

"What are you talking about?"

"We were just fooling around," Dylan said.

"She wanted a turn. It was an empty parking lot. Nobody was going to get hurt."

"She was good at it, though. Real good."

Chrissy had been driving, they were telling her. Leigh pulled the comforter up to her chin.

"But here's the thing," Dylan said next. "I can see her driving, but I can't see her lying about it to the cops. She wouldn't let Kip take the fall for something she did."

"Right!" Zack said, like *Bingo!*

The same reaction rang inside Leigh's head. If Chrissy was driving—*if*—she would have owned up to it.

"So he's gotta be lying," Zack said, coming full circle.

"I guess," Dylan said.

"But still. It's not Pete's fault. Right, Mom?"

"Of course not."

"Then why won't you let him come home?"

"Why won't—*I*?" Now she'd come full circle. "What did Peter tell you?"

"He said you need some space."

That was the opposite of what she needed. She had too much space. There was nothing but space and emptiness here in this hollow house. Even this long stretch of silence over the telephone line held too much empty space.

"Mom?"

"It's not that. It's just—he needs to be with Kip right now."

Their silence told her she hadn't quite answered their question. She sank deeper under the comforter. Negotiating the rapids of this conversation had sapped all her energy.

"Well, what should *we* do? About Pete, I mean."

She never had to tell them before. She never even gave them the standard lecture about respecting and obeying their new stepparent just as they would a parent. They took to Peter from the start and got there all on their own.

"That's up to you," she said.

"Oh," they said, nearly in unison, and they sounded so dejected that she knew she must have said the wrong thing again.

"Well." After a moment Dylan cleared his throat. "I know this much. It's the last thing Chrissy would want."

"For this to tear us apart," Zach said. "Right?"

Tears burned in Leigh's eyes. No, the last thing Chrissy would want was to be dead. "Right," she said thickly.

"So . . ."

"I guess."

"Yeah."

And then it was good-bye.

She spent hours in the family room loading the old home videos in the DVD player and watching Chrissy de-age from teenager to infant. Ted was a sloppy cameraman and he never seemed to get the audio on right, so the early videos were jerky and soundless, like old-time silent films, except in color. Vivid color. Chrissy's persimmon curls and cornflower eyes lit up the screen and left Leigh convulsing with sobs. It was supposed to be cathartic to cry. *Let it out*, people always said, *you'll feel better afterward*. But she only ever felt worse. Chrissy was still dead, and no amount of crying could change that.

She wished she could rewind life as easily as she did the family videos. She'd go back to that Friday night, only this time she wouldn't call home on their way back from the Greenbrier. They'd arrive unannounced. Chrissy would be in bed and Kip wouldn't be, and Peter would pace and worry and yell at him when he finally stumbled home in the morning, and that was the worst thing that would have happened.

But no, she needed to rewind further than that, back to the day she decided they had to take an anniversary trip. What was she thinking? Leaving two teenagers home alone, one of them a notorious troublemaker and the other only fourteen years old. They'd never done it before, not even when the twins were still home. It wasn't even a good time for Peter to leave his project, but she'd insisted on it. They needed a getaway, she told him, a little romantic jaunt, but it was only herself she was thinking of.

These thoughts were the worst torture of all, for she couldn't escape the mutilating realization that Chrissy's death may have been Kip's crime, but it was her fault.

Peter had always resisted texting before. It was for kids, he said, and besides, he'd rather hear her voice. She wanted to hear his, too, but she still couldn't pick up when he called. So it wasn't long before he stopped calling and took to texting instead. Every evening after dinner. *OK 2day?* he'd ask, and she'd reply, *Fine. U?* Like idiotic mutes.

Chapter Fifteen

When the phone rang Saturday morning, Leigh ran for it as usual, and froze as usual until the caller's name appeared on the display and she saw that it wasn't Peter. It was Carrie Dietrich.

"Leigh, I am so sorry," Carrie said. "I hate to be bothering you like this, but I don't know if there's someone else in your office I should call, and all hell's breaking out over here—"

"What is it? Is Jenna all right?"

"She took off, that's what. She said she was going to disappear and now she's gone and done it. But Hunter's not having it. He called the cops, and they're here and he's here with his lawyer, and there's a TV van out front, and we don't know what—"

"I'll be right there."

The Dietrichs' farm was on Hollow Road, not half a mile from Peter's job site. They operated it as a nonprofit retirement facility for aging horses that were literally put out to pasture. Chrissy had volunteered there twice a week, mucking out stalls and hauling hay bales, hard labor for a young girl, but she considered it the price of admission for the chance to stroke the graying muzzles of the old horses and whisper fondly in their ears. Golden Oldies was the name of the farm, but Kip always called it The Glue Factory, just to get a rise out of Chrissy, which always worked. He'd volunteered there, too, in the office, only long enough to get the semester's credit.

Three TV vans were in the drive when Leigh arrived, and ten or so other cars were parked haphazardly along the shoulder of Hollow Road. She slalomed a course around the vans and looped to the left to park by the barn. An unexpected sight stood in the meadow beyond it: a helicopter in a circle of flattened grass, its pilot leaning against the landing skid with his arms folded and his laconic gaze on the crowd by the house.

"Stay," she said, and Shep whined pitifully as he plopped his rear down in the seat and thrust his head out the window to track her path to the house.

It was an old-fashioned country farmhouse with a wide front porch and white-railed stairs lined with pots of red geraniums. A couple dozen people thronged across the lawn at the foot of the stairs, some with microphones and others with shoulder-mounted cameras aimed like grenade launchers at the porch. Three steps above them stood Hunter Beck.

When he held his press conference on the courthouse steps last month, reporters from all the major outlets attended, in numbers never before seen in Hampshire County. Today he was at a private house on a rural road that most GPS systems had trouble finding, and still he'd drawn a huge media presence. Not many private citizens could command that kind of attention, maybe not even many billionaires, but this one was a special breed. Not yet forty, Beck was widely regarded as a visionary in the mold of Steve Jobs. His Intellocity internet utility program had made him a hero to everyone for whom web pages could never load fast enough. Her own boys spoke of him with the kind of awe they usually reserved for sports figures and rock stars.

But it was something else that drew this many reporters. The story was heartbreaking. Five years ago, Hunter's first wife had just learned the gender of their baby, and she was so excited to share the news with him that she dashed across the street to the sidewalk café where he was waiting for her—right into the path of an oncoming cab. Her body landed ten feet from where he sat, and a hundred cell phones recorded the moment as he fell to his knees beside her howling his shock and anguish. The videos went viral on YouTube until someone finally had the decency to take them down.

The idea that Hunter might now be losing his second family, too, had to be more than the reporters could resist. They lobbed their questions at him in a frenzy as he stood before the bouquet of microphones. He was an unsmiling man with an intense gaze behind black-rimmed glasses, and he was dressed for a day in the country, in a canvas jacket over a T-shirt and blue jeans.

Leigh was still dressed in the yoga pants and baggy shirt she'd slept in. She gave a wide berth to the crowd and headed for the back porch as Carrie beckoned to her from the door. "Welcome to the madhouse," she said.

Leigh ducked inside. "Where is she?" she whispered. The vestibule was draped with barn coats and rain slickers on hooks, and lined up below them were two dog bowls and a dozen pairs of boots in various sizes—paddock boots and muck boots and knee-high riding boots made of hand-tooled leather polished to a high gleam. The mudroom of a working horse farm.

"She won't say." Carrie raked her fingers through her short blond hair. She looked more frazzled than worried. "She doesn't trust us not to let it slip to Hunter, and I can't say I blame her after this." She pointed Leigh through to the kitchen. "We woke up this morning and she was gone but her car was still here. So we figured either Hunter took her or she went back to him. The way her mood's been swinging? Nothing would surprise us. So that was our first call." She held up the coffeepot and poured herself a cup when Leigh shook her head no. "Big mistake," Carrie said. "Jenna called five minutes later. Turns out she's been planning this for weeks. Lining up a place to live, leasing a new car. He never cut off the money, you know. She's been squirreling it away for a while."

"Did you tell Hunter that?"

"Yep. Didn't make a bit of difference. He called the cops anyway and reported her as a missing person and flew straight down here in his chopper. So now the cops are searching her room and taking our statements like we're some kind of criminals."

Even in the kitchen the reporters' voices could be heard shouting out their questions at the front porch. "And he alerted the media," Leigh said.

Carrie rolled her eyes.

Leigh followed another set of voices coming from the living room. Fred Dietrich was at the front window, on his feet with his fists clutching the casing as he stared through the glass. Three other men were seated around the coffee table. She recognized two of them. "Sergeant Hooper," she said as the uniformed officer shot to his feet.

"Mrs. Conley?" He was clearly confused by her arrival on the scene.

"It's Ms. Huyett today, Sergeant. Attorney for the Dietrichs." She looked down at the two men in suits still seated on the sofa. "Rob," she said to Hunter Beck's attorney.

"Leigh." Rob Canaday was an excellent lawyer notwithstanding his embarrassing defeat in this case. She didn't beat him because she was the better lawyer. She beat him because he was young and eager. It made him too malleable in the hands of a demanding client.

The third man got to his feet and flashed an ID from his inside coat pocket. "Detective Jim Denton. Investigating a missing persons report concerning Jenna Beck."

"She's not missing. Her parents spoke to her this morning."

"But they don't know where she is."

"She's twenty-five years old, Detective. Do your parents know where you are?"

The detective's expression remained stony. "An investigation is called for whenever there are serious concerns for the safety and welfare of a person whose whereabouts are unknown."

"What concerns?" Leigh looked to Carrie where she leaned in the kitchen doorway. "Mrs. Dietrich, do you have any concerns for Jenna's safety and welfare?"

Carrie folded her arms. "Nope."

"Mr. Dietrich? Do you?"

Fred turned from the window. "Not so long as that son of a bitch stays away from her."

"Her husband has concerns," the detective said.

"You mean the husband who hasn't resided with her for more than two months? Who's had no communication with her for more than two months. And who therefore knows nothing about the state of her safety and welfare."

"He knows that she's pregnant," Canaday said.

"Believe it or not, Rob, that's not a disability."

"She's shutting him out and now she's taken off—"

"Because she's an adult woman who has a constitutional right to the privacy of her own body as well as the freedom to come and go as she pleases." She turned back to the other man. "There's nothing to see here, Detective. And certainly no basis for a criminal investigation. I'm afraid Mr. Beck's been wasting your time."

The young lawyer blustered. "He has legitimate cause to be concerned—"

"Be honest, Rob. His only concern is that she'll try to keep the baby from him. But like the judge said, that's not a cognizable concern until the baby's born. Until then he has no right to see her, to touch her, or even to know where she is."

"We have an appeal pending."

"Which you know full well you're going to lose. Meanwhile there are some actual rights being violated here today." She turned to Fred. "Mr. Dietrich, there's a large number of people on your front lawn. Did you invite them here?"

He clenched his jaw. "I did not."

"Did you give that helicopter permission to land on your property?"

He snorted. "I sure as hell did not."

"Then I suggest you go out there and tell them they're trespassing and they have five minutes to vacate. I'm sure Sergeant Hooper will be happy to back you up on that."

Fred didn't hesitate. He stomped to the front door, and to his credit, Sergeant Hooper followed with not even a glance back for permission from the two men in suits.

The detective picked up his notepad from the coffee table. "Mrs. Dietrich, you'll let us know if you hear from her—"

"She's under no obligation to do that," Leigh cut in, and Carrie gave a curt nod.

"Just to close out our file—"

"Let's do this instead. You close it out right now as REPORT UN-FOUNDED. Or we'll make a formal complaint that you're working as a private investigator for Hunter Beck. At taxpayer expense. Meanwhile, if the Dietrichs ever have any concerns for their daughter's safety and welfare, they'll call you then. How's that?"

The detective stared hard at her a moment before he turned and wrenched the front door open. Fred's voice carried in from the porch. He was shouting at the reporters to get off his lawn, while Hooper's voice underscored it with a mild, "Move along, folks. You heard the man." Rob Canaday followed the detective outside but not before sending a parting look at Leigh—*This isn't over*, he seemed to say.

After they'd gone Leigh sank down into the sofa they'd vacated. She was trembling, not so much from emotion as from simple exertion. She felt so tired.

"Let me get you something," Carrie said. "Coffee, or a cup of tea or what?"

"No, thanks. I'm fine."

"Better than fine, I'd say. I can't thank you enough. Coming out here on a minute's notice and only three weeks after—" She stopped with a hand to her throat. "I felt sick about even calling you."

"No, you did the right thing." Leigh looked up at her. "But promise me you're really not worried about Jenna."

Carrie waved a dismissive arm. "She left most of her clothes, which means she'll be back. And she took her prenatal vitamins, which means she's taking care of herself. The only thing that ever worried us was this idea in her head that he was stalking her. So if she's got herself somewhere that feels safe to her, what's there to worry about?"

"You can't help it, though, can you?"

"Nope." Carrie sighed. "Not from the second you know you're carrying them."

"Please tell her to call me the next time you hear from her."

"I will."

When the front door opened behind her, Leigh assumed it was Rob Canaday, returning to get in a delayed last word. But it wasn't the lawyer, it was the client. Hunter Beck stood framed in the doorway, his face pale and his gaze penetrating behind his glasses. He looked like a man of the people in lug-soled work boots and a canvas field coat, except that the boots were Dolce & Gabbana and the jacket was Burberry and each retailed for more than a thousand dollars.

"I'm not a bad guy." His voice, as always, was low and restrained.

"I never suggested otherwise," Leigh said.

"Maybe my marriage is irretrievably broken. I don't know. I hope not."

"Mr. Beck, I can't talk to you without your lawyer present."

"But here's the thing," he spoke over her. "No matter what happens between me and Jenna, I don't want to lose my child. I can't lose my child. Not after— You of all people"—he looked straight at Leigh—"should understand that."

Her face froze. He knew? He knew, and he was using it as a weapon against her. She stared up at him, too stunned to speak.

If she was speechless, Carrie wasn't. "How dare you!" She lunged at him with pointed finger. "Barging in here and bringing up her—her tragedy! You get out of my house this minute, you—you—"

He turned and left before she could muster up an adequate insult.

Chapter Sixteen

L eigh left soon after. The porch and the lawn were clear by then and
the helicopter had lifted off with a deafening blast of air that made
the geriatric horses kick up their heels and scatter like mustangs
across the pasture. But the cars and TV vans were still out on the road. She
felt too exhausted to run that gauntlet, and she stopped on the back steps
with a weary sigh.

"Take the tractor road," Carrie said.

"Good idea," she said and gave Carrie a quick hug good-bye.

She drove around the paddock and past the second barn to a dirt track
that ran between the fencerows past pastures of horses who seemed to
know the best part of their lives was over. They were all good horses once,
champions some of them, but no one needed or wanted them anymore.
They'd outlived their usefulness, and there was nothing to do but stand
and snooze in the sunshine and wait for their time to run out.

She drove through the meadows and up over the ridge to the woods.
She hadn't realized how close this road came to the site of Peter's project,
but as she reached the top of the hill, she could see the back of Hollow
House less than a hundred yards away. Her foot eased off the gas and she
stopped and stared at it through the trees.

Construction was further along than when she last saw the place, but it was still only a shell of a house. The gaping doors and windows looked like open wounds, and the fluttering white sheets of Tyvek were like bandages coming unwrapped. It was obviously uninhabitable. It was absurd for Peter to live here when he could be in his own comfortable home. So what did it say about her that he would choose this instead?

The crew was on-site. She could hear the sound of hammering ringing out over the hillside. It was the best sound in the world, Peter always said. It was the sound of something being built.

A ruddy-faced man came around the corner of the house and stopped to squint into the woods. Leigh froze. It was Kevin, Peter's foreman, and he recognized her at the same moment. He gave a grin and a wave. "Hey, Pete," he shouted. "The missus is here!"

Leigh jerked and fumbled for the shifter, but before she could put the car in gear, Shep scrambled into her lap and thrust his head out her window. She tried to shove him back into his own seat, but his tail was wagging so hard it slapped her in the face.

Peter came jogging around the corner of the house. His stubble was now a beard, and he had a hitch in his gait that made her wonder if he'd injured himself. Then she saw the black hair streaming out behind him and realized he was carrying Mia piggyback.

She started at the sight of the little girl. She'd forgotten that this was their visitation weekend. Every other Saturday he picked her up at Karen's and dropped her off with Leigh before he went to work. That was always their routine. But today he brought her here instead. She shouldn't have been so shocked. He was the one with the visitation rights, after all. Mia was his daughter, not hers.

Shepherd spotted them, or sniffed them, and he bunched up his legs and leaped through the window like a circus dog. Mia squealed with delight as he streaked through the woods toward her. She slid off Peter's back to hug him, and a moment later Kip was there, too, dropping to the ground to wrestle with him. The dog barked and wriggled in delirium as he darted from Mia to Kip to Peter. It was one big joyous family reunion, and the pressure of tears started to build behind Leigh's face like a steam engine. "Shepherd! Come!" she called.

The dog ignored her, but Peter spun, searching for her through the dappled sunlight. He couldn't see her, but she could see him, clearly. He looked like a stranger with his thick black beard.

Kip stood up beside him and looked for her, too. The tears flooded her eyes and his face blurred out of focus, and the light around him started to bend and shimmer. A flash set his hair ablaze and a smile lit up like a thousand suns, and it was Chrissy again, in the place where Kip stood. In the place where she should have been.

Peter saw her then and started toward her, and she took off so fast that dust clouds detonated from her tires.

She drove blindly, and she had to stop behind the Hermitage and wipe her streaming eyes before she could see to go on. She looked up in the mirror, but no one was following her, not Peter, not even Shepherd. She looped around the far side of the Hermitage and down the hill, and she was starting to pull out on Hollow Road when another car suddenly rounded the bend in front of her. She slammed on the brakes as a dusty old Saab rolled past with a priest behind the wheel.

Blink and she almost missed it. The driver wore a black coat and a clerical collar, and she stomped on the gas and took off after him.

It was ridiculous. She didn't even believe Kip's story about the priest, and here she was chasing a man down Hollow Road for no reason other than he wore a Roman collar. But still she followed him. She had to know. If he did happen to be on the road that night, if he did happen to see anything, she had to find out.

The Saab reached the end of Hollow Road and turned onto Providence, and Leigh merged into the traffic and followed from two cars behind. She'd never tried to tail a car in her life, but in a law practice that sometimes required proof of adultery, she'd often hired investigators to follow the wayward spouse, and she had a general sense of how they did it. Hang back a few car lengths but keep him in sight. If the target glanced in the mirror too much, if he seemed to get suspicious, speed up and pass and follow from ahead for a while.

The Saab looked like it must be twenty years old. There were pits of rust around its undercarriage, and the trunk lid bounced with every bump in the road. The priest drove five miles below the speed limit and so did Leigh as the cars behind her zipped around to pass. After a few miles, she pulled out and stole a glance inside as she passed him. He had thick hair going to silver and he sat up very erect with both hands firmly on the wheel. His lips were moving, and she thought he must be talking on a Bluetooth until he threw his head back with his mouth wide open and she realized he was belting out a song.

She dropped back. After a few more miles, he took a turn west, deeper into the countryside, and she followed past horse farms and vineyards until he turned onto a narrow rural road. No other cars turned with him, so Leigh had to follow right behind as he turned again through a pair of stone pillars that opened onto a long curving drive. A quarter mile ahead on the top of a hill she could see a gleaming white manor house with a columned portico, but the Saab turned before it got there, onto a gravel road through a patch of deep woods. The road twisted around a bend and arrived at a little stone house that was probably once the caretaker's cottage for the estate up on the hill.

Leigh pulled in behind the Saab as the driver got out and looked back at her with a quizzical smile. "Can I help you?"

She hadn't mistaken his priest garb. Under his suit coat, he wore a black clerical shirtfront and a crisp white Roman collar. He was tall, and handsome in a patrician sort of way, like an English gentleman in tweeds and wellies on his weekend farm, or one of the older male models in a Brooks Brothers catalog, the ones who wore a golf shirt on one page and a white dinner jacket on the other.

Leigh stood behind the shield of her car door. "I'm sorry to intrude," she said. "But I wonder—could I ask you something?"

"Certainly."

"Three weeks ago," she began. Was that right? It seemed like yesterday, but it also seemed like it was something she'd been living with forever. "Three weeks ago last night, there was an accident on Hollow Road. I saw you driving there just now, so it occurred to me— I mean, it wasn't an accident exactly. A truck went off the road into the ditch and hit a tree. There were two teenagers inside, a boy and a girl?" She paused. Her throat was closing up again.

"Yes?" he said, still smiling his encouraging smile.

"And I was wondering—if you were driving past—? If you saw it happen?"

His smile faded. "I'm sorry," he said. "I wish I could help you."

She put a hand to her shaking mouth. Of course he couldn't. She was such a fool to follow him here. She was such a fool to hope.

He started toward her. "Did something happen—?" He stopped, and his face went suddenly still. "You've lost someone."

She put her hands over her face and started to cry.

He came up and touched his hand to her elbow. "Please. Come inside. Have a cup of tea."

The little stone cottage had a glass sunroom on one side, curiously, since the surrounding woods crept in too close for any sunshine to penetrate. The sunroom had its own entrance, and the priest steered her there, carefully, as if she'd suffered a bad fall and might have broken something. Leigh hid her face as he guided her through the door and into a deep-cushioned chair. She was humiliated by her tears in front of this stranger. Humiliated by the way she'd followed him like some kind of psycho stalker. This is not who I am, she wanted to tell him, I haven't been who I really am for a while now. But she couldn't speak through her tears, and anyway, he was doing all the talking, telling her in a soothing voice to sit back, relax, here's a stool, put your feet up, I'll go and pop the kettle on.

He ducked through a doorway into the main house, and she took her hands from her face and wiped her eyes and blew her nose. Her chair was covered in a plush burgundy fabric worn shiny with age. The stool was a faded needlepoint, and the stone floor was crisscrossed in overlapping layers of Oriental rugs. The wall the priest disappeared through was crammed full of books on floor-to-ceiling shelves, and hundreds more were stacked on the floor, the coffee table, the desk, and every other dusty dark wood surface. The room had the look of an old-time study except that the ceiling and the other three walls were made entirely of glass. The trees overhead and the greenery all around made her feel like she was in an inside-out terrarium.

He returned with two teacups rattling in their saucers and set hers on top of a stack of books on an end table. Leigh murmured her thanks as he settled into the chair beside her. "I'm so sorry," she said. "For breaking down like this."

"No, don't. We should never apologize for grief. It doesn't mean we're weak. It's simply the price we pay for love."

It was too high a price. It was costing her everything. "This room," she began. She looked up and around the space. The light filtering through the foliage overhead was soft and tinged with green, like sunshine through a wisteria arbor. "It reminds me of a fairy tale."

He smiled. "I often wonder if the woods sprang up after the sunroom was added, or if they planned to cut down the woods but lost heart. I'm only renting here, but I foolishly brought my whole library with me, and this was the only space that would accommodate it. So into the sunroom I moved it. It looks odd, I know, but I've come to think of it as a metaphor for the civilized mind. Educated"—he waved toward the wall of bookshelves—"but open to new and different ideas." He swept an arm to take in the three walls of glass. Then his eyes twinkled. "If you'll forgive the self-aggrandizement."

"No, I love it. This room, I mean."

"My Snuggery I call it, at home or wherever I go." He took a sip of his tea. "Though my ex-wife liked to call it the Growlery when she thought I was being grumpy."

"You were married? But—I thought—"

"That I was a Catholic priest? No, I'm the Episcopal variation. Catholicism without celibacy as they say."

"Oh, I should have realized. I was raised as an Episcopal. Though we always called it Catholicism without the guilt."

His laugh was a little rueful. "We've done a fair job of minimizing shame, but I'm afraid the guilt's still with us."

"I'm not sure I know the distinction."

"I like to frame it this way. Shame is what you feel when society is judging you. Guilt is what you feel when you judge yourself."

"Ah." She nodded and took a tentative sip of tea. It was nothing fancy, just a strong brew of good hot tea. "Which is worse, I wonder?"

"Oh, I'd have to go with guilt. Nobody can punish you like you can punish yourself. But the question is, do we want to eliminate it? Yes, it hurts, but it serves a purpose. Where would the conscience be without it?" He held out his hand. "I'm Stephen Kendall, by the way."

"Leigh Huyett. And I'm so sorry for barging in on you this way."

"I'm not."

"No, really. This isn't like me. I hardly recognize myself these days. I'm driving everyone away from me. And now chasing after strangers on the road. I've turned into a crazy woman. A bitter, ugly, old crazy woman."

"Not old, surely," he said. "And not ugly by a long shot. As for the rest—" He spread his hands. "I don't know you well enough yet to say."

It wasn't the flattery that made her relax, because she didn't believe it, not with her rumpled clothes and uncombed hair. It was the *yet*. As if it wouldn't necessarily be awful to get to know her better. She settled a little deeper in her chair. It was so comfortable here, in this room full of books and greenery.

He picked up his cup and took another sip of tea. "Was it the boy or the girl?"

"Excuse me?"

"The one you lost in the accident. Was it the boy or the girl?"

"Oh! The girl. My daughter." A fresh rush of tears came to her eyes. "She was only—" She shook her head helplessly. "I'm sorry, I shouldn't—"

"Maybe you should," he said. "For some people it helps to put the pain in words. If you feel like talking, I definitely feel like listening."

After living in near silence for so long, speaking to no one and listening to nothing but Shepherd's ceaseless whining—yes, she did feel like talking, especially here in the Snuggery with the Good Reverend Brooks Brothers. But she didn't know where to begin, and her uncertainty must have shown on her face, because he put his hand over hers again. "Perhaps you'd like to tell me about the accident on Hollow Road?"

She told him, even though it meant she started to cry again. She told him the whole story, starting with Kip's first DUI last New Year's. She told him about their anniversary getaway to Greenbrier and Kip's partying on a suspended license and Chrissy's pajama-clad bike ride. She told him about the accident, the night in the police station, and the morning in the hospital.

"It was all my fault," she said, weeping. "I insisted on a long weekend away. We left them home alone. We never did that before, not overnight. None of this would have happened—I was so selfish! If only— My daughter—"

"No. Stop. Please." He put his cup down. "Your daughter was how old? Fourteen? People hire fourteen-year-old babysitters all the time, and leave them alone in a strange house with small children to care for. You left your daughter in her own house with an eighteen-year-old. There's no blame to be found there."

"But none of this would have happened—"

"See what I mean about guilt? You're punishing yourself for something no one else would raise an eyebrow at. Something everyone does, all the time."

She squeezed her eyes shut and shook her head.

He put his hand over hers. "There's no best way to grieve," he said. "But the worst way is to blame yourself. I've seen it too many times. *I should have kept after him about his cholesterol. I never should have put her in that nursing home. I shouldn't have let him get on that plane.* That's the worst kind of mourning. It halts the healing."

His hand was warm and enveloping over hers. Leigh blinked her eyes open. "Is there a best kind of mourning?"

"As I say, it's different for everyone. When I lost my son—"

"Oh! I'm so sorry." She felt a hot flush of embarrassment. Carrying on as if she were the only person in the world ever to lose a child.

He didn't seem to notice. "When he died, what helped me most was to talk about him. People shied away from even mentioning his name to me, but I relished the chance to talk about him. To anyone who cared to listen."

Leigh thought how seldom anyone had spoken to her about Chrissy these last weeks. She remembered how careful Carrie was this morning not to speak her name out loud. And Peter never mentioned her at all. To spare her feelings, probably, but maybe because he'd already moved on.

"I care to listen," he said. "If you'd like to tell me about Chrissy."

For a moment she thought about trying. But it was too raw. She shook her head.

"Not yet, then," he said. "Someday perhaps."

She gazed at him. His eyes were blue, she noticed. Not the bright welding-torch blue of Chrissy's eyes, but three shades quieter. A still mountain lake. Even when he smiled, as he did now, there were such dark depths there.

"Not yet," she agreed. "But thank you."

By then the sun had climbed high enough to shine through the overhanging tree limbs. Suddenly the room was lit up, and all its dim corners were on display. Stephen switched off the lamp on the table between them. "It only lasts twenty or thirty minutes," he said. "So I try to savor the sunshine while I can."

Leigh rose to her feet. "I'll savor it on my drive back home. I've intruded on you far too long."

"Not at all. I've enjoyed meeting you."

"Me, too."

He walked her outside and down the drive to her car. At the door, she turned and held out her hand. "Reverend—"

"Stephen." He took her hand and held it in both of his. "And again, I'm so sorry I couldn't help you."

"You have helped me. A little."

"May I give you a blessing?" He winced an apology. "It's what I do. But I promise I won't proselytize."

She laughed. "Go on then. If you must."

He placed a hand on her head. "Leigh. May you know the peace that passes all understanding and may it guard your heart and mind, always and everywhere."

Those words coiled through in her mind as she drove out the narrow lane to the road. Always and everywhere. Her *I love you* words to Peter and the kids. She'd forgotten they came from the Bible, if she even knew. It was simply a phrase inculcated in her during her childhood, the same as *goodness and mercy*. They were only ever words to her, a familiar phrase that made for clever names for her two barn cats. But now they seemed to have come to life, personified in that gentle man. Goodness and mercy.

A car was parked at the end of the cottage lane, a black SUV, and she had to cut around it to reach the road. A man sat behind the wheel, and as she drove past him, she had a feeling, a little low zap like static electricity that made her eyes dart up to the mirror. But the man wasn't looking at her at all. He had a camera to his face and was snapping pictures of the rolling countryside on this beautiful spring day.

And it was a beautiful spring day. The sun was spilling a pale gold over the new green grass, and the roadside rhododendrons were blooming in brilliant bursts of pink and purple, and Leigh did feel some measure of peace as she drove to the highway. Not enough to pass all understanding, but something. She'd fallen out of the habit of going to church—weekends were always so hectic in their household—but she thought she might enjoy attending one of Stephen's sermons. It would be nice to see him again, to listen to his soothing voice and feel that little bit of peace settle into her soul. It was too bad she didn't get the name of his church.

Her phone burbled with an incoming text, and at the next stoplight she took a glance. It was from Peter, sent more than an hour after she stumbled on his happy family scene. *Sry I miss U OK?*

This was why they never used to text each other. She couldn't tell what he meant. *I'm sorry. I miss you? Are you okay?* Or only *Sorry I missed you, okay?* Two very different messages. She could parse through the language of a complex statute and discern the legislative intent with the best of them, but the meaning behind those five near-words eluded her.

OK, she replied.

Chapter Seventeen

"Put that away. Pay attention." Pete rapped his knuckles on the table. He was spending thousands of dollars for the opinions of the doctor and lawyer across from them, and there Kip sat playing with his phone.

Shelby and the doctor exchanged a *hoo boy* look, and for a second Kip's face flashed dark with defiance, like he was ready to pick up his phone and stomp out of the conference room. But only for a second. "Sorry," he mumbled. He slid the phone across the polished wood-grain surface of the table and let it fall into his lap. His expression when he looked up again was perfectly bland.

Dr. Harold Rabin was a neurologist who used to specialize in brain aneurysms, and now, Pete gathered, specialized in court testimony. He had curly white hair that grew in a dense mat around his bald spot so his head resembled one of the sugar-frosted crullers laid out on the credenza. He'd reviewed all of Chrissy's medical records and for a further fee was prepared to give expert testimony that her death could not be causally connected to the accident because it was equally likely that her aneurysm was congenital.

"Isn't that kind of a big coincidence, though?" Kip said. "If she was walking around with this thing in her head for fourteen years, and it didn't burst until ten hours after she bumped her head in the truck?"

"Stop." Shelby threw up a hand like a crossing guard. She was wearing a bronze silk suit today, and it made her green eyes look almost yellow. Like a tigress. "There's no evidence she bumped her head in the truck. Nothing beyond your own statement that she *might have* and what—?" She looked to the doctor. "A faint contusion on her scalp?"

He nodded. "Which could have been sustained in any other minor injury in the previous twenty-four hours."

"Remember, it's the Commonwealth's burden. And the standard is beyond a reasonable doubt. Not simply possible, or more likely than not."

The burden of proof, she meant, but every time Pete heard her say it—*the burden's on their side*—he wanted to object. *It's on us. The burden's all on us.* The expense for sure, but also the fear, the loneliness, the shame.

"And a congenital abnormality is only one alternative possibility," the doctor said. "The aneurysm could have resulted from any previous injury. According to the medical history, the young lady sustained other injuries over the years. Two years ago she fell from a horse."

"She only broke her wrist." Pete remembered that day. He was in the garage when he heard the cry from the pasture. Everybody heard it, and they all went running outside, Leigh, all three boys, even Shep, and when Chrissy looked up from the ground at the circle of frantic faces above her, she started to laugh through her tears. *Oh, no!* she said, cradling her arm. *Am I dead?*

"But she could have bumped her head in that fall, too. Or any other time she fell from a horse. And there was another ER visit." The doctor flipped through his notes. "What was it? A soccer injury?"

"That was only a sprained ankle."

"Ah, but she played soccer. That's the significance. Head injuries are common in soccer. She could have developed the aneurysm from a ball to the head and no one ever knew it."

"Hold on." Pete turned to Shelby. "You're not gonna bring up these other accidents in court?" Shelby was tapping the keys on her laptop, and she answered without looking up from the screen. "We have to. Any alternative explanation."

"But if Leigh thinks it was soccer or riding that did it—I mean, she was the one who got Chrissy into all those activities. If she thought—I mean—it'd kill her."

"Pete." Shelby looked up then, and her eyes lasered across the table. "I understand your concerns. But Kip's the one on trial here. He's the one we need to protect."

Pete scrubbed a hand over his beard. Kip was watching him closely, like he was waiting for a call from a tennis line judge. "Yeah," Pete said finally. "Of course."

Next Dr. Rabin delivered a tutorial on the geography of the brain, complete with slick, interactive illustrations projected on a screen. Eight hundred dollars an hour bought all the bells and whistles. He pointed out the cerebrum, cerebellum, brainstem, the hemispheres, the lobes, then pinpointed the precise location of Chrissy's aneurysm in the left parietal lobe.

"The left side?" Pete leaned forward in his chair. "And that's where this contusion was?"

"That's right."

"So how does somebody sitting on the right side of a vehicle injure the left side of her brain?" He snapped his gaze between Shelby and the doctor. "The right side of her head would make sense, if she bumped against the passenger window or doorframe. Or the top of her head if she bounced up against the ceiling. But what does she hit the left side on?"

Shelby looked intrigued. "Unless she was on the left side. In the driver's seat."

"Exactly."

The doctor interrupted to mention something he called *coup contre-coup*, how an impact on one side of the head would sometimes result in injury to the opposite side of the brain. "You should hire an ergonomics expert to model this," he said. "Set up a test."

"Like a crash dummy test?" Shelby said.

"Yes, and the dummy would have a simulated brain to register the points of injury according to the different impact scenarios."

She nodded and typed rapidly on her keyboard. "We'd video each scenario and have you testify about the location of each resulting injury."

"Which could prove Chrissy was the one driving," Pete said. "Even if we never find the priest."

Despite the media blitz, the witness still hadn't come forward. Pete didn't like to think about why that might be. If the priest was willing to stop and help on the road that night, he damn well ought to be willing to step up and help now. Unless he was off on a missionary trip to Siberia. Unless he didn't exist.

The doctor completed his dog-and-pony show, gathered up his materials, and after a round of departing handshakes, left the room. Another expert shortly took his place. He was the accident reconstructionist, a licensed engineer about Pete's age named Neal Grenier. His subject was more in Pete's wheelhouse, but he got lost when the guy starting throwing around terms like EDSMAC and delta-V and yaw-plane analysis and co-efficients of static friction. Like the doctor, he came equipped with some slick visuals—computer-generated simulations showing a dozen different scenarios of a truck swerving to avoid a dog. The variables were vehicle speed and distance from first sighting of the dog, which Kip estimated at a hundred feet. Not to mention dog speed. But in the end his conclusion was that the truck would not have left the road if it had been operated at or below the speed limit by an attentive driver with normal reaction times.

"What if it was operated by an inexperienced driver?" Pete said.

Grenier shrugged. "Inexperienced, distracted, intoxicated. All the same."

Pete sat back with a nod as Shelby rose to her feet. "Thanks, Neal. We'll be in touch."

The expert packed up his materials and shook hands all around before the paralegal escorted him from the conference room.

"We can't use him," Shelby said as soon as the door closed.

"What?" Pete gaped at her. Not only did he spend thousands of dollars for that dog-and-pony show, but it was the best news he'd heard yet. "This helps prove that Chrissy was driving."

"Only as one of the possibilities. If the jury doesn't buy it? Then all we've done is establish the others: that Kip must have been speeding and/or drunk. We'd be handing the Commonwealth the nails to build our own coffin."

"Mine," Kip mumbled.

"Excuse me?"

He didn't answer. "So that's it?" he said instead. "We're not going there? We can't find the priest so we're not gonna say Chrissy was driving?"

"No, come on." Pete turned to Shelby. "We're not abandoning that." He didn't mean it as a question, and he was chagrined that it came out sounding that way.

"We'll cross that bridge later," she said.

It wasn't the answer he was hoping for. He was hoping there wasn't even a bridge to cross. Kip Wasn't Driving. The End. Why wasn't that the Commonwealth's burden? he'd asked her earlier. Oh, it was, she explained, but they already met it when Kip told the officer he was driving. Now the burden had shifted to Kip to refute his own statement. The burden of proof, the burden of persuasion, the burden of fear and accusation. It was a good thing Karen wasn't being included in these meetings, Pete thought, not for the first time. She would have collapsed under the weight of all those burdens.

"Frank has some more ideas on that front," Shelby said. "Let's get him in here."

Her paralegal picked up the phone to summon him, and Frank Nobbin came in the room and set a laptop down on the table. Last week, he told them, he led a squad of investigators on a door-to-door canvass of the residents of Hollow Road, asking if anyone had been visited by a clergyman the night of the accident. None had, even though they hit every house along all five miles of Hollow Road. "Except that fortress next to your construction site," he said to Pete. "Nobody answered the buzzer at the gate. I can't find a telephone listing for that location either."

Pete wasn't surprised. "I don't think anyone's living there."

"Remember I saw lights, though, that one time," Kip said.

"On a timer, I bet," Pete said. "Same as the cameras."

"Cameras?" Shelby looked up. "Like CCTV?"

Nobbin shook his head. "It's a dead end. The cameras don't rotate to the road."

"Besides," Pete said, "wouldn't the tape be erased by now?"

Kip rolled his eyes. "It'd be digital, not tape, and if nobody's living there, it'd be saved to the cloud. Like, forever."

"Let's get a subpoena out." Shelby nodded at her paralegal. "Maybe the cameras caught something."

Nobbin obviously thought that was a waste of time. He was already moving on to his next agenda item. He turned to Kip. "Since you struck out trying to pick out the guy on that first photo array, I expanded the geographic perimeter of the churches. I also added in all the ordained clergy I could find who don't have a church. They teach or do counseling or play golf, whatever." He opened his laptop and slid it across the table to Kip. "Close to five hundred faces here. You need to go through them all."

Kip groaned as he opened the slide show on the screen.

"I have to be in court." Shelby glanced at her watch. "Take all the time you need."

Pete had a meeting with his own lawyer that afternoon, to review the closing documents for Rose Lane and to discuss the payment terms of the Millers' contract and get a fix on his rights and remedies. Five hundred dollars later, the answer was exactly what he suspected. Yes, he had the right to the progress payment, but no real remedy. What was he going to do, sue the guy and guarantee that the next progress payment wouldn't come either? He could stop work and lay off his crew, but even if he was willing to do that, most of the men would find other work and he'd lose them forever. Those who didn't would collect unemployment, and he couldn't afford the hit to his premiums.

He called Kip on his way to the parking garage. He was ready to leave, too, so Pete arranged to pick him up on the corner in front of Shelby's building. A couple of emails had come in while his phone was off, and before he started the engine, he scrolled through them. Scheduling matters. Money matters. Scheduling the money matters.

But here was a surprise: emails from Zack and Dylan. They'd been staying in touch, but always by phone, not email. Now they'd both emailed, within minutes of each other.

He opened Dylan's first. He'd been thinking a lot about summer break. He had a great time working for Pete last summer, but he was thinking about something different this year. He had a line on a cater-waiter gig doing summer weddings and parties. *Free leftovers!* he wrote and tacked on a smiley face. He hoped this wouldn't leave Pete in a lurch.

Zack's email was almost word-for-word the same. They must have called each other to coordinate their messages and synchronized their watches for the moment to push SEND.

It would leave him in a lurch, but that wasn't what stung. Those boys were like his own, and he'd been looking forward to having them around this summer. The plan was that they'd live at home with Leigh but spend all day with Pete on the job, and he'd harbored some hope that they'd bridge the two households. Give him an excuse to drop by now and then.

He was supposed to drop by every day, that was what he thought they'd agreed on, but he hadn't been back since that first day. He'd brought Kip along, thinking for sure she'd go out and coax him inside and they'd all have a nice dinner together. But the plan backfired on him, big-time. She stiffened up when she realized Kip was out there, thrust some fast-food coupons at Pete, and even turned away from his kiss. He made allowances at the time—he'd caught her off guard, she didn't mean to be so frosty—but when she wouldn't take his calls after that or answer his texts with anything more than *OK*, it became pretty clear that he needed to keep his distance for a while. The standoff would end, he thought, once the twins were home and working for him. He'd pick them up in the morning and drop them off at night and maybe bring along a pizza, and one of those nights, she'd tell him to come in and help them eat it. That was what he'd been counting on.

But if the twins didn't want to work for him, there was nothing he could do about it. They weren't his own, Kip was, and the battle lines were drawn. *Ours is the most perfectly blended family I've ever seen,* Leigh used to boast, but they were completely separated now. Oil on top, vinegar down below.

He exited the garage, paid the ransom at the booth, and cut across town to Shelby's building. Kip was on the corner out front. It looked like he was being hassled by a panhandler. A white guy with dreads was up in his face, and the kid was shying away like a skittish horse. His big-time felon son.

Pete tooted the horn, and Kip broke away from the panhandler and jumped in the passenger seat.

"Any luck with the photos?" Pete asked as he eased back into traffic.

"No."

"Too bad." He tried not to show his disappointment. Or was that even the right word for it? Royally pissed off might be more like it, and scared shitless might come even closer. Because they couldn't identify the priest, Pete was going to have spend more money he didn't have hiring another expert and making a crash dummy video.

"It gets worse," Kip said. "I got an email from the governor's office."

"Saying what?"

He affected a pompous politician tone. "In light of recent developments, we regret that we no longer have a place for you in our summer internship program. Good luck with all your future endeavors. Fuck you very much."

"Hey," Pete said, but the rebuke was mild. He knew the disappointment must be hitting him hard. The internship would have been a major résumé-builder for Kip, and the icing on top was that he would have spent the summer on his own in Richmond, in an apartment with the other interns. "I got an email today, too," he said. "Two of them, in fact." He handed over his phone.

Kip's face flushed as he skimmed the twins' parallel messages. "So they'd rather wear a bow tie and pass canapés than spend any time with me."

"That's not it. It's just—they're in a tricky situation."

"Yeah," he muttered. "Join the club."

They were rolling past the Washington Monument, the reflecting pool, the Lincoln Memorial, the most glorious sights in the country, but Kip's eyes were firmly fixed the other way, looking out at nothing. Pete wondered what was hitting him hardest—losing the internship or losing the twins. Despite their spats and scuffles, they got along as well as most biological brothers did, and in any case they were the only brothers he'd ever have.

"Anyway, it all works out," he said as they reached the end of the Mall. "You don't have a summer job, and I don't have any summer help. But now we both do."

Kip groaned. Construction gofer work didn't quite compare to hobnobbing with politicians. "But where are we—? Are we gonna live at the site all summer?"

"Bathroom fixtures'll be in soon. We'll be in the lap of luxury."

"Awesome."

"Call your mom," Pete reminded him, and he groaned again as he scrolled through his phone for her number.

Chapter Eighteen

There was no right way to grieve, the Good Reverend Brooks Brothers told Leigh. But there must be a wrong way, she thought, and this had to be it. Sleeping all day, wandering the empty house all night, setting foot outside only to turn the horses out in the morning and to bring them back in at night. Speaking to almost no one.

She'd managed to live in the world without Chrissy for more than thirty years. She'd managed for more than twenty years without Shelby, and more than forty without Peter. There was no reason why it should be so crippling to live without them now. She was her own person, an educated woman, strong and independent. She had to be more than the sum of her relationships with other people. There had to be something left of her on her own.

She remembered spouting off once at a book group meeting, protesting that all their selected works seemed to have titles like *The Watchmaker's Daughter, The Photographer's Wife, The Dry Cleaner's Fiancée. Doesn't the woman ever get to be something in her own right?* she'd railed at her friends, who rolled their eyes at one another with a *Here she goes again* look. But it was a serious question. A woman shouldn't be defined solely by who she was to somebody else.

Leigh was a wife, a mother, a daughter, and a friend. At the bottom of that list she would have added *lawyer*. But when everything else fell away, the bottom was what was left.

So, that was the answer. She had to work.

Those words were her constant refrain in the weeks after Ted took off. She had to work because she had three children to feed and clothe and educate. She had a mortgage plus a construction loan plus a building contract already signed and sealed. She had to work to pay the bills.

This time she had to work because she didn't know what else was left of her.

She couldn't face the office, not yet, but every morning she forced herself to sit down at Mission Control in the kitchen and face the daily deluge of emails. She began to respond directly to clients and opposing counsel. She became more attentive to Polly's summaries of phone messages and was able to dispatch most of them with a written reply. She put together a property settlement proposal, conducted all the negotiations in writing, and wrapped it up in the space of a week. She even managed to field a few phone calls, including one from Jenna Dietrich that Polly transferred from the office. It was placed, Polly told her, from a number marked WITHHELD.

"Jenna!" Leigh said when the call connected.

"Mom said to call you." The girl sounded as sullen as a teenager caught out after curfew.

"Are you all right?"

"Yes."

"Where are you?"

"I'm not telling. Anyone."

"Jenna. You know I won't tell Hunter."

"He could make you tell."

"How? By waterboarding? Come on. I need to be able to reach you in case there're any developments in the appeal."

"What developments?" the girl scoffed. "They file some papers, you file some papers, then a bunch of old men read them and decide what happens to my body. Right?"

Leigh winced a little. That assessment wasn't far off. "We're going to win the appeal," she said. "You don't need to be afraid of that."

"That's not what I'm afraid of." Now the sullen teenager voice was dark with portent. She sounded like an actress in a movie melodrama.

"The last thing Hunter would do is hurt you."

"Sure. Until the baby's born. Then what?"

"Are you planning to stay away until then?"

"Maybe I'll just stay away forever."

Leigh dropped her head into her hand. There was nothing she could say to talk her out of her paranoia. "Are you someplace safe?"

"Oh, I'm safe, all right. This place I'm staying? It's like a fucking fortress. I even got one of those Bluetooth panic buttons."

"Okay, good." She'd read about those. Push a button on a key chain or a piece of jewelry, and the device automatically dialed 911, sent out a GPS signal, and transmitted the audio from the crime scene. That sounded like a good security blanket for Jenna.

"And I'll tell you what else." There was a self-congratulatory smugness in Jenna's voice. "I got a gun."

"Oh, no. Jenna. That's too dangerous. You'll end up hurting yourself."

"I know what I'm doing."

Leigh didn't believe that at all. She sighed. "Do you have enough money?"

"I was stockpiling cash for months before I took off. It'll last me until the divorce comes through and I get my settlement."

"Well, what about medical care? You need to keep up with your obstetrical visits."

"I am. I found somebody else. Somebody who doesn't know me or Hunter."

"Well—" She didn't know what else she could do. "Promise you'll call me. Every week."

"God, you sound like my mother."

Leigh flinched, and for a moment she couldn't respond. "So I can keep you updated on the legal proceedings," she said tightly.

"Whatever."

Leigh felt so drained after that call she had to drag herself up the stairs and burrow deep into Chrissy's comforter.

She woke to darkness, with no clue what time it was or even what day. She'd drifted in and out of sleep and somehow lost her bearings on both the calendar and clock. She lifted her wrist and squinted at the glowing digits on her watch. It was after nine. PM, but which one? It was the weekend, she thought, but was it Saturday or Sunday? She'd forgotten to eat, she had no idea for how long, but she had a nagging sense she'd forgotten something else.

She hauled herself off the bed and wandered through the maze of the house. A dozen chores needed to be done, but that wasn't what nagged at her. It wasn't until she got to the kitchen and looked out to the back garden that she remembered. She'd forgotten to feed the horses. She'd forgotten to bring them in. And if this was Sunday, she'd forgotten for more than thirty-six hours.

She jammed her feet into her shoes and ran out the kitchen door and over the lawn to the gate. The horses' silhouettes rose black against the dusk on the far side of the pasture, as still as statues in a midnight garden. Leigh clucked her tongue, but they wouldn't come—punishment for her forgetfulness—so she had to go and fetch them and lead them into their stalls. They had plenty of grass in the pasture and the water trough was still half full, so they hadn't suffered from her neglect. But it wasn't until she grained and watered them that they deigned to acknowledge her with head-butting nuzzles against her shoulder. Goodness and Mercy paid her no mind at all. They sat on their perches up in the rafters, their eyes unblinking and glowing yellow in the dark.

She should sell the horses. Nobody was riding them, and the expense simply couldn't be justified. She nearly sold Licorice once before, after Ted left and the feed and veterinary bills threatened to overwhelm her. But it would have broken Chrissy's heart, so she dawdled and delayed until along came Peter, and they didn't have to sell him anymore, and not long after that they even added Romeo to their stable. Not to mention Shepherd. Those were the days when their household seemed capable of infinite expansion. Like those little hydrogel balls the kids used to play with. Drop them in a bowl of water and they expanded to two hundred times their size. But take them out of the water and they shriveled down to nothing. Eventually they disintegrated altogether.

She slid the bolt on the barn door and latched the gate and headed back to the house. It was a warm night, nearly summer, though still too early in the season for the fireflies to come out. Too early in the night for the stars to come out either, and the gloom was sinking in darkly over the pasture and lawn. There was nothing but a square of light from the kitchen window to guide her way back to the house. The peepers were in the tall grass and sounded like a chorus of sleigh bells as they sang their nighttime songs. Another few degrees hotter and the crickets would be chirping, too. That was when it would be time to reverse the horses' routine and keep them out of the heat in the barn during the day and turn them loose to graze at night.

The path from the pasture gate to the house curved around the big weeping cherry tree in the garden. For a moment the beacon of kitchen light was extinguished behind it, and in the sudden blackness Leigh heard a noise. Or more like—felt it. She strained her ears to find it again, but all she could hear were the chorus frogs singing in the weeds and the slam of a car door in the Markhams' driveway down the road. Still the skin crawled at the nape of her neck.

She broke into a run around the cherry tree and across the lawn to the kitchen door. Inside, she threw the dead bolt and ran to each of the open windows and closed and locked them, too. She peered out the front window, but all she could see was her own reflection in the glass. She switched off the lights and looked again. There were no streetlamps on their road, and the only illumination came from the distant glow of other houses.

Her hands shook as she poured herself a glass of water at the sink. If only Shep were here. If anyone were creeping around outside, anyone whose scent or sound he didn't recognize, he'd be at the door with a growl buzzing through his whip-tense body. But Shep wasn't here. He had to choose sides, and he chose Peter.

She should have had the baby they talked about the first year they were married. A small child wouldn't get to choose; it would simply be hers. But Leigh was past forty by then and their house was already overflowing with children to love and they decided no. Now, though, Peter might not have left if they had a child together. It would have been harder to split up a shared genome than it was to divide up their separate clusters of chromosomes.

She crossed the darkened kitchen to the rear window and gazed out into the backyard, through the wispy shadow of the cherry tree and past the hazy outline of the clematis arbor and the pineapple fountain standing dry in the middle of the garden. And there, above the bench, came a tiny burst of light.

It was only a brief flare, like someone struck a match and quickly shook it out. Almost like a firefly, except it couldn't have been, not in May in Northern Virginia. She grabbed the phone and dialed 911. Someone was out there, she knew it.

Stay by the phone, the dispatcher said, so Leigh kept it in her hand as she ran through the rooms, turning on all the lights. Somewhere in the house were baseball bats, lacrosse sticks, tennis rackets, and she ran to the kids' rooms before she remembered they were all stowed out in the garage, a breezeway away from the house. She ended up arming herself with a golf umbrella from the hall closet, and she was still holding it, pointy end out, when the phone rang in her hand.

It was the 911 operator, reporting in a monotone that an officer had arrived at her address, parked down the street, and was currently approaching her rear garden on foot. She should remain inside. Leigh ran to the front windows, then the back, but all she could see was herself in the glass. It was ten minutes before the operator called again, this time to tell her the officer was approaching her front door and to please disarm any weapons.

Leigh propped the umbrella in the corner when the doorbell rang. It was strangely comforting to hear a woman's voice call "Police!" through the door, and even stranger to open it and see Officer Ballerina Bun on the doorstep.

"Evening, Mrs. Huyett. I'm Officer Mateo."

"Yes. Yes, I remember."

"I conducted a search of the property, the yard and the pasture and the barn, but I didn't find anyone out there. Would you like me to search in here?"

"No, no, that won't be necessary. I was in here with the doors locked when I saw him strike a match— Did you look for a match in the garden by the bench?"

"Yes, ma'am. I couldn't see one. And no tracks in the garden soil either that I could see."

"Oh."

"I'd be happy to take a look around inside. Just in case."

"Yes, all right."

"Is anyone else at home?"

"Not at the moment, no."

She trailed after the young woman as she swept through the house. It wasn't like on TV. She didn't unholster her weapon or shout *Clear!* at every threshold. She moved through the rooms like a casual shopper at a Sunday open house, one who was only looking, thanks, but took the time to peer in every closet. When she finished the ground floor, she climbed the stairs and did the full circuit of the second floor, too, but it was obvious there was nothing amiss up there either, nothing beyond the unmade bed in the master bedroom and the rumpled comforter in Chrissy's room.

It was at the threshold of Chrissy's room that Officer Mateo stopped and looked at Leigh. "I don't see any sign of an intruder, ma'am."

"No." Leigh flushed and tucked a loose strand of hair behind her ear. "I'm sorry to have bothered you. I was so sure there was someone—"

"No need to apologize. That's what we're here for. If you like, someone could come out in the daylight tomorrow and take a closer look in the garden."

"No, that won't be necessary." Leigh followed her down the stairs to the front hall. "I must have imagined it." Maybe she had. She was so groggy from her lost weekend she could have seen anything.

The officer hesitated at the front door. "Mrs. Huyett, I never got the chance to tell you how sorry I am for your loss."

"Oh." Leigh went still. "Thank you."

"She seemed like a very special young lady. That night at the station? Before you and your husband arrived? You could tell she was scared, but she was being so brave about it. And yet still so courteous to all the officers. I thought at the time what a lovely girl she was."

"You're kind to say so."

"Later I found out she went to school with my husband's niece, Lacey. She couldn't say enough good things about her. Like that club she started, the antibullying thing?"

"The Defense League, right." The Spring to Everyone's Defense League, Leigh used to call it.

"My husband, he's hoping it's a girl, but I always thought I wanted a boy. Until I met your daughter."

It took a moment for Leigh to understand. "You're pregnant?" She dropped her eyes to the woman's waistline, but it was too thick with her equipment belt to reveal anything.

"I'm only four months along. We don't know what it is yet. But I've been thinking how lucky I'd be, if we have a girl and she turns out anything like yours."

The radio crackled on the officer's shoulder, and that finally moved her out the door. It was late now and the night was completely black outside. Leigh switched on the porch light, and it shone a warm glow over the front walk and its tidy edging of little globe boxwoods.

"Don't hesitate to call if you hear or see anything again."

"Thank you, but I'm sure it was nothing. The wind probably."

"Good night, then."

"Good night. Good luck with your baby."

Leigh locked the door and went through the house, turning off all the lights she'd turned on earlier, first floor up to second. When she reached her own room, she hit that switch, too, but switched it back on an instant later. It was a disgrace how long she'd left the bed unmade, and she was embarrassed that Officer Mateo saw it. She stripped off both sheets in one violent pull and carried them down the back stairs to the laundry room and crammed them in the washer. The water came on with a cleansing whoosh to fill the tub.

At the bay window in the darkened kitchen she knelt on the window seat and gazed out at the spot where the bench stood in the night garden. The wind could explain the noise she heard, but what could explain the spark? She knew she hadn't imagined that. It was like a little wink of fairy light in the darkness.

Chapter Nineteen

"Daddy?" Mia studiously stirred her ice cream to soup. "Did Kip do something bad?"

Pete threw a startled look at his daughter then a wary glance at the other families in the booths around them to check that no one was eavesdropping. "Well, what does Mommy say about it?"

This was the protocol he'd learned since the divorce. The parent with primary custody got to set the rules regarding bedtime, diet, TV, and what the child was allowed to know and not know. In the early years Mia arrived every other weekend with a set of printed instructions like a new appliance. But Karen hadn't passed on any instructions on this subject. How to couch her brother's arrest for homicide.

"Mommy says she can't talk about it. And Gary says I don't need to know. So does that mean it's really bad?"

Her face was the same shade of pink as her Hello Kitty T-shirt. They'd spent the day at the zoo, and it looked like he hadn't applied enough sunscreen. She had the coloring of her Irish ancestors—black hair and pale, pale skin—and even in May, she burned easily. He should have been more vigilant, or, better yet, planned an outing that didn't subject her to the sun all day. But he was still new to this kind of visitation and so far not very good at it. Things were so much easier when she came to the house every other weekend and they simply lived their ordinary hectic weekend lives. But after he moved to the job site, Karen vetoed overnight visitation. What he had to do now was drive to Karen's every Sunday to pick up his daughter and drop off his son. Mia skipped out to the truck while Kip trudged to the front door, and a high-five in passing was the sum of their sibling interaction.

"He made a mistake," Pete said finally. "It wasn't bad. But he broke some rules."

She considered that while she swirled a stripe of chocolate syrup through the cream in her dish. "And Chrissy died 'cause of it?"

"No!" He checked himself to add in a softer tone, "No. Chrissy died because she had a problem inside her head. The accident had nothing to do with it." He didn't know whether he believed that or not, but the important thing was for Mia to believe it. "Sometimes bad things happen and it's nobody's fault at all. It just—happens."

Her pale eyes bored straight into his. "Did God make it happen?"

"I don't know. Maybe."

"But why would he?"

Kip never asked questions like these at her age—or ever—but Mia was a different, more contemplative child. He wished he could give her some kind of answer. Something better than *mysterious ways* or *Deus Vult*. He remembered something his grandmother had said at the funeral of a teenaged cousin when Pete was maybe six or seven. *God likes to have pretty young flowers in his garden, too.* Even as a little boy, he saw the flaw in that argument. *Then why doesn't he just make the old ones young again?* "I don't know, sweetie," he said.

"I bet Leigh knows. She knows all the hard stuff. Let's call her."

He wondered. If Leigh heard Mia's voice on the machine, would that finally make her pick up? "No, we shouldn't bother her. She's going through a really hard time right now."

"Is that why I'm not allowed to see her?"

"It's not that you're not allowed—"

"Mommy says I can't go there."

"Just for a little while."

"But I miss her."

"I know." He cleared his throat. "Me, too."

Mia sighed and let her spoon sink into the liquid. "I miss Chrissy, too. Most of all. At night in bed I close my eyes and put her face inside my eyelids so I can remember her. But I'm afraid someday she'll just—flicker out."

Pete sat back against the hard vinyl of the booth. What a thing for a ten-year-old to say. He had no idea how to respond. Finally he pulled out his wallet and flipped open the photo strip. Chrissy's photo was there, right next to Leigh's. He slid it out and passed it over the table. "Would you like to hold on to this?"

Mia pursed her lips. "It's not the same," she said, but she tucked it into her tiny Hello Kitty pocketbook anyway.

After the divorce, Karen and Gary had moved to Silver Spring, into a new development of mass-produced, cookie-cutter houses called "executive-style" that came with small lots and zero character. It wasn't where Kip grew up or where his childhood buddies lived, and even in the best of times he didn't much enjoy his every-other-weekends there. Today he was waiting out front with his hands in his pockets and Karen was behind him hugging her ribs and Pete could read their body language from the end of the driveway: there'd been some kind of blowup with Gary. He leaned over to kiss Mia good-bye in the truck.

She wrinkled her nose. "Are you always going to have a beard now?"

"I don't know. Maybe."

"Nothing's the same anymore." She sighed and slid to the ground.

Kip swung up to take her place and slammed the door harder than necessary.

"Trouble?"

"Friggin' asshole." He scowled and slumped against the door.

"Seat belt," Pete said as he backed away.

Chapter Twenty

On Monday, Leigh's email from Polly had an attachment: Rob Canaday's opening brief in the case of *Beck v. Beck*. Leigh read it through in an hour. It was nothing more than a rehash of the arguments she'd already shot down in the lower court, and one of her young associates could easily draft the responsive brief. But she decided to do it herself. More than ever she felt that the mother-child relationship was something primal, sacred even, and not to be intruded upon by others. Even by the father. After all, his connection to the child was solely genetic. All he did was contribute half the blueprints. While the mother supplied an equal part of the design along with the building site, the construction materials, and all of the labor. She was connected to the baby through blood and nerves and every corpuscle of her being.

She didn't write any of that, of course. The only issue on appeal was whether the lower court erred in denying Hunter Beck access to his unborn child, and she confined herself to the legal reasons why that ruling was correct. But there was a force behind her writing that was new, and the words seemed to pour out of her. She finished the brief in half a day.

Another email arrived from Polly on Tuesday: *Ashley Gregg called again. Please call ASAP*. She'd called before, Leigh vaguely remembered. The last message said *You'll know what it's about*, but she didn't, and she never responded. Now she had an embarrassed flash of recall. Ashley Gregg was the personal shopper at Saks. Leigh's only conduit to the other crazy bereaved lady, Sheikha Devra.

She rummaged through the desk to retrieve the business card of that young woman who delivered the flowers, Emily Whitman. Sheikh Mazin Al-Khazrati was the name of her late boss, and she googled it and in ten seconds confirmed that he had died in January after suffering a heart attack while speaking at an energy symposium at Georgetown. He was a former OPEC minister from Saudi Arabia but not a member of the royal family, as she might have thought. It seemed that *sheikh* wasn't exclusively a royal title; it was an honorific bestowed throughout the Muslim world on tribal leaders and clerics, too. There were literally thousands of sheikhs out there. But no sheikhas. Their wives, singular or plural, had no internet presence at all, and a search for *Devra* anywhere in proximity to *Al-Khazrati* came up empty.

It was morbid curiosity that made her reach for the phone and place a business call for the first time.

"Oh, Mrs. Huyett," answered the young woman at Saks. "I've been trying to reach you."

"I'm sorry. I had, uh." Leigh cleared her throat. "A death in the family."

"Oh, I'm sorry," Ashley said but only in the breezy way of a social convention. "Our mutual friend is anxious to set up another meeting with you."

Our mutual friend. Ashley must have imagined their phones were being tapped. Or more likely, Devra imagined it, the deranged widow.

"Have you known her very long?" Leigh asked. "I was wondering."

"Oh, yes. She's been one of my best customers this last year or so. Such a stylish woman. She has truly exquisite taste."

"Did you ever meet her husband?"

"No, not yet. Why do you ask?"

"Oh, just curious." Leigh debated what kind of message to relay back to Devra, but everything she thought of came off as too brusque. *I'm un-*

able to take on this matter, or *I suggest you not pursue this further*. Those words were too unkind for a woman so obviously unhinged by her grief. The message should be delivered more gently, in person, and who better to deliver it than Leigh herself? The woman who hallucinated holographic images of her dead daughter. "When would she like to get together?"

They set a date for the following morning at the same location.

It wouldn't be a first client meeting this time—it wouldn't be a client meeting at all—but Wednesday morning Leigh dressed as if it were, in a suit and heels as before. No pearls this time, though. They'd come unstrung, and she didn't know what had become of them.

It was strange to be out in the world, dressed and groomed and on the road. Except for her demented chase after the good reverend, she hadn't been this far from home since the funeral. Except for a few grocery runs, she hadn't left the house at all. It was like staggering out of a cave into the blinding sunlight. The letters on the road signs faded in and out of focus like the charts at the eye doctor's. Better here? Or here? The windshields of passing motorists reflected shards of sun glare, and she had to squint to see their faces through the distortion. They looked unreal to her, like museum specimens behind glass, a diorama of harried D.C. commuters. Everyone in such a hurry to be somewhere else, all of them so busy with their busy lives. Their worlds spinning on.

She negotiated the heavy inbound traffic and parked by the entrance to Saks, in the same no-parking zone where Ashley directed her before. It was the same spot where she turned on her phone that morning and saw the missed calls from Kip and Peter and the hospital, and that memory was all it took for the grief to billow up and smack her like a wall of water.

She'd come to think of grief that way, as a giant swell rising up in an otherwise calm sea, cresting into an enormous wave that came crashing down over her. If she was on her guard, if she kept watch for it, she could sometimes see it coming and paddle furiously ahead to miss the worst of it. But too often it came out of nowhere and there was nothing she could do but choke and sputter and gasp for breath.

The young woman, Ashley Gregg, was waiting at the door. Leigh pretended to be busy checking her phone long enough to pull herself together. She stepped out of the car with a shaky greeting.

"The sheikha's already arrived," Ashley told her as she hurried her along through cosmetics and jewelry and into the elevator. "If you wouldn't mind carrying this—?" She handed Leigh a hanger holding a plastic-bagged gown, and at Leigh's blank look, she added, "To—uh—you know."

"Oh. Of course." Leigh maneuvered the gown to conceal the briefcase on her arm as the elevator doors opened.

The same bodyguard stood at attention outside the door of the designer wear salon. His eyes raked over Leigh as he held the door open, and with a short nod she brushed past him.

Devra rose from the divan and extended both hands toward her. She'd already removed her black outer coverings, but she was clad in black underneath, too, in a form-fitting sleeveless sheath that revealed a flawless figure. "Leigh. Thank you for meeting me," she said. "Please, won't you sit down?"

"Thank you." Leigh perched on the edge of the divan. "And thank you also for the beautiful flower arrangement."

"I'm sorry?"

"The flowers. Your assistant delivered them."

The sheikha's brow furrowed.

"Emily Whitman. Your assistant?"

She looked more and more confused. "I don't believe I know anyone by that name."

Leigh didn't know how to proceed. If she tried to press too much reality on her, the sheikha might have a complete psychotic break. Hesitantly she said, "Back in January—did your husband suffer a heart attack?"

Devra gaped at her. "Why would you ask such a thing?"

"I saw it in the newspaper." Leigh pulled the printout of the obituary from her briefcase and handed it to her.

The sheikha read it and looked up with a frown. "I don't understand. This is about the death of Mazin Al-Khazrati."

Gently Leigh said, "Your husband."

Devra stared at her a moment. Then she threw back her head and let out a peal of manic laughter. "Al-Khazrati is not my husband! Where did you ever get such an idea?"

"From Emily Whitman. Your assistant." Leigh reached in her briefcase for the young woman's business card.

Devra shook her head as she read it. "I do not know this person." She passed the card back. "This confusion is obviously my fault. I should have told you everything from the start." She rummaged in her handbag— today it was a crocodile Chanel—and came out with a business card of her own. "Here. This is my husband."

Leigh took the card from her and read it:

His Excellency Faheem bin Jabar

Ambassador Extraordinary and Plenipotentiary

Embassy of the State of Qatar in the United States

2355 Belmont Road NW, Washington, DC 20008

She looked up. Carefully she said, "Your husband is the Qatari ambassador to the United States."

"That is correct, yes." Devra folded her hands, as if pleased that the misunderstanding had been so swiftly resolved.

Leigh couldn't imagine any reason for the widow of a Saudi sheikh to carry the business card of the Qatari ambassador. But she also couldn't imagine any reason for Emily Whitman to lie to her. "And this is your address?"

"That is the address of the embassy," Devra said. "We have living quarters there, of course, but we spend the weekends at our country estate here in Virginia."

"Where, exactly?"

"In Hampshire County."

Leigh blinked. "That's where I live."

"Oh?" Devra didn't seem to register the unlikelihood of that coincidence. "During our last meeting," she went on, "you told me I couldn't seek a divorce in the District of Columbia unless I was first separated from my husband. But in Virginia, separation is not required if certain fault grounds exist. Is that correct?"

"That's all correct." And cogently summarized, too, Leigh had to admit.

"So would I be permitted to file for divorce in Virginia rather than Washington?"

Leigh didn't know how to answer. Devra seemed perfectly rational, but if she wasn't deranged, it meant that Emily Whitman had lied, which made no sense. But if Leigh didn't know *how* to answer, at least she knew *what*. "Only if you've been a domiciliary of Virginia for at least six months. *Domicile* means your fixed, permanent home. You can reside in several places, but you're only domiciled in one." She ticked off the factors the Virginia courts would examine: where she voted, was employed, banked, participated in community activities, and insured her automobiles, as well as the state that issued her driver's license and car registration.

Devra looked helpless when Leigh finished the litany. "I've never done any of those things," she said. "Anywhere."

Of course she hadn't, Leigh realized. The test for domicile wasn't designed with cloistered wives in mind. "We might persuade the court to make a more subjective examination, in your case. To determine which residence is more truly your home."

"As between Washington and Virginia? Virginia. Clearly. The embassy is an office building full of functionaries on computers and strangers standing in line. We do not own it and it is not our home. Or at least not mine. My husband seems content enough there."

"Your husband"—Leigh read from the business card—"the Extraordinary and Plenipotentiary." It sounded as grandiose and mythical as the Great and Powerful Oz.

"That is his title, yes." Devra pushed the buzzer beside her chair, the signal, Leigh now recognized, that their meeting was over. "If you would please give some consideration to the domicile question, perhaps at our next meeting I will be prepared to go forward. Meanwhile, I have arranged for the sum of a hundred thousand dollars to be wired to your firm's bank account. I hope this will suffice for your initial retainer."

A knock sounded on the door, and Ashley Gregg came through with another rolling rack of dresses, and the three women went through the same routine as before, pretending Leigh was a fashion consultant for the sake of the brooding bodyguard posted outside.

"Until next time," Devra said, clasping her hand warmly.

The charade was so elaborate, pretending a marriage to the Qatari ambassador, setting up clandestine meetings, carefully parsing out the venue requirements for her divorce from a dead man. As soon as Leigh got home, she sat down at the computer in the kitchen and pulled up the website for the Qatari embassy. There he was, Faheem bin Jabar, a gray-bearded man with an unsmiling face, wearing a dark business suit and a starched white *ghutra* on his head held in place by a corded black *agal*. He was indeed the ambassador from Qatar, having formally presented his credentials to the president at a White House ceremony last year. But nothing on the embassy website mentioned his wife or any other information about his family.

She telephoned her office for the first time in weeks and asked for Miguel Gonzalez. He was the head of the firm's government relations department—their euphemism for lobbyist—and he had a vast network of contacts in virtually every branch of the federal government. She announced herself to his secretary, and to her surprise, Gonzalez himself came on the line. Ordinarily he wouldn't take her unscheduled call, but her bereavement must have stirred enough sympathy for him to overlook the difference in their places within the firm's hierarchy.

"Leigh," he said in a pained whisper. "I can't tell you how sorry Gina and I are. We just can't imagine."

Leigh had never even met Gina, but men like Gonzalez seemed to shy away from expressing any emotion as their own; they always thrust their wives out front and center in conveying the sentiment.

"Mike, who do you know at State?" she asked without preamble.

"Why, quite a few people." It took him a second to recover his footing. "What do you need?"

"I'm looking for some information on the ambassador from Qatar."

"Be more specific."

"The name of his wife. Or wives."

"Hmm. You probably want to talk to the Office of Protocol. They liaise with all the foreign diplomats and organize the various ceremonial affairs. I'll switch you back to Shirley and she'll get you the number of my best contact there."

"Thank you, Mike."

"Oh, and while I have you. I have a new matter for you. A custody case."

Leigh was too startled to respond. Gonzalez had never referred a case to her before, and she couldn't believe he'd choose this time to begin.

"He's a very impressive young man. An honest-to-God war hero. Special Forces. John Stoddard's his name. He was awarded the Silver Star last week, and Congressman Breating held a little dinner for him afterward. We got to talking, and he mentioned his domestic situation, and I told him we have the perfect lawyer for him."

"I'm sorry, Mike. I'm really not ready—"

"Of course. I understand. You need time. Let me set something up for, let's see. I'll get him in here in a week or so. Until then, take it easy. Take care of yourself. And again, Leigh, our deepest condolences."

Leigh stared at the phone in disbelief. There was no way she was going to represent a man who wanted to take a child away from her mother. War hero or not.

Gonzalez's assistant came on the line with the name and number of his contact at the Office of Protocol. Leigh dialed the number and waved the magic wand of Miguel Gonzalez's name to get through to the chief, who promptly transferred the call to a subordinate responsible for maintaining the Diplomatic List. The List was a State Department publication detailing the names of everyone having diplomatic rank in every foreign mission in the country, along with their spouses. The subordinate located Faheem bin Jabar's name on the list but told Leigh there was no spouse name below it.

"So that means he's unmarried?"

"Or he left her behind in Qatar. Or he elected not to publish her name."

"But there'd have to be a record of any diplomatic passport issued to a spouse."

"That would be classified."

She made one more attempt. If Devra and her husband had purchased a country house in Hampshire County last year, there'd be a record of the property transfer. She called a paralegal in the real estate department and asked her to do a record search under the name bin Jabar, and also, just in case, under the name Al-Khazrati.

The answer came back in thirty minutes. There were no recorded property transfers in Hampshire County under either name in the past year or, in fact, ever.

She was ready to give up. Devra didn't exist in the real estate records, or on a driver's license, a car registration, the voter rolls, or the Diplomatic List. It was as if she left no footprints in the world. She might as well be a ghost.

But at that moment her computer pinged with an incoming email. A notification from the Accounting Department that the sum of $100,000 had been wired into her client trust account that day. From an anonymous, numbered account in Vienna.

Ghosts didn't wire money.

She leaned back and thought for a while before it came to her. There was an easy way to find out if Devra was the ambassador's wife, and she was an idiot not to have done it sooner. She reached for her phone.

"Hello," she said when the embassy operator answered. "Could I speak to Devra please?"

She could hear a whispered exchange before the operator returned to the line. "The sheikha is not receiving calls. You may leave a message."

"No, no message."

So. Devra was who she said she was. It was Emily Whitman who wasn't. She located the young woman's phony business card and dialed the number. The call went directly to voicemail with no override option to an operator. "This is Leigh Huyett," she said. "And I'd like to know why you lied to me. Call me back. At once."

The phone didn't ring until that evening, and it wasn't Emily Whitman. It was Jenna Dietrich, two days later than promised and twice as surly. Leigh asked about her health, her safety, her finances, until the girl snapped, "God! I already went through all this shit with my mother. Why don't you two coordinate and save me the hassle of saying it twice?"

For a moment Leigh was stung silent. "You're right," she said finally. "I'm only your lawyer. But all these questions are pertinent to your divorce case. You'll have to answer them before custody and visitation are decided."

"I guess we'll see about that."

"Meanwhile, I have Canaday's brief and a draft of our response I'd like to send you."

"What for?"

"You're the client, Jenna. You have the right to see their arguments and sign off on ours."

"Oh, like suddenly I have rights?"

Leigh sighed. "You've always had rights. The lower court said so, and the appellate court will, too, as soon as we get this brief filed."

"Then file it already. Jeez." Jenna snapped and hung up.

Such a difficult girl, Leigh thought as she put down the phone. She did not envy Carrie her daughter.

But no, she thought an instant later. No, she did.

Chapter Twenty-One

"Good news," Shelby shouted through the speaker on Kip's phone, and for two seconds Pete let himself hope. The priest came forward, Kip's statement was corroborated, the Commonwealth's Attorney was dropping all charges. He threw a quick glance beside him in the truck. Kip was staring at his phone with the same hope. His breath sounded in rapid little pants.

"We got a trial date," she said. "August tenth."

"Oh."

"It's exactly what we asked for," she reminded him.

"Right." He glanced over again. Kip's face had turned to stone.

"So it's all hands on deck," Shelby said. "I'm setting up interviews with the ER doc and the neurosurgeon and the neighbor who called 911, and Frank's circling back to the kids at the party. We'll get all the witnesses nailed down."

Kip mumbled something. He was staring out the window, and Pete couldn't hear him above the roar of the tires on the asphalt. Shelby didn't hear him at all. She continued, "And we need to green light the ergonomics guy if we're going to."

"The crash dummy test," Pete remembered. This would be the simulation to determine whether Chrissy's brain would have been injured in the left parietal lobe if she were riding in the passenger seat.

"Right. Is it yea or nay?"

It was *yea* if they believed Kip's story, *nay* if they didn't want to waste any more time and money on it. "Yea," Pete said.

"I'll need a check."

"I'll get it to you."

"I'll be in touch."

The call disconnected, and for a mile there was no sound in the cab but the whoosh of the wind passing them by.

"This is good news," Pete said finally. "It means it'll all be over in time for you to report to first-year orientation on the eighteenth."

"Yeah." Kip didn't turn his face from the window. "I wonder what kind of orientation program they have in prison."

"Hey! None of that, now." Pete swung out his arm to swat him on the chest. It was the same way he always threw an arm out in front of the kids when he had to brake suddenly. Despite air bags, the instinct was still there. "Remember what Shelby said. Even if we lose, there's no real chance you'll do jail time."

"Right."

"We have two months of hard work ahead. You gotta keep your spirits up."

"Right," Kip said again, and slumped so low in the seat he couldn't even see out of the window he pretended to be staring through.

Pete thought back to an article Leigh had shown him a couple years ago about the physiology of the teenaged brain. *This explains everything*, she said. *Everything* meaning the often mystifying behaviors of their assorted children. Until about age twenty, the article claimed, the neural connections between the prefrontal lobes weren't fully developed. This supposedly led to wild mood swings, poor impulse control, the inability to foresee consequences, and easy distractibility. It read like a case history of his own son. He could never understand how someone so smart could do so many stupid things. *It's like you don't think!* he'd railed at him more than once. But if this research was correct, Kip was thinking, all right. It was just that the thoughts weren't connecting from one side of his brain to the other.

The boy's silence lasted all the way back to the job site, and when he got out of the truck, he dropped his backpack by the door and headed up the hill to the woods.

"Where are you going?" Pete called after him.

"For a walk."

"Don't forget. You've got that history paper to write."

"Yeah, yeah, I'm on it."

A hundred pages in and only a week before the due date, Kip had ditched his original idea of examining what started the Crusades to focus instead on what ended them. That was the more interesting question, he told Pete. How did the imperative to wage war for the glory of God disappear? What made the Christians decide they didn't need to bother anymore? What made the command of *Deus Vult!* become *Yeah, whatever?* But Pete didn't see any reason to assume such fatalism. Maybe they simply found more productive things to do with their lives.

"I'm heading out to do some errands," he called as Kip trudged up the hill. "What d'you want for dinner tonight?"

Kip kept walking. "Whatever."

Pete didn't actually have any errands to run. What he did instead was drive home. Or rather, drive past home. It was what he did almost every night on his food run, just drive by and eyeball the place. Make sure no shutters were hanging loose or rain gutters overflowing. A quick glance to see if the car was in the garage or the lights were on in the house.

It was yes to both today. It was more than a month since the funeral, and as far as he could tell, Leigh hadn't gone back to work or anywhere else. He knew from their joint bank account records that she was keeping up with the bills, and either she'd hired a lawn service to fill in for Kip or she was cutting the grass herself. So it seemed she was functioning okay. She simply never left the house.

There were things he wanted to get—some summer-weight clothes, now that warm weather was here, a spare coffeemaker, the TV from Kip's room. But Leigh was always there, and he couldn't bring himself even to pull in the driveway. He didn't know how to go about it anymore. Would he use his key like he had a right to, or ring the bell like he didn't? Obviously he couldn't call ahead, not since she refused to answer his calls and the sum of their marital relations was reduced to text messages. *OK?* he asked. *Fine. U?* she answered. They'd have clearer communication with a string and two tin cans.

He drove on. But fifty yards down the road, he slammed on his brakes. Romeo was out of his pasture again and stretching his neck to tear the leaves off the Markhams' red maple tree. "Aw, dammit," he muttered.

He parked on the shoulder of the road and jumped out. Romeo flicked his ears in recognition and trotted his way, and he snagged him by the halter and led him back to the pasture and gave him a slap on the hindquarters to shoo him through the gate. Then he walked the entire perimeter of the fence. If there was a rail down, he couldn't see where it was. Maybe Romeo could jump over all three rails now, in which case he should run a strand of electrified wire along the top. That was the remedy, if it was even still his right.

The weeping cherry was dripping its pale petals onto the lawn, the azaleas were blooming along the back of the border, and the feathery sprays of astilbe added their own intense shades of hot pink and purple to the mix. But the serpentine curves of the flowerbeds were empty. Leigh always got the annuals in the ground by this date in May, but not this year. Pete hadn't done his usual winter cleanup or spread any mulch either. Their garden wasn't going to be much to look at this summer. The bird feeder was empty, too, though the birds were swooping in for a look anyway. Hope and habit died hard.

A light flashed on in the kitchen, and he shrank back into the tree line like some kind of stalker. A Peeping Tom spying on his own wife.

There she was, gliding past the big bay window. She was dressed in jeans and that green T-shirt he liked so much, the one that lit up the reddish gold in her hair and clung so nicely to the underside of her breasts. And great, now he was having sexual fantasies like a real Peeping Tom. Except his didn't lead to a happy ending. His ended with their last night together and the shame of remembering how he pumped to climax while his wife lay sobbing beneath him. No wonder she woke up the next morning with a burning desire to live apart.

He watched her another moment as she moved about the kitchen, and for a second he fantasized about joining her there. Sitting down together. Talking. But about what? The only subjects that mattered were Chrissy and the trial, and they were both minefields. One wrong step and everything would blow up.

He crouched down out of sight and stole back to the truck.

Dusk had fallen by the time he returned to Hollow Road. He switched on his headlights and they bored two cones of bright light straight ahead but cast the roadsides into darkness. Which was why he almost missed the car pulling out of the Hermitage with its headlights off.

He slammed on his brakes, and the car braked hard, too, barely in time. The two vehicles lurched to a stop with their front fenders only inches apart.

Pete's chest heaved, both from the near-miss and from the shock of seeing those gates open for the first time in ten months. Shelby's process server struck out three times trying to serve a subpoena on this address, and it was everybody's conclusion that the place was unoccupied.

He threw the truck in park and got out. The car was a green Toyota and behind the wheel was a bald guy with a goatee. He lowered the window as Pete approached.

"I just wanted you to know—your headlights are off."

"Oh, jeez." He fumbled for the switch, and as the lights flashed on he started to close his window. "Thanks, man."

"While I have you."

"Yeah?" He stopped the window at half-mast.

"I'm Pete Conley. I'm building the house next door?"

The man looked blank.

"I wanted to ask you." The gates stood wide open behind the idling car, and Pete cut a quick glance that way. It was his first view inside the compound, but all he could make out in the dim light was an entry court paved with cobblestones and, set back a couple hundred feet, a mansion built of the same red brick as the perimeter wall. "By any chance do you know a priest who drives a big dark car?"

"I'm just the Uber driver, man." The man jerked a thumb over his seat back.

Pete hadn't noticed the woman in the backseat. She was a posh-looking blonde in a Burberry trench coat with her hair in a stylish up-do. She lowered her own window. "Sorry?"

He repeated the question. "A priest or some other kind of clergyman? The reason I'm asking—my son was in an accident down the road last month, and the only witness was this priest or whoever. We're really hoping to track him down."

"No. Sorry."

"Maybe your security system caught something?"

She tossed a quick look at the camera mounted by the gates. "I don't actually live here, you see. In fact, I'm just on my way to the airport now."

"Oh." He glanced again through the gates and caught a glimpse of the front door—double doors, actually, topped by a broken pediment and flanked by columnar evergreens in big concrete pots. "If you could give me the name of the owner, I'll contact him."

"It's a corporation, I think. I'm sorry. I really must be off now. International check-in, you know."

Her window whined shut.

Pete moved the truck out of the way, and the gates clanged shut as the Toyota pulled out and turned down the road in the other direction. He squinted at the mirror as the taillights receded. The occupancy of that estate had been a mystery for ten months, and meeting this woman did nothing to solve it. He looked back at the security camera. It was pointed down, to the window-level height of any vehicle that might approach. Frank Nobbin was probably right. It was a waste of time pursuing the footage.

He put the truck in gear and drove on down the road and up the drive to Hollow House. Where Drew Miller's silver Porsche sat glowing in the dark by the garage.

It was weeks since King Midas had been by the site, and weeks longer since he made his last payment. If he was here tonight, it would only be to look for enough problems or defects to justify his default. Pete parked and headed for the back door, bracing himself for more of Miller's carping and demands.

A giggle sounded from somewhere in the dark. A huskier voice said something that elicited another light, teasing giggle. Pete stopped. Both voices were coming from the woods.

A big expanse of undeveloped property ran behind both the Hermitage and Hollow House. It was owned by a nature conservancy and preserved into perpetuity, a feature that made the Millers' lot particularly valuable. The conservancy tract included the woods at the top of the hill and an open field down the other side. Pete had never seen anybody back there except the Dietrichs, who mowed the meadow a couple times a year in exchange for the hay. If the local teenagers were using it as a lovers' lane, Midas was bound to throw another fit.

Two figures emerged from the gloom of the woods, and Pete started up the hill to cut them off—to warn them off, too—when he saw that one of them was his own teenager and the other wasn't a teenager at all. She was Yana Miller.

"Hey," he called. "What's going on?"

"Oh. Hey," Kip said.

"We ben inwestigating," Yana said in a la-di-da lilt. She was wearing a fluttery white blouse over skinny white jeans and her pale hair was long and loose down her back. As always, she walked in a weird loping gait, one foot crossing over the other in exaggerated steps like she was on a fashion runway. Kip stumbled along behind her like he'd forgotten how to walk altogether.

"Just so you know, your property ends there." Pete pointed to the line, but Yana didn't even bother to turn around and look. Boundaries meant nothing to her.

A door slammed behind them, and Miller came charging out of the house. "There you are," he said, stomping up furiously to Pete. He was practically foaming at the mouth. "What the fuck, Conley? It looks like somebody's *living* in there."

"Yes, sir." Kip stepped up to answer before Pete could. "Me and my dad are staying here to keep an eye on the place. Make sure everything's secure. You know." He jerked his chin in the direction of the Hermitage. "Just in case."

"Huh." Miller squinted hard, like an unexpected thought was hatching out of the smooth shell of his head. "That's kinda going above and beyond."

Kip gave an eager nod. "Dad likes to look out for his customers."

"Oh." Slowly Miller's hackles went down. "Well. I appreciate that."

Pete had to marvel at this kid sometimes. One minute he was tripping over his own feet in the presence of a female. The next he was de-fanging a pit bull. Two hours ago he was hanging his head in despair. The mysteries of the teenaged brain.

"But it's all cool," Kip went on. "Turns out nobody's even living there."

"Huh."

Pete held his tongue as Miller turned to study the place next door. Another thought seemed to be hatching, but after a minute he stirred himself and clapped Pete on the back. "Place looks good."

"Yeah, we've been making good progress this week." Pete emphasized the word *progress*.

"Yeah, yeah, that reminds me. I'll get you that payment tomorrow."

"That'd be great, thanks."

"Yana, you ready, babe?" Miller squeezed himself behind the wheel of the car.

She didn't answer him. She simply turned and walked her loopy walk to the Porsche and, with a strange twitch of her mouth that was something like a parting smile, she folded her long legs and got into the car.

Kip's own mouth hung open as they drove out of sight.

"What a fruitcake," Pete said.

"Are you kidding? She's the hottest girl I've ever seen!"

It was King Midas that Pete was speaking of, and he almost laughed at how Kip's mind sprang immediately to the Queen. "Hardly a girl," he said. "She must be thirty."

"Do you think her magazine spreads are online?" Kip didn't wait for Pete to answer. He was already tapping the search terms into his phone.

"Hey, listen," Pete said. "You should stay out of those woods."

"What? Why?"

"Because they back right up to the neighbors, that's why, and I told you to steer clear of the place, remember?"

"Yeah, yeah." Kip walked away with his screen lit up.

Chapter Twenty-Two

Once there were elaborate rules and rituals for mourning. The bereaved wore black clothes or armbands. They pulled the curtains and stopped the clocks and draped all the household mirrors. They hung a wreath of laurel tied with black crape on the front door. They ordered stationery with a black border. For some strictly regimented period of time, they didn't sing or dance or attend amusements or otherwise go out in society.

Today the public rituals of mourning were no longer observed. Today the bereaved wore whatever color they liked and after three days, maybe seven, they went back to work. Any open display of grief after that was unseemly. Self-indulgent and inconsiderate of the sensibilities of others. It was like an amputee going out in public with an empty sleeve. He should wear a prosthetic whether it helped or not. Fill that emptiness with something artificial so as not to disturb other people.

Karen called on a Friday. It was more than a month since the funeral, so she could skip the sympathetic preliminaries and get right to the point. She wanted to stop by the next morning to pick up Mia's things.

"I'm sorry?" Leigh said.

"Her toys, her clothes. Anything she left there. If you could pack it up for me, I'll stop by tomorrow." When Leigh's silence went on too long, she added, "She misses her things. Is there a problem?"

Leigh swallowed hard. "No. No problem. I'll have it all ready for you."

She had the box waiting in the front hall when Karen rang the doorbell the next morning. She was a frail-looking woman, very pretty, but with a timidity that made it hard to imagine she'd ever been audacious enough to have an extramarital affair. Though as Peter told it, she was simply a movable object in the path of Gary's irresistible force.

"Let me carry it out for you." Leigh hoisted the box through the door and out to the driveway. She was hoping that Mia might be waiting in the car, but Gary was alone in his big Mercedes. He gave her a mock salute from behind the wheel.

"Did you already drop Mia off?" Leigh asked as went around to the trunk.

Karen gave a tight-lipped nod. "I didn't want to. It's really not safe there, with all those tools and nails and splinters. Not to mention all those strange men."

"I'm sure Peter watches out for her."

"It's no place for Kip to live either."

Her tone had never been so frosty, and Leigh knew she must blame her for Kip's exile. She must be the wicked stepmother who banished him to the woods. "I know," she said.

Karen slammed the trunk lid shut. "You know, I always thought I'd get him back at the end of that first year. I thought he'd get it out of his system and want to come home and Pete wouldn't have a leg to stand on in court." She stopped beside her door. "Then he went and married a divorce lawyer and I lost all hope."

Leigh blinked with surprise. This was nothing she'd ever heard before. "Karen, I never advised Peter on custody. I never got involved."

"You did, though. In more ways than one."

The narrative was changing by the moment. Now Leigh was an interloper. "I never tried to take your place with Kip."

"Didn't you?"

Leigh stood speechless as a UPS truck rumbled into the driveway. Behind the wheel Gary threw his hands up in disgust—he'd be blocked for the two minutes it would take the driver to complete his delivery.

"Sorry," Leigh said and hurried to take the package. She didn't know what it could be. The time for flowers and fruit baskets had long since passed. The driver hefted an oversize carton off the truck, and it wasn't until he handed her the electronic signature device that she remembered. It was Kip's surprise graduation present.

Every college-bound student wanted a new computer, but Kip had a wish list of special requirements, and over the course of many stealthy conversations she figured them out and ordered it custom-built to his specifications. It took many phone calls and thousands of dollars, but it was pure pleasure for Leigh as she imagined his usual smart-aleck cool dissolving into stunned joy as he unwrapped it.

"I'll carry it to the door," the driver offered while Gary fumed.

Leigh looked down at the box, then over at Karen. "I wonder if you could take this, too?" she called to her.

"What is it?"

"I don't know," Leigh said. "Something Peter got for Kip's graduation." In truth it would be a surprise for Peter, too. He'd come up with the golf clubs for Kip's birthday but left it to Leigh to think of a graduation present.

"Oh, all right," Karen said with a put-upon sigh, and as the UPS truck backed out of the drive, Leigh loaded it into the backseat of the car.

On Tuesday Leigh returned to the office. She had no choice. Miguel Gonzalez refused to take *not yet* for an answer and went ahead and put a meeting on her calendar with John Stoddard, the war hero who now wanted to wage a custody battle. She wasn't going to take the case, she hadn't changed her mind about that. But if Gonzalez wouldn't take no for an answer, she could see to it that Stoddard would. She'd take the meeting but make herself so discouraging, so dismally skeptical of his chances of wresting the child away from her mother, that he'd storm out after ten minutes. She'd earn herself a few black marks in the process, but she hardly cared.

She left the house early enough to avoid the worst of the commuter crowds on the Metro and arrived at the office in time to avoid any awkward encounters in the elevator. The corridors were dark as she wended her way around the perimeter of the building past the open doors and cluttered desktops of her colleagues. Her own office door stood uncharacteristically closed, and when she pushed it open, a musty odor rose up, like a spritz of gloom diffused through the air.

She closed the door and sat down at her desk. This was always her favorite time to work, in the still of the early morning, the quiet before the storm of phone calls and *Got a minute?* head-pokes around the door. A leaning tower of accumulated, nonurgent mail overflowed her inbox. She was able to make quick work of most of it, and quick work of the administrative messages piled up in her electronic inbox, too. Except for one. A request from Accounting that she account for the $100,000 wire transfer from Austria.

Either she should open a new client file for Devra or she should refund the retainer, but she couldn't decide which. It wouldn't be an easy case. She'd have to establish Virginia domicile based only on a weekend getaway, then she'd have to step carefully around the thorny question of diplomatic immunity. The Vienna Convention protected foreign diplomats from any legal action in their host country. The purpose was to ward off politically motivated prosecutions, but technically the immunity extended even to private domestic relations cases between the diplomats and their spouses. In practice, the home country typically waived the immunity defense so the divorce action could proceed in a U.S. court, but the procedure for obtaining that waiver was cumbersome. And even when diplomatic immunity was waived for purposes of dissolving the marriage, it was often resurrected to shield the diplomat's assets. In effect, the foreign sovereign told the diplomat's spouse: yes, you may have your divorce but not a penny of settlement or support. If the government of Qatar followed the same course, it would jeopardize Devra's entitlement to her *mahr*. The Virginia court might order the ambassador to pay her the agreed sum, but the order would be unenforceable against any of his assets in the United States. And the Qatari courts wouldn't enforce the order because her American divorce wouldn't be recognized there. The final complication was how she'd even serve the divorce complaint on the ambassador. The embassy was technically the property of the government of Qatar, and the Foreign Sovereign Immunities Act would render it off-limits for Leigh's process server.

Even apart from the legal hurdles, so many other questions remained. Why wouldn't Devra just leave her husband when she had at least $100,000 at ready disposal? And who was Emily Whitman, and why would she concoct such an elaborate lie?

She dug out the phony business card and punched in the young woman's number, but as before, the call went straight to voicemail. She left a terse message and was hanging up the phone as her office door swung open.

She whirled in her chair. Polly teetered under an armload of files, and they both gasped their surprise.

"Polly!"

"Leigh! Oh, my God, I had no idea you were back!"

"Sorry. I wanted a quiet morning."

Polly put the stack of files on the worktable across the room. She was a stout woman of sixty with six grandchildren and three daughters who called her every day. She was also a crack assistant-cum-paralegal who knew more about the minutiae of divorce filings than anyone in the city. If she'd had the same opportunities as Leigh growing up, she would have been Leigh's most formidable opponent instead of her indispensable assistant.

"Can I get you anything?" Polly asked. "Coffee?"

They'd worked together nearly twenty years and Leigh had never once asked her to fetch coffee. Now she must have FRAGILE. HANDLE WITH CARE stamped on her forehead. "No, thanks. I'm fine."

"It's so good to see you back."

"It's good to see you, too. And thanks again for everything you did while I was out."

"Well." Polly shifted her weight awkwardly. "I thought you had enough on your plate."

"Yes."

"You let me know if you need anything. Anything at all."

Leigh smiled weakly. This was more solicitousness than she could bear.

"Shall I close the door?"

"No, it's fine. Leave it open."

She paid a price for that small vanity. The open door invited a stream of well-wishers to stop by and deliver their platitudes, and she had to nod and smile and try to remember who sent flowers and who made charitable contributions in Chrissy's name so she could thank them again for their kindness. They were kind, all of them, and she knew they meant well, but after a dozen visitors, she couldn't face another. She closed her door and buzzed Polly to say she was in conference and couldn't be disturbed.

When her door nonetheless swung open again an hour later, she turned around with her eyes flashing and a rebuke on her tongue.

"Hold your fire!" Shelby cried, throwing her arms in the air. "I'm on your side!"

Leigh wasn't sure that was true anymore, but she got up with a shaky laugh and embraced her anyway. Shelby was wearing a sleeveless jumpsuit in marigold yellow. Leigh could never get away with wearing something like that, not in this firm and not with her untoned arms and pasty white skin either. On Shelby it looked fabulous. "How'd you know I was back?"

"Are you kidding? The drums are beating all over the city. Husbands, hide your assets. Leigh Huyett is back!"

An old joke, but Leigh managed a laugh.

Shelby held her back at arm's length. "I made a reservation at Ebbitt's, but now I think we better go to Medium Rare instead. You need some red meat, darling."

The idea was nauseating. Strolling into a fine restaurant, shaking out her napkin, and pretending to peruse the menu while the hubbub of other voices built to a loud buzz inside her head. "Oh, thanks, but I can't. Really. I have so much—" Leigh waved an arm at her desktop.

"I thought you might say that." Shelby leaned into the corridor. "Polly, go ahead and bring that in, would you, hon?"

Polly entered a moment later with takeout bags, and Shelby handed one to Leigh. Inside was a turkey club sandwich.

Leigh smiled. "You remembered."

"Of course."

This was her standard lunch fare back in their days at Penn. They ate together nearly every day in law school, discussing their future careers and their present boyfriends in identical tones of what-if speculation. Their career paths had diverged wildly since then, and Shelby had had about a hundred boyfriends while Leigh had two husbands and five children. By the time they were ten years out of school, they had nothing in common anymore. But they never grew apart. At least not until one of those children died.

Shelby reclined in one of the two client chairs in front of the desk. Her own lunch was a small tray of sushi, which she picked up with delicate pinches of her chopsticks. "I'm sorry about you and Pete," she said.

Leigh's sandwich froze an inch from her mouth. He told her. She didn't think he would. She thought their split would be as secret and shameful and inexplicable to him as it was to her. But she supposed he had to tell her. *Don't send your bills to the house. I'm not living there anymore.*

"And I'm sorry, too, that I couldn't talk to you about the case. But you know the rules as well as I do. I can't reveal any information relating to my representation of a client."

A rule lawyers routinely violated with every war story told at every cocktail party. Leigh put the sandwich down. "Is there anything you can tell me?"

"Such as?"

"Is there a plea offer on the table?"

"Not yet."

"It's going to be the minimum, suspended, plus fine and community service, right?"

"Hopefully."

"Then why won't he put an end to this? Why won't he tell the truth?"

The deltoids rippled on the caps of Shelby's shoulders as she shrugged. "Maybe he is."

"Come on."

She tweezered up another sushi roll and popped it in her mouth.

"I can't believe you're wasting your time on it. Not to mention Peter's money."

There was a trick with Shelby's eyes that Leigh had witnessed dozens of times over the last twenty-five years. The irises turned from green to citrine when her blood was up. The warning lights were flashing now. "Here's something I *can* tell you," she said, putting down her chopsticks. "When this file hit the Commonwealth's Attorney's office, the intake attorney, Andrea Briggs, made a *nolle prosequi* recommendation and sent it to her boss to rubber-stamp. You remember her boss. Commonwealth's Attorney Boyd Harrison. He gave it his usual cursory review until one name jumped out at him from the hospital records. Leigh Huyett. As soon as he saw that, he stamped a big veto all over the *nolle pros* memo."

Leigh stared at her. "You can't possibly know that."

"I got it straight from Andrea's mouth. The only question Harrison asked: *Is this the same Leigh Huyett who's the divorce lawyer?*"

"Why—why would he do that?"

"He wants to destroy your family the same way you destroyed his."

"I didn't—! What are you saying? This is all my fault?"

"I'm saying the man holds a grudge. And Kip's paying the price for it."

"He's paying the price for his own— He brought this on himself!"

"Sure, and he would have gotten a slap on the wrist for it. If you weren't his stepmother."

It was the second time in two days that Leigh could hear the unspoken *wicked* in there. "Is that what you told Peter? Is that why—? How dare—!"

She cut herself off before she said something worse, but it was already too late. Shelby pursed her lips and slid the rest of her sushi back in the bag. "I can see this was a mistake." She rose to her full height and strode to the door.

Leigh got up, too. "No, Shelby, wait—"

The intercom buzzed. "Mr. Stoddard's here," Polly announced over the speaker. "He's waiting in the Steadman Room."

"There's my cue," Shelby said, as if she weren't already out the door, and then she was. Leigh stood alone, staring at the after-flash of marigold-yellow as it blinked and disappeared.

Chapter Twenty-Three

The Steadman conference room was one flight up and on the other side of the building. By the time Leigh arrived, it was empty. Apparently John Stoddard couldn't be kept waiting ten minutes even when custody of his child was at stake. Just as well, she thought. It saved her the trouble of getting rid of him.

She turned to leave as a voice sounded from somewhere inside the room. "Negative. Negative," it said. "Not until we have eyes on. No visual, no go. Confirm."

She edged back inside. No one was seated in any of the dozen chairs around the long conference table, and no one was standing at the window to admire the view either. The speakerphone sat on the center of the table, but the light was off, so that wasn't the source of the voice. Slowly she circled the table and lurched to a stop. On the rug between the table and the credenza lay a man's rigid body.

"Roger that. Stand by." The body levitated a foot off the floor, then lowered back down, then up again in effortless rhythm.

It was a man doing push-ups as he carried on a conversation into a Bluetooth mic. Leigh let out her breath in a puff of relief. At the sound, his head came up and his elbows locked. "Stoddard out," he said.

He got to his feet. Not with a hop or a haul, but in a smooth rise from horizontal to vertical. Probably six foot four of vertical. He pushed a button on what looked like dog tags around his neck, and the light on his earpiece went out. "Mrs. Huyett. I'm John Stoddard."

She looked up at him as his big hand enveloped hers. He had a plain square face with close-cropped brown hair, and he wore a green Polo shirt that, despite the push-ups, was neatly tucked into dress slacks. The shirt was a size too small, chosen deliberately, she thought, to show off a hard, muscular torso.

"Sorry, ma'am," he said with a finger-point at the earpiece. "I'm running ops on a security detail today."

"This needn't last long." Leigh tossed her legal pad on the table. "I can summarize in five minutes the unlikelihood of your ex-wife losing custody."

His lips curled in a humorless smile. "She already lost custody," he said. "On account of being—you know—dead."

Her face froze in horror. "Oh. I'm sorry. I must have misunderstood the situation. Who is it then who now has custody of your child?"

"His father."

"I'm sorry?" she said again, then "Oh!" It never would have occurred to her that this combat-ready man would present that kind of domestic situation. Her biases were showing, and she hurried to hide them. "Oh. I see." And suddenly her interest was piqued. The most cutting-edge issues in family law were coming out of same-sex marriage. She ought to at least hear him out. "Please. Have a seat."

His humorless smile stretched to a grin. "I'm not gay."

She frowned. Was this some kind of game? "Then I'm afraid I don't understand. He's the father of *your* child?"

"That's what they tell me. That in the eyes of the law, he's the boy's father. It's my blood in his veins, but he's his legal father. I tried to live with that while Heather was alive, but with her gone, it can't be right anymore. I need to know if it's true."

"Ohh." Finally she understood. "Your parental rights were terminated?"

"Yes, ma'am."

"Maybe if you started at the beginning, Mr. Stoddard."

"John." He pulled out her chair with a surprising courtliness and sat down beside her to tell his story.

When he was twenty, a buck private in the army on the eve of his first deployment, his girlfriend Heather announced she was pregnant. They had a hurry-up wedding, and six months later, when he was in Fallujah, he got the news that Bryce had been born. He came home on leave as soon as he could and every chance he could get after that, but it was never enough, not while he did another tour in Iraq plus two in Afghanistan. Heather was miserable with the life of an army wife, and they divorced when Bryce was six. John was recruited into Delta Force soon after, and didn't make it home much at all for the next few years.

Leigh reached for her legal pad and started to take notes.

Two years ago Heather contacted him to announce she was getting married. She wanted him to sign a termination of parental rights so her new husband could adopt Bryce. She wanted to start fresh, she said. She wanted to make a real family. He was about to embark on a new mission deep in-country—there was a decent chance he wouldn't come out alive. So he consented. The papers were filed and a guy named Bill Gunder became Bryce's legal father.

Late last year Heather was killed in a car accident. John was two weeks away from re-upping when the news reached him. He mustered out instead and got an apartment close to where Bryce was living with Gunder in Bethesda. But Gunder wouldn't let him see the boy. He was his father now, he said. John was the guy who gave up his parental rights and stopped paying child support. He had no more right to see Bryce than a stranger would.

"So I gotta know." Stoddard spread his hands. "Is that true?"

Leigh put down her pen. "I'm afraid so. So long as he's the sole custodial parent, he alone decides who can visit his child."

He pushed to his feet and strode to the window and stood with his arms crossed, staring out into the city. "And I'm supposed to live with that."

"Unless you can prove that he's unfit to make parental decisions. In which case you could sue for visitation rights. For custody, for that matter."

He spun a pivot. "But how? I signed my rights away."

"Custody doesn't turn on the rights of the adults. It turns on the best interests of the child. Anyone can petition for visitation rights or for custody. Grandparents, for example, but even a stranger if he can prove the custodial parent is unfit and it would be in the best interests of the child to make a change."

He uncrossed his arms. "Like, even a real stranger?"

She held up a cautioning hand. "There is a parental preference presumption, so the burden of proof is on the stranger." But even as she said it, she wondered which way the presumption would cut in this case. John Stoddard was the biological father and until two years ago, the only father. The parental preference doctrine was based on the strength of the parent-child bond, and who had the stronger bond here? The natural parent, she thought, the one who was there from birth. Stepparents could never feel the same kind of primal connection. Peter was the best evidence of that. He loved Chrissy, he was wonderful to her, but how easily he went on with his life without her.

But she mustn't project, and she mustn't give Stoddard false hope either. "That means you'd have to convince the court that Gunder's an unfit parent," she said.

Stoddard sat down again and studied the surface of the table. "I've been hearing things," he said after a moment. "From a couple old buddies who still run around with Heather's friends. Stories about Gunder drinking too much, knocking Heather around sometimes. There were some rumors about that car accident, that he might have been drunk when he ran off the road. No charges were filed, but there might be something there."

"That might help, if it's true," Leigh said. "I could put an investigator on it."

"No, I can do it myself. I've got some pretty good connections."

"Oh?"

"I'm working private security now. You get your fingers in a lot of different pots." Suddenly he frowned, said a curt "Excuse me, ma'am," and swung out of his chair. "Report," he barked as he paced back to the window.

As a low muttered conversation took place behind her, Leigh looked over her notes. The situation wasn't what she'd expected when she'd walked into the room. John Stoddard was every bit as impressive as Miguel Gonzalez advertised, and his case looked like it could be interesting. Maybe even rewarding, if she could succeed in getting custody away from a drunk driver who had killed the child's mother.

Stoddard ended his call with "Stoddard out" and returned to the conference table. "Let me run this down," he said. "See if there's anything to these rumors before we meet again."

He was assuming she'd agreed to represent him. Maybe she had. "Sounds good," she said and got up to walk him to the elevator.

Back in her office the message light was flashing on her phone, and Leigh hit the playback button as she settled into her chair to go over her notes.

"I hear someone's been sleuthing," came a singsong greeting.

Her head snapped up.

"Yes, this is Emily Whitman," the message continued. "And yes, Devra's husband is very much alive. I do apologize for the disinformation, but you have to understand, divorce is simply out of the question. So please, stand down. Save yourself a lot of time and trouble. A *lot* of trouble."

Leigh stared at the phone, her mouth agape. She'd been warned off cases before, there'd been some thinly veiled threats over the years, but never anything as bald-faced as this. Disinformation? These were outright lies.

She pushed a button to replay the message with the envelope information. The call was received at 1:15 today from a blocked number. She dialed the number on Emily Whitman's business card again, and again the call went to voicemail. It was obvious she worked for the ambassador, though, so Leigh telephoned the embassy next and asked for Emily Whitman.

"There is no such person here," replied a man with a heavy accent.

"The ambassador's assistant. A young woman. Blond?"

"There is no such person," he repeated and hung up.

She googled Whitman's name and got hundreds of results, but none had anything to do with Qatar or the embassy. Emily Whitman could have been privately employed by the ambassador, but her name wasn't linked to any detective agencies or investigative services either. Still, the conclusion was inescapable that she'd been hired by the ambassador to spy on his wife and to dissuade anyone from representing her. She tried first through lies and ploys and now through outright threats.

Which just backfired. Spectacularly. All of Leigh's uncertainty and hesitation were gone. Now she was determined to get Devra her divorce, and every penny of her *mahr* as well.

And suddenly she realized: she was back to work. Today wasn't merely a one-time drop-by. She had two new cases, and she was ready to work them both.

She spent the balance of the afternoon brushing up her research on the Virginia domicile requirements for Devra and the Maryland custody rules for Stoddard. It felt good, being back in the saddle again, turning her brain out for exercise the way she might run Romeo on a lead line. Let him stretch his legs a bit, fill his lungs, get some traction under his hooves.

Then she spun in her chair to reach for a file, and her brain stopped. There was Chrissy, smiling out at her from the lineup of photos on the credenza. In her tutu and her soccer jersey and her riding breeches. Midair on Romeo's back and sitting cross-legged on the floor last Christmas.

All of the day's mental gymnastics came to a crashing end. Leigh stared at the photos. She barely saw herself and Peter in the frames or any of the other children, his or hers. All she could see was Chrissy. A beautiful child on her way to becoming a lovely young woman.

Becoming. Unbecoming. Never to be.

The house was so quiet that night. She reheated some leftovers in the microwave, and the sound of the electromagnetic waves oscillating through the chamber roared like a jet engine blasting through the kitchen.

The bell dinged when it was done, and the silence swelled up again as she removed her plate and carried it to the table.

Four chairs were pulled up to the table, and one blink of the eye filled them with the other three occupants. Chrissy bubbling over with some story from school that day, Kip interrupting with his wisecracking commentary, and Peter grinning at the pair of them while Leigh basked in the glow of her perfectly blended family.

She sat down at her solitary place at the table and gazed at the three empty chairs while she picked at the pasta on her plate. It was like looking at a picture hanging crooked on a wall. So out of balance it disturbed her inner equilibrium, and she had to stop what she was doing and cross the room to straighten it. Those three empty chairs disturbed her even more. She got up and dragged one of them into the laundry room.

When she returned the table still looked cockeyed, so she dragged another chair to the laundry room and stacked it teetering on top of the first.

How pathetic would it look, she wondered, if she left only one chair at the table. She wondered what people did who always lived alone. Did they keep an empty chair or three at their kitchen tables? She couldn't imagine it. She'd never lived alone in her life. She lived with her parents, then college roommates, then Shelby in law school, then Ted and marriage and children, then Peter and remarriage and stepchildren. She didn't know if she was even capable of living alone.

No, of course she was, she tried to tell herself. She was a strong, capable woman with a busy, fulfilling profession.

But she was a wife and mother, too, her other voice answered. At least she used to be.

No, this was silly. She gave herself a shake. She was still a mother, of two fine sons who would be home from school before she knew it. They wouldn't be working for Peter as originally planned, which was too bad— if they were on-site, she'd have an excuse to drop by with their lunch now and then—but at least they'd be living here with her. There'd soon be plenty of family meals around this table. She went back to the laundry room and dragged one of the chairs to its place, then returned for the fourth chair and slid it under the table, too.

There. She sat down again and stared into space until the pasta turned cold and gelatinous on her plate.

She went to the desk and put her hand on the phone. She could call the twins, but they were in finals now and she shouldn't cut into their study time. She could call her parents, but it alarmed them to receive phone calls after nine, and she couldn't risk shaving even a minute off their lives. She could call Shelby Randolph and apologize for their quarrel today. She could call Peter and beg him to come home and bring Kip with him and somehow they'd all learn to walk on the eggshells strewn between them.

No. She couldn't do any of those things.

She pulled her hand from the phone and sat down at the computer and typed a name into the search window. Reverend Stephen Kendall.

Chapter Twenty-Four

Kip finished his AP History paper at midnight on the night before his extended, absolutely final, no excuses deadline. They didn't have a printer on the job site, so Pete drove him to a twenty-four-hour FedEx Print Center and sat next to him at the worktable and proofread the hundred-plus pages as they slithered out of the machine. He was too exhausted to absorb much of the content of the paper, but it looked like Kip was positing some new theory for the real reason why the Crusades ended. It wasn't because the Christians lost some crucial battles, though they did. It was because they lost their willingness to forgo earthly life for the sake of some heavenly reward. They began to believe that their hopes of securing a place in heaven depended less on martyrdom and more on living a good life in the here and now.

Pete was all for living a good life, but he wasn't sure he liked Kip's take-away from all this. "Live in the present is the moral of the story," the boy said on the drive back to Hollow Road. "Carpe diem, you know? What's the point of giving up what you want to do in the present for the sake of some future payoff that might never happen? Live for the moment is the only logical way to go."

"That's stupid," Pete said. "If we only lived for the moment, we'd still be huddling in caves and eating nuts and berries. It's working toward the future, building things for the next generation—that's what makes the world tick."

"But what about when the future's full of uncertainty? Who can say where we'll be next month or next year? So why not party down?"

"And just give up? The thing to do is to control the future. Shape your own destiny."

"That's an illusion. We don't have any control over what happens to us."

There was something Pete wanted to say to that, but it was two in the morning by then. He let it go.

The next day was a tough one on barely four hours' sleep, but he powered through on slugs of coffee and willpower. Kip, though, looked like he was dozing on his feet when Pete picked him up at the end of the school day. He leaned his head back against the seat and closed his eyes with a sleepy little smile on his face.

But he woke up fast when they reached the site and found Yana Miller in the driveway. She was standing next to a beauty of a car, a vintage Jaguar convertible, gleaming white on the outside and a deep cherry red on the leather upholstery. Kip sat up straight and jumped out of the truck before Pete could even put it in park.

"Hey," Kip called, loping up to her.

"Hey yourzelf." She leaned back against the rear bumper of the car. She was wearing a black sundress with a flared skirt and a tight bodice that left her white shoulders bare. It looked vintage, too, the dress of a 1940s movie siren.

"Is Drew inside?" Pete said.

"No, ees only me," she said, and Kip laughed like a fool. "I come to ask fawor."

"What's that?"

"I must begin organize for when we move, yes? But zhere's too much clutter. In garage and attic and basement. Too much for me, but we don't want for strangers to touch our zhings, you know? So Drew, he say, why don't hire Keep for few weeks to geeve hand?"

Kip blinked wildly, like someone flashed a searchlight in his face.

"He's still in school," Pete said. "Until the tenth."

"Starting next day zhen. You do us such fawor. Ten dollars an hour, eef zhat ees fair."

Kip turned a look on Pete he hadn't seen since the boy was eight years old and pleading for a puppy. "He can't drive."

"I can drive heem. Ees no problem."

Pete hesitated. He'd been planning on putting Kip to work on the job this summer. But grunt work was grunt work, and a change of scenery might be good for him. And if it kept the Millers happy, so much the better. "Okay with me if it's okay with him."

Kip was all but swaying on his feet. "Um, sure!" he said to Yana.

She gave him a wide smile in her angular face. "I see you the eleventh zhen." She got in the convertible and drove off, and Kip stood and watched her go until Shepherd came bounding around the corner of the house with a Frisbee in his mouth. Kip laughed and snatched it from him and sent it sailing up toward the top of the hill.

Pete decided to call ahead before he drove to the house the next day. Let her know he was coming. That way he could sidestep the question of whether to use his key or knock like a stranger. If she was expecting him, the door would be open and he could walk right in. Assuming she said yes, that is. Assuming she even picked up the phone.

He thought about it all day, what he should say and what she might say, but he waited until he was a mile from home to make the call. He brought Shep along as an icebreaker, and the dog was squirming with excitement, his head hanging out the window, sniffing in all the familiar scents as they got closer to home.

It was seven o'clock by then. He wondered if she still bothered to cook, now that it was dinner for one instead of four. His thumb hovered over her name on the screen of his phone, and finally he touched it.

"Hello?"

He startled at the sound of her voice. It seemed like years since he heard it. "Hi! I was wondering if I could swing by the house and pick up a few things."

"Yes, of course."

Her tone was perfunctory, like she was talking to a neighbor or a deliveryman, but the important thing was she said yes. "I need to pick up Kip's suit and mine," he said. "Graduation's coming up." He'd planned that part carefully, to give her an opening to say she wanted to come to the commencement exercises, too.

"I'm on my way out right now, but you know where they are, right?"

Out? Where? They never went out in the evenings unless it was with each other. Where would she even go? To a movie, to sit alone in the dark? Or maybe to pick up her own dinner. "Okay, so—"

"Bye."

She didn't realize how close he was. He could be home before she left, and maybe they could go get dinner together. He put the phone down and drove a little faster.

The turnoff to their road was a quarter mile ahead, and his long-range vision was pretty sharp. Sharp enough to see the Volvo ahead at the intersection. She was already on the road. He pressed down on the gas as the Volvo turned and headed the other way. He was still close enough to catch up with her, but what then? Tail her until she spotted him in the rearview? Honk the horn until she pulled over? But what if she didn't? He eased off the gas and she disappeared from sight down the road.

He made the turn onto their road and pulled into the driveway and used his key to open the kitchen door. Shep pushed in ahead of him and stopped to sniff at the floor where his bowl usually stood. Pete stopped and sniffed, too. There were none of the usual cooking aromas, but he caught Leigh's favorite fragrance in the air. It was his favorite, too, a scent he would always associate with the soft skin between her earlobe and her collarbone, the spot he liked to nuzzle.

Shep was making the rounds of the first floor, and Pete did the same. Everything in the place looked tidy, and he supposed that was a good sign—no deterioration in cleanliness to suggest depression—except the place was normally a little untidy, the way any busy household full of kids and working parents tended to be. Now it seemed more like a museum exhibit. The Relics of a Fractured Family, circa 2015.

Upstairs was better. Clothes were strewn across their bed, and she'd left the light on in their bath. The clothes were all dresses, he saw, tried on and rejected and left where they lay. He ran his fingers over the fabrics. These weren't the kind of clothes she wore to work. These were the dresses she wore to receptions and dinner parties. So where was she going? Her makeup case was open on the bathroom vanity, and three different lipstick tubes rolled loose on the marble top. A dressy dress and lipstick on a Thursday night.

He packed up his own clothes and grabbed some things for Kip, too. He threw the bags in the truck and went back upstairs for Kip's TV. Shep was whining at Chrissy's door when he came down the hall, and he balanced the TV against the wall long enough to push the door open and show him she wasn't there. The curtains were drawn at the windows, and the room was dim in a way it never was. They were always open when Chrissy lived there. The blinds were always up.

He kneed Shepherd back and closed the door.

There were some chores he needed to do. The AC filters had to be changed, and while he was at it, he changed the refrigerator and oven hood filters, too. He did a walk around the outside of the house. Whoever was cutting the grass wasn't trimming the edges very well, so he got the Weedwacker out of the garage and ran it along the front walk and around the flowerbeds. The motor had run dry on the fountain pump, so he primed it and got the water flowing again. He filled the bird feeder with black oil sunflower seeds.

The horses were nickering at the fence, and he went back and let them nuzzle his palms. Romeo lifted his tail and let three or four big turds plop to the ground, and Pete had a sudden flashback of the kids stringing a net in the pasture and playing badminton. Half the point of their game was to hit the birdie in such a way that the opponent couldn't avoid stepping in manure to return the volley. As if that wasn't hard enough, they usually played after dinner as twilight fell so they could barely see the piles they were dancing to avoid. They hooted and hollered whenever someone misstepped, and up on the patio, Pete and Leigh used to laugh, too, to hear it. The sound of the kids' laughter ringing out through the pasture was a sound he'd always associate with summer nights. That and the sound of the hose running afterward to wash off their shoes.

Another flashback, to the first time he brought Kip and Mia here. They kept their kids apart while they were dating—Leigh knew too many children who got to know a prospective brother and sister, learned to share toys and meals and often bedrooms, only to watch them leave after a month or a year when things didn't work out. No child should have to have an ex-sibling, she said. So they waited until they knew it was forever and arranged a big get-to-know-each-other dinner for the kids. It was late winter but unseasonably warm so they grilled out on the patio. Mia at five was desperately shy around strangers, especially those loud, lumbering, fifteen-year-old giants, so Leigh took her under her wing. She sat next to her at dinner and made ketchup smiley faces on her plate and stuck five candles in her cupcake to make up for all the birthdays she'd missed. By the time dessert was over, Mia was in her lap and Leigh was reading her one book after another by the fading light of the day. That was when the twins set up the badminton net in the pasture. Chrissy was yanking on her barn boots to play the first set when she looked up at Kip and suddenly clapped her hands in delight. *Hey!* she cried. *We don't have to take turns anymore! Now we can play teams!* Three players were now four, and the world became perfect in her eyes.

The horses ambled away and so did he. He sat on the glider on the patio and watched the light fade from their garden. Their house, their home, and he wanted it back, all of it. The perfect life they'd built here. It still could happen, he told himself. Kip would soon be done with school. He could go stay with Karen, and Pete could move home. Live civilized again. End the campout and sleep on a real bed. With Leigh.

Except that Kip was barely tolerating his Sunday visits to his mom's. There was no way he could live there full-time, and who would help him deal with Shelby and the case? Who would keep the lid on his wild mood swings? Not Karen and sure as hell not Gary. As for Pete moving back home— He looked up at the windows of the house, every one of them black and forbidding as dusk fell. Leigh wouldn't even talk to him on the phone for more than thirty seconds. She wasn't going to throw the doors open for him now.

He put his head in his hands. Kip was nearly grown and out of the nest. Leigh was the one Pete was supposed to be spending the rest of his life with. Forsaking all others, their wedding vows said. But when it came down to it, he chose Kip. Yes, the kid was having the worst time of his life, but, God, so was Leigh. *Blood will out*, his mother had said acidly when he told her a little of their situation, and maybe that was all it came down to. Despite a thousand years of civilization, the tribal mentality still prevailed.

He went back in the kitchen for Shep, but the dog didn't want to go. He jumped up on the window seat and circled it three times and flopped down with a sigh. Pete called him and snapped his fingers and even hooked a hand in his collar and gave a tug. But Shep wouldn't budge. "Have it your way," he said.

Back in the truck he took a moment to text Leigh so she wouldn't be startled when she got back. *Shep's in the kitchen*, he typed. *He didn't want to leave home.*

Neither did I, he added, but the words glowed too brightly on the screen, and he hit the back arrow until they disappeared.

Chapter Twenty-Five

A photograph of the Reverend Brooks Brothers appeared on a poster outside the auditorium, along with his actual name: STEPHEN H. KENDALL, PHD, DD. Below that was the title of tonight's lecture: "Truth and Consequences: The Ethics of Lying." The university had billed the event differently on its website. "The Morality of Affluence, or How Much Is Too Much?" was the advertised title. There must have been a late-breaking change, after the posters were printed. The original title still appeared in spectral letters behind the plastered-on new one.

Leigh had googled Stephen Kendall only to find out where his church was, but it turned out he was on sabbatical from his parish in Chevy Chase and was now teaching Ethics at George Washington. The university was in summer recess, but this was a free lecture open to the public. Waiting in line for the doors to open were the usual white-haired retirees who tended to fill the seats of such lectures, but also businessmen straight from the office, women like Leigh who'd overdressed for the occasion, and a surprising number of young people.

One of them stood ahead of Leigh in line, a girl in shorts and sandals with a streak of bright turquoise through her dark hair. She was pulling a rollaboard suitcase behind her as they inched toward the door. "Sorry," she yelped when it bumped against Leigh's foot. "I didn't have time to drop this off at my hotel."

"You're from out of town?"

The girl slid her sunglasses on top of her head. "I'm home in Boston for the summer. But when I heard Professor Kendall was speaking tonight, I dropped everything and hopped on the Acela."

"You know him?"

The sunglasses bounced with the vigor of her nod. "I had him for Ethics in the Online World last semester. But I knew about him before that. I mean, he's like a total rock star."

Leigh smiled. "Not something you hear very often about a minister."

"Oh, he's a lot more than that. He's an ethicist and a philosopher—I don't know—a thinker, you know? Like Emerson. Or Voltaire."

"Wow." Leigh blinked and laughed.

"Seriously. And the cool thing is, he's such an awesome dude. Good-natured and really funny sometimes. It's amazing, considering." The girl lowered her voice, her eyes gone wide. "You know about his son?"

Leigh had to look away as she nodded. She'd devoured the story after she found it online. Two years ago Reverend Kendall's son Andrew was shot to death when he came home late one night and stumbled in on a burglary in progress. His parents were asleep upstairs, and they ran down to find the burglar gone and Andy on the floor in a pool of blood. He was only twenty-three.

Leigh felt sick with shame to think of it. The way she carried on that day in Stephen's library, sobbing and wailing as if she were the only parent in the world to ever suffer the loss of a child. She didn't know how he kept himself from screaming at her to pull her head out of her ass and see that others had endured horrors worse than hers. Instead he offered her tea and kind words and the first bit of comfort she'd felt since Chrissy's death. "I don't know how he goes on," she said to the girl in line.

"I know, right? He's like a total inspiration."

But she meant the question literally. How could anyone go on after something like that? How could he not be consumed by grief and hatred and a thirst for revenge? Somehow Reverend Kendall not only went on, but also found a way to bring something good out of the tragedy. After he buried his son, he made a public appeal—not for information leading to the capture of the killer, as many parents would do—but rather for an all-out effort to stem the tide of gun-related deaths across the country. Donations poured in, and today the Andrew Kendall Research Center on Gun Violence was a leading sponsor of research on the epidemiology of firearm deaths and injuries.

The doors opened and the line shuffled ahead into the building and across the lobby and into the auditorium. A single lectern stood on one side of the stage, like a pulpit in a church. The girl from Boston followed Leigh into a row and sat down with her rollaboard wedged in front of her and her knees tucked up to her chest. The auditorium buzzed with voices as people settled into their seats, but at a single chime, everyone hushed, and a moment later, Reverend Kendall took the stage to a burst of applause.

He wore a suit and tie, not a clerical collar, and he leaned easily against the lectern in a halo of yellow light. "Good evening, everyone," he opened. "Welcome to Lying 101." A titter of laughter rippled through the audience. "As some of you may know, I'm an ordained minister." Even amplified through the microphone, his voice was as quiet and soothing as it was that day in his Snuggery. "And if you're wondering what I know about lying—am I even qualified to teach this course?—well, let me tell you a story.

"One day I was walking down the street near my home in Maryland when I saw a circle of boys surrounding a dog. I was afraid they might be abusing it, so I burst in and demanded to know what they were up to. 'This dog is a stray,' one of the boys told me. 'We all want him, but only one of us can take him home. So we decided whichever one of us can tell the biggest lie gets to keep the dog.'

"Well, as you can imagine, I was appalled. 'You boys shouldn't be having a contest telling lies!' I said. 'Don't you know it's a sin to tell a lie? Why, when I was your age, I never told a lie.'

"The boys looked at each other and scuffed their shoes in the dirt, and I thought I'd actually gotten through to them. Then one of them gave a sigh and said, 'All right, give the old guy the dog.'"

A surprised burst of laughter rolled through the auditorium, and Leigh startled herself by laughing along.

"The moral of the story? Everyone lies. Anyone who says he doesn't is lying, and that applies equally to members of the clergy. Let's begin, then, shall we? With an exploration of exactly what a lie is."

Leigh looked around at the attentive faces throughout the audience. Some people were even taking notes, like the girl from Boston in the seat beside her, who scribbled furiously on a tiny reporter's pad.

He began by attempting to define what a lie was. Was an affirmative statement required or could silence alone amount to a lie? He talked about the paradox of a truthful lie—a true statement made with the intent to deceive.

"Is lying always wrong?" he said next. "Well, it must be; the Bible says so, right?" He let a beat of silence pass as he gazed out at his audience. "Wrong."

Beside Leigh, the girl's head snapped up.

"Let's start with the Ten Commandments. In both Christianity and Judaism, the Commandments are considered God's universal and timeless standards of right and wrong. The Eighth Commandment—Ninth in the Talmud—says: *Thou shalt not bear false witness against thy neighbor.* That's a blanket prohibition against lying, right? Well, let's think about that. All you lawyers out there, parse through it with me. It doesn't say *Thou shalt not lie*, or *Thou shalt not deceive*. No, it forbids us to *bear false witness*. That's a testimonial term. And the rest of the commandment puts it in context. *Against thy neighbor.* This commandment is a prohibition against libel and slander. Lies intended to harm the reputation of another."

Leigh had never thought of this, but once he said it, it was so obvious. This was classic tort law language. Conduct causing harm to another that gave rise to a common law cause of action. Usually bodily harm, but in the case of libel and slander, harm to the reputation was the requisite.

"So out of all the Ten Commandments, there's only one rather narrow prohibition against lying. Don't go around bad-mouthing your neighbor. Unless it's true, and he really doesn't keep up his property."

Another titter of laughter from the audience.

"This is a commandment having more to do with law and commerce than it does with truth and honesty. There's a parallel commandment in the Qur'an: *Give full measure when you measure, and weigh with a balance that is straight.* In other words, be an honest merchant. Don't cheat your customers. Islam doesn't have a blanket prohibition against lies any more than Christianity and Judaism do. Muhammad himself took the view that deceit is permitted in three situations: to reconcile two or more quarreling parties; between husband and wife; and in war."

Stephen paused for effect. "Some of you may see some redundancy there.

"So," he continued when the laughter receded. "In the central moral code of all three major religions, there is no absolute prohibition against lying. Against defamation, yes, and against dishonest trade. But not against other kinds of lying.

"But surely there must be some prohibition somewhere. Weren't we all brought up with the notion that lying is wrong? So let's look elsewhere for the source of that notion. Start with St. Augustine, whose writings shaped not only Christian theology but also much of Western philosophy. He maintained lying was always wrong. God gave us speech so that we can make our thoughts known to others. If we lie, we're using speech to do the opposite of what God intended. But even St. Augustine allowed for some wiggle room. Some lies are okay, he said. Lies that hurt nobody and protect someone else from harm are at the top of his list, and lies that hurt nobody and benefit someone else come next. Lies that hurt nobody is the common refrain."

The girl from Boston tucked a turquoise strand of hair behind her ear and jotted that down—*hurts nobody—benefits somebody.* Leigh stared at the words on the notepad. Was that how Kip rationalized his lie? Chrissy couldn't be hurt anymore, and he could save his own skin. His lie hurt nobody and protected himself, he must have thought. But he didn't think of Leigh. He didn't think about how much she'd be hurt.

Her attention had wandered, and by the time she brought it back, Stephen was talking about Plato's concept of the Noble Lie. Political lies supposedly told for the greater good of the populace. "The economy is fine," for example, to avoid a run on the banks. And then there were the pious fictions—religious tales presented as true but almost certainly concocted, albeit with an altruistic motive. The Book of Daniel, for instance.

Immanuel Kant was his next topic. Kant was an absolutist who professed that lying was always wrong. Even if it harmed no one, and no matter how noble the goal might be, lying to acquire or accomplish something was in denigration of the humanity of the person lied to and thus a violation of universal law.

"John Stuart Mills saw it differently. He was a consequentialist. A utilitarian. If telling a lie leads to a better result than telling the truth, it's right and good to tell the lie. Let's take an example. You're hiding Anne Frank and her family in your attic when the SS knocks on your door and asks if you know where the Frank family is. You say no. That's a lie, but it's a good lie under Mills and utilitarianism.

"But it's not always easy to predict the consequences of a lie, and you also have to ask for whom the expected result is better. Not for the SS officer, obviously, in my Anne Frank example. Let's imagine you're harboring a different fugitive in your attic, a neighbor boy who's suspected of having set off a bomb that killed dozens of innocent people. There's a huge manhunt under way. He swears he's innocent, but the level of hysteria in the streets is so high you're afraid he won't get a fair trial if you turn him in. If he even makes it to jail alive. The police knock on your door and ask if you've seen him. What do you do? In Kant's world, you say yes, here he is. In Mills's? You have to do a lot of crystal ball gazing to guess what the consequences might be. What if you lie and he's not innocent, and he escapes and goes on to kill again? But what if you don't lie and he is innocent and he's killed while allegedly trying to escape police custody? It's a tough call, isn't it? As between absolutism and consequentialism.

"The modern philosopher Sissela Bok suggests a third alternative. She rejects the Kantian absolute prohibition, but she also rejects Mills's utilitarianism. It's not enough for the liar himself to balance the benefits and harms that might follow from the lie, because he can't account for the damage that might be done to the overall level of trust in our society. Not to mention the damage to his own credibility. A liar's house is on fire but no one believes him, goes the old proverb. No, Bok says, the better test is the court of public opinion, or at least a panel convened for that purpose. The would-be liar should consult with friends and colleagues and particularly with people of allegiances different from his own to see if they concur that the lie is justified under the circumstances presented."

Leigh tried to imagine such an exercise. Convening a panel to test the ethics of Kip's lie. They could assemble a jury made up of Peter and Leigh and the twins, and all right, even Karen and Gary, and let Kip put the question to all of them. Should he lie and say Chrissy was driving? It would save him from a trial and allow him to go on to college and pursue his career and live the rest of his life without the taint of a criminal conviction. It would save Peter money that he could use in his business or to pay tuition or to care for Mia. It would save Karen immeasurable heartache. But it would cause—was causing, this minute, every minute since he first spoke the words—immeasurable heartache for Leigh. How would the majority of the panel vote?

The answer hit her like a punch. She'd lose.

At the end of the hour, Reverend Kendall took some questions from the audience. A student volunteer moved through the aisles with a microphone and reached over rows to hold it to the faces of those who stood up. A series of so-called hypotheticals followed. The doctor tells you your elderly mother has a terminal disease. Should you tell her and probably accelerate her death and increase her suffering and despair? Or keep her in blissful, medicated ignorance, but with no opportunity to make her peace with the world before she leaves it? The next question was political: you believe the enemy possesses weapons of mass destruction but you are unable to confirm it; should you lie about it as a means to justify an invasion? And finally a question designed only to get a laugh: my wife asks if these pants make her look fat, and in fact they do. Should I lie?

That last question was the only one Reverend Kendall answered definitively. "God help you if you don't!"

Leigh didn't join in the laughter that time. She was still thinking about the truth panel and how the votes would come in. Even if the panel were expanded to include strangers with no stake in the outcome, she knew she'd lose. Even if she put it out to the whole world. A mother's grief wouldn't count for anything in their deliberations. Not when weighed against the future of a bright young man.

Cookies and coffee were available in the lobby afterward, but Leigh didn't want to linger. The girl from Boston was rooting through her suitcase in search of some books she hoped to get signed, so Leigh said good night and skirted the other way to the aisle, then outside into the summer night. Some smokers were out there already, sucking up a quick hit of nicotine before they rejoined the crowd inside, and she hurried past them and down a shrub-lined path to the parking lot. She turned on her phone as she reached her car. A text lit up the screen in the dark. From Peter.

"Leigh! Leigh, wait!"

She spun around. Stephen Kendall was loping down the path after her.

"Oh! Hello."

"I thought I spotted you in the audience, but the lights were dim and I was afraid I'd imagined it." He smiled. "I've been hoping to see you again."

"I was hoping to see you, too," she said. "Then I saw a poster about your lecture tonight."

"You're not leaving already?"

"I'm sorry. It was very interesting. But I really have to go."

"Have you had dinner?"

"Well, no, but—"

"Dine with me, won't you?"

"Oh," she said, startled. "No, I don't think—"

"Please. You'd be doing me a big favor." His eyes twinkled imploringly in the streetlight. "Because otherwise I'm about to get roped into some stuffy trustee meal."

"Well." She smiled a little. "I wouldn't want to be responsible for that."

He beamed. "Wonderful. I'm promised to sign a few books, but I won't be ten minutes. If you'd like to wait for me here? Or at the restaurant."

"Why don't I go on ahead?" That would give her time to reconsider. She could send him a text in ten minutes—*Something came up. Sorry.*

"Great. Do you the know the Acropolis?"

Leigh nodded in surprise. She was expecting him to name some sedate café, the kind of place where intellectuals went to pick at salads and have cultured conversations. Not a noisy Greek diner where the menu was twenty pages long and you could get breakfast all day.

"Wonderful." He took her hand and squeezed it. "I'll get away as soon as I can."

He ran back up the path as she got in the car. This was a bad idea, she decided as she exited the lot. She didn't even need ten minutes to think better of it. She was in mourning. She didn't do casual social affairs, and certainly not with a man she barely knew, no matter how kind he was. She pulled over in the next campus parking lot and took out her phone, but even before the screen lit up, she realized she didn't have his number. She couldn't call it off.

The text from Peter glowed on the screen. *Shep's in the kitchen. He didn't want to leave home.*

If only Peter felt the same way, she thought. But he'd rather sleep on a cot in a half-built house than come home to her.

She put the phone away and drove on to the diner.

Chapter Twenty-Six

"Hey there, Padre," the elderly proprietor called out when Stephen came through the diner door. "The usual?"

"Not tonight, Nick." He spotted Leigh in a booth and gave her a wave. "I'm trying to impress my lady friend here, and it won't do to dribble a gyro all over my tie."

The proprietor laughed, but he gave Leigh a careful once-over, and so did the waitresses behind the counter. She could see that Stephen was not only known here, but he was also liked, and they were protective of him. They knew his history, too, she suspected. His terrible personal tragedy.

He slid into the vinyl bench across from her. "Are you hungry?" he asked as he opened the laminated menu. "Public speaking always makes me hungry. Which is a real occupational hazard when you're both a preacher and a teacher." He gave a rueful pat to his stomach.

They were both overdressed for the diner, Stephen in his suit and Leigh in her silk dress. The young people crowding into the booths around them probably thought they'd met on SeniorMatch.com and were trying to impress each other on their first in-person date.

"I enjoyed your talk tonight," she said. "Though the topic was a surprise. I thought you were going to talk about the one-percenters."

He gave a shrug as his eyes skimmed the menu. "Lecturer's prerogative. I tend to talk about whatever's most on my mind at the moment."

"Lying's been on my mind a good bit, too."

His gaze rose to her face. "Did I say something to upset you? I was afraid— I thought you looked troubled when I saw you in the audience."

She was spared a response when the waitress presented herself for their orders. A spinach pie for Stephen, an egg white omelet for Leigh. She changed the subject as the waitress bustled back to the kitchen. "I have a confession to make. I didn't actually see a poster for your lecture. The truth is, I googled you."

"Oh?" He shook out his paper napkin like it was cloth and placed it on his lap. "What's the internet saying about me these days?"

"Nothing bad, I can tell you that. You have quite a loyal following. In fact, I sat next to one of your groupies tonight."

"Oh, the girl with the, uh—?" With a grin he drew an imaginary streak through his hair.

"I can only imagine how devoted your parishioners must be."

"They're a little impatient with me, to tell the truth. My sabbatical's already lasted longer than any of us contemplated."

"You don't want to return to your church?"

"Someday, of course. But for now, my extracurricular work seems more important than preaching to two thousand comfortable souls in Chevy Chase."

"Two thousand!"

"Don't be impressed. They're not all regulars. Many of them we see only twice a year, at Christmas and Easter. And quite a few we see only three times in their lives." His mouth twitched. "You know the saying? We hatch 'em, match 'em, then dispatch 'em."

Leigh gave a guilty laugh. That expression more or less described her own church attendance record over the last many years. Baptisms, weddings, funerals. "I meant to ask you," she said. "The day we met, when I followed you home?" She flushed at the memory of her madness that day, but pushed through to the question that had been on her mind since then. "Could I ask what you were doing out there?"

"Where?"

"On Hollow Road. In St. Alban."

"Visiting a friend," he said. "What about you? What brought you there?"

She hesitated. She couldn't talk about her litigation against Hunter Beck, and she didn't want to bring up Peter and his construction project. "I was visiting a friend, too. She owns a retirement horse farm there."

"You don't mean Golden Oldies?"

"You know it?"

"Only to drive past. But I always think what a worthy project it is, giving those old horses a comfortable exit."

"My, uh, my daughter—Chrissy—did volunteer work there."

"What a lovely thing for her to do."

Tears rose in her throat. She was about to sabotage a pleasant conversation by crying. She dug her nails deep into her palms to hold back the tears until the waitress rescued her with the delivery of their orders. For a few minutes, she could busy herself with her napkin, the salt and pepper, a sip of her water until the threat receded.

"Tell me about your work," Stephen said next, rescuing her completely. "What kind of law do you practice?"

"Divorce." She was surprised to hear her own answer. She never answered that way, because it usually brought guffaws or shudders or jokes about taking men to the cleaners. She tended to offer the more palatable *matrimonial law* in its place. But in truth, even when she advised couples contemplating marriage, divorce was what they were really contemplating.

Stephen didn't guffaw or shudder. "We have something in common then," he said with a thoughtful nod. "We both see people at their worst. When they're angry or hurt or guilt stricken or desolate. And we do our best to help them get through to the other side."

Leigh gave a startled smile. He'd managed to take a career that always had a taint of shame about it and turn it into a calling almost as noble as his own.

They skimmed the surface of their own divorces after that. Hers from Ted seemed a lifetime ago, and she could sum it up with a handful of quips and barbs that had lost all their power to sting. But Stephen's was more recent—only a year ago. After their son died.

She wasn't sure what to say. "Something like that—it would put a horrible strain on a marriage."

He paused to reflect. "What I find in my work is that some couples' bonds become even stronger after they face tragedy together. But others crumble under the added weight. Especially when the foundation was already cracked."

She bit her lip and looked away. She hadn't told him anything about the state of her own marriage, but obviously he'd guessed. Her failure must be written all over her face.

"I'm afraid that was the case with Claire and me."

"Oh." He was talking about himself. She was embarrassed at how self-absorbed she was, always imagining everything was about her. "Yours had cracks?"

"Mmm. It's not easy being a pastor's wife. She comes from a wealthy family and never quite adapted to life in a parsonage, even a well-to-do parsonage like ours. And she was always unhappy with what she called my crusades, especially the time I devoted to our inner-city ministries. She was terrified that *those elements*, as she called them, would follow us home. And then—and then when it happened . . ." His voice trailed off.

"But you don't know that the burglar came from the city."

"No. No, he was never found."

He picked up his fork and for a few minutes they ate in silence. Leigh couldn't erase the image she'd conjured in her head, Andy sprawled on the floor, Stephen dropping to his knees in the puddle of his blood, his face frozen in shock and anguish. Instead of probing into Andy's death, she should ask about his life. "What was he like?" She added, "If it's not too painful to talk about him."

"Not at all," he said. "There's nothing I like better. Though that wasn't always the case. I used to cringe whenever I heard his name. Because it was always, *Reverend Kendall, Andy's been smoking in the nave again.* Or, *Reverend Kendall, Andy's drinking the communion wine.*"

"Oh, dear." Leigh laughed.

"He was your typical preacher's kid. Raising hell for the hell of it. Sarah was never like that, but Andy felt the stigma more, I suppose. Claire and I were on the brink of despair more than once while he was growing up.

"But eventually he grew out of it. In fact, after college he thought he heard the call to the ministry. He planned to spend a few years working with our Columbia Heights mission before going on to seminary."

"I'm so sorry."

"No, wait," he said with an unexpected chuckle. "After only a few months, he decided that the last thing these people needed was more spiritual care. What they really needed, desperately, was legal advocacy. He'd just been accepted to Yale Law."

"Oh, Stephen, I'm so sorry." All that young promise, his whole bright future, gone.

"No, don't be. It makes me happy to talk about him. To think about him."

They were finishing their meals when Nick, the proprietor, came over to ask if everything was to their liking, then he lingered at their tableside to talk baseball. He was a Yankees fan and Stephen liked the Red Sox, and the two men pretended to argue about their teams' respective merits and faults with an intensity that matched the age-old rivalry between the two ball clubs. Leigh listened with a smile to the heated exchange. Stephen was a man for all seasons, she thought. Equally at home pontificating at a lectern and bullshitting in a diner.

Nick slapped the check on the table, and Stephen grabbed it before she could and insisted on paying it. He allowed her to leave the tip, then there was nothing to do but stand up and say good night.

"How about a nightcap?" he said.

"Oh, no, I—"

"I have an excellent cognac back in the Snuggery. A snifter would be the perfect end to the evening."

It was the Snuggery that persuaded her, not the cognac. That wonderful inside-out terrarium. "Maybe a quick one," she said.

She followed his Saab along the back roads to his cottage. He'd left the lights on, and the Snuggery glowed through its glass walls like a jewelry store window in the dark woods. When he ushered her inside, she felt as if she'd climbed into the window, and all the rich jewels of books and rugs were hers to touch.

"Sit, please," he said, and she sank deep in the plush velvet chair while he went to the bookcase wall. He opened one of the cabinet doors to reveal a very-well-stocked bar. "I'm an *Episcopal* preacher, remember," he teased as he splashed some Godet into two snifters and handed one to her.

Behind another cabinet door was a sound system, and he pushed a button and a symphony swelled out into the room. He settled into the chair beside her and clinked his glass against hers. "To new friends."

If he were anyone else, she would suspect an ulterior motive. The bar, the sound system, the soft upholstery—it was a scene set for seduction. But it was impossible to find any predation in the eyes of this gentle man. She took a sip and settled back in the chair as the smooth burn rolled down her throat. The music was something classical but nothing she recognized. It was lyrical and melodic and reminiscent of an old folk song notwithstanding the layers of orchestration. She tilted her head to one side, listening closely. "Who is this?"

"Ralph Vaughan Williams. The composer to the Church of England, some call him." At her blank stare, he said, "You probably know this one. 'Hail Thee, Festival Day'?" He sang a few bars in a boisterous baritone, and she nodded as she recognized the hymn. "But he also wrote symphonies and operas, and even movie scores. Wait." He got to his feet and went back to the sound system to push another button. "Here's one you may like." He returned to his seat beside her as a solo violin slowly began.

"What is it?"

"One of his secular pieces. Called *The Lark Ascending*. Can you see it?"

Leigh closed her eyes, and yes—yes, she could. The notes from the violin rose up and up like a little fluting bird beating its wings skyward. She took another sip of her cognac, and as the sweet warmth flowed down her throat, the orchestra came in softly below the fluttering flight of the violin.

She laid her head back. The violin melody soared up and up, so high that at times there was barely a shimmer of sound from the strings, and the orchestral accompaniment lilted richly below it like the rolling countryside beneath the bird's flight path. The bird swooped down, skimming the treetops and entwining itself playfully around the branches before it soared upward again, higher and higher in the sky until she felt it would break through the firmament.

"This is beautiful." She sighed.

"Hmm. Uplifting but also so peaceful."

"Yes."

"I wonder if now you could tell me what it was I said that upset you during my talk?"

The question startled her out of her trance. "Oh." She sat up straight and took another sip of her drink before she answered. "It wasn't you. I was thinking about my stepson. His lie about Chrissy being the driver. If a panel of people were convened the way you discussed, they'd declare it to be a good lie, wouldn't they? No harm to Chrissy, not anymore, and plenty of benefit to Kip."

"Perhaps."

"But what about the harm to me? Shouldn't that count for something in the calculation?"

Stephen swirled the liquid in his glass. "I think the question to ask yourself," he said finally, "is why are you hurt? What is it about that particular statement that causes you harm?"

"Because—" She faltered. "Well, because—"

"If it's a lie, how does it hurt you?" If he were opposing counsel, she'd object that he was badgering the witness, but his voice was too soft for badgering. "What hurts is if it *isn't* a lie. Because then you'd have no one to blame for your loss."

She stared at him.

"You need someone to blame, and you can't blame your stepson if he wasn't driving."

"That's not it. I know it was an accident. I don't blame him for that."

"Of course you do. You might forgive him, but you still blame him. It's the most natural thing in the world. It's how we all cope with grief. Find someone or something to blame. But you can't blame Christopher if he wasn't driving. That's what's causing you so much pain."

She put her glass down on the table between them. There was something familiar in what he was saying, but it was familiar the way the tune of "Hail Thee, Festival Day" was familiar. Remote, and unconnected to her. "If that's true," she said finally, bitterly, "what does that make me?"

"Human."

"You didn't need to blame anyone to get through your grief when your son was—when you lost your son."

"Of course I did. I'm as human as anyone else. When I couldn't blame the killer, I blamed the gun. All the guns and the companies that make them and the legislators and lobbyists who allow them to proliferate. I blamed all of them. It was the only way I could get through my grief to get anywhere close to forgiveness."

"Do you?" she asked. "Forgive them?"

"I try," he said. "Every day. I try to see their viewpoint. The manufacturers are businesses with shareholders to satisfy. The legislators have voters to placate. They're all just trying to do their jobs. My hope is that the research we're funding will develop arguments and alternatives that might persuade them there's a better way to do their jobs."

"I think." She stopped to clear her throat. "I think you're a better person than I am."

He shook his head. "I doubt that. I doubt that very much."

She had to look away from his gaze. Warm and gentle as it was, it was so probing. He could see straight through to her darkest thoughts. She didn't want him to see the worst of her. "Oh, look at the time," she said, twisting her wrist. "It's late. I have to go."

Outside the night was dark and the woods were still with only a faint rustle coming from the treetops as a soft breeze stirred them. Stephen walked her to her car. "Come back again. We'll talk some more. Would you like that? I would."

Leigh looked back at the little jewel box of the Snuggery. "I think I would, too."

"Saturday morning?"

"I'd hate to impose."

"Eleven o'clock?"

"Yes. All right."

"Wonderful," he said and clapped his hands as if to seal the deal.

Chapter Twenty-Seven

Here and now. That was Kip's new credo. Don't dwell on the past or worry about the future. Live for the moment. In the moment.

At this moment the *here* was the football field of St. Alban High School and the *now* was the graduation exercises for the Class of 2015. Kip was a floating island in a sea of blue caps and gowns. *Floating* thanks to the joint he smoked behind the bleachers before commencement commenced. *Island* because, even packed as they were in tight rows of folding chairs, his classmates managed to avoid all forms of contact with him. Speech, of course. Eye contact. Even shoulder brushes.

It was hard to believe that only two months ago he was the guy everybody wanted to know. Then came his arrest, and overnight he went from Mr. Popularity to Mr. Pariah. Not because of the manslaughter charge—that would have given him some outlaw panache. It was because Atwood's party got raided by the cops, the best night of everybody's life turned into one of the worst, and they all blamed him for it. For twenty-four hours after the party his phone blew up with slurs and threats and circulating gifs: a cartoon Kip with a rat's face, another cartoon being broomsticked. *See how you like it, Loser*. Then abruptly, nothing. Radio silence.

Ah, the irony. The one thing he was actually innocent of was the one thing that got him blackballed. Not to mention blueballed. He was this-close to nailing Ava diFlorio that night, but it looked like that was the last shot he'd ever have in this lifetime, with her or any other girl at St. Alban High.

But whatever. He couldn't change the past or control the future. Here and now was all that mattered. Sensations. The warmth of the summer night. The smell of fresh-mown grass under his feet. The feel of fresh-smoked grass inside him. The tinny strains of music broadcast through the stadium. He leaned back in his chair and free-floated through the band's rendition of "Pomp and Circumstance" and hummed along to the choir's attempt at "Defying Gravity." He gazed dreamily at the giant cloud puffs in the sky.

His mom and dad and Mia were in the audience, and if he squinted hard through the haze he could just make them out up there in the bleachers. Just the three of them. Gary was off at some dentistry boondoggle in Vegas, and his mom decided not to send invitations to Leigh and Zack and Dylan. *Under the circumstances*, she said. No biggie—they wouldn't have come anyway. So it was only his own original nuclear family in attendance, but that was the way it was supposed to be. If they'd stayed together, if his mom hadn't gone crazy and fallen in love with her dentist— her dentist! God, nobody else even *liked* their dentist—none of this would have happened. His dad wouldn't have married Leigh. Kip wouldn't have moved into their big crazy household. Chrissy wouldn't have become his sister. She wouldn't have died.

He wished Leigh were there, wished it with a sudden piercing ache that made his eyes burn. Of the whole Gang of Four, Leigh was the only one who got him. She'd understand why he had to get high to get through tonight. She'd bust his balls but she'd get it. She got his friends, too, and she'd march right up to Brad and Ryan and Ava and the rest of them and say something that sounded pleasant but was full of hidden barbs that would make them stammer and shuffle their feet with embarrassment at how they'd ostracized him. *Don't you think you owe him an apology?* He could hear her voice saying it. He'd heard it a hundred times.

Or maybe he was only longing for Leigh as a proxy for Chrissy. If she were here, she'd be up there woo-hooing in the bleachers. Trying to make everyone do the wave. He could hear her voice, too, and the tears pricked like hot needles behind his eyelids.

No—he swiped his fists over his eyes. He couldn't think about Chrissy now. Don't dwell on the past. Live in the moment, and at this moment Norman Chu was speaking. He was their valedictorian, and his speech was all about the future, or at least the next four years of the future. He had lots of ideas about how to get the most out of college, and most of them came down to *design your own independent study*, which made Kip wonder why they all killed themselves trying to get into the top colleges. They could have stayed home and dreamed up their own curricula.

Kip finished second to Norman in the GPA race. Any other year that would have made him salutatorian, but this year the administration decided to streamline the proceedings by dispensing with the second student speaker. It was just as well. If he gave a speech, all he'd want to say is *Here and now, people. Enjoy it while it lasts.*

Dr. Dairy Queen was up next, droning on about hopes and dreams and hard work and discipline. Kip leaned back and closed his eyes and turned the volume down on the principal's voice until it faded to a low hum. He wasn't the only one tuning out the principal's speech. Conversations were buzzing all around him. Kids to his right talking about whose parties to hit that night, who was going to have kegs and who was always good for some weed. Some dude to his left still angsting about his place on the waiting list of his number one pick. A gaggle of girls behind him obsessing over how their asses looked in their bikinis; they were all headed to senior week at the beach tomorrow.

As for Kip, tomorrow he was headed for his new job of cleaning out the clutter at the Millers. It would be dirty, sweaty, and mind-numbingly tedious, but at the beginning and end of each day, he'd get to ride in a car with Yana Koslov, the hottest girl in the world. A fantasy girl, he knew that, but with his real-girl action cut off, fantasies were all he had. And at least now he was able to indulge them. The staircases were finished in Hollow House, and he finally got to sleep upstairs in his own room with a door that actually closed.

He flipped idly through the commencement program until he came to the page listing the academic prize winners. The English medal to Sondra Brill, math to Sanjay Patel, physics to Norman Chu, and what do you know, history to Christopher Conley. His Crusades paper was what did it, which was funny, considering he almost didn't bother turning it in. What was the point? The DA wasn't going to drop the charges when he saw all his AP credits. The governor wasn't going to give him back his internship. The once-bright ribbon of his career potential wasn't going to unspool before him, ever again. He'd been busting a gut his whole life, it seemed, to build up credits for the future, when all that really mattered was life in the present.

But in the end he turned it in. What the hell, it was done and he knew it was a winner, so why not throw his parents a bone? Give them one small flicker of pride in their otherwise reprobate son.

He half-dozed through a couple more speeches until at last it was time to march across the stage and do the handshake and tassel-flip. *Hold your applause to the end*, Dr. Fulton said, but the parents ignored him as happily as the kids did. Every name called out elicited a burst of clapping and fingers-in-the-mouth whistles. The laughter came even louder than Kip's when Damian Callahan's dad hollered "Get a job!" as Damian crossed the stage.

Christopher Conley came next, and abruptly the laughter died and so did the applause. The arena was silent except for a buzz of whispers—*Is that the kid who . . . ?*—and six hands clapping too hard in an audience of two thousand. Dr. Fulton's face was impassive as Kip walked across the stage toward him. Kip gave him a lopsided grin and took his diploma and marched on.

His family joined him on the field afterward. His mom gave him a big hug, and his dad clapped him on the back. Gifts were being bestowed all around them. Flowers thrust into the girls' arms. Watches unwrapped. For a few lucky ones, car keys dangled. Once that might have been Kip. Last year his dad gave him a *We'll see* when he asked for a car for graduation. But that was before his first DUI, and definitely before the second one turned into a manslaughter charge that was costing him a fortune. But he shouldn't complain. He'd already gotten his graduation present, a sweet customized computer with a souped-up processor and enhanced graphics and the Intellocity browser and all the rest of his dream specifications. *Thank your father*, his mother said, then his dad said, *Thank your mom*, which meant for once they'd been able to agree on something. Collaborate even. So there was something to celebrate.

He watched the other parents and kids as they said their good-byes, the parents heading home and the kids heading off to their parties. He wasn't going to any of the parties. He was going to a restaurant instead, with his little original nuclear family.

Just as well, though. He had a serious case of the munchies.

Chapter Twenty-Eight

"Grief doesn't have a timetable," Stephen said during the first of their Saturday sessions in the Snuggery. "It takes its own sweet time, and it's no use trying to rush past it. It'll jerk you back in a heartbeat."

"But don't I have to move on at some point?" Leigh said, wondering *Do I?*

"Don't put your grief on a countdown clock. It won't end simply because you tell it to."

She swallowed a hard lump in her throat. "Does it ever end at all?"

He shocked her with the bluntness of his answer. "No. Never." But then he laid his hand over hers and spoke more softly. "It does change. It changes into something more bearable. Give yourself time to let that happen."

But time was in short supply at the start of that summer. All the matters she'd farmed out to her colleagues during her bereavement came home to roost within days of her return to the office. And not all of them had been well tended in her absence. She had delinquencies to cure, pleadings to amend, apologies to tender. She worked through lunch most days and ordered dinner in and seldom made it home before nine.

The boys were home from school but already at work at their cater-waiter jobs and out every evening past midnight. Leigh was asleep by the time they got home, and they were asleep when she left in the morning, and she saw little more of them now than when they were away at school. And heard even less. They no longer indulged her with live-voice telephone calls. It was back to texts again. *Outta milk. U c my ipad?* She couldn't even count on the old standby of home-cooked meals to lure them in. They were getting all they could eat at work.

On Saturday they were booked for an afternoon wedding reception, so she was surprised to find their old Honda in the driveway when she returned home from her session with Stephen. Surprised and so delighted she didn't even mind that they'd blocked the garage door. She parked on the street and was halfway to the house when she realized the old Honda wasn't theirs. A woman was behind the wheel, on the phone. She had a file open on her lap and looked like she was sweltering in the afternoon heat even with all the windows open. Leigh could hear her exasperated voice. "No. I told you, not until you clean your room. I don't care what Courtney's doing. You're not going anywhere until you clean that room."

Leigh smiled to herself. The harangue sounded like a replay of a hundred of her own. *I'm not going to tell you again*, but she always did anyway, three or four times more.

She came up to the driver's door. "Oh! Sorry," the woman yelped, then muttered into the phone, "I'll see you when I get home."

She heaved herself out of the car, a thickset woman of about forty in a wrinkled pantsuit. "Ms. Huyett?" She held out her hand. "I'm Andrea Briggs."

Leigh usually had no time for unannounced sales calls, but this harried working mother rang a sympathetic chord in her. She shook her hand. "What can I do for you?" It couldn't be Mary Kay, not with that heat-blotched complexion. She hoped it wasn't Amway.

"I'm from the Commonwealth's Attorney's Office. I'm prosecuting Christopher Conley."

Leigh's smile faded.

"We'd like to bring you up to date on the case."

"Oh. Of course."

She should have been eager to hear her out—this would be the conversation Shelby refused to have—but she felt a rising dread as she unlocked the door and ushered the woman to the living room. "Iced tea?"

"Oh, thank you." Briggs accepted a glass with a deep sigh of gratitude and sank onto the sofa. "You have a beautiful home."

Leigh said nothing as she perched on the chair opposite.

"It's such an honor to meet you. I've heard so much about you over the years. Your reputation at the bar—it's first rate."

Leigh recognized the bald-faced flattery. She didn't practice criminal law and only occasionally appeared in Hampshire County courtrooms. There was no reason why this woman would know anything about her.

"I'm sorry I haven't been out to see you sooner. I usually try to visit with the victim's family right after the arraignment, but with this case on such a fast track—"

"Why?" she interrupted. "Why is it on a fast track?"

"The defense requested it." Briggs tilted her head. "Didn't you know?"

"No." Apparently Peter couldn't squeeze the information into a text.

"We have a trial date already. August tenth."

So soon. Chrissy wouldn't even be four months in the ground.

"That's the first thing I wanted to alert you to. So you can clear your calendar."

Leigh's hand went to her throat. "I don't have to be there, do I?"

"Oh, yes. It's vital. Not only your presence, but your testimony."

"My—what could I possibly testify to? I wasn't there. I didn't see anything."

"Not about the accident. You'll be the face of the victim. It's important that the jury get to know Christine, what she was like, her hopes and dreams. What a truly special girl she was."

There was no way she could talk about that, to anyone, let alone a courtroom full of strangers. "I don't understand. Why are you taking this to trial?"

"Oh, we might still reach a deal. My boss has my plea proposal on his desk. But meanwhile we have to prepare for trial. You know how it is." She said the last with a little wink to remind her they were sisters-in-arms.

"Your boss. That would be Boyd Harrison?"

"The Commonwealth's Attorney. Yes."

Leigh cleared her throat. "Is it true—you recommended no charges be brought?"

The splotches on the woman's face went redder. "I'm afraid that's confidential."

"I'm your client, you said."

"Yes, but it's different. This was the exercise of our prosecutorial discretion—"

"You wrote up a *nolle pros* recommendation and Harrison vetoed it when he saw my name in the file. Is that right?"

Briggs bit her lip. "I may have spoken out of turn to Ms. Randolph."

Leigh stood abruptly and went to the window. It was true, then. Kip's arrest, the trial—this whole ordeal was because of her.

"I shouldn't have mentioned it. It's really none of my business if Mr. Harrison's charging decisions happen to benefit a friend."

"A friend?" Leigh wheeled on her. "You think he's doing this as a *favor* to me?"

Briggs squinted up. "Maybe I'm not privy to the whole story—"

"Obviously!"

"I don't understand." Briggs looked flustered and genuinely confused. "What side are you on?"

Leigh stared at her until Briggs put down her glass and gathered up her file. "I apologize for upsetting you. Perhaps this was too soon after all." She heaved to her feet. "But please, do consider testifying, won't you? It could make all the difference."

She was only doing her job, Leigh reminded herself, and she was taking time away from her children on a Saturday to do it. She didn't deserve to be treated like the enemy. "I'll think about it," she said as she showed her to the door.

But afterward all she could focus on was what Peter must be thinking. That this was all her fault. No wonder he moved out. No wonder he stopped coming by after only a single visit.

Her car was still out on the street. She went out and moved it into the garage, and sat there with the engine idling a long moment. She could barely remember the details of the Harrison divorce. Had she been too aggressive? Had she crossed any lines? Obviously Harrison must think so, to be pursuing this vendetta, and Peter must think so, too. That she'd brought this down on all of them.

She backed out of the garage and headed out to Hollow Road.

The landscape had changed since she was last here. Now it was the height of summer and the trees were in full leaf and the roadsides choked with ditch weeds and tiger lilies. Everything looked so different that she thought she might not even recognize the accident scene, but no, she did. There it was, the tree, the creek, the little driveway bridge. A shiver rolled up her spine, and she clutched the wheel and reminded herself: it was an accident, it wasn't his fault, it could have happened to anyone.

I'm afraid it's a package deal, Peter had said when they first started to discuss a future together, and she smiled and said *Two for the price of one! What a bargain!*

Ahead she saw Fred Dietrich peering into the mailbox at the end of the Golden Oldies lane. He straightened and grinned and flapped his fistful of mail to wave her down. "Hey, there, Leigh," he said, stooping to the window. "You just missed Carrie. She's off to Richmond."

"That's okay. I'm just passing by on my way to Peter's job site."

"Oh, sure. Boy, that place looks amazing. I bet it'll be in a magazine when it's done. He is some craftsman, that husband of yours."

"What's going on in Richmond?"

"Some charity function. Carrie figures if people already have their wallets open, they can shell out a few dollars for the farm." He frowned at the sheaf of bills in his hand. "God knows we could use it."

"Donations down?"

He gave a grim nod. "You know who we really miss around here?"

Her throat tightened. Of course she knew. Chrissy was missed everywhere.

"He was a huge help with our fund-raising."

She blinked. "Who?"

"Your boy Kip. What a whiz he was at getting donors to give. Dialing for dollars, he called it. I used to listen to him work his magic. That boy could charm the birds out of the trees."

Of course. How could she forget Christopher Con Man? Always running some kind of scam. Sometimes for good, most times not. "Yes," she murmured. "Well, bye, Fred."

A lump formed thick in her throat as she drove on. Package deal, she remembered, but the price had gone up since then.

Another half mile brought her to the site. The last time she saw the house it was little more than a shell, but now it was nearly finished, and it was beautiful. King Midas's first vision for the place was straight out of *Gone with the Wind,* but Peter had slowly coaxed him into something more organic to the site. Three stories tall but built into the hillside like it grew there. It was made of stone and stucco and copper flashing that winked in the sunlight, with a hundred muntined windows and doors, a gabled pergola at one end, and a vast bluestone terrace at the other. Peter always did beautiful work, but she could see that he'd outdone himself this time.

It was late afternoon, his crew was gone, and she was able to pull all the way up the drive. But when she reached the top of the hill, she saw that Peter's truck was gone, too. She should have called ahead. Music was playing from somewhere nearby. She could feel the heavy bass line vibrating through the floorboards of her car. A shadow passed by one of the open windows of the house. Kip was in there, alone, blasting his music like cannon fire through the countryside.

She sat idling. It was Peter she came to apologize to, and she wasn't sure what to say to Kip. That she was sorry, but for what? That she did her job and represented an emotionally abused wife to the best of her ability and didn't foresee that years later Boyd Harrison might take it out on a stepson she didn't even have at the time.

After a long moment, she put the car in reverse and backed slowly down the drive.

She still owed an apology, though, to someone else, and after she returned home, she steeled herself to make the call.

"I'm so sorry," she said as Shelby answered at the same moment with the same words.

They met for lunch on Monday at a new place near Foggy Bottom. It was a long walk from both their offices, but Shelby said it was worth the hike. Farm-to-table, she told her, a real comfort-food restaurant.

Leigh arrived first to the faux-rustic space and was shown to her seat at a rough-hewn plank table. The place was packed, and as she settled in to wait for Shelby, a party of boisterous young people caught her eye on the other side of the restaurant. There were six or eight of them, young men in shirts and ties and young women in office skirts and dresses. They looked like a lot of the young people that populated Washington—Hillrats or White House interns or GS-9s in some government agency. They seemed to be having some kind of reunion, and Leigh speculated that they went to school together and all came to Washington with their big dreams and high spirits. Ambitious young hopefuls. Kip would have been one of them in five or ten years.

Shelby swept in ten minutes later wearing a lime-green romper. One of the most respected lawyers in the District and she was dressed in a style Leigh stopped putting Chrissy in at age five. It looked unbelievably sexy on Shelby, and heads swiveled to watch her as she navigated the restaurant in her long-legged stride.

Leigh stood up to hug her, and Shelby held her back and looked her over, up and down. "You look wonderful," she decided. "You're practically glowing."

"I believe that's called sweat," Leigh said as they took their seats.

Shelby ignored the deflection. "Does this mean you're feeling better?"

"A little. Being back to work helps. I might have a new custody case that looks interesting. And I'll tell you what else—promise you won't laugh?"

"Cross my heart."

"I've been meeting with a minister."

"How nice." Shelby opened her menu and let her lips curve behind it. She had the usual sophisticate's disdain for religion.

Leigh laughed. "I saw that."

"Oh, whatever works, darling. Just promise me you won't start selling flowers in the airport. Or wear homespun dresses, God forbid."

Their server arrived, and after they put in their orders, Shelby picked up her water glass and said, "So tell me about this minister of yours."

"Well, he's really more a professor than a minister, at the moment, at least. He teaches Ethics at George Washington, and he's written some interesting books—"

"Wait." Shelby slammed the glass to the table. "Are you talking about Stephen Kendall?"

"You've heard of him?"

"Of course. The gun control guy. I don't agree with a thing he says, but, honey"—she affected a southern-belle drawl—"ah do declare ah admire the way he looks while he says it."

"I know." Leigh was a little sheepish. "I used to think of him as Reverend Brooks Brothers."

"No, that's not right." Shelby tapped her chin. "Let me think. Not Clooney. We need to go back to the golden age of Hollywood. Gregory Peck? No, your reverend has more of a twinkle in his eye. I know! Cary Grant! But without the transatlantic accent."

"Okay, stop!" Leigh laughed.

"So exactly *how* are you seeing him?"

Leigh knew she was teasing her, but she tried to answer anyway. Her relationship with Stephen was more than simple friendship, but the extra dimension was hard to define. It wasn't priest-penitent, not exactly. She didn't confess everything to him, and he never preached at her and certainly didn't grant her absolution. Sometimes she thought of it as a therapist-patient relationship, but Stephen confided too much about his own struggles for that to be accurate.

"It's like we're in AA," she said finally. "And he's my sponsor."

"Huh. So what is it you're addicted to?"

Grief was the obvious answer, but she was spared speaking it as their plates arrived. She changed the subject, to the new man in Shelby's life. He was a complete departure from her usual type. He was black, for one thing, and older than she was, and as a senior cabinet official, he had an even more distinguished career. "So what's he like?" Leigh asked. "More Denzel Washington or Idris Elba?"

Shelby pretended to deliberate. "Morgan Freeman," she said finally.

Leigh sputtered a laugh, and Shelby joined in until they sounded nearly as raucous as the reunion table of young people across the room.

That party was starting to break up. They were all on their feet and going through an exchange of elaborate good-byes around the table. One of the young women turned to one of the men and presented her cheek for a peck, but he grabbed hold of her instead and bent her backward like the iconic sailor and nurse in Times Square on V-J Day. He dipped her so low the girl's wheat-blond ponytail swept the floor. Everyone laughed, and she joined in good-naturedly, straightened her dress, and headed for the door.

A beat too late Leigh recognized her. She jumped up from the table and ran for the door and burst out on the pavement as the ponytail fluttered around the corner at the end of the block. By the time she reached the corner, Emily Whitman was out of sight.

Shelby came up behind her. "What the hell was that about?"

Leigh struggled to catch her breath. "I thought I recognized somebody."

"Who?"

She searched the skyline of all the familiar Foggy Bottom landmarks. The Kennedy Center was nearby. George Washington University, the World Bank, the State Department, and the notorious Watergate hotel complex. The mysterious minister of disinformation could have disappeared into any of those buildings. "Oh, nobody important," she said finally. "Shall we go back and pay the check?"

"Already taken care of," Shelby said and linked arms with Leigh for their walk back to work.

⸻ ∞ ⸻

Leigh received a call that afternoon from someone named Deborah con-
firming her appointment with Dr. Alfarsi the next day.

"You have the wrong number," she said and started to hang up.

"Wait—isn't this Leigh Huyett?"

"Yes, but I'm not a patient of your practice."

"I was told—" Some papers rustled on the other end of the line. "Oh.
This is *Devra* from Dr. Alfarsi's office calling to confirm your appointment."

"Oh!" Leigh took down the address the woman recited. "Yes, tomorrow at nine thirty. I'll be there."

Dr. Alfarsi was a gynecologist, and his office was in a brick town house
shrouded in tangled vines of ivy on a quiet, tree-lined street in Alexandria.
Leigh announced herself at the reception desk and was immediately ushered down a wainscoted hallway and into a small examining room. The
walls of the room were hung with posters illustrating the development of a
fetus from blastocyst to zygote to full-term infant. "Have a seat," the nurse
said. "The doctor will be right with you."

The *doctor* meaning Devra, but the subterfuge was so much like a real
doctor's visit that Leigh wouldn't have been surprised if they gave her a paper gown and made her put her feet in the stirrups. The examination table
took up most of the room, but there were two chairs, and she took one of
them and pulled out her notes. She'd done some further work on the Virginia domicile issue and had a list of questions for Devra to complete the
analysis. One of them she could cross off already. Receiving her medical
care in Alexandria would be one point on the Virginia side of the scale.

The door opened again, and Devra swept in. Gracefully, as if in a
dance, she removed her abaya. Beneath it she wore a sleeveless, full-skirted
dress with elephants embroidered in gold thread around the hemline. Her
hair was styled differently today, in a sleek French twist, and she had dark
circles under her eyes that her elaborate makeup failed to conceal.

She held out both hands to Leigh. "Thank you for meeting me here. I
was afraid my Saturdays at Saks were becoming too regular. Hassan"—she
nodded in the direction of the waiting room—"could become suspicious."

"He may already be," Leigh said.

Devra's brow furrowed as Leigh told her about Emily Whitman and her threats. "I don't understand. Why should this woman care about such a thing?"

"She must work for your husband. He must suspect that you've been meeting with me."

Devra's eyes went wide and fearful.

"I took the liberty of getting this for you." Leigh handed her a pre-paid, disposable phone. "My numbers are programmed in. Office, home, and mobile. Whenever you need to talk to me, call me on this."

Devra took it gingerly. "I don't know if this is possible. There are people . . ."

"Take it in the bathroom," Leigh suggested, remembering a hundred different spy movies. "Turn the shower on."

Devra still looked doubtful. Leigh wondered if she'd never used a mobile phone or if her doubts went deeper. "That is, if you've decided to go forward?"

"I have." Devra straightened. "I wish to file immediately in Virginia on grounds of adultery."

She'd gotten ahead of herself on both points, and Leigh hurried to rein her in. Virginia jurisdiction was still uncertain, she told her—they needed to examine the domicile issue more closely. And a claim of adultery wasn't certain either.

"But you told me—" Devra sounded betrayed. "You told me his second and third marriages would not be recognized by your courts."

"That's correct, but he could assert a defense known as condonation. If you continued to have sexual relations with him after you knew about the other wives, then you're considered to have condoned his adultery. So the crucial question is, when did you learn of his subsequent marriages?"

Her erect carriage collapsed. "I attended the weddings," she said helplessly. She looked up from her bowed shoulders. "So I am lost?"

"In Virginia, there's still the alternative of no-fault divorce. You mentioned you have a country home there?"

"Yes."

Leigh took out her notes. "What's the address there?"

"I don't know."

Her head came up. "You don't know your address?"

"How would I know it?" A defensive tone crept into the sheikha's voice. "Someone else drives me there. Someone else handles the mail. Why should I concern myself?"

"Well, if you could move there and live apart from your husband for a year—"

She sighed as if she were trying once again to explain something to a slow pupil. "This is impossible. He would not allow it."

Leigh forged ahead. "There's another alternative. In the District, you'll recall, separation from bed and board can suffice. You could continue living with your husband but sever all sexual relations—"

"This is even more impossible!" Devra looked appalled. "A wife may not refuse sex! My husband would—" She broke off with a hand to her heaving chest.

"He would—what? Would he hurt you?"

"I have never given him cause. But a husband has that right."

Another idea started to take shape in Leigh's mind. "You're afraid he might exercise it?"

"Of course I'm afraid. But it's more than that. It would be a sin for me to refuse him. The angels would curse me!"

Leigh nodded but it was only the first part that interested her, her admission of fear. "Another fault ground is cruelty."

"No. He has never once struck me."

"The law requires only that you have a reasonable apprehension of bodily harm."

"It feels dishonest to claim such a thing." Devra's black eyes stared unfocused into the middle distance, as hazy as if she were looking through the veiled slit in her niqab.

Leigh followed her gaze to the posters on the wall, and a half-dozen embryonic children gazed back at her. "You can leave him, you can refuse sex, or you can sue for divorce on the basis of cruelty. I'm afraid I don't see another alternative."

"Except to stay with him." Devra stood up so abruptly that the elephant embroidery on her dress swayed like a swinging trunk. "I must reflect further on these things."

Leigh rose to her feet. "Of course."

Devra rewrapped her abaya and opened the door a crack. "Someone will contact you." She peered out into the hallway. "Please wait here until we've gone."

Leigh waited ten minutes before she left, though it probably didn't matter anymore. She wasn't sure she'd ever hear from Devra again, on the prepaid phone or otherwise. In the rules of their world, Devra's ability to divorce would always be defeated by the sheikh's unwillingness to let her leave him.

Though maybe it wasn't cultural, she reflected on the drive back to the office. Maybe it was simply that some husbands held on tighter than others.

Chapter Twenty-Nine

Two weeks into summer Kip mutinied. "I'm done with all that," he announced from his cot Sunday morning. This was his version of taking a stand: lying flat on his back. "I'm not going."

"You damn well are," Pete said, because he had to, not because it would make any difference. Short of dragging the kid out of bed and wrestling him into the truck, there was no way he could force him to spend the day with his mother. He was eighteen now, a theoretical adult, and all the carefully negotiated and sometimes hard-fought visitation protocols were out the window. Kip didn't have to visit anybody he didn't want to anymore.

"What're you gonna do, stuck here all day?"

He scrunched up his pillow and flopped over. "Catch up on my z's."

Fair enough. He'd been working long days for the past two weeks. It was hard for Pete to believe the Millers could have so much clutter—they must be major-league hoarders—but Kip seemed to like the work. He tore out to the Jag every morning when Yana arrived to pick him up, and he staggered back every night looking wrung out but happy, the way a guy should look after a good day's physical labor.

"Suit yourself," Pete said, but he gritted out the words to show he was still pissed.

Karen answered the door and looked past him to the driveway, smiling her tentative smile at the truck until she saw that Kip wasn't in it. Her eyes filled with tears.

Pete leaned in and spoke in a low voice. "Call him. It's not you he's avoiding."

She blinked and looked away.

"Daddy!" Mia squealed as she pranced down the stairs in her party dress, and he caught her up in his arms and gave her a twirl.

Pete didn't have to come up with any ideas for today's outing. It was already ordained: she had a birthday party to attend. He drove her to her friend's house on the far side of the school district and followed behind as she skipped to the front door clutching her gift like the ticket to admission. "Hello, Mia!" the friend's mom cried out in a voice like a circus ringleader. "Hurry! Come see what's out back!" She prized the gift from Mia's hands and waved her inside, then stepped aside to hold the door open for Pete. "Come in, Mia's daddy!" she cried at the same volume. "The men are in the man cave! The game's already started!"

Ten years ago a birthday party meant a free afternoon. He'd drop Kip off and get some work done or run some errands. These days it seemed the parents were expected to stay. Calliope music was playing, and through the rear-facing windows of the house he saw that the backyard was set up like a carnival, with food stalls and game booths and bouncy houses. A dozen children were streaking from one attraction to another as a dozen women stood in little chatting knots to watch them. In the shade of an oak tree in the corner of a yard stood a pony with a daisy-chain halter, his head hung low like a boxer steeling himself for the next round.

"Go on down."

The woman flung open a door, and the unmistakable roar of a stadium crowd came up from the basement. Pete followed the organ music downstairs and around a corner to the glow of a giant TV. The game was up on the screen—Orioles versus the Padres today—and three men sprawled in leather recliners in front of it. One of them squeaked upright to shake Pete's hand and introduce himself along with the other two guys, who thrust out their hands without rising. The host handed Pete a beer and waved him into the fourth recliner.

Maybe times had changed for the better, Pete thought as he pushed back and watched his legs elevate before him. He popped the tab on his beer and took a cold swallow. This was as relaxed as he'd felt in two months. Sunday afternoon, kicking back and watching the game, no pressure to make conversation, just good ol' silent male companion-ship. Mostly silent, anyway. The other two guys were divorced dads, too, and between their intermittent play-by-plays, they exchanged a few commiserating quips about visitation hassles. And all four men exchanged their job titles like business cards passed around a Japanese conference table. *IT*, for one. *Government* for another. *Government IT* for the third. "Construction," Pete said when his own turn arrived. "Ah. Real work," the host dad said, while the other two gave approv-ing nods.

It was a respite to spend time away from St. Alban, with people who didn't know anything about Kip or Chrissy or what their family was going through. Nobody was looking at him funny, wondering what it must be like, watching for him to crack under the pressure. Here he was just an or-dinary dad with an ordinary kid. He finished his beer, dipped a few chips, and let himself relax. The Orioles were three up when his eyelids drooped to half-mast and the stadium sounds faded to a peaceful drone.

"Mr., uh—Mia's daddy?" the lady ringleader shouted from the top of the stairs. "Could you come up a sec?"

He lurched out of the recliner and trotted up the stairs. "What's up?"

The woman made a sad-clown face. "Mia's not having very much fun, I'm afraid."

He followed her outside into the whirling dervish of the carnival kids. It took a minute for him to pick out his own. She was huddled under the cake table, behind the flapping skirt of a pink paper tablecloth, her face hidden against her knees.

"Hey, sweetie, what's going on?" His knees creaked as he squatted beside her.

She shook her head without lifting it.

"She's afraid of the pony." A little girl stood behind him with her hands on her tiny hips. "We're supposed to take turns riding him, but she won't do it."

"Is that right?" he said to Mia. "Well, you don't have to ride if you don't want to."

"But it's part of the party," the other child insisted.

"There's other parts you can do. Do you want to come out and do some of those?"

Mia shook her head against her knees. "I wanna go home," she whispered.

He reached for her under the table and she came into his arms and buried her face in his shoulder as he cracked his knees straight again. "I guess we better go," he said to the hostess.

"I'm so sorry! I never would have guessed she'd be so scared. I mean, he's only twelve hands high!"

"Thank you for having her," he said and bore his sobbing child out to the street.

She calmed down after they were in the truck and he promised her ice cream. It was a bad reflex on his part, he knew, consoling her with ice cream every time she got upset. But it was a relief to see the tears subside, and even better to see a smile flicker over her face as she put tongue to chocolate cone.

"Mia—honey—I know you don't like horses, and that's fine. Lots of people don't. I don't much like cats."

"Even Goodness and Mercy?"

"All of them. So I avoid them, and it's fine for you to avoid horses and ponies, too. But here's the thing. You don't need to be afraid of them. You just say no thank you and do something else."

"I was afraid they'd laugh at me."

"So what if they do? You just laugh back. You don't need to be afraid of those kids. You don't need to be afraid of anything. I'm always going to protect you and keep you safe."

She stared at him while a drip of melted ice cream trickled down her hand and puddled on the table. "You're not always there."

Neither was any dad, but Pete's noncustodial guilt still made him flinch at the reminder. "But somebody's always there. Mommy and Gary. Or Grandma, or your teachers. Right? You're never alone. All of us are there to keep you safe. That's our job."

She considered that as she licked a trail up her hand. "For how long?"

"What do you mean?"

"Until I'm twelve, or fifteen, or how old?"

"Forever."

Her stare turned suddenly accusing. "Chrissy was fourteen and nobody kept her safe."

Fuck. Why did he not see that coming. His mind churned for a response. "Well, that was because something was wrong in her brain—"

"Kip's eighteen, and he's not safe. He might have to go to jail! Gary says—"

"No." Goddam that Gary March. "He's wrong. Kip's not going to jail."

"'Cause you're going to protect him?"

"I am," he said. "Absolutely."

Kip was in the dining room when Pete got back to the site, his fingers clattering at hyperspeed over his fancy new ergonomic keyboard. Pete was still amazed that Karen had sprung for such a high-priced setup and even more amazed that Gary let her.

"What are you working on?" School was out.

"My manifesto," Kip answered with a smirk and kept on typing.

"Funny man." Pete headed for the kitchen for a drink of water.

"Hey, Dad? Can I make a charge on your card?"

"How much?" he hollered back.

"Nineteen-ninety-nine."

"What for?"

"There's this new app I need."

"What for?"

"It increases the functionality of the graphic interface and facilitates incremental updates to improve system stability. Let me show you—"

Pete was already lost. He tossed his credit card on the table as he passed through the room again. "Talk to your mom?"

Kip made a face and reached for his phone.

Chapter Thirty

Leigh's meetings with Stephen became a standing appointment. Every Saturday at eleven she drove to his cottage and he met her at the Snuggery door with tea—iced tea, now that hot weather was upon them, topped with a sprig of mint from his garden—and she settled deep into the worn upholstery and they talked. About everything. Current events. Gun violence, of course—the subject was unavoidable with all the shootings in the news and Stephen with such a personal stake in the debate—but they also talked about books and movies and whatever was on last week's Must-See TV. And mostly they talked about Leigh's grief and how to chart her course through it.

She could talk to him about it in a way she couldn't with anyone else. Here was someone who understood her loss, who'd suffered his own and somehow endured it. She told him the worst of her thoughts, the ugly, bitter ones, and he told her all the times he'd thought and felt the same after Andy's death. There were no platitudes, no *Time heals all wounds* from Stephen. He never shied away from her pain. He never shied away from speaking her daughter's name either.

"Tell me about Chrissy," he said as he always did.

As always she felt the swell of grief billow in her chest. "I can't. I don't know—"

He took her hand and gave her fingers an encouraging squeeze. "Not about her death. Tell me about her life."

But her life led to her death. They were all of a piece. Leigh had a million beautiful stories to tell about Chrissy, but every story led to the same unbearable ending. What was the point in telling a story, any story, when the ending was all wrong? She didn't understand how he could talk so cheerfully about his son. Andy was meant to become an advocate for the poor and make his mark on the world. He was meant to be a husband and a father and a grandfather, too, but none of that ever happened. His murder in his parents' home that awful night deprived him and everyone else of the man he was meant to be.

Chrissy was meant to be—what? Alive, long enough to figure that out for herself. Long enough to have the ending she deserved. "I'm sorry, Stephen," she said finally as she always did. "I can't."

He relented and asked about the twins instead, and that was easy. They were such all-American boys, ordinary in the best sense of the word. Being twins made them special enough, so they never felt any need to prove themselves in other ways. Even when they played sports, it was without that bloodthirsty competitive drive that many athletes possessed. They didn't play to win; they played for fun. They were happy with who they were, and she was happy with who they were, too.

"It's the children least like ourselves we're able to enjoy the most," Stephen said. "Sarah, my artist, has nothing in common with me, and all I do is glory in her differences."

"I suppose that's true." She took a thoughtful sip of her tea. She never had anything like Chrissy's sparkling cheer, yet how richly she enjoyed it.

"Kip, now, he sounds the most like you."

She put the glass down with a clunk. "He isn't mine."

"No, of course. Not by birth. But he sounds most like you in intellect and disposition. And—dare I say it? He has the same irreverent sense of humor."

Was that true? No one could make her laugh the way Kip did, and no one laughed at her own jokes more than Kip did either. They always seemed to understand each other. *You get it, don't you, Leigh?* he'd say during every disagreement with his father, and even when she couldn't say so, she always did. But—"No. I was a good kid. Not a hell-raiser like Kip."

"Never?" A smile pulled at Stephen's mouth. "I can't believe there weren't a few hijinks in your otherwise well-spent youth. Some elaborate prank?"

A memory stirred. That time she tucked a note inside the gas tank door on her boyfriend's car. *Please help me! I'm being kidnapped!* it read. The gas station attendant had poor Sammy in a headlock and the manager was dialing 911 by the time she clapped her hands and hollered *April Fools!*

"Ha! I knew it!" Stephen laughed, and she gave up and laughed along, too.

It was always past noon by the time they finished their talks, and he always persuaded her to join him for lunch at the Acropolis. He liked to sing as he drove, with the radio or not. One day he felt inspired to sing what seemed like the entire Beach Boys songbook, belting out the tunes in the same rich baritone he used for "Hail Thee, Festival Day." And because every Beach Boys song begged for harmony, Leigh had no choice but to join in. What a sight they must have presented to the people passing them on the road. Two middle-aged people in an old Saab, pretending they were in a T-Bird as they belted out the lyrics to "Fun, Fun, Fun."

John Stoddard called on Monday. He'd come up with some intel he hoped might help his chances on custody. He asked if he could come in and show it to her.

Leigh had done her own homework since they last met. Research on Maryland custody laws, of course, but also on Stoddard himself. The details were classified—very little information on Delta Force operations was ever released to the public—but between survivor accounts and reporters' blogs, she'd pieced together some of the story. Last year ISIS captured more than forty reporters, Kurdish fighters, and foreign aid workers and held them hostage in a makeshift prison in the northern Syrian town of

Al-Bab. Negotiations for their release were attempted, prisoner swaps were offered, but all efforts failed. The matter was at a standoff until one day last October when eye-in-the-sky surveillance photos showed backhoes at work, digging what appeared to be mass graves around the perimeter of the compound.

That night a team of Delta Force operators stormed the prison. Seven ISIS soldiers were killed in the firefight that followed, but all of the hostages were rescued. Those who spoke afterward reported that Master Sergeant John Stoddard led the charge and single-handedly took down five of the prison guards. The Pentagon would neither confirm nor deny those statements, but upon his return stateside, Stoddard was awarded the Silver Star for gallantry in military action against an enemy of the United States.

Leigh met him in Reception late that afternoon and brought him to her office. He was dressed as before, in a tight golf shirt and crisply creased slacks, but there was no earpiece today and no electronic dog tags around his neck. Instead he carried a cross-body courier-style briefcase, the kind with a built-in lock and a fire-resistant inner bag. He opened it and extracted a thin folder that he placed carefully on her desk blotter. Then he went to the window and stood with his hands clasped behind his back and waited for her to read it.

She opened the folder. Inside were two separate incident reports from the Bethesda police involving complaints of domestic abuse against William Gunder, forty-two, by Heather Gunder, thirty-three. Subsequently withdrawn by the complainant. Next was a rap sheet from the Metro Police showing Gunder's DUI arrest in August and another from the Virginia State Police showing a second DUI arrest in September. Below that was a Maryland State Police report of a single-car traffic accident on the Capital Beltway in December. It included a lab report showing Gunder's BAC level well above the legal limit, and the coroner's report of the fatal injuries sustained by Heather. The final document was a *nolle pros* report: the government declined to prosecute Gunder for vehicular homicide in view of the intrafamily relationship.

Leigh looked up in amazement. Somehow Stoddard had managed to tap into the records of four different police departments in the space of only two weeks—records that were either exempt from public disclosure or required miles of red tape to dislodge. No one in her usual stable of investigators could have accomplished this.

"It's not enough, is it?" he said without turning from the window. "That he used to drink and beat his wife. I have to show that he still drinks and he beats his kid."

"Yes." She was impressed all over again, that he'd figured this out on his own. He was fast becoming her favorite client. "Or something else to show he's an unfit parent."

"Then I'll keep looking." He was silent for a moment, staring through the glass over the rooftops of the city. "I saw him yesterday."

"Gunder?"

"Bryce. He was in the park, by himself, kicking around a soccer ball."

"No—John—you mustn't approach him."

"I was a hundred yards away. I had a scope."

"Okay, but you have to be careful. You don't want Gunder to suspect you're investigating him, and you certainly don't want to invite charges of trespass or harassment. You need to keep your distance. Stay out of sight."

He turned from the window with a tight smile. "All due respect, ma'am, but I know how to conduct covert surveillance."

She let out an embarrassed laugh. "Yes, of course you do."

He gazed past her, to the credenza behind her desk. "He's a big kid for his age," he said. "He's gonna be as tall as me." He slipped the file in his courier bag, but he was still looking past her. "He seemed so lonely."

"Maybe we can change that." She stood up and held out her hand.

He nodded as he shook it. "You have a beautiful family."

She glanced back at the family photographs on the credenza. "Oh. Thank you."

"I'll be in touch."

After he left, she sat down and slowly spun in her chair. There they all were. Dylan and Zack and Kip and Mia, and front and center, Chrissy, captured midair on Romeo's back as they soared over a jump. She picked up the photo and held it close, so close her breath steamed the glass. She could see every drop of sweat on Romeo's neck. She could even see the little pink tip of Chrissy's tongue between her teeth. It was what she always did when she was concentrating hard on a task, whether it was homework or frosting cupcakes, though Leigh warned her again and again not to do it on horseback—one jarring bump and she'd bite right through it.

The things she worried about then.

The twins' Honda was in the driveway when she got home that night. Their catering gig must have been canceled, which meant a whole evening to spend with her sons. They could order takeout and find something to stream on Netflix and she wouldn't even care if they chose a superhero movie. They were sitting at the kitchen table when she came in, their handsome young faces so pinched and drawn that her heart did a skip. "What happened?" Somebody died, she thought. Don't let it be somebody died.

"Everything's fine. We just wanted to talk."

"Sure!" With a relieved smile she pulled up the third chair at the table. They glanced at each other. Dylan gave a nod, and Zack cleared his throat. "Dad called today."

"Oh?"

"He just booked a big charter sailing a couple rich dudes around the New England coast. It's for the whole rest of the summer."

"Good for him. I'm glad."

"He wants us to crew for him."

"Oh." They were watching her closely. She mustn't let her shock show. "Well, what about your catering job?"

"We just quit."

"It wasn't really our thing."

"No." Slowly she nodded. "I can see that." They must have been like young bulls in a china shop, bumping into partygoers, knocking over wineglasses and fumbling serving trays. They probably would have been fired soon anyway.

"But listen—Mom—we don't want to leave you here all alone."

"Me?" She gave a little shake and smiled at them. "Don't be silly. With my schedule these days? I'm hardly ever home. No, you should do it. This could be the last free summer of your lives. You may never get to spend this much time with your dad again."

"Yeah, that's what we were thinking. And after losing Chrissy . . ."

Zack finished Dylan's thought. ". . . it just seems like you need to keep family closer than ever, you know?"

"Absolutely," she said.

"So—we thought we'd head out first thing tomorrow. . . ."

She pushed back from the table. "Then you'll need to make an early night of it. Why don't we order in some Chinese and watch a movie?"

They glanced at each other, and she could see they'd already made other plans for the evening. But in their silent twin language, they canceled them on the spot. "Hey, you think *Captain America*'s on Netflix?" Zack said, and they jumped up and shoulder-checked each other through the doorway as they ran to the family room to find out.

Chapter Thirty-One

The Millers selected glazed lava stone for their kitchen countertops, in a color called *châtaigne* that looked a lot like gray to Pete. The material was incredibly expensive—it was quarried from the crater of an inactive volcano in France—so he was there himself to guide the installation. They'd just finished setting the slab on the ten-foot island when his phone rang. The display read: SHELBY RANDOLPH.

He stepped outside to take the call.

"Pete, I've been trying to reach Kip."

"He's at work, but he should have his phone with him."

"He's not answering. I was hoping he could come in today. Both of you. I just got off the phone with the prosecutor."

"About—?"

"Let's discuss it in person. If you could track him down—"

Any hope he had sizzled out in an instant. She wouldn't make him wait for good news. "I'll pick him up. We can be there by"—he glanced at his watch—"eleven?"

"Great. See you then."

He tried Kip's number, but he couldn't get through either. He ran upstairs and changed clothes and had a quick huddle with Angelo about the rest of the lava stone and another quick huddle with the sub installing the lap pool in the basement, then he got in the truck and headed out for the Millers' house in McLean.

He was expecting a shipment of Macassar ebony flooring planks to-day, from a mill in Alabama. The flooring crew was slated to start work first thing in the morning, and he was still waiting on an ETA on the eb-ony. He drove with his phone in his hand and kept cycling through Kip's number and the mill in Alabama. Kip didn't answer, but at last a woman at the mill did. The shipment should arrive at the site by six, she told him, seven at the latest. His crew would be gone by then, which meant he'd have to off-load it himself, but one way or another, he'd have it ready to go in the morning.

He turned into the Millers' driveway and punched Kip's number one more time. He studied the house as he waited through the rings. It was nothing like the house he was building for them now. This one was a midcentury modern, all straight lines and jutting angles in glaring white concrete. It had the look of new money. What Midas wanted now was the look of old money. In their first meeting, Pete had asked him about his style preferences—did he like traditional or modern, Greek Revival or Williamsburg Colonial. Miller thought for a while then said, "High-End." Like that was an architectural genre.

"Jesus, where have you been?" Pete yelled when Kip finally answered his phone. "If I'm paying your phone bill, the least you could do is pick up when I call."

"Um, sorry, I was busy, um, working.'Sup?"

"Shelby needs to see you. I'm right outside."

"Outside—*here*?" Kip's voice broke on the word, like he was thirteen again.

"Make your excuses to Mrs. Miller and get a move on, okay? We're due there at eleven."

It was five minutes before Kip came trotting around the side of the garage and jumped breathless into the cab. His hair was wet and his shoe-laces untied. "What'd you do?" Pete said, eyeing him. "Go for a swim?"

"She lets me jump in the pool to cool off."

"First thing in the morning?"

"It was hot."

"You're not goofing off, I hope. We need to keep these people satisfied."

"I am."

"Which?"

"Huh?"

"Forget it," Pete said and backed out of the drive.

Shelby's assistant showed them to the conference room, and ten minutes later, Shelby came in. She wasn't wearing one of her wild Parisian outfits today. She wore a gray suit, and except for the sky-high heels, looked as sober as a judge.

She began without preliminaries. "I spoke with the Commonwealth's Attorney this morning. They've presented us with a plea offer."

Pete leaned forward and waited for it.

"You plead guilty to involuntary manslaughter in exchange for a sentence of two years."

Pete waited for her to finish. "Suspended," he said when she didn't.

"No." Her face was a mask. "I'm afraid not."

He rocked back in his chair. For a minute he couldn't speak. She was talking about real jail time. Kip didn't speak either. He looked like he'd been clobbered with a two-by-four.

"Let me remind you," she said. "If he's convicted, the judge can impose a sentence of up to ten years."

Pete wasn't sure how much worse that would be. Two years or ten, the boy's life was ruined. Even if he came out unscathed, Duke would be off the table forever, and so would any elected position or government job. Or doctor, lawyer, banker, newspaperman, any kind of profession. He'd be an ex-con for the rest of his life. He'd have to work for Pete when he got out. The kid who couldn't hammer a nail in straight.

"You don't have to decide now. There's no expiration date on the offer. We can think about it. Let's begin now by reviewing all of the witness statements."

"What witnesses?" Kip was blinking wildly. "They're weren't any."

Pete shot him a look. "Except for the priest, you mean."

"Right." The boy flushed. His hair was dry now but loose and unstyled. It made him look about twelve. "Except for him."

"Trial witnesses," Shelby said. "Not eyewitnesses." She opened a folder on the table in front of her. "All their statements and reports are in now, so we know exactly what the evidence will be. First up is Stanley Fisher." She looked at Kip. "The gentleman whose tree you hit."

"The dude who called nine-one-one?"

She nodded. "He says he heard the crash shortly after midnight, got up, looked out the window, and dialed nine-one-one. He's also going to testify there was no other vehicle on the road, and you were the one behind the wheel of the truck. And before you ask—" She held up a hand. "His vision is twenty-twenty."

"By then I was behind the wheel," he said. "And the priest was already gone."

She went on. "Next is the arresting officer, Diane Mateo. She responded to the nine-one-one dispatch, found the truck in the ditch and you spinning your tires trying to back up. She detected the smell of alcohol on your person and noted that your speech was slurred—"

"That's a lie—"

"—and had you exit the vehicle to administer a standardized field sobriety test." Shelby looked up from the page. "She reports that you fell."

"It was raining! I slipped in the mud!"

"Then we have a statement from the ER physician that you told him Chrissy banged her head in the accident and one from the neurosurgeon that her injuries were consistent with a trauma of that nature."

"Consistent with," Pete said. "Not caused by."

"That's right. They'll have the right to call their own expert rebuttal witness after we put on our medical testimony, in which case it turns into a battle of the experts."

"So who wins?"

"Too soon to say. Let's move on. The next two statements are from Kip's friends at the party that night. Ryan Atwood, your host, who admits there was beer, vodka, and tequila at the party, and Ava diFlorio, who says you drank at least two beers—"

"Like I said—"

"And you also had a shot of tequila and smoked marijuana."

A beat of silence passed before Pete spoke. "What?"

Kip was suddenly fascinated by the whorls of wood grain on the conference table.

"Hey." Pete snapped his fingers at him. "Answer me."

"I don't remember drinking any tequila."

Bad answer. "And the marijuana?"

"Somebody brought some," Kip said, shrugging. "I had a couple hits."

Pete closed his eyes with a grimace. He and Leigh liked to congratulate themselves on how they got the boys through high school without any drug trouble. Looks like they jumped the gun with this one. "Jesus, Kip."

"Hey, it's not like I'm a stoner. It's just a party thing, you know? It's no big deal."

"No big deal? Considering it's gonna be used against you in a homicide trial, I'd say it's a pretty big deal. It's a goddam huge deal!"

Kip reddened and went back to studying the whorls on the table.

"The tequila would explain how your BAC came in at point-oh-five-five," Shelby said. "The marijuana would explain why you failed the field sobriety test."

"I didn't!"

"And I'm afraid it all paints a certain picture for the jury."

Pete knew that picture. The dissolute frat boy wannabe. The privileged white kid wallowing in his privilege. Devil may care and get out of my way. And lie about it when you get caught. That was what hit him next. "You lied."

"Nobody ever asked me about marijuana."

"God," he muttered.

Shelby closed the file and folded her hands on top of it. "There are three witnesses we won't be hearing from. The accident reconstructionist couldn't help. Our work with the ergonomics expert was inconclusive. There's no way based on the location of Chrissy's injuries to prove she was the one driving. And finally, despite aggressive efforts, we've been unable to locate the priest."

"You tried again to subpoena the people next door?"

"We did. No one answers at the gate, and our letters to Resident come back Undeliverable."

Pete massaged his beard. He should have grabbed that woman in the Uber car and demanded that she let him in. He could have turned the place upside down until he found the video files. But there was little point if the security footage didn't show the road. Even less point if there was never any priest on the road to begin with.

"So," Shelby said. "As things now stand, our defense consists only of your testimony, Kip, if we decide to put you on the stand, and the testimony of Dr. Rabin on medical causation."

"What d'you mean—*if* you decide to put Kip on?"

"If he testifies, it opens the door to credibility attacks. The prosecution would have the right to elicit evidence of every other occasion when Kip is known to have lied. So we'll have to consider that very carefully."

Pete put his head in his hands. Two years. Two versus ten.

"As I said, there's no time limit on the plea offer. Not yet." She rose to her feet. "Think about it."

"Wait," Kip said before she reached the door. "Can I take another look at those priest mug shots Frank put together?"

She frowned. "Didn't he send you the computer file?"

"Yeah, but I want to go through it again. Here, on your computer, if it's okay."

"All right," she said, shrugging. "I'll get Britta to set you up at a work station."

Pete waited in the coffee shop downstairs and tried to think about it. Two years. It seemed barely that long ago that the boy was born. He remembered it like it was last week, and what he remembered most was how scared Karen was. She was scared of labor, and scared she'd embarrass herself by being scared of labor, and even scared to hold the baby when it was all over. He was too tiny, she might break him. Pete pretended to find it all funny, but secretly he worried there was something wrong with her. No one should be that afraid of parenthood. Now he knew she was right to be so scared. It was terrifying, being responsible for the life of another human being. He didn't know why anyone would ever volunteer for it. He couldn't remember why he did.

His coffee was cold in the cup by the time Kip appeared at the door. Pete sent him the question with a look across the crowded shop, and when Kip shook his head, Pete got up and dumped the cup in the trash.

It was a little after noon. There was enough day left for both of them to get back to work. Kip plugged in his earbuds in the truck and Pete turned on the radio, and they rode out of the city without speaking. Pete thought about the plea offer the whole way. He had no idea what Kip was thinking about.

Chapter Thirty-Two

"I don't want to think about it," Kip said.

Yana shrugged and didn't ask again. She was already naked on the chaise and racking up lines on a mirror. He peeled off his clothes as he walked to the edge of the pool, and he dove in and swam two lengths underwater without coming up for air. She was waiting poolside when he surfaced. "Hev leetle heet." She held the mirror out to him. "Mek you feel bitter."

He already felt bitter, but he hauled up out of the water and took a quick snort before he flipped over and swam away again. The pool was painted black and it made the water look black, too, and soon he was rocketing through galaxies of shooting stars as the coke raced through light-years of capillaries and veins and arteries and burst into supernovas inside his brain. Here and now. Pure sensation. Live for the moment. Carpe diem. Live. Feel. Just don't think.

The water felt like silk against his chest and shoulders as he torpedoed through it. It felt like silk against his dick, too, and it wasn't long before he was ready. She was ready, too, splayed out on her back in the black-and-white-striped cabana, long and lean and built like no human girl he'd ever known. An alien from some alien world. Her skin so pale it glowed with its own white light against the black canvas of the chaise.

He fell dripping on top of her. He didn't have to think about it, because she did all the thinking for him. She always did, from the first day of this make-believe job when she led him back here and stripped off her clothes. He didn't have to think about how to undress because she reached for his zipper and undressed him herself. He didn't have to think about being safe, because she had the condom ready to roll on. He didn't have to think about timing or positions, because she stage-directed the whole thing. All he had to do was fuck, and he did, with his mind as empty and free as it ever was. He didn't have to worry about what she'd say to her friends afterward or what he'd say to his, or whether this meant they were dating and he'd have to take her to the prom. He didn't have to think about anything except not blowing his wad too soon, and she managed to control even that and kept him hard until she came. And then it was whiteout time as he rippled into an explosion of pure thoughtless pleasure.

This was week three of pure thoughtless pleasure. Day after day fucking the hottest girl in the world and swimming in her black-water pool. Doing a bump of coke in the morning and a toke of weed in the afternoon and slurping vodka out of her navel any time in between. Anybody with a pair of balls would jump aboard and enjoy this ride, whether he was headed to prison or not. He wasn't going to second-guess why she picked him out of everybody in the world or wonder if she was a cokehead or worry that her husband would walk in or his father would find out. He was living for the moment, here and now. He wasn't going to think about anything but the slapping rhythm of his hips against hers.

"I can't do this anymore," he said as he flopped off her.

She snickered, just as she did every other time he said it.

His cargo shorts lay crumpled on the pool deck. He staggered up and stepped into them as Yana yawned and stretched and rolled over to sleep.

Inside the house was cool, black marble and white upholstery, and so still and quiet all he could hear was the hum of the refrigerator and the clink of newly hatched ice cubes dropping into the dispenser. He lay flat on his back on the zebra-hide rug in the living room and tried to empty his mind until it was as blank as the pure white ceiling above. But it was

like holding his fingers in a dike, all ten, and new leaks kept on spring-
ing and he didn't have any fingers left to plug them, and all the thoughts
flooded into his brain until he was swamped.

He flopped over on his belly. *Don't dwell on the past.* There was nothing he could do to bring Chrissy back. There was nothing he could do to
make Leigh and the twins stop hating him. *Live in the present.* Yeah, that's
the game plan, but exactly how's that working out for you, dude? *Don't
worry about the future.* Fair enough, don't worry about it, but how about
trying to fucking change it?

He got up and went to the kitchen for a Red Bull and took it to
Midas's office at the far end of the house. The desk was a slab of petrified
wood with nothing on it but a double-monitored computer and a framed
black-and-white head shot of Yana peeking through the wet strands of her
hair. Kip tapped a key and both monitors lit up. He located the program
he installed last week and found it still well hidden among the spread-
sheets and porn that comprised most of Miller's downloads. He clicked
to the IP address he'd already sussed out with the scanning app, and the
program started up, belching out a random barrage of letters and numbers
and symbols and combinations of all three at the log-in screen. It ran at
hyperspeed, but as always, failure was almost instantaneous. Kip didn't
even have thirty seconds to scroll through Miller's porn collection before
the server timed him out.

He dropped his head into his hands as a busty blonde writhed on
one screen and the circle-backslash symbol lit up on the other. *Prohibited.*
He'd been trying every day, from this computer, his own, his dad's, even
Shelby's, but he struck out every time. He might as well give up, on this
and everything else.

Yana was still asleep when he went back outside. He stripped again
and plunged headfirst in the pool and swam lap after lap through the bottomless black water. Here and now, he reminded himself. He recited it
rhythmically in his mind, like a mantra; he swam until his arms burned
and his lungs heaved for breath; but it was like everything else he did these
days. A total failure.

He dried off and got dressed. In the pocket of his cargo shorts was a thick roll of twenties. It was every dollar of the money Yana had paid him for this pretend job, and he placed it gently on the taut white skin of her abdomen. He looked around for a pen and paper, and when he couldn't find any, he sent a text to her phone. *I can't do this anymore.* Then he booked an Uber ride to Hollow Road and went out front to wait for it.

Chapter Thirty-Three

The phone jangled on the bedside table, and Leigh bolted upright, her heart stuttering. Somebody died. Don't let it be somebody died. She lurched across Peter's side of the bed and grabbed up the phone and gasped a breathless "Hello?" A boating accident, a heart attack on the golf course, a nail gun shooting wild.

There was no answer. A prank call at what?—she squinted at the luminous digits on the alarm clock—3:00 a.m. She started to hang up as a faint sound perforated the speaker. White noise in the background. It sounded like the distant roar of a waterfall. Or the blast of a shower.

"Devra?"

Another noise, this one red hot. It was the rupture of a sob.

"Devra, what is it?" She groped for the lamp switch. "What happened?"

"I—I did as you advised. I refused him—"

"Did he hurt you?" The background noise was no longer faint. She could hear shouts, the hammer of fists, men's voices, guttural snarls in another language. "Are you someplace safe?"

"Leigh, my friend, please! I want to leave. Help me—please!"

She heard the crash of splintering wood, a bellow and a long, piercing shriek before the line went dead.

In fifteen minutes she was racing for the city. She tried calling as she drove, cycling between Devra's burner phone and the embassy switchboard. No one answered on the burner, and the switchboard answered with a recording in Arabic, followed by one in English advising that business hours were Monday through Friday, 9:00 a.m. to 5:00 p.m. Her next call to the burner was answered by a recording, too. *We're sorry. Your call cannot be completed as dialed.*

Her next call was to the police.

"Nine-one-one, what's your emergency?"

"A woman's been attacked. She'd being held prisoner—"

The operator cut her off. She wanted her name—*Leigh Huyett*, she shouted—and location—at that moment, speeding across the Key Bridge into the District. "She's being held against her will at this address: 2355 Belmont Road Northwest. Her name is Devra bin Jabar. I'm her attorney. She locked herself in the bathroom and called me for help, then two or more men crashed through the door and her phone went dead. I haven't been able to reach her since."

"A patrol car has been dispatched. Are these men are armed?"

She felt certain they must be. "Yes!"

"Pull over. Do not approach the scene."

She drove on, east on O Street, north on Massachusetts. The embassy was in the Kalorama section of the city, one of Washington's most elite residential neighborhoods, and Belmont was a tree-lined street of century-old architecture. She looked for the flashing red-and-blue lights on a Metro police car, but the only spots of light on the dark street came from the mercury-vapor bulbs glowing through the decorative streetlamps.

She cruised slowly down the block in search of number 2355 until she found it mounted in brass numerals on a pair of steel gates. She cut in close to the curb and parked in a NO PARKING zone. A guardhouse stood just inside the gate, and beyond it a circle drive looped around to a gray stone mansion. Spotlights shone on a fountain in the middle of the circle spurting a geyser of sparkling water toward the sky. On a brick pillar beside the gate was a modest plaque identifying the complex as the Embassy of the State of Qatar. Below that was a buzzer. Above it, a security camera.

She pressed the buzzer, and a man emerged from the guardhouse. He wore a long dishdasha, a white *ghutra* and a long jewel-encrusted dagger at his waist. Ceremonial, she hoped. He said something to her in Arabic. "My name is Leigh Huyett," she said. "I'm the attorney for Devra bin Jabar, and I demand to see her at once."

He turned with a flap of his robes and picked up a phone in the guardhouse. He watched her closely as he listened, then returned to the gate. "Business hours are nine a.m. to five p.m.," he said in careful English.

"I'm not here on embassy business. I'm here on Devra's personal business. She called me an hour ago and asked me to come get her. I demand to see her."

"The sheikha is in bed."

"If she is, it's against her will. Open these gates. Let me in."

"You leave. You leave now. Come back at nine a.m."

Another man came trotting down the drive from the mansion, this one dressed in Western attire. Half-dressed, anyway. He was buttoning his shirt as he ran. The guard whispered to him in furious Arabic punctuated with repeated finger stabs at Leigh. The second man listened and nodded and stepped around him. "You are trespassing on the sovereign territory of the State of Qatar," he said in unaccented English. "Leave at once or we will have the police remove you."

"I've already called the police. Diplomatic immunity doesn't give your boss the right to assault his wife or to imprison her. What's your name?"

"I am attaché to the ambassador, and I command you to leave."

A third man ran up—Hassan, fully dressed in a dark suit. She grabbed the steel bars. "Hassan, where is the sheikha? Go tell her I'm here. Bring her to me."

A light switched on in the mansion across the street. Hassan turned his back on her and spoke in a mutter to the attaché. That man nodded once, and Hassan thrust his hand in his suit coat and turned back with a gun trained on Leigh.

She lurched back from the bars. Something flickered in the corner of her eye, then flashed red and blue. A patrol car was turning down the street. She ran out to meet it, flapping her arms in giant semaphores to signal it to stop. It let out a single belch of its siren and pulled in behind the rear bumper of her own car. Two officers emerged and two more neighbors' lights came on.

"I'm Leigh Huyett," she shouted to the cops. "That man just pulled a gun on me."

"You were directed not to approach," one of the officers said, a well-built man with a shaved head gleaming pink before he put on his uniform hat.

"Yes, but—" She glanced back. Hassan had holstered his gun, and all three men were standing calmly behind the gate.

The cop squinted at the plaque on the brick pillar. "This is a foreign embassy?"

"Yes, but diplomatic immunity doesn't apply—"

"Where's your vehicle?"

She pointed to it. "Officer, my client's being held captive in there. They won't let her leave, and they've disabled her phone. I believe she's been beaten—"

"Officers?" The embassy man beckoned from behind the gates. "A word, if you please."

"Get her in her vehicle," the first cop said to his partner.

"This way, ma'am," the second cop said.

She didn't resist. She let him take her elbow and steer her to her car, but she wouldn't let him close the door until she told him the whole story. He showed no reaction, only kept cutting his eyes from her to the other conversation in progress.

After a few minutes the bald cop stepped away from the gates and his partner shut Leigh's car door, and the two of them went into a huddle on the sidewalk, exchanging their he said/she said reports, Leigh imagined. The bald one stepped out of the huddle. "Lemme call this in to the watch commander," he said, reaching for his radio handset. "Let him make the ruling."

"No." She jumped out of the car again. "I'm a lawyer. I can tell you what the rules are. You can't arrest the ambassador, but I'm not asking you to. I'm asking you to rescue my client. You have a duty to do that much." She scoured her memory for the official language. "To prevent further grave crimes from being committed."

"Back in your vehicle, ma'am."

This time she did resist. She planted her feet and stood firm. "I have a right to be on a public sidewalk."

The bald cop jerked his chin at the trio of men behind the gates. "They've accused you of harassment and making terroristic threats. So either you get back in your vehicle, or we can cuff you and put you in the back of ours."

She returned to her car, fuming, as a man in a seersucker bathrobe stepped out on the porch next door. "What's going on?" he called out to Leigh.

"The ambassador kidnapped a woman," she called back. "He's holding her captive in the embassy."

"Get back in your vehicle!" the cop roared.

She retreated to her car. The cops climbed back in their cruiser, and the neighbor pulled a cell phone from the pocket of his robe and snapped photos of the scene before he got bored and went back inside.

An hour passed. A second police car arrived, and an older, gray-haired officer got out. He didn't wear the same blue uniform shirt that the first two did; his shirt was white with gold insignia displayed on the shoulder epaulettes. He conferred briefly with the patrol cops, and all three returned to their vehicles as the sun started to glow a rosy pink over the rooftops to the east.

Leigh typed up her notes on her phone while she waited. She recorded the time of her 911 call and the five-digit license plate number of the patrol car still parked behind her. She wished she could have gotten the names of the two other men behind the gates or snapped their photo. She made a note of the address of the picture-taking neighbor; later she'd follow up and see if he'd captured them on film. She started to draft a habeas petition, though she knew it was a stretch. Devra was a detainee but she wasn't being held by the government. Not this government, at any rate.

She felt sick with fear for Devra. Her cries of *Help me*, that final ear-splitting scream as the door crashed in—they played in an unrelenting loop inside her head. She felt sick with guilt, too. She was the one who told Devra that the way to establish separation from bed and board was to refuse sex. Devra took her advice and her husband beat her for it. For the first time in twenty years he raised his hand to her, and it was all Leigh's fault.

A trash truck rattled down the street. Men in sweatpants emerged from their houses with tiny dogs on leashes that scurried ten paces for every two of their masters'. A housekeeper arrived at one of the mansions, hauling her own vacuum cleaner up its marble steps. Blinds were raised in upstairs windows, and faces peered out at the scene on the street.

Shortly after six Leigh caught a movement in the rearview mirror, and her head snapped up as the three cops converged at the side of her car. They formed a phalanx so tight there was barely room for her to open the door. "You need to move along," the senior officer said.

"I need to see my client. She's being held in there against her will. She's been beaten—"

"There's nothing we can do about it," he said. "He's got immunity. We can't arrest him, charge him—"

"I'm not asking you to!"

He set his jaw. "—or enter or search his residence. We got an official State Department ruling on the matter. It's out of our hands."

She demanded to know who made that ruling, but they were under no obligation to tell her, and they didn't. She protested, she took down their badge numbers, she threatened to sue the department, but it was like shouting into the wind. There was nothing she could do to convince them to breach the embassy walls and rescue Devra.

The State Department was her only recourse. She went straight to the office dressed as she was, and as soon as the government switchboards opened, she called the main number and asked the operator to connect her to the Office of General Counsel.

"Do you mean the Office of Legal Adviser?"

"Whatever you call it, I want to talk to a State Department lawyer. Now."

There were probably hundreds of them there but none who would take her call. She asked next for the country desk for Qatar and learned there wasn't one. After a long hold, she was transferred to the Bureau for Near Eastern Affairs. There she was punted from one lowly bureaucrat to another as she pressed to talk to someone, anyone, willing to discuss the Qatari ambassador and his actions outside the scope of his diplomatic duties. It played like a game of hot potato as her call was passed from one harassed-sounding bureaucrat to the next, all of them responding that the issue of diplomatic immunity for the Qatari ambassador was way above their pay grades. Three different people told her there was nothing they could do to help; the fourth suggested she call the police.

"Yes, what is it you want to know?" snapped the fifth person she was transferred to.

Leigh blinked at the phone in her hand. That voice— "Emily?"

There was a beat of silence before a soft chuckle sounded over the line. "Why, Ms. Huyett, you've found me out."

She lurched to her feet. "You—you work for the State Department? What possible interest does State have—? This is a private matter between Devra and her husband!"

"Who happens to be the ambassador of a country with great strategic value to us in our war on terror. And who does not wish for his wife to pursue a divorce."

"You're interfering with her lawful rights!"

"You mean the laws of Virginia? You interfered with sharia law and the laws of the State of Qatar. Not to mention the Vienna Convention. I warned you divorce was impossible."

"Are you honestly telling me that the State Department would prevent an ambassador's wife from divorcing him?"

"Officially? No. Some matters are necessarily handled off-book."

Leigh plopped back in her chair. Now she understood. Emily was moonlighting. Serving as facilitator/henchman for the ambassador. "And compensated off-book, too, I assume."

"Don't be vulgar, Ms. Huyett. The currency in Washington is favors, not money."

"Oh, I get it." She clamped the phone to her shoulder and brought up the State Department website on her computer. "You scratch the ambassador's back, and he rewards you with—what? What's the ambitious young bureaucrat looking for these days? Chief lobbyist for the government of Qatar?"

"Watch this space," the woman said coyly. "But don't really watch it," she added. "I'll have security evict you if you try to come over here and find me."

Leigh clicked vainly through the State Department website. She already knew Emily Whitman wasn't her real name, so she wasn't going to find her listed there. She probably worked at main headquarters in the Truman Building, not far from the restaurant in Foggy Bottom where she spotted her that day, but an estimated eight thousand people worked in that building. Short of standing at every exit all day every day and scanning every employee who passed through, she'd never find out who Emily Whitman really was. She felt hot with frustration. "I won't forget this," she swore.

Emily abandoned her breezy nonchalance. "You'd better. You may not be afraid of your own government, Ms. Huyett, but trust me. You do not want to tangle with the State of Qatar."

She hung up, and Leigh stared flabbergasted at the phone. She dialed the State Department again and tried to retrace her steps through all the employees she'd been transferred to and from, and when that didn't work, she called her own office switchboard to see if they could identify each of the extensions she'd been connected to. But they didn't have that technology and it all came to nothing. In the end all she could do was call the Qatari embassy.

"Tell the ambassador I know all about his cozy arrangement with the woman at State," she said hotly to the clerk who answered. "And if he doesn't want to be exposed and have his credentials yanked, he'd better call me back at once."

She could hear a hesitancy in the man's murmurs as he took down her message. For a second she hoped she might actually get through to the ambassador this time. Until in halting English, the clerk asked, "How does this word *cozy* mean?"

Chapter Thirty-Four

"Your witness," Shelby Randolph said and returned to her seat at the defense table.

Her counterpart rose to his feet across the aisle. He was Jonathan Garcia, a former Justice Department lawyer still in his thirties but already famous for winning convictions in high-profile cases across the country. He strode to the lectern, and Kip shifted his weight in the witness stand, watching warily as the prosecutor squared his notes and looked up at the judge. "Your Honor."

"Proceed, Mr. Garcia."

He turned toward Kip. "Good morning, Christopher."

Kip didn't answer. Shelby had drilled that into him. *Wait for the question.*

"The night of the accident, you told Officer Mateo you were driving, didn't you?"

"Yes."

"Later, at the station, you also told Sergeant Hooper you were driving, didn't you?"

"Yes."

"You told your father you were driving. You told your stepmother you were driving. I expect you even told your attorney you were driving."

"Objection," Shelby said mildly without rising from her chair. "Privilege." Garcia went on without skipping a beat. "Today you told this jury you weren't driving."

Kip waited.

"So please help us all understand. Are you lying now or were you lying then?"

"Then," Kip said. "I was lying then."

"To protect your stepsister."

"That's right."

"You're blaming her now, but you were supposedly protecting her then."

"I'm not blaming her. I'm just telling the truth about who was driving."

"Your fourteen-year-old stepsister."

"Yes."

"The one who didn't have a driver's license."

"Right."

"The one who never before drove on a public road at any time in her short life."

"I don't know. I guess."

"The one who's dead."

Kip sat silent, and Garcia fixed his gaze on him and waited.

It was a drill, Pete reminded himself from his seat in the first row of spectator benches. This was only a drill. Kip needed to be prepared for the torture of cross-examination, and Shelby had trotted out one of her firm's best and brightest to play the role of torturer. "It'll be expensive," she warned when she called to set this up. "I'll have to charge you for my partners' time, too. But I think you'll find it a valuable exercise. It'll help expose any weakness in our case."

She already knew what the weakness was. Kip's credibility. The only point of the exercise was to make them see it, too.

"Is there a question," Kip said finally, and Shelby sat up and made a jagged note on the legal pad in front of her.

"Yes, there's a question. Do you expect this jury to believe you lied to protect your dead stepsister who can't even be here to defend herself?"

"Yes. I do." Kip looked at the empty jury box. "'Cause if they thought a dead person could be here to defend herself, they'd be crazy."

"Your Honor," Garcia said, pained, while Shelby made another angry note.

Shelby's other partner stirred in his perch on the moot court bench. He was obviously working on his own files while he sat up there and pretended to preside. "Answer the question, young man."

The AC was pumped up too high in the practice courtroom. It was fine for Shelby and her partners in their suit coats and judge's robe, but Pete was wearing a golf shirt, and Kip looked like he was shivering in his T-shirt and shorts.

"Okay, yes. They should believe it," he said. "'Cause it's the truth."

"You don't have a very close relationship with the truth, though, do you, Christopher?"

"I don't think it's a *spatial* thing."

The fake judge didn't need to be prompted to scold this time. "Mr. Conley, answer the question. Without the sarcastic commentary."

Kip looked up at him, then back at Garcia. He shrugged. "I think I have the same relationship with the truth as anyone else."

"Yet at school you lied repeatedly to your teachers and principal, didn't you?"

"If repeatedly means more than once, then probably. The same as any other kid."

"They amassed quite a file on you at St. Alban High, didn't they, Christopher?"

"I wouldn't know. They never let me see it."

Garcia walked to counsel table and picked up a thick sheaf of papers. "Would you like to see it now?"

"Not really."

"Because you know what's in it, don't you? Cutting classes, smoking on campus, an incident when you stole a farmer's goat and put it on the roof of the gymnasium?"

"Objection, Your Honor," Shelby put in. "High school disciplinary infractions are hardly relevant to the charges before the court."

"Goes to credibility, Your Honor. Because in every single incident, the defendant lied to the administration about his involvement."

"Objection overruled. Answer the question."

Kip set his jaw as he looked back to Garcia. "There was never any—what d'you call it?—adjudication. So who can say whether I was lying or not?"

"Oh, is that your definition? It's only a lie if you get caught?"

"No, I didn't mean—"

"Then let's talk about a time or two when you *did* get caught. When you lied to Officer Mateo and Sergeant Hooper on the night of your arrest, that wasn't the first time you lied to the police, was it?"

Shelby had prepared him thoroughly for that question, but Kip still flinched a little as he answered. "No."

"Let's go back to last year. July eighteenth. You lied to the police then, too, didn't you?"

Pete sat up suddenly. He'd never heard about anything happening last July.

When Kip didn't answer, Garcia gave a prompt. "You and your friend Brad Farrell?"

Kip squirmed a little in the witness stand. "Yes."

"Tell the jury what happened that night."

Kip looked at the empty jury box. "I, uh, I told the officer I didn't know anything about some missing lacrosse sticks."

"But you did know, didn't you? Because you're the one who broke into the sporting goods store and stole them!"

Pete felt dazed. How did he not know about this?

"I did it on a dare," Kip said mulishly. "I didn't really steal them. I didn't have any, what d'you call it, intent to keep them. I mean, they were *girls'* lacrosse sticks."

"Which you tossed in a Dumpster before leading the officer on a ten-block foot race?"

"He let us go. He knew it was only a prank."

"You weren't let go the next time, though, were you?"

"Objection," Shelby said.

"I'll rephrase. January first of this year. At two a.m. You lied to the police then, too, didn't you?"

"Yes."

"Different officer, same question. Have you consumed any alcohol tonight? And what did you tell him?"

"I said no."

"That was a lie, wasn't it?"

"I was scared."

"I understand. You were scared, so you lied. Tell me, were you scared the day you were arrested for manslaughter?"

"Yes."

"Were you scared when you had to spend that night in jail?"

"I guess."

"You guess. Tell the truth. It was the scariest night of your life, wasn't it?"

Kip looked down at his lap as he answered. "Yes."

"So the very next day, the day after the scariest night of your life, that was the first time you came forward with this story that it was your stepsister who was driving. You were scared, so you lied, isn't that right?"

"It's not a story. It's the truth."

"You made it up, didn't you? You even made up a witness who wasn't there."

"I didn't make him up. The priest was there."

"The priest was there," Garcia mocked him. He stepped back from the lectern and spread his arms wide. "Then where is he now?"

It was too cold in this room. Pete couldn't take it anymore. He passed a note to Shelby as he left the room. *Tell Kip to call me when he's done here.* Because Pete already was.

He rode the elevator to the lobby and stepped outside into the scorching afternoon sun. It was too cold inside and too hot out. Welcome to summer in the city. *Hot town, isn't it a pity.* The brim on his ball cap did little to block the glare of the sun, and even after he crossed over to the shady side of the street, he felt no relief.

Leigh called it from the start. *You want to believe it, so you do.* It was like believing in God. There was more hope for the world if you believed in a higher power, so you made yourself buy into it. There was more hope for Kip if he wasn't the one driving, so Pete made himself buy into that, too. Worse than that, he committed to it—with Shelby and her team of investigators, with the high school principal, and worst of all, with Leigh. He'd staked their marriage on the word of a kid he didn't believe half the time himself.

He needed to see her. That was the only thing he could be sure of. There were things he should do, phone calls to make, a truckload of home electronics to track down, but all he wanted was to see Leigh. Her office was only a few blocks away, and it was almost five o'clock. If she would come down out of her tower, they could meet for a drink someplace. He took out his phone and pressed her office number before he got cold feet on the blistering sidewalk.

"Ms. Huyett's office."

"Hey, Polly."

"Pete! Well, hello, stranger! Where you been keeping yourself?"

So—she didn't know they were separated. Leigh hadn't told her. He tried not to read too much into that.

"I guess you've been busy, huh?" she said when he didn't immediately answer. "Building some big fancy house."

"Next one's for you, Polly."

"Ha! Don't I wish. Listen, Leigh's been in a deposition all day over at One Franklin. It's probably breaking up about now if you want to try her on her cell."

"Thanks. I'll do that."

"And don't be a stranger, you hear me?"

"You bet."

One Franklin Square. He knew that building—it was one of the few high-rises in Washington—and he knew the route she'd take from there back to her own office. He remembered a sidewalk café along that route. She'd have to go right past it.

He jogged across the street and up another block to the café. All the tables were empty on the pavement; it was too hot to sit outside even under the big yellow market umbrellas. He went in and ordered two iced teas and carried them out to a table in the deepest shade he could find. He ought to call her or text her to meet him here so she wouldn't see it as an ambush. But if she knew he was here, she might take a detour to avoid him. He left his phone in his pocket.

The glasses sweated and so did he. It was after five by then, and every building up and down the street was spitting out its hourly workers in staccato bursts of their revolving doors. The people wilted as they walked, but they all kept moving in a steady stream to the Metro station on the corner or the bus stop down the street or the parking garages all over town.

Twenty minutes later, the ice was melted and the tea was warm when his phone rang in his pocket. He pulled it out. Kip's name was on the screen. "Yeah."

"I'm done. Where are you?"

That was the moment he spotted her. She was walking down the pavement toward him in her rhythmic high-heeled stride with her phone to her ear and her briefcase swinging at her side. "Wait out front," he said to Kip. "I'll get there when I can."

"It's ninety-five frigging degrees—"

He disconnected and stood up at the table. She'd gotten her hair cut since he last saw her, and it fell in two smooth curtains sweeping the shoulders of her black suit jacket. He usually thought black was too severe for her, but he had to admire the way it lit up the gold in her hair. He used to joke about the day all that gold would turn to silver, the same way she used to joke about the inevitable retreat of his hairline. Aging wasn't so bad if you could face it together.

She saw him then. He could tell by the instant deceleration of her footsteps. "May I call you back?" he heard her say into the phone. "Yes. Yes, I'll take care of it." Her hand fell to her side. "Peter," she said. "What brings you to town?"

That was the subject he'd hoped to avoid. "Um, we had a meeting with Shelby."

"Oh. Of course."

"Can you sit for a minute?" He waved a hand at the glasses. "Have some iced tea?"

She looked at her watch. "For a minute." Before he could pull out the chair beside his, she took the far seat and dropped her briefcase into the one between them. She placed her phone directly in front of her on the table.

"You look good," he said, meaning *wonderful, gorgeous, I miss you*.

She shrugged off the compliment. "I got my hair cut. And I see you grew a beard."

"Yeah. For the duration." He remembered his ball cap then and jerked it off. His hair was sweaty under it and plastered to his head. He didn't know how she managed to look so cool in this heat. "I've been hoping to see you."

"You know where I live."

"You never seem to be home. Working late nights, I guess?"

She nodded and took a sip from her glass.

"Saturdays, too, seems like."

"I'm always home on Sundays."

"That's my day with Mia now."

"Oh." Her expression softened. "How is she?"

"She's fine. She misses you." It was Chrissy she really missed, but he didn't dare speak her name to Leigh. This was the closest thing they'd had to a conversation in two months. He wasn't going to rock the boat, not when it was already riding so low in the water.

"I miss her, too. Maybe you could bring her by some Sunday?"

"Sure." That could work. Kip was used to spending Sundays alone now. They could have a nice peaceful day together, he and Leigh and Mia. Kip would only be the invisible elephant in the room, instead of the visible, audible, palpable, unavoidable one he otherwise was. He forced a smile. "Hey, what do you hear from the old sea dogs? They having a good summer?"

"I'm not sure. They called last week from Newport and went on a big rant about the one-percenters and their mansions and their fancy cars. I think their rich clients are getting to them."

Pete snorted. "Tell me about it."

"Speaking of—how's the Millers' house coming along?"

"We're in the home stretch now. It's looking good. You should come by." But he remembered what happened the last time she came by. One look at Kip and she went roaring off so fast she made dust clouds fly. He'd always be between them. He was there now, as solid a barrier as her briefcase on the empty chair. It was time to stop pretending he wasn't. "Listen, Leigh. I wanted you to know— This business about who was driving? That's off the table. It won't be part of the defense."

She looked down. With the tip of her straw she submerged the lemon wedge in her glass and watched closely as it bobbed to the surface again. "He's recanted?" she said finally, her eyes still on her tea.

"Well, no. But the thing is—he's not going to testify, and there's no other proof, so that's just—gone."

She looked up with a puzzled squint. "Why wouldn't he testify?"

"This thing with Shelby today? It was like a mock trial to see how he'd do on the stand. And he totally blew it."

"Oh." Slowly her face changed. He'd watched it happen many times before, this transformation, when her everyday face of wife and mom dissolved and she reorganized her thinking and put on the face of a lawyer. "Let me guess," she said. "The prosecutor was played by Shelby's partner, Jonathan Garcia?"

"You know him?"

"He's a superstar. He teaches master classes in cross-examination all over the country. The actual prosecutor won't perform anything like Jonathan."

"It was Kip's performance that was the problem."

"But remember drama club? He always flubbed his lines in dress rehearsal and absolutely shone on opening night. He needs the pressure of the real thing to do his best."

"Maybe."

"Come on. That boy can charm the birds out of the trees. He's his own best witness."

But he wasn't the boy Leigh remembered. Whatever charm he once had was gone, along with all of his self-confidence. "Shelby thinks it would be a mistake."

"Well. I shouldn't second-guess her." Her gaze shifted to the pavement and the commuters rushing past them to get home to their families. "She may have her own reason to keep him off the stand."

"If he's lying, you mean."

"And if she knows he is. It's called suborning perjury. She could be disbarred."

"Right." It was what he'd guessed.

"But that's assuming this even goes to trial. I assume there's a plea of-fer on the table?"

He nodded. She watched him, waiting for the rest of it, but there was no way he was going to put that on her. The silence stretched out like a filament between them until she dropped her gaze to the phone on the table. She stared at it like she was willing it to ring and reprieve her.

Incredibly, at that moment it did. She let out a huff of relief like it was a bell ending a boxing round. She answered without even bothering to look at the display. "Leigh Huyett."

Her face changed again. A slight frown of confusion came first. "Yes?" Then she blinked, and it was like a mask slipped off. Her tight lawyer face was gone, but so was her everyday face. Her eyes seemed to sink into her skull, and her mouth hung so slack that for a second Pete was afraid she'd stroked. "Yes." Her voice was faint. "Yes, that's me."

"What?" he said. "What is it?"

She didn't hear him. "No," she whispered. Her eyes fell shut. "I haven't heard from them since—since last Thursday."

"Leigh—what?"

She didn't answer, either him or the caller whose agitated voice was shouting, "Hello? Hello?" Pete took the phone out of her limp fingers. "This is Pete Conley. Who's this?"

"Conley? Hey, you're my next call. Number two on the contact list."

"What list?" He reached for Leigh's hand. Her skin was ice-cold. "Who is this?"

"Harvey Brodsky. I'm dockmaster up here at the Camden Yacht Club.

The Porter boys left their float plan with me, and it says if I can't raise them on the marine radio, I'm to call Leigh Huyett first and Pete Conley second."

"Call for what?" He watched as Leigh's jaw began to quiver. It set off little seismic ripples under the sagging skin, and she pulled her hand out of his and pressed her knuckles to her mouth like she was holding back an eruption.

"If they miss check-in," the man said. "And they did. Two days ago."

He booked their flights before they left the café table. The dockmaster wasn't sure which Coast Guard station would serve as SAR headquarters—it could be anywhere from Lubec, Maine, to the Hamptons—so Pete booked multiple flights, to Portland, Logan, and JFK, and he reserved rental cars at each of those airports, too.

Leigh was on her own phone, cycling through the twins' mobile numbers and Ted's, leaving messages on each one to *call, please call the second you get this.* She had some of the twins' friends in her phone contacts, or at least their parents, and she cycled through all of those numbers, too. *If you hear anything, anything at all.* The quiver was in her voice now, too. She was fighting hard to keep control. "This can't be happening," she whispered.

"It isn't." *Wear your life jackets*, he told them. *Wear your climbing harness.* As if falling overboard was the only thing that could go wrong at sea. It never occurred to him that the whole fucking boat could go down. "They're fine," he told her. "By the time we get up there they'll be docked and we can give them hell for missing check-in. All of them," he added. That goddam Ted Porter.

"It comes in threes," she whispered.

"What does?"

"Death."

He stood up abruptly. "Let's get to the airport. We'll figure out which flight to take when we get there." He picked up her briefcase and pulled out her chair. "Where'd you park today?"

She looked up at him through glazed eyes. "I don't—I can't—"

"Never mind. We'll take the truck."

She swayed as she got to her feet, and he caught her by the elbow to steady her, then stopped and put both arms around her and held her tight. "It'll be all right," he said.

Her whole body trembled against his as they walked the five blocks to the parking garage. They were almost there when the phone rang in his pocket. This was the number he gave to the dockmaster for updates, and he dove to answer it. But it was only Kip's name on the display.

Shit. He forgot about Kip, and he felt a flash of irritation at the reminder. He didn't have time to deal with him now. In a couple curt sentences, he filled him in on what was happening. "No way," Kip said and peppered him with a dozen follow-up questions. Pete answered as tersely as he could. Leigh was growing more and more upset with each response and by then they were at the garage.

"Listen," he cut him off. "You need to go to Mom's tonight. Call her and tell her—" But Karen wouldn't drive into the city; it was one of her many fears. Kip was an adult, though, right? He could make his own way out to Maryland. "Take the Metro out to Silver Spring and tell her to pick you up there."

"Umm—"

"What?" he snapped. "You take the red line. You know that."

"Yeah, but I don't have any money."

Pete cursed. "Right. Okay, I'll swing by before we head to the airport. Wait there. Don't move."

The elevator in the parking garage was out of service. He steered Leigh up five flights of stairs to the rooftop deck where the truck sat broiling in the late-day sun. He lowered the windows and turned the AC on full blast, but the sweat still poured off him as he circled down the concrete ramps to the exit. Leigh was on the phone again, cycling one more time between the boys' numbers. He reached out a hand to cup the back of her neck. Her skin was so cold he wanted to plunge his face into it.

It was rush hour, and it took fifteen minutes to crawl the few blocks to Shelby's building. Kip was out front where he was supposed to be, phone to ear arranging his ride with Karen, Pete hoped. He pulled over to the curb, and Leigh slid over on the seat to make room.

"Here." Kip held his phone out to Leigh as he climbed in. "It's for you."

She stared at him in bewilderment, not moving.

"Who is it?" Pete said.

Kip placed the phone against her ear. Her features sharpened and something quickened in her eyes. She burst into tears.

"What?" Pete yelled. The dread stabbed into him. "Who is it?"

Her own phone was ringing then, and Kip took it from her lap and pressed the answer key and held it up to her other ear. She cried even harder.

"Answer me, damn it!" Pete hollered. "Who is it?"

"It's the twins," Kip said simply. "I found them."

Chapter Thirty-Five

Zack and Dylan were speaking over each other into the two separate phones and Kip was explaining over her head to Peter, and Leigh could barely follow any of it. Kip said something about getting the dockmaster to send him the float plan and how he put together a timeline of all of their ports of call, then there was something about finding out where to get free Wi-Fi in each town and who served the best pizza. And somehow, from nothing more than that, he tracked down a waitress on Nantucket who knew who the twins were and also knew where they were at that very moment—pricing out new phones at the computer store on Old South Road.

The twins explained the rest. They went snorkeling a few days back and forgot to take their phones out of their pockets. They would have called her from a landline as soon as they docked in Nantucket, but they didn't know anyone thought they were missing. Their dad said he'd do their last check-in, and they thought he had. He also said he'd have somebody look at the corroded cable connections on the marine radio, and they thought he'd done that, too. As for why he wasn't answering his own phone now, their voices trailed off into mumbles. It had something to do with a woman or with a bar, or most likely, Leigh thought, a woman in a bar.

She didn't care. All she cared about was the sound of their voices, coming through loud and clear, in stereo, as she held both phones to her head. *Head-phones*, she thought, and she laughed even louder as the tears poured down her face. She must have sounded hysterical, but she didn't care about that either. They were safe. Nothing else mattered.

Pete wanted to talk to them next, and she surrendered the phones to him. "Where are you? You're okay?" he said before his voice turned stern. "You check in with us from now on, you hear me? Not some random dockmaster. You call your mom, and I'm talking every day. And you get that radio fixed. This can't ever happen again. You hear me?" He grinned at Leigh as their stammered assurances came through the speakers.

She wiped her face and turned the other way to Kip, this boy genius who sleuthed out the twins' location and saved her from hours of heart-stopping terror.

"Kip," she said softly. She took his face in her hands. "Thank you." Then she flung her arms around him and hugged him tight. "Thank you!"

He let out a shaky breath in her ear as Peter reached around to squeeze his shoulder.

There were flights to cancel and car rental reservations to relinquish and Peter got honked out of his illegal parking space at the curb and had to find another place where he could pull over to finish all his calls. By that time Leigh remembered where she'd left the car: at the Metro station in Reston.

"Great," Peter said. "We'll take you there." He let his hand drop to her thigh as he pointed the truck out of the city. She put her hand on top of it and laced her fingers through his. His thumb rubbed against her wedding band as he drove. She glanced over at his left hand, where it gripped the wheel at eleven o'clock. A band of gold glinted there, too.

Kip had his phone back now and was busy tapping out texts. She glanced over as the bubbles lit up on his screen. *How much trouble we in?* Zack texted him. *Always a distant second to me, bro,* Kip replied.

———⌘———

All her life Leigh had loved living in the country and never so much as tonight. The deeper they drove into the Virginia countryside, the lighter the
traffic became and the greener the fields. All the world was at peace out here,
out of the hustle and chaos of the city. She was at peace, too, here between
Peter and Kip. They banded together today, the way families do in a crisis.

But as they got closer to Reston and the end of this ride, she couldn't
help remembering that it was a crisis that drove them apart in the first
place. She doubted they could forget it either. Peter spotted the Volvo in
the parking lot and pulled up alongside it, and Kip jumped out and held
the door for her, and her heart sank as she slid to the ground. Their happy
little reunion was over. This was how it would all end. They'd deposit her
here and go back to Hollow House and she'd go home alone.

"There's pizza in the freezer," she said.

"Sounds good," Peter said. "We'll see you at home."

That was all it took to settle the matter. A couple DiGiornos in the
deep-freeze, and she had her family back.

For the evening at least. Part of them, anyway.

Shep fired out of the house like a launched torpedo when she opened the
kitchen door. He streaked back and forth between Peter and Kip, yipping
with joy to see them again. Kip dropped to the ground to wrestle with
him, and Peter stepped around them to follow her into the kitchen. He
stopped on the threshold. "I don't like the way this door's sticking." He
opened and closed it with a frown.

"It's the humidity."

He went to the garage for his tools, and she went ahead of him into
the kitchen feeling as nervous as a bride on her in-laws' first visit. There
were dirty dishes on the counter and kibble scattered around the dog dish,
and she hurried to tidy up. This was a celebration, after all—the boys were
safe!—and everything should be perfect. She popped the pizzas in the
oven and uncorked a bottle of wine as Peter returned with the toolbox and
squatted to work on the door hinges.

From the front window she could see Kip rolling around with Shep out on the lawn. He used to tussle with Dylan and Zack in that same spot, and she remembered how Peter used to yell at them to take it out back before the neighbors called the cops. She remembered all four of them playing in the garden or the pasture on summer nights like this one. They'd set up volleyball nets or soccer cages, every night after dinner, playing until nightfall and even later, stumbling around in the dark and blindly slamming into each other. Laughing hysterically the whole time. Chrissy's laugh was always so easy to pick out. She could hear it now—a little light tinkling sound dancing gaily above her brothers' snorts and guffaws.

The oven timer dinged and she shook herself out of her reverie and slid out the pizzas. She rapped on the front window, and when Kip looked up from the lawn, she crooked a finger and beckoned him inside. Peter was still fiddling with the back door, and Kip cut around him and stopped uncertainly in the middle of the kitchen floor.

"Go wash up," she told him. "Dinner's ready."

"That's better," Peter said as Kip took off down the hall. He got to his feet and opened and closed the door a few times before he packed up his tools and went back to the garage to put them away.

She set the table, three places at a table with four chairs. She stood back and surveyed it, but it looked so off-balance that she stacked up the plates again.

"You know what?" she said when Peter came back in from the garage. "Let's eat in front of the TV tonight."

"Great," he said and headed there.

The family room was always his favorite place to unwind, and he was already on the sofa with the remote in hand when she set the pizza on the coffee table. She came back with a Snapple for Kip and poured out two glasses of wine as she sat down next to Peter. Kip flopped on the floor and sat cross-legged at the coffee table to eat. He peeled the olives off his slice and tossed them to Shepherd, who leaped in the air and caught each one between his snapping jaws.

It used to be Chrissy who snagged the olives off Kip's slice. He hated them, and he used to accuse her of ordering their pizzas with olives just to provoke him. She always looked up at the ceiling and airily said, *Who, me?*

Leigh heard the ring of her laughter again, as clear and true as if her ghost were there in the room with them. She felt her flopping between them on the sofa. *Isn't there anything else on?* Diving for olives off Kip's pizza. Feet pounding on the stairs. *I'll get it!* The sparkle of her laugh amid the flash and wink of the fireflies in the garden. Her ghost wisping through every room of the house.

No. She reached for her glass and took a gulp of wine. She mustn't think about Chrissy tonight, not now that everything else was right with the world. Dylan and Zack were safe, Peter and Kip were back. She mustn't ask about the case either, that other elephant in their room. This reunion was too fragile; it could disintegrate with talk of witness statements and plea negotiations.

She made herself concentrate on the news instead, but it was awful, as always. Another terrorist attack in Europe today. Another mass shooting in America last night. Events that used to be so shocking that time seemed to stand still until it could finally sink in they had actually happened. Now the networks could broadcast the same clips in a loop and no one would notice that the news hadn't changed.

Kip polished off his pizza and got to his feet. "I'm going up to my room. I mean"—he caught himself and looked at Leigh—"is it all right if I go up to my room?"

Was it still his room? he was asking. Peter pulled his eyes from the news and watched her like he was taking the temperature of her reply. "Of course," she said.

His footsteps pounded up the stairs, and she got up and cleared the plates to the kitchen. It was such a precarious truce, she thought as she rinsed them off and loaded them in the dishwasher. One wrong move, one careless word, and it could all be over in an instant.

She returned to the sofa, and Peter put his arm around her shoulder and pulled her close, and when the news cut to a commercial, he put a hand under her chin and tilted her face up to his and kissed her.

His beard felt strange against her skin. Not scratchy. Just different. Different enough to underscore how long they'd been apart. They kissed like teenagers, nervously, as if their parents might switch on the lights at any moment. But also like teenagers in another respect. They'd been chaste too long, and their kisses soon took on a backseat-of-the-car urgency. She slipped her hands under his shirt and tried to remember if he still had a toothbrush here. If he had to go back to Hollow House for anything, this spell might be broken. It would be so much easier if they could climb the stairs at the end of the evening and fall into bed without a second's thought or discussion. Their bodies would remember what to do. It was the thinking and discussing that might bring trouble.

Kip thundered down the stairs again, and they scrambled apart, panting a little, but laughing a little, too. "Hey, Leigh, could I use your laptop?" he called on his way to the kitchen.

"Help yourself," she called back.

Peter returned his attention to the news. This was when Chrissy usually came running downstairs after her bath, and the sweet fragrance of strawberry shampoo would scent the room as she pulled up the stool at Leigh's feet. She could smell it now. She could feel the slide of the comb and the spring of each corkscrew curl around her fingers. She could see her hair shimmer into a halo as she let go.

"Dessert?" She started to get up. "I could thaw something."

"Relax," Peter said and pulled her down, her head in his lap. She stretched out her legs, and he stroked her hair through the market report, the sports wrap-up, the week ahead in weather. Her eyes fell closed, the voices droned, and she drifted slowly off to sleep.

She dreamed of Chrissy. She often did, but this dream was different from the rest. She was all grown up in this one. Leigh was sitting at the kitchen table with a cup of tea while she watched Chrissy unload the dishwasher. Her back was to the room, and her strawberry-blond hair fell like a veil over her face as she bent to pull out the dishes. She sorted the flatware and slid the plates in the rack and put the glasses on the shelves one by one. "There. All done," she said, and she was just starting to turn around, her grown-up face was almost in view—when suddenly Stephen Kendall was there in the room, too. He was saying something to her, but—*Wait. Just a moment,* she said and leaned to look past him. It was too late, though. Chrissy had already flickered out of sight.

Her eyes flashed open. The dream was over, but somehow Stephen was still there. She sat up and sent a confused look around the room. She could hear his voice so clearly. "Oh!" she said when her gaze reached the TV screen. "Look—it's my friend Stephen."

Peter cocked his head. "Who?"

"A new friend. Stephen Kendall."

He clicked the volume up. Stephen was at a news desk with a mic wired to his tie. He was being interviewed about gun violence. *No, I wouldn't call it an epidemic,* he was saying. *Pandemic's the better word.*

"Hey, is there any ice cream?" Kip hollered from the kitchen.

"Only one way to find out," she hollered back.

More than two hundred mass shootings so far this year alone, Stephen said on screen. His name appeared below his super-size face. *Rev. Dr. Stephen H. Kendall.*

"He's a priest?" Peter said.

"Yes, and a professor, and he's the director of a research center on gun violence."

"Mint chocolate chip," Kip groaned in the kitchen. Ice cream shouldn't be green, he always griped, but it was Chrissy's favorite. *It's cool and refreshing. Like me*! she used to say.

"But he's also a priest."

"Yes. He has a church in Chevy Chase."

Suicides, accidental shootings, domestic violence. All deaths resulting from guns kept in the home for self-defense. But the numbers make it clear: We're not defending ourselves with these guns. We're killing our loved ones and ourselves.

"You've been going to church in Chevy Chase?"

She shook her head. "We met—elsewhere."

"Elsewhere where?"

"He was driving past the Hermitage one day. We stopped and introduced ourselves." Not the whole truth, but she couldn't admit that she followed him home.

"On Hollow Road?" Peter suddenly muted the volume on Stephen's voice. "You know a priest who was driving on Hollow Road and you never mentioned it?"

Kip appeared in the doorway with his hand plunged deep in a bag of potato chips.

"He's not—"

Peter got to his feet. "Do you know how hard we've been looking—? Hey." He snapped his fingers at Kip and pointed at the TV. "Take a look at this guy."

"He's not that priest." Leigh got up, too. "He wasn't on Hollow Road that night."

Kip squinted at the screen and went closer.

"How do you know?" Peter said.

"Because I asked him. And he said no."

Peter pressed the remote and Stephen's voice filled the room again. *You've heard the saying, Guns don't kill people; people kill people. That's perfectly true. Mentally ill people kill people. Toddlers kill people. Careless shooters kill people. Depressives kill themselves. But what's the common denominator? Guns. Easy access to guns.*

Kip's brow furrowed as he listened. "I don't know. He could be the guy."

Leigh threw up her hands. "He's not the guy. I told you—I already asked him. What possible reason would he have to lie?"

Kip studied the face on the screen. "Maybe he was doing something he didn't want anybody to find out. Like, I don't know, maybe he had a girl in the car. Or I know—a little boy!"

"Stop it," she said tightly. "He's an esteemed scholar. He's the kindest man I've ever—"

"You knew about him this whole time," Peter said. "And you never bothered to mention he might be the guy we've been beating the bushes to find?"

"Oh, for God's sake, Peter," she burst out. "Face facts: there was no guy!"

He took a step back, away from her.

"There was," Kip said. "I swear I'm telling the truth."

She wheeled on him. "What does that even mean to you, Kip? Seriously. Do you even understand the concept?"

She put her hand over her mouth, but it was too late. Kip flinched, and Peter stared at her like she'd slapped the boy.

No one spoke for a long time. They stood in the middle of the kitchen like three sides of a triangle, watching one another across the empty space in the middle. The image of a triangle took hold in Leigh's mind, and Chrissy's ghost was back in the room, kneeling at the coffee table, working through one of her geometry lessons. But this triangle wasn't equilateral, it was isosceles, and Leigh was the odd one out. Peter and Kip formed a right angle and she was the hypotenuse opposing them. She could hear Chrissy reciting the formula: the square of the hypotenuse is equal to the sum of the squares— But her voice faded away, and Leigh couldn't remember the rest of it. All she knew was that nothing was ever going to square up right again.

Kip broke formation first. He edged for the door. "I'm gonna go call Shelby."

"Hold up," Peter said with a last look at Leigh. "We'll call her together from the road."

Shepherd jumped down from the window seat and trotted after them out the back door and hopped up in the truck to ride with them as they drove away.

Chapter Thirty-Six

It was everything they'd been hoping and praying for. It was worth every gamble. It would solve all of their problems. Right up until the moment it didn't.

He wasn't the guy.

Shelby called from the road to deliver the news on her way back to the city. She and Frank Nobbin drove out to Kendall's house that morning to question him, and they both came away convinced he was nowhere near Hollow Road that night.

The trackhoe was on-site excavating for the swimming pool and it made such a racket that Pete waved Kip down to the basement to take the call. They put the phone on speaker and crouched over it like they were peering into a crystal ball. Kip's face was white with a layer of fine plaster dust. Ever since his job ended at the Millers', he'd been pitching in with whatever work was under way. Today it was the finish plaster crew.

Kendall was a lovely man, Shelby told them. He couldn't have been more gracious. He invited them into his study and offered them tea and answered every one of their questions. He knew about the accident, of course, from Leigh, and he was truly sorry he couldn't help. As for where he was that night, he couldn't remember after all this time, but he gave Frank his day-planner to peruse while he poured their tea, and there it was—he was in New York at a fund-raiser for the Andrew Kendall Research Center on Gun Violence. It came back to him then, and he went to his computer and printed out the guest list for the event, complete with email addresses and telephone numbers. And he seemed to recall there might be a video—yes, there it was, posted on the foundation website, a video of the speech he gave that night, time-stamped 9:30 p.m.

"I'm gonna call some of these guests to confirm," Frank said.

"But really, there's no question. He couldn't have been on Hollow Road that night."

For a minute Pete couldn't speak, the news hit him so hard. He'd fought with Leigh, *he'd walked out on her*, and all for nothing. Kip didn't even recognize the man on the TV screen, but Pete pounced on the possibility anyway, and look where it got them. Nowhere.

"Wait. Hold on," he said. "The day Leigh met him. What was he doing on Hollow Road?"

"That's the one thing he wouldn't share with us. Seal of the confessional or whatever. Not that it matters."

"Wait. He's saying it was official business? Frank, your people canvassed everybody on the road and not one person said a priest visited them. Then or ever, right?"

"I guess that seal works both ways."

"No." He couldn't let it go. "Something fishy's going on."

Shelby's sigh drifted through the speaker. "Fishy or not, who cares? Maybe he was on Hollow Road a hundred times before, but he wasn't there that night. He couldn't have made it from New York to St. Alban in two hours. So he's not the guy. End of story."

After a minute Pete mumbled a grudging, "Right."

She rang off soon after, and he and Kip stayed where they were, on their haunches staring at the phone in heavy silence.

Kip finally spoke. "He coulda helicoptered down."

Pete gave him a withering look. "This isn't some comic book, Kip. This is your life."

The boy's cheeks flushed pink under the plaster dust. "I know that."

The silence swelled, and after a minute Pete realized why. The trackhoe wasn't running. He ran upstairs and found the pool guys waiting for him. They'd run into a problem, and he followed them outside to see that they'd unearthed a massive boulder in the exact space where the spa would go. They'd need a crane to get it out of there, and that would have to be an add-on to their contract price. While they were haggling over that, the landscaper came up to eyeball the boulder. He thought he could work it into his design for the roadside border, and for the next hour Pete dealt with that and tried not to think about the case and how they were losing it. Or Leigh and how he'd already lost her.

He picked sides last night, and so did she. The trouble was, neither of them had picked each other.

Leigh was at the office when Stephen called with the same news. It was what she'd been hoping and praying for all these months—now Peter would have to accept that Kip was lying—but her victory felt hollow. This wasn't going to solve their problems. They couldn't simply chalk this all up to a misunderstanding and move on. Say a blithe *I'm sorry* and *I forgive you.* So many times she'd made the children speak those words to each other, and finally she understood why they always resisted. Hurt feelings didn't just evaporate. Wounds didn't just disappear.

"I'm so sorry they dragged you into this," she told Stephen.

"A good lawyer chases down every lead, right?"

"Not one that's so obviously a lie."

"I don't believe it is a lie."

"What?"

"If he's lying, why would he say it might be me? Knowing I'd deny it. The poor boy must be telling the truth that someone was on the road that night."

"Or he's sending up trial balloons and watching to see if they fly."

"Maybe," he said. "Or maybe his house is on fire. He's telling the truth this time, but no one will believe him."

"You're too charitable, Stephen."

He chuckled. "Occupational hazard."

At home that night she walked the whole circuit of the house, upstairs and down, but it was no victory lap. It felt more like a farewell tour. They should sell it, she thought suddenly. Now, before the divorce. Buyers always lowballed their offers when they learned the sellers were divorcing. They'd get a better price for it before the papers were filed.

Once she would have shocked herself for even thinking the word *divorce*, but not anymore. The reason two-thirds of all second marriages ended in divorce was that divorce survivors knew when it was time to stop fooling themselves that things were going to work out. Hope had to surrender to experience. The way Peter turned on her last night, how quickly he jumped over to Kip's side of the giant fault line that opened between them—that told her everything she needed to know about the state of their marriage.

She had no appetite for dinner. Instead she took a bottle of wine into the family room and loaded a home video into the DVD player. But she didn't select one of Chrissy's baby videos this time. Tonight she chose the wedding video.

She poured a glass and curled up on the sofa as the old country church lit up on the screen. The camera panned across the lawn in the misty morning light, then dollied in through the double doors, and there they all were on the screen, her perfectly blended family. The twins at fifteen already looking like young men as they ushered the handful of guests to their seats; tiny Mia with her flower basket balking at the aisle until Peter's mother got up and coaxed her along; best man Kip and maid of honor Chrissy grinning at each other through the whole ceremony, already thick as thieves; and finally Peter at the altar, so handsome in his blue suit, his gaze on her so warm and steady as she walked down the aisle to join him, his voice so full of love as he recited his vows.

Forsaking all others. That was what he vowed to do.

Tears spilled, and she hastily wiped them away. She couldn't blame him for choosing Kip over her. She'd probably do the same thing in his situation. No one should be forced to decide whether to be a parent first or a spouse. If this were a traditional nuclear family, if she and Peter were the parents of the same shared children—these problems would never have come up. It was divorce that was at fault.

It was an ironic admission for a divorce lawyer to make, but there it was.

The real reason two-thirds of all second marriages ended in divorce? No couple could ever hope to forsake all others, not when their hearts already belonged to the children who came before.

That week she received notice that the appellate court had scheduled oral argument in the matter of *Beck v. Beck* for the first Tuesday in October. The next day she received notice that Hunter Beck was dropping his appeal.

It was the logical move. The baby would be two months old by then and a whole new set of rules on custody and visitation would apply. Nonetheless it was a surprise: Hunter hadn't done anything logical before this. He'd just paid his lawyer tens of thousands of dollars to write seventy-five pages of argument only to call *Never mind*.

Still, it was good news, and she called Carrie as Jenna's proxy to relay it.

"Yeah, he told us he was dropping it."

Here was another surprise. "You've talked to Hunter?" The last time she saw them together Fred was chasing him off his lawn.

"Oh, all the time. Would you believe he and Fred call each other just to talk?"

"About what?" Leigh couldn't imagine.

"What else do men talk about? Sports and politics. But he talks about Jenna to me. He gave me a letter to read to her the next time she calls. Of course I read it right away. He loves her, he misses her. Please forgive him. She's the only one who matters."

Ah, Leigh thought. Here at last was the reason Jenna left him, and there was nothing mysterious about it. It was a tale as old as time. Hunter cheated on her.

"He said he's called off the hounds. The lawyers, the investigators, all of them."

And there was his second admission. Jenna might be paranoid but she hadn't imagined that Hunter's goons were stalking her.

"You know," Carrie mused. "Get past all of Jenna's drama, and he's really not a bad guy."

Those were the same words Hunter used to describe himself. Leigh hoped there wasn't some kind of Svengali effect at work here. "Well—I'd still be on my guard."

Carrie snorted. "Jenna's on guard enough for all of us."

John Stoddard called later that morning. He'd dug up some new intel on Bill Gunder, something pretty useful, he thought. He wanted to come in and show it to her. "Would six thirty be too late?"

"Not at all. See you then."

She hung up with a smile. It was such a pleasure working with a can-do client like John. It saved her from thinking helplessly about Devra and the nightmare she must be living at the embassy. She was still haunted by the words Devra choked out over the phone. *I want to leave. Help me, please.* She tried to help: she began every day with another round of phone calls to the embassy and the State Department—*dialing for Devra*, she thought of it—but her persistence was pointless. She never got through. It was her biggest failure.

No, not her biggest, she admitted, but the prospect of John Stoddard's arrival saved her from having to think about that, too.

The reception desk was unattended after business hours, so as six thirty approached, Leigh took some files and went there to work. Reception was a space meant to impress visitors and it was fitted out accordingly, with floor-to-ceiling windows overlooking the boulevard and cool travertine floors and furniture covered in buttery soft leather. After hours a grate of steel bars descended from the ceiling to block access from the elevator lobby. The grate was in place now, and Leigh tapped in the access code on the security panel to get through. She spread out her papers on a coffee table and settled in to wait.

At precisely six thirty the elevator chimed, and she glanced up through the grate as a man in a tuxedo stepped off. One of her partners must be making a pit stop on his way to some black-tie event. She bent her head back to her work.

"Ma'am?"

She looked up again, and her mouth fell open. "John?"

He grimaced through the gridwork of the gate. "It's the penguin suit, right? I'm working security at some fancy party tonight. They want us to blend in, but I look like a moron."

She laughed as she got up and unlocked the access door. "You look just fine," she said and shook his hand as he came through.

He waited for her to sit before he pulled up a chair beside her and opened his courier bag. "I did some digging on Gunder like we talked about." He spread out some papers on the desk. "He works for the State of Maryland. The Budget Office. I was able to get my hands on his personnel file."

"How?" In a city full of government employees, she knew all too well that civil service files were practically sacrosanct.

"I have some good connections. Please, take a look."

She skimmed through the pages as he passed them to her. Gunder's file was thick with warnings and adverse actions relating to his poor conduct and job performance. He'd been written up repeatedly for absenteeism and insubordination, and there were three reports of intoxication on the job, the most recent only last month.

"So he's still a drunk," John said.

Leigh nodded. She was amazed that he'd been able to obtain these documents. She'd worked with some good private investigators over the years, but none of them could have unearthed material like this in this time frame.

"So what next?" As always, John was focused on the mission. "What else do we need?"

She closed the file. "We'll have to show that his drinking has a deleterious effect on Bryce. There are high-functioning alcoholics who somehow manage to raise their children. We need to show that Gunder isn't one of them."

He considered that. "I've got a lead on Bryce's school records," he said. "If they show any kind of medical issues or behavioral problems, would that help?"

That was another set of records that should have been inviolable. She wondered if locks simply fell open for war heroes. "Possibly," she said. "Or if there's any evidence that his drinking puts Bryce in physical danger. For example, if he drove drunk with Bryce in the car—"

"Begging your pardon, ma'am, but I couldn't let that happen. Covert or not, I'd have to step in if I saw that happening."

"Of course you would." She put a reassuring hand on his arm. "I meant if you hear of such things from anyone else."

He nodded like he'd received a set of orders. "I'll see what I can find out."

He packed away the file and got to his feet. She looked up at him towering over her in his tuxedo, ready to head off to his next assignment, so calm and capable. An idea struck.

"John, I wonder—could I hire you to do some investigative work for me?"

If he was surprised, he didn't show it. "Sure." He sat back down. "What's the job?"

"I have this client—" In broad strokes she told him about Devra's imprisonment and the mysterious Emily Whitman and the showdown at the embassy gates. "I need to find out who this State Department employee is. If I can figure out a way to expose her arrangement with the ambassador—"

"—then State'll lean on the ambassador, spring the wife, and fire this Whitman woman. That about it?"

"That's my hope."

"Got a photo?"

"Sorry," Leigh said but did her best to describe her. "Oh, and she drives a little red car. A Mini Cooper, I think."

"License plate?"

"No, sorry." She felt foolish. Obviously this wasn't enough information for him to launch any kind of investigation.

He tucked his notes in the breast pocket of his tuxedo. "I'll have to
book this through my employer if that's okay. I don't moonlight."

"That's fine."

"Then I'll be in touch."

"Leigh," Stephen said the next day. "There's something I have to say
to you."

"Yes?"

They were driving back from the Acropolis and he'd been boisterously
singing along with the Met's Saturday afternoon broadcast—*Fidelio* was
today's performance. He reached to the lower the volume on the Saab's old
radio. "It might make you angry," he warned.

She couldn't imagine. "What is it?"

"It's about Chrissy. I've been thinking about what a delightful, wonderful child she must have been. Truly exceptional. I wish I could have
known her."

"Me, too." It was crushing to know that he never would. That the
whole world would never have the chance to know her. World without
Chrissy. Amen.

"But here's the thing," he said. "It's a mistake for you to canonize her."

Her mouth fell open. "I—I'm not," she sputtered. "I haven't—"

"Don't burden her memory with impossible standards. She was a
brave, generous girl but she wasn't a saint."

"I never said she was!"

"She was magical. That's the word you always use to describe her, but
you have to remember it's only a metaphor. She wasn't magic, she was
human."

"I never—I never said otherwise!"

"You think it, though. That's why it's so hard for you to accept that
she may have done one selfish act in her young life. That's why you can't

believe Christopher might be telling the truth. Because it would mean that for once she put herself ahead of someone else. She stood by and let him take the blame."

Her mouth trembled. This was such an unjust accusation. She never said Chrissy was a saint. That wasn't the reason she couldn't believe Kip. It was simpler than that. Chrissy didn't drive, and if she had driven, she never would have lied about it, because—because—

"I knew you'd get angry. But please, consider the idea, won't you?"

She turned her head to the window, and he turned up the volume on *Fidelio* and drove on without singing or speaking. The idea lodged like a lump in her throat—that Chrissy stood by and let Kip take the blame. That she lied to protect herself. Stephen was right. She couldn't believe it. She thought back to the scene in the police station that night. She remembered Kip in the interview room, looking so small and scared with the cops looming over him and Peter yelling at him. She remembered Chrissy at her side, looking into the same room, blinking back tears at the same scene.

They were nearly back to his cottage, and the "Prisoners' Chorus" was on the radio. Stephen made the turn through the stone pillars to the lane. On the distant hill ahead gleamed the old porticoed plantation house as he turned into the woods.

"You're right," she said at last.

"Ah." He beamed at her.

"I don't believe Chrissy would have lied."

His smile faded.

"If you'd been there that night, if you'd heard the charges they were threatening Kip with and you saw how scared he was? Chrissy saw and heard every bit of it, and there's no way she would have stood by and let him take the blame for her. You have to remember: She wasn't drinking and she didn't have a suspended driver's license like Kip did. She wasn't facing anything worse than a scolding. It wouldn't take a saint to tell the truth in that situation. Just an ordinary decent person. Which is what she was."

He turned into the drive. "What a fool I am," he said with a smile, "to even think of arguing with a lawyer."

Then he slammed on his brakes. A blue station wagon was blocking his driveway. A woman was slumped behind the wheel, her legs half-in, half-out of the car. She staggered to her feet as the Saab lurched to a stop behind her. It was a hot summer day, but she wore a long tattered cardigan that she clutched with both hands around her ribs. She was barefoot and her hair stood out in a wild gray frizz. If not for the late-model car and her stylish eyeglasses, she could have been mistaken for a homeless woman. From fifty feet away Leigh could see that she was crying.

Stephen stared at the woman through the windshield. He cleared his throat. "I'm afraid I'll have to say good-bye here."

It had never occurred to Leigh that he counseled other bereaved people. "Of course."

Her car was wedged in the drive beside the station wagon, but with a little maneuvering she could back out without everyone having to shuffle places. She circled around to her driver's door as Stephen approached the distraught woman. He said something in a low voice and put a hand on her elbow to guide her to the house.

Halfway there the woman stopped and wrenched a look back at Leigh. "I know you!"

Leigh stopped. "I don't think so—"

"Let's get inside." Stephen put his hands on the woman's shoulders.

"I know you. Don't I? You're their mother, yes? That sweet girl. And that poor boy." Her hand fluttered to her mouth as her face twisted with a sob. "That beautiful, beautiful boy—"

"Claire. Come inside. Now."

Claire? Leigh's mouth dropped open. She shot a look at Stephen, but he didn't look back. He steered the weeping woman to the front door. "I'm sorry. I'm so sorry!" she wailed as he shut it firmly behind them.

Chapter Thirty-Seven

Pete didn't bother driving by the house that week. What was the point? Leigh had her *new friend* now. Her *esteemed scholar*. Even Shelby was taken with the guy. *A lovely man*, she called him. He kept turning over the way Leigh spoke his name—*Stephen*—like he was too good for plain old *Steve*. Okay, so she also called him *Peter*, but still. *Stephen* was the reason for the lipstick and the dressy dress. He was the reason she was out night after goddam night. Pete wasn't even going to try to compete. He missed the warning signs seven years ago when Karen was suddenly so taken with her new dentist; he wasn't going to suffer that humiliation again.

Saturday night he picked up some takeout and headed home with the windows open and the summer breeze blowing through the cab of the truck. He passed a park where a Little League game was in progress, and it brought back a wave of memories, of other summer nights like this, when Kip was little and life was easy. Stretched out in a lawn chair behind the backstop, cheering him on, wincing a little when he struck out or missed an easy fly ball but always covering it up before he turned around to see. Giving him a big thumbs-up that made the boy duck his head in embarrassment but not before Pete saw him smile.

He wasn't any good at covering up his reactions these days. The government's plea offer had knocked him on his ass, and after two more strike-outs this week—Kip's lousy performance on the stand and the busted lead on the priest—the dread had to be showing in everything he said and did. Two years or ten. In prison. He couldn't even wrap his head around it.

Back at Hollow House, he let himself in the kitchen and hollered for Kip to come and eat. He hollered again as he got out the paper plates and unwrapped the burgers, and when Kip didn't answer the third holler, he went looking for him.

He was probably sacked out on his cot, Pete thought as he trotted upstairs. But he wasn't in his room or anywhere on the second floor, or on the third floor or even in the basement. He wasn't anywhere in the house.

Pete called Kip's phone as he climbed up the basement stairs, and from the kitchen came the answering ring tones. "Where've you been?" he yelled. But Kip didn't answer, on his phone or otherwise, and Pete followed the rings all the way to the island, where Kip's phone lay quivering on the glazed lava stone.

He stared at it. Kip never went anywhere without his phone. He took it with him to the john. He'd take it in the shower with him, too, if he could figure out how to waterproof it.

He went outside and yelled for him, but the whole place was quiet, inside and out. He headed up to the conservancy land behind the Millers' property and hiked into the woods at the top of the hill. The trees were in full leaf and so dense it was like the sun switched off as soon as he passed under them. He called Kip's name again as he walked through the gloom.

Still no answer. He stopped and turned a slow revolution, then leaned his head back and looked up. The trees in this stand of woods were old hardwoods, oaks mostly, thick-trunked and tall, with good strong horizontal limbs. The thought of those horizontal limbs made his heart clutch, and he broke into a run.

He wouldn't—of course he wouldn't. It was one thing to be kind of bummed out and a totally different thing to be— No, he wasn't going to say the word, not even in his head. He kept running and yelling Kip's name, squinting through the forest murk, his head spinning as he scanned every limb on every tree. What would he even use? There wasn't any rope on the job site he could recall. Nothing but a few leftover coils of electrical cable in the tool trailer, and that was when he remembered the nail guns.

Oh, Jesus. He stopped dead with his chest heaving. He should have checked the trailer first. He wheeled around and tore back down the hill the way he came. There might still be time. He might still get there in time.

Something creaked as he burst out of the woods. A metallic sound like a hinge or a rusty chain. His feet stuttered to a stop and his head snapped around, and there he was. Not dangling from the end of a rope but at the wall of the place next door, halfway up an extension ladder propped against the bricks.

"What—what the hell?"

Kip froze, one foot suspended in the air above the next rung.

Pete's relief was displaced by a red-hot boil of anger. "What are you—? After I told you to— Get your ass down here! Now!"

Kip scrambled down. It was an aluminum ladder pilfered from the tool trailer, and draped over the electrified wire on top of the wall was the rubber bed mat from the back of the truck. Pete felt the steam building so hot it could have blown out his ears. He didn't wait for him to reach the ground. He pulled him off the ladder and flung him around and pinned him against the wall. "What the hell do you think you're doing?"

"Nothing. I was just—I don't know—curious."

"You could've gotten electrocuted! Or—God!—shot!"

"I grounded the electricity, okay? And there's nobody there to shoot at me."

"You don't know that." Pete grabbed him hard by the shoulders. "I told you to stay away from that place!"

"Okay." Kip squirmed in his grip. "All right!"

"You would've set off the alarms. The cops would've been here in three minutes."

"So?"

"So?" Pete gave him a shake. "They'd arrest you for trespassing. No, for breaking and entering!"

"Big deal. So I get another three months. On top of two years."

His hands fell from the boy's shoulders. He lurched back a step. "Nobody said we're taking that deal."

"On top of *ten* years, then." Kip slid down the wall until his butt smacked the ground. "'Cause if we don't take the deal, that's what I'm gonna get."

"Aw, jeez." Pete turned away with his hands on top of his head and walked two laps of a tight circle before he rounded back on Kip. "You're not doing ten years or two or even a week. You hear me? I'm not letting you go to prison!"

Kip looked up at him, his eyes defiant through the shine of tears. "How do you think you're gonna stop it?"

"You let me worry about that." Pete grabbed him under the arms and hauled him to his feet. "You just keep your head down and do as you're told." With a shove toward the house, he added, "And you stay the hell away from that place!"

The temperature hit a hundred that day, and it was midnight before it dropped back below ninety. The AC wasn't hooked up yet, and Pete lay sweating on his cot, watching his phone for the degrees to drop, watching the minutes crawl by. He thought he heard a wobble in the ceiling fan overhead—that bolt might need tightening—and he tried to move that to the front of his digital worry screen. But it was no use. There was only one thing on his screen, and it didn't scroll, it strobed in hot stabbing flashes of light. The memory of how his heart seized up at the thought of ropes and nail guns.

They were locked up now and so were the saw blades and everything else he could think of. No harm in taking precautions, even if Kip's self-destructiveness was taking a different bent.

Two years versus ten. Jesus Christ.

There was no hope of sleep. He got up and crept across the hall and cracked open the door to Kip's room. He could just make out the sprawl of his body in the moonlight. Softly he closed the door again. It was years since he'd felt the need to do bed checks on his son, but if that was what it took now, that was what he was going to do.

He padded down the staircase. He'd spent eighteen years protecting his family, peering through windshields, scanning hilltops, always on the lookout for danger—and after all that he was supposed to sit by and let them haul his kid off to jail? Nobody ever went to prison and came out the better for it. No matter what happened inside, he'd come out a different boy—man—than he went in. He'd be scarred in a hundred ways, and there was no way Pete could let that happen.

He opened up his laptop on the lava stone counter and did a search for countries that didn't have extradition treaties with America. The list came up: Afghanistan, Bahrain, Morocco, Senegal, and Tunisia. He added in countries with no diplomatic relations: North Korea, Iran, Bhutan.

That was the universe of choices. War zones and totalitarian states where Kip would be safe from extradition but not much else. And they'd stand out like two sore thumbs in any of those countries. They wouldn't speak the language, they wouldn't know the customs, they wouldn't have the right skin tone.

Canada was the only place he could think of where they'd blend in. But Canada did have an extradition treaty with the States. He clicked through the Google results in search of a loophole. There were none, legally speaking, but the statistics were promising. It looked like the United States seldom made an extradition request to Canada for anyone other than murderers and drug dealers. Manslaughter cases made up only about one percent of the total. Another click told him that only about a hundred people a year were extradited from Canada. Which meant at most one person a year was extradited for manslaughter. Not much comfort if that one person happened to be Kip, but odds of a hundred to one sounded a hell of a lot better to Pete than the odds they were facing now.

He closed the lid of his laptop. That was it, then. They'd head for Canada. Find work in construction or the oil fields. Assimilate and keep their fingers crossed.

So okay. He had a backup plan. Maybe now he could get some sleep.

Chapter Thirty-Eight

Leigh thought she'd hear from Stephen that weekend. He'd want to confide in her, now that she knew a little about his ex-wife and her situation. Or maybe confess that Leigh had served as a kind of proxy for Claire, that he was helping her work through her grief because he couldn't help his own wife. It would be a difficult conversation, she thought, and when the phone finally rang Sunday afternoon, she steeled herself as she answered. "Hello?"

"Sorry to disturb you at home, ma'am."

"John?" She was startled, not only because it wasn't Stephen, but also because she'd never given Stoddard this number. Though that shouldn't have surprised her. His intelligence gathering skills had been amply demonstrated by then.

"I've completed that assignment you gave me. I didn't know whether you wanted to wait until office hours or—"

"You mean—on Emily Whitman?" It was only two days since they last spoke.

"Yes, ma'am. Or I should say Lindy Carlson."

He'd found her. Her pulse quickened. "Can you come over right now?" She gave him her address, though she probably didn't need to bother with that either.

An hour later he pulled in the driveway in a decidedly unmilitary-looking minivan. He was dressed casually today, in camo pants and a tight black athletic shirt with the familiar Nike swoosh at the middle of the neckline. "Come on in," she called from the breezeway.

He hesitated by his car. "I don't want to intrude on your family." He hitched a rucksack over his shoulder.

"It's fine. No one's home." She led him into the kitchen. "Something to drink?"

"No, ma'am. Thank you."

He opened the rucksack and pulled out a file and placed it on the table. She meant to show him into the living room, but his body language made it clear that the kitchen was as far as he would go. She sat down at the table and waved for him to sit, too. "How did you ever manage it?" she asked as she flipped the file open.

"I surveilled the Qatari embassy yesterday, and at fourteen hundred a blonde in a red Mini Cooper went through the gates. I didn't think there could be two of them. So I followed her when she came out, and the rest of the pieces fell into place after that."

He made it sound so simple, but there was nothing simple about the contents of the file he'd assembled. It was practically a dossier on Lindy Carlson, aka Emily Whitman. A copy of her driver's license was clipped to the left side of the folder, and on the right were photos of the front and back of her car displaying Virginia license plates. It was parked in front of a suburban town house with a yellow front door and a basket of pink and purple fuchsia hanging from a hook beside the house number plaque. A Post-it on the photo showed an address in Fairfax.

"This is where she lives?"

"She owns it with her boyfriend. Copies of the deed and mortgage are in there."

So was a photo of the boyfriend, an intense-looking young man in glasses. "Joshua Landrum," John said. "He's a legislative aide to Senator Brockhurst." The file included screenshots of Landrum's LinkedIn profile and the staff directory on the senator's website. Lindy's profile was there, too, showing her current position in the Office of Protocol of the State Department. Below that was her college transcript from Wellesley, and below that her grad school transcript from Harvard.

"I got some long-lens shots." John shuffled through time-stamped photos of Lindy getting in her car, standing at her mailbox, with her boyfriend at a restaurant, and driving in and out of the gates of the Qatari embassy. One of the photos showed her passing an envelope to the man in the guardhouse.

The final document was a copy of the incident report of Leigh's 911 call and the standoff at the embassy gates. It contained a capsule summary of Leigh's accusations against the ambassador and the attaché's cross-accusations against Leigh, then noted that a State Department official named Lindy Carlson confirmed that diplomatic immunity prevented any entry onto or search of the embassy premises. The attaché agreed not to press charges against Leigh, and the matter was closed.

"She's not assigned to the Near Eastern desk," John said. "There's no official reason for her to have this kind of relationship with the embassy."

"Off-book, she called it."

"Unauthorized, I'd call it, and maybe illegal. Depends on what's in those envelopes."

Leigh looked up from the file. "This is amazing work, John. I can't thank you enough. When you send me your bill, be sure to give yourself a bonus."

He leaned back in the chair. "Can I ask—what are you planning to do with this intel?"

"I'll take it to the police and force them to reopen the investigation."

He nodded. "Then best case—what?—they go to some other State Department official for clarification? Is that your end game?"

She saw where he was going. The ruling on diplomatic immunity would be the same, even if it came from a legitimate source inside the State Department. "Then I'll take this to Justice."

"Okay, but what then? Best case, they charge Lindy with something and the ambassador gets expelled."

That was the last thing she wanted. If bin Jabar was sent back to Qatar, he'd take Devra with him, and she'd be under sharia law again with no ability to ever divorce him. "Then I'll go to Emily—Lindy—and threaten to expose her if she doesn't—" Leigh broke off. No matter how cozy Lindy's relationship was with the embassy, she couldn't possibly have enough influence to secure Devra's freedom. "I don't know," she said finally, helplessly. "I have to do something."

"Could I suggest something *else*?"

She eyed him. "Such as?"

"Extraction."

She let out an astonished laugh. "What?"

"Go in and pull your client out of there."

"This isn't Syria, John. We can't breach the gates with a dozen armed men."

He smiled sheepishly. "Yeah, sometimes we went in loud," he admitted. "But sometimes we went in real quiet."

She cocked her head. "How?"

"With a Trojan horse." He tapped a finger on the file. She looked down. He was pointing at a photo of Lindy Carlson.

Early Monday morning Lindy Carlson emerged from her cheery yellow door looking chic in a white peplum blouse over a turquoise pencil skirt. She came down the stairs and crossed the parking lot in the brisk, purposeful stride of a smart young professional. She was halfway to her car when she stopped, stared, and did an abrupt about-face back to her house.

"Oh, would you rather do this inside?" Leigh called from where she leaned against the bumper of the Mini Cooper. "In front of Josh? In which case, perhaps we should invite the senator to sit in, too."

Lindy tried and failed to form a smirk as she turned around. "What do you want?"

"I'm here to trade in your currency, Ms. Carlson. Favors, right? You do a favor for me, and in return, I won't ruin your life." Leigh plucked the car keys from the girl's hand and pointed her toward the sliding door of the van parked beside the Mini Cooper. "Please. After you," she said as John Stoddard reached out and jerked the girl inside.

At five fifteen that afternoon, Lindy pulled up to the gates of the Qatari embassy in her little red car. She pushed her oversize sunglasses back on her head, and the guard greeted her with a nod of recognition as he scanned the entries on his clipboard. "The ambassador is expecting you."

She nodded. She'd exchanged her skirt and blouse for a bright orange dress with a cobalt blue scarf tied over her head, bold colors so eye-catching they all but eclipsed her features.

"Who is this with you?" the guard asked.

"A friend. Alsama Kouri."

"ID please."

Leigh could barely see through the small mesh screen in her burka. She had to grope for the tote bag at her feet to pull out the passport from the Islamic Republic of Afghanistan. The man took it into the guardhouse to photocopy, and Lindy's breath caught as he paused to study it.

"Careful," Leigh warned her. "Don't screw this up."

"I *won't*," Lindy hissed.

Not deliberately, Leigh was certain of that much. It took the girl only thirty minutes that morning to appreciate that she had a greater investment than anyone in the success of Devra's extraction. She spent the whole day cloistered in a conference room at Leigh's office without a phone or a computer and nothing to read but her own dossier. While John was out organizing the supplies they'd need, Leigh walked her through the pages, now neatly tabbed and annotated for ease of reading. Multiple copies of the same file were spread out over the table in envelopes addressed to Lindy's boss, his boss, and his boss, all the way up to the secretary himself. With courtesy copies to Senator Brockhurst and the FBI. Copies of the delivery instructions were there, too: if Devra wasn't safely away by the end of the day, the files would be hand-delivered to the addressees in the morning. All the envelopes were in the firm's fire safe now, with the delivery instructions in the hands of Polly and two of Leigh's partners.

The guard returned with the passport, a counterfeit John procured that day from a source he declined to reveal. The photo was of some anonymous Afghan woman, and the guard held it open to that page as he bent to peer into the vehicle. This was the moment of truth; the mission would nose-dive if he asked Leigh to remove her head covering. But John had watched other veiled women pass through these gates unchallenged during his surveillance, and he felt confident this would work.

The guard closed the passport and handed it in. "Go through."

Lindy put her sunglasses back on and drove through the gates to the circular drive and looped around the burbling fountain to the visitors parking lot. She parked and passed the car keys to Leigh, who dropped them in the tote bag, a red polka-dotted carryall that was as distinctive and hopefully distracting as Lindy's outfit. She gathered up her burka and stepped carefully out of the car and up the stairs to the entrance of the embassy. It was difficult to manage the steps through the long folds of fabric and even more difficult to see where she was going through the mesh over her eyes She felt like she was inside a character costume at Disney World, clumsy and disconnected, with only a narrow tunnel of vision out into the world.

A few members of the embassy staff were at their desks inside, the men in Western attire, the women in hijabs. A young man in a business suit sat at the reception desk, and Leigh recognized him: he was the attaché who had run up to the gates buttoning his shirt the night of Devra's distress call. He greeted Lindy by name. "The ambassador is in his office," he said. "You may go up."

"Thanks, Fadi."

Leigh followed her into a small elevator. Lindy pressed the button for the second floor, and as the doors slid shut, Leigh leaned around her and pressed the button for the third floor.

Lindy stared ahead as the elevator cranked to life. "I want all the copies, too," she said.

"You'll get them. The day the divorce is final."

"Not that you care? But it's not like I was passing classified documents in those envelopes. It was basically celebrity gossip for the Mideast diplomatic set. Who's dining with whom, who got invited to the White House. It was nothing."

"You're right," Leigh said. "I don't care."

The bell dinged, and Lindy got off at the second floor without another glance at Leigh.

The doors closed again and the elevator rose to the third floor. It opened directly on the foyer, a small room with heavy hangings draped on the other three walls. Leigh pulled the fabric aside on one wall and found a door. Two other doors were hidden behind the other hangings. She could hear the clang of pots and pans behind the door on the right, and the center door was most likely the entrance to the formal rooms. She hoped the door on the left would lead to the bedrooms and other private rooms. That was where she thought she'd find Devra.

She slipped through that door into a smaller hallway. From behind another door on the right, she could hear the tinny sound of studio audience laughter. She opened it a crack. A TV glowed blue in the dimly lit room. A game show was on the screen, and a dark figure lay on a chaise in front of it.

Leigh came through and pushed the door shut, and as Devra's gaze swung her way, she pulled off her head covering.

Devra's eyes flared wide. She struggled to pull herself to her feet. "Leigh! What are—?"

Leigh put a finger to her lips. Devra wore a loose caftan that didn't disguise how much weight she'd lost since their last meeting. Her cheeks were hollow, and dark circles hung under her eyes. "I can get you out of here," Leigh whispered. "There's a car waiting outside and I've booked a hotel room for you. The question is: Is that what you want to do?"

Devra stared at her. This was the real moment of truth. When she cried *Help me, please help me! I want to leave!*—was it a momentary impulse that she'd thought better of since? It was the basic question that almost every client of Leigh's faced. Did she really want to leave the known world for the unknown? Could she face the uncertainty of a new life on her own?

Devra pressed her hands to her gaunt cheeks. "Yes!" she cried. "I do!"

Leigh stripped off the burka. Under it she wore an orange dress identical to Lindy's, albeit two sizes up. In the tote bag was a blond wig and a cobalt blue scarf, and she put them on and handed the burka to Devra. "Put this on." She looked at her watch as Devra pulled the garment on over her caftan. "You have five minutes to pack, but you can only take as much as you can fit in this tote."

"There is nothing here I want."

They crept out to the foyer. The elevator had returned to the ground floor, and they had to wait frozen and silent until it rose to the third floor again. They hurried on and Leigh lunged to press the button and close the doors. She put on a pair of oversize sunglasses as the elevator descended to the first floor.

"Walk slowly," she whispered as they stepped off, and Devra matched her pace to hers as they approached the reception desk. The attaché named Fadi glanced up from his screen. "Have a pleasant evening," he said, and Leigh waggled her fingers in farewell. Devra nodded and clutched the tote tight.

A few embassy staffers were departing for the day and heading for their cars in the parking lot. They nodded greetings to Leigh and Devra as they passed, and one of them stared a moment at Leigh's orange dress, but no one paid any particular attention to Devra as they walked to the Mini Cooper and got in.

Leigh checked her watch one more time before she started the engine. It was five forty-five, and by the time she looped around the circle drive, the FedEx truck was at the gate, as it was every day at this time. The guard was huddled with the driver, checking the list of packages and envelopes against his clipboard, and Leigh drove around them and out into the street.

They traveled two blocks before Devra let out her breath. It whooshed like a gust in a wind tunnel inside her headdress. "No one follows?"

Leigh glanced up at the mirror. "Not yet. But just in case—" She pulled over to the curb behind the blue minivan as John jumped out from the driver's side and opened the passenger door for them.

"Who is that?" Devra cried in alarm.

"A friend," Leigh assured her. "A very good friend."

An hour later Devra was settled into a luxury suite in a hotel five miles away. The room was booked under an alias, as if she were a movie star, and the staff had already been briefed on the protocols for their guest's privacy. Her meals would be delivered to her room along with anything else she might desire. She wasn't to contact anyone other than the hotel manager, the concierge, or Leigh herself; whatever she needed would be routed through one of them.

The suite was exquisite. Nearly two thousand square feet in tasteful tones of celadon and robin's egg blue, with two bedrooms, a living room, separate dining room, and full kitchen, all with panoramic views of the Tidal Basin. A golden cage, but still a cage, Leigh thought grimly, no better than her quarters at the embassy or her harem at home. But at least now the countdown clock could start on her divorce proceedings. Six months from today, Leigh could file the petition, and the cage door could begin to open. Assuming Devra could hold out that long. Not to mention the $100,000 retainer that was paying for all this.

The chief concierge arrived with the room service waiter and a dinner cart. Her name was Simone, and her hair was lacquered and her nails polished to a high sheen so that she gleamed like a fine automobile. She would see to Devra's day-to-day needs for as long as she was in residence. They reviewed the details of those needs while Devra picked at her meal and stared out the floor-to-ceiling windows. Ten stories down people were enjoying a bustling nightlife, but they looked tiny and artificial from up here, like CGI figures in a battlefield epic.

"I hope this is all to your satisfaction," Leigh said when it was time to take her leave. "If anything isn't what you want, please tell me."

Devra seemed dazed by all that had transpired in the last several hours. "I didn't know enough to want this," she said. "Any of this. It's like a dream."

"Take your time. Get some rest. We'll talk in a few days about where we go from here."

John was waiting outside, and when Leigh emerged from the hotel lobby, he flicked a cigarette into the gutter and opened the door of the minivan for her. "Everything go okay?"

"Perfectly."

"What floor's she on? I'll go up and do some recon."

"Oh, John, you've done enough already. More than enough."

"You sure? I don't mind."

"No, it's fine, really." She sank into the seat with a sigh. It had been a long day, but the hard part was over now. "John, seriously—what can I do to thank you?" she asked as they pulled out from the curb. "Besides handling your own case for free."

"You mean it?"

"Of course. Have you had any luck yet?"

"Hmm?" He was distracted by a traffic snarl in front of the Washington Monument.

"With Bryce's school records."

"Oh. Right. No, I hit a brick wall. I'll have to figure something else out. But at least we had a good day today, didn't we?"

"We sure did."

He merged onto Seventeenth Street, and she settled in for the ride, relaxed and happy with the satisfaction of a job well done. It was the best she'd felt since—she didn't know how long.

No, she knew. It was he best she'd felt since then.

Chapter Thirty-Nine

Pete got another email from Duke that week, this one inviting him to a southern-style barbecue at the Gazebo Quad during parent-family orientation week. All summer he'd been getting news and announcements and reassurances for parents, and now that August was here, the emails were coming in fast and furious. Kip had to be getting his own emails, too, but he never mentioned them. He must have received his roommate assignment by now, too, but he didn't mention that either. When the twins started college, they had most of their gear packed by this date. They'd had long conversations with each of their prospective roommates and made almost daily runs to Bed, Bath and Beyond for plastic storage cubes and beds-in-a-bag and unauthorized minifridges. So far Kip hadn't even opened a duffel.

But he was still *In*. The admissions office either didn't know or didn't care about the manslaughter charge, and they hadn't yanked his grant money either. It was right there as a deduct on the first-semester tuition bill. A bill that Pete didn't plan to pay until after the due date. Not because he was running behind on all his bills, though he was, and not because he'd have an easier time paying it with the bail refund he'd receive after Kip's case was closed, although that was also true. No, he was delaying payment for the same reason Kip hadn't gone out sheet-shopping. Because

Duke might not happen. And to his shame, Pete had done the calculations: it would be cheaper for him to pay the point-and-a-half late fee on
the tuition bill if Kip was acquitted than to wait for a refund and lose the
time-value of his money if he wasn't.

He wasn't sure what Kip's calculations were. Whether he was scared
or resigned or too paralyzed to think. Though *paralyzed* wasn't the right
word. Lately he'd been working like a demon around the job site. That
morning he helped the painters tape up their plastic sheets and spread
their drop cloths, and now he was out digging holes with the landscapers.
Pete didn't tell him to do either one, and he wouldn't have, anyway. Those
were both fixed-price subcontracts, so Kip's free labor wasn't saving him
a dime. It must have been saving Kip, though, from having to think too
much about what was coming after August 10.

What was coming now, on August 3, was Shelby Randolph in her
black BMW. The driveway was blocked with half a dozen trucks, so she
parked down on the road and picked her way through the gravel in her
lethal-looking heels. Kip's spine snapped up like a rubber band when he
saw her. He dropped his shovel and trudged up the hill in a parallel path
to Shelby's. "I'll go wash up," he said to Pete at the door and brushed past
him into the house.

The paint fumes were too strong for an indoor meeting. Pete showed
Shelby to the makeshift table on the terrace—a plywood sheet over
sawhorses—where the men ate lunch and took their coffee breaks. It was
set up under the pergola, and the sun shone through the slats and laid di-
agonal stripes across the striated surface of the plywood. Shelby sat down
and swung her legs under the table.

"You met with the new prosecutor?" Until last week a middle-aged
woman named Andrea Briggs was running the case. Now some kid named
Seth Rodell was in charge. That was good news, Pete had thought, a down-
grade, until Shelby quietly shook her head. Andrea had been bumped
down to second chair. Rodell was the rising star.

"Let's wait for Kip, shall we?" she said now.

Right. Kip was the client. Her adult client. This little fiction they
maintained.

She swept her gaze over the rear elevation of the house across the bluestone patio, past the pool, and up to the windowpanes winking in the sunlight. "Place looks good," she said.

"Have you seen Leigh?"

She kept her eyes on the house. "I'm not going to talk to you about Leigh, Pete."

"I only want to know if she's okay."

"Of course she's not okay. Her daughter died and her husband left her."

His fists clenched under the table. "You know that's not the whole—"

"Of course I know. When she asks if you're okay, I say *No, his son got arrested and his wife kicked him out.* Both statements are true, but it doesn't solve a damn thing. So I have nothing more to say on the subject, okay?"

"Okay," Pete said, stung.

"Look," she said. "It's an impossible situation. For both of you, but also for me. She's my best friend. I should have been beside her, helping her get through these few last months. But Kip's my client, and I had to be there for him, too, and it turned out I couldn't do both. I should have withdrawn when he changed his story about who was driving, but I didn't realize how bad things were going to get."

"Nobody did."

"In any case, it's too late now. There's nothing to do but get through it."

Get through it. She made it sound like crawling through a tunnel and coming out into sunshine on the other side, and maybe that would be true for her. When this case was over, her life would revert to normal. Back to her glamorous life and her billion-dollar cases in the city. But Kip's tunnel might come out somewhere even darker.

He came out of the house with his arms scrubbed up to his elbows. Droplets sprayed off his hair like a dog giving himself a shake. "Hey," he panted as he sat down next to Pete on the bench seat. "'Sup?"

"I had a meeting with the prosecutor today," Shelby said. "He's put an expiration date on their plea offer. We have until Thursday nine a.m. to say yea or nay."

"Why so soon?" Pete thought the offer would be good until the minute before the jury returned a verdict.

She shrugged. "The usual. He doesn't want to prepare for trial if he doesn't have to."

Everything was usual for Shelby. She couldn't appreciate how unusual this experience was for anyone else. To have to decide in three days—less—whether your kid goes away for a guaranteed two years or rolls the dice and risks five times as long. To have to decide if you were going to let him go away under any circumstances. Take off for Canada and both become felons.

"We exchanged exhibits and witness statements today. There were no surprises. So let me preview exactly what their case will consist of." She picked up her notes. "First they'll put on the neighbor who called nine-one-one. We know what he's going to say. Next up will be the arresting officer, Denise Mateo. Then your two friends from the party. Then the ER doctor to testify about Chrissy's condition when she arrived and about Kip's statement that she hit her head. Finally, the neurosurgeon to establish the nature of the injury and to offer his opinion as to the cause of death." She looked up from her notes. "That's a capsule of the prosecution case."

"What about Leigh?" Pete said. "Her name's on their witness list."

"Yes, but apparently they're not calling her."

"Really?" He wondered what that could mean.

"I'll cross the government's witnesses, of course, and hammer away on reasonable doubt. Then for the defense case—Pete, you'll testify first, paint a picture for the jury of Kip and his accomplishments and all his prospects. Then I'll call Dr. Rabin to testify about all of the other possible causes of the aneurysm." She paused. "Then we rest."

"Wait." Kip's eyes darted from Pete to Shelby. "What about me?"

He had a streak of dirt behind his ear, Pete noticed. It was the spot he routinely missed as a little boy. They were always sending him back to the sink for another go before dinner.

"We can't put you on the stand, Kip. You saw what happened during our practice run. If you don't testify, the only picture the jury gets of you is that nice-looking boy at the defense table with the proud parents sitting behind him. Evidence of your previous arrest and all those other incidents will be inadmissible. This will look like the first time you ever got into trouble. You cooperated with Officer Mateo, and you were helpful to the ER doc. That's all the jury ever has to know about you."

"But—but then how will they know I wasn't driving?"

Shelby folded her hands on her notes. "I'm sorry, Kip. We have to abandon that line of defense. The neighbor will testify that you were behind the wheel when he looked out, and the cops will testify that neither you nor Chrissy ever said anything different. We never found a corroborating witness, which means we only have your word for it. Your inconsistent word. Putting you on the stand will do far more harm than good."

"It's my decision, though." Kip looked from Shelby to Pete. "I mean, I'm the client."

Pete's eyes met hers. How long were they going to play out this pretense? Duke was emailing suggestions to parents on how to guide their children through homesickness, and somehow they were supposed to maintain this facade that Kip was an adult who could make these life-changing decisions all on his own?

"You have the right to testify, certainly," she said. "But I strongly advise against it."

Kip traced a finger along the stripes of light that lay across the plywood. "What if we found that witness? Would it be too late?"

Pete shot him a look. "What are you talking about?"

Kip didn't answer. His eyes were on Shelby, who replied cautiously. "The judge could allow us to amend our witness list. Depending on the circumstances that caused the delay."

He nodded. "So what about the security footage from next door?"

"What about it?" Pete said with a snap of impatience in his voice. They'd run this down and ruled it out weeks ago.

"Oh, about that." Shelby shuffled some papers. "Frank finally dug up the owner of that place. She lives in England. A woman named Deidre Cookson."

Pete remembered the woman in the Uber car. "I think I saw her. A ritzy-looking blonde in her fifties?"

"Sounds right. We sent her a polite request, which she politely ignored."

"So subpoena her already," Kip said.

"Serving a subpoena overseas is expensive and takes forever. We'd never get it done before trial. Besides—" She looked to Pete. "The cameras don't cover the road. Didn't we already confirm that?"

Kip jumped up from the table. "Wait here, okay? I'll be right back."

He ran for the house, and Shelby turned an irritated face on Pete. "What's this about?"

"You got me."

They watched the door Kip disappeared into until he appeared out of it again. He loped back to the table carrying his laptop.

Pete sat up straight. "You picked out the priest? From the mug shots?"

"No." Kip wore an expression Pete had never seen on him before. One part shit-eating slyness, three parts hope. "But I got his car." He flipped open the computer lid. "We can enhance it and get the license plate, then we got him." He touched the trackpad and lit up the screen.

"What do you mean, you got the car?"

Kip held up a flash of silver. A thumb drive. "It's the security video." He nodded toward the Hermitage. "From next door."

"What?" Pete and Shelby spoke at the same time, but she had razors in her voice.

"I got the video feed from that night and just before midnight there's the car. I knew it as soon as I saw it." He inserted the thumb drive into the slot and a grainy video began to play on the monitor. "You can send it to one of those labs, and we'll be able to ID the driver. Then you can add the driver to the witness list and subpoena him or whatever, and it'll be over." He pulled his eyes from the screen and looked from Pete to Shelby. Now his expression was one part smug satisfaction and three parts hope. "Right?"

Shelby reached across the table and slammed the laptop lid shut. "How'd you get this?"

Pete stared at him. "Did you—that day I caught you—did you break in?"

Kip shook his head. "I thought I might have to. I kept getting timed out on the server before the password generator finished running. But last night I finally cracked it."

"You mean, hacked it." Shelby's eyes shone like a laser freeze ray across the table.

"What?" Pete pushed back from the table so violently the plywood sheet rocked on the sawhorses. "Jesus!"

"You hacked into a private CCTV system."

Kip stuck out his chin. "It's not like you were getting anywhere your way."

"My way was the only way it would be admissible," she said. "I can't put on evidence that was obtained through criminal activity, and even if I could, we don't have a witness to authenticate it."

"You don't need to play the video in court. Just use it to ID the driver of the car."

"You think it won't come out how we found him? The evidence will be thrown out, you'll be charged with cybercrimes on top of everything else, and I'll be dragged up on disciplinary charges."

Kip squirmed. "At least watch it. Then decide."

"No. No." Shelby stood to her full looming height. "Even watching it makes me complicit in your crime." She looked down at Pete. "The same goes for you. Destroy the files and hope no one ever finds out. Agreed?"

Pete gave a curt nod as Kip clenched his jaw and looked away.

She closed her briefcase. "Think about the plea offer. We'll talk tomorrow."

They watched her pick her way down the driveway. When she passed out of sight, Kip turned pleading eyes on Pete. "Dad, I had to try. I couldn't just do nothing."

Pete didn't move.

"Dad—"

"Quiet." He waited until he heard the growl of the BMW engine before he stood up. "Give me that thing," he said and grabbed the laptop off the table.

"Dad! No—come on!"

Pete went inside and downstairs to the basement. Angelo and his crew were setting the tile along the coping of the lap pool. Pete turned the other way into the media room and shut the door. The reclining theater seats weren't installed yet, but all the electronics were in. He set the laptop on the console and ran the connections, and the video lit up the jumbo-size screen on the end wall of the room.

Kip was at his side by then. "Thanks, Dad," he said in a voice full of feeling.

"Shut up. You were stupid and reckless and I told you—"

"I had to do it." He reached for the keyboard. "Finding this guy's my only chance."

"This better be worth it."

Pete dimmed the ceiling lights and Kip hit a button on the laptop and four different videos started to play in a quadrant of split images on the screen. It took Pete a minute to make out what he was seeing. The images were washed in an eerie greenish light—the cameras must have been equipped with infrared night vision—but all they showed were the bushes and trees outside the Hermitage walls.

"The cameras don't point at the road," Kip said. "Frank was right about that."

"Then what am I even looking at?"

"You know that dirt road that loops around from the Glue Factory?"

Pete looked at him blankly until he remembered his stupid joke name for Golden Oldies Farm. "Yeah?"

"It comes out on the far side of the Hermitage. Watch."

Kip hit another button. The split-screen disappeared and a single video played across the jumbo screen. He hit another button and the footage blipped and blurred. "Hold on," he said, freezing it. Then, "There. You see it?"

Pete walked closer to the screen. He couldn't see anything but grass and trees and a date and time-stamp at the bottom. Then something moved at the top of the screen—a vehicle materialized in the pear-colored light of the night-vision filter. It was coming out of the conservancy woods up on the hill. A Jeep Wrangler, he pegged it. It could have been blue or green in that strange light but was probably black. It drove slowly down the dirt track until it disappeared out of the frame at the bottom of the screen.

"Play it again."

Behind him Kip hit another button.

It was a Wrangler, Pete confirmed on the second viewing, with the four-door upgrade, and it was driving with its headlights off. "Again," he said.

On the third viewing he saw that there was no license plate mounted on the front of the Jeep. Virginia required plates front and back. Maryland and the District, too. "You got it from any other angles?"

"Yeah. Hold on."

One other camera picked up the Jeep that night, but it didn't show the rear bumper either. "There's no license plate," Pete said. "There's nothing to enhance."

"Wait. Watch this." Kip froze on a single frame. "See the driver?"

Pete squinted hard. He couldn't make out anything but a black shadow behind the wheel. "Can you lighten it up?"

"No, but look at that flash of white. Right where his throat would be. That's the priest collar I saw."

"That could be anything."

"It's him. I know it. He came out and turned left and drove down Hollow Road to where we went in the ditch."

"This tractor road. It doesn't go anywhere but around to the Dietrichs' place."

"Right."

"So why would he take the back way out of the Dietrichs' only to turn left and drive right past their front gates? If he was going that way anyway, he would've gone out their front drive."

"It's him. I know it is."

"A priest wouldn't be driving a back road at midnight with his lights off. It's probably just some kids going up to the woods to smoke dope."

"Dad, I swear it's the priest's car. I'd know it anywhere."

Pete let out a heavy breath as he turned from the screen. "Except in a photo array."

"Huh?"

"That binder Frank put together? It had a photo of this same car, the same model, and you didn't recognize it then."

"Was it the same? I don't remember—"

"I do. And I remember Frank already canvassed the Dietrichs, and they didn't have any visitors that night." He reached to switch off the video player and the screen went dark. The whole room went dark. "Why would they lie about that?"

"Why would I?!"

That was the question. Why would he make up a witness who would never be found? Why point out a car that couldn't be traced? Maybe for that exact reason, Pete couldn't help thinking. It was like running a long con. If you told a lie that made no sense to tell, nobody would think it was a lie. Pete felt for the thumb drive and pulled it out of the port and dropped it in his pocket. "You risked your neck for nothing. This is just another dead end."

He tramped upstairs. The paving contractor had arrived to pour the base for the driveway, and he had to round up everybody to move their trucks so they could get to work.

Chapter Forty

Dialing for Devra became *dialing Devra* in the days following her extraction from the embassy. Leigh's first call every morning was to the new prepaid cell phone she gave her. In order to avoid eavesdropping or any other security breaches on the hotel switchboard, she'd removed all other phones from the suite. She was concerned, too, that Devra might reach out to some old friend in Qatar who turned out to be a better friend to the sheikh. The burner phone was insurance against any such call being traced.

Devra's dazed relief the night of her escape had already given way to bored restlessness and was sinking fast into loneliness. "I'm fine, everything's fine," she always said. "I simply don't know what to do with myself all day."

"Well, what did you do when you were living at the embassy?"

She sighed. "I never knew what to do with myself there either."

Leigh arranged for books and DVDs to be delivered to her suite, and the concierge took tea with her every day, but it wasn't enough. Her friends were all in Qatar, the one place she could never return to. She knew no one in this country except her lawyer and her personal shopper. Speaking of which, there were some clothes she needed. Would it be all right if she called Ashley at Saks?

"That's too risky. Tell me what you need."

The list was lengthy—she'd obviously come to regret leaving the embassy with nothing.

"Tell you what," Leigh said. "I'll get this order in and deliver it to you myself."

"And stay for a visit, I hope?"

"I'd love to."

She missed a call while she was speaking with Devra, and a message was waiting in her voicemail box. It was Stephen. Regretfully he'd have to cancel their session this Saturday. Andy's foundation had just released some important new data, and he was scheduled to appear on a radio program to discuss it.

It was the first she'd heard from him since the encounter with his ex-wife in his driveway. They still hadn't had that difficult conversation about Claire, and when Leigh's return call went straight to voicemail, she couldn't help wondering if he was avoiding her. She wouldn't blame him. Some subjects were open wounds: the instinct was to wrap them in layers of bandages even when exposure to the air was what they needed to heal. She did a quick Google search for the radio program he was scheduled for and put it on her calendar. If she couldn't talk to him on Saturday, at least she'd be able to listen to him.

Her next call was to Saks.

"Ms. Huyett!" Ashley said in a horrified whisper. "Has something happened to the sheikha? Those men were just here. That bodyguard and two other men, too. They wanted to know if I've heard from her."

Leigh was dismayed but not surprised. After everything the sheikh did to impede Devra's efforts even to consult a divorce lawyer, he wasn't going to take her desertion lying down. "She's decided to leave her husband," she said. "She's living in seclusion for the present."

"Oh! I hope I didn't say the wrong thing. I told them to call you."

An image flashed behind her eyes, of the gun in Hassan's hand pointed straight at her through the embassy gates. She shook it off. "That's fine," she said. After all, the ambassador already knew who she was. He knew where she lived and worked. If he wanted to intimidate her, he would have done it already. "Now—there're a few things the sheikha needs." She read off Devra's shopping list: fine silk lingerie, luncheon suits, cocktail dresses. Devra knew only one way to dress, even if it was only for herself. Her life in a golden cage.

Leigh had a committee luncheon that day, and when she returned to the office, the receptionist called to her across the lobby. "Ms. Huyett? You have a visitor."

She tensed as she turned to scan the half-dozen people in the waiting room, but Hassan wasn't among them. "Who?"

The receptionist pointed discreetly to a woman in a beige suit on the couch by the windows. It was the prosecutor Andrea Briggs, and Leigh's tension turned to nausea.

"Oh, Ms. Huyett." The woman tried to shoot to her feet, but the backs of her legs stuck to the leather upholstery, and she had to heave herself to get free. Her hair was damp with perspiration and her suit was wilted. "Forgive me for coming unannounced." Her flustered hands tried to smooth out the creases in her skirt. "I was in the neighborhood and thought I'd stop by for a chat."

She worked in Hampshire County. She wouldn't have been *in the neighborhood* of K Street. She deliberately came here unannounced, to ambush her. "Chat about what?"

"Your daughter's case. You know we start trial on Monday."

"My daughter doesn't have a case," Leigh said in a voice as chilly as the air-conditioning. "You mean Kip's."

"I think of it as hers. I like to think of myself as speaking for the victim."

Leigh didn't want her to speak at all, and certainly not here in front of other waiting visitors. "Come this way," she said.

She led her into one of the small caucus rooms that opened off the reception area. The woman seemed to wilt even more under the harsh fluorescent panels in the ceiling. She must have taken the Metro in and walked three sweltering city blocks to Leigh's office. She dropped heavily into a chair at the small round table. "I'm hoping I can persuade you to reconsider testifying at trial."

Leigh was exasperated. "Why are you even taking this to trial? Offer him a plea and be done with it."

"Oh, we have. He refused it."

"Oh." She sat down then, too. "What was the offer?"

"Two years."

That didn't sound so bad. Peter should have grabbed it and saved them all this misery. "Any strings attached?"

"The usual. He'll have to stay sober and check in regularly with his parole officer."

"His probation officer, you mean."

"No." The woman looked confused. "His parole officer. After he gets out."

"Out?" Leigh repeated. Then her eyes flared wide. "Out of *prison*?"

"Well—yes."

"Oh, my God!" She shot to her feet again. "You mean two years *in prison*?"

The woman blinked under the severe light. "The statute authorizes up to ten years. Two years is reasonable for a drunk driving homicide."

"Kip was barely drunk! He swerved to miss a dog!"

"There's no evidence of that. Beyond his own word, and we all know what a liar he is."

Leigh flushed hot. *How dare you*, she almost said before she bit back the words. She was losing her direction in this conversation.

The woman sensed her vacillation and leaned in to press her point. "Please reconsider. Testify for the Commonwealth. We need someone to tell the jury about Chrissy. Describe who she was and what she was like."

Tell me about Chrissy. If she couldn't do it for Stephen, she certainly couldn't do it for a courtroom full of strangers. "Exactly what are you trying to accomplish here?"

The prosecutor folded her hands on the table. "It's important to put a face to the victim."

Chrissy had her own face. A bright, shining, beautiful face. Leigh's grief-ravaged face was no stand-in for hers. "I mean, what are you trying to accomplish by seeking jail time for Kip?"

"Justice for Chrissy."

"Putting Kip in jail is the last thing she'd want."

She didn't think the words until she spoke them, but their truth hit her so hard it was like the caucus room ceiling crashed down on her. Not in a million years would Chrissy want to see Kip go to prison. She'd fight like a hellcat to stop it. Whether he was driving or not driving or lying or not lying—it wouldn't matter. Chrissy would fight to save him.

Tears thickened in her throat. She couldn't stay another second in this tiny room. She flung the door open. "I'm sorry. I can't help you."

"Ms. Huyett," Andrea called after her. "Please. Just think about it."

Leigh hurried past the elevator to the stairwell, and once in her office she closed the door. Behind her was the credenza displaying its array of family photographs, but she couldn't bear to face them. Prison. Two years in prison. Now she understood why Peter was fighting so hard for Kip. Now she even understood why Kip was lying. Maybe his lie harmed her, but—my God!—he had to protect himself.

She picked up the phone. "I just had a visit from Andrea Briggs," she said when Shelby came on the line. "She told me about the plea offer. Two years?"

"I can't discuss this with you, Leigh."

"When was prison even on the table? You told me suspended sentence and probation!"

"I told you probably. It's what we all thought."

"You have to do something!"

"Besides defend him to the best of my ability? What do you think I'm doing here?"

She put her head in her hand. "I know. I'm sorry. It's just—there has to be something you can do—"

"Well—" Shelby's tone was suddenly wheedling. "There's something *you* could do."

"What?"

"Testify for the defense."

"Me? What could I possibly say?"

"Tell the jury about Kip. Tell them that he graduated at the top of his class. He won the history medal. He played Hamlet. He raised money for that horse farm and redesigned their website. Stories that show the kind of kid he is."

"Can't Peter testify to that?"

"Better from you, don't you think?"

Probably so, Leigh had to concede. She understood Kip better than Peter did, better than any of them. Of the whole Gang of Four, she was the only one who got him.

But Shelby meant something else entirely. "You can say something Pete can't say."

"What?"

"That you don't blame Kip for your daughter's death."

Leigh fell silent. Slowly she spun her chair to face the photographs on the credenza. *I know it wasn't his fault*, she'd told Peter and Stephen and everybody. *I don't blame him.* But was that a lie? "I don't . . ." Her voice faded.

"Think about it. Even if you don't want to testify, if you'd just sit next to Pete in the courtroom, if I could point you out to the jury in my opening. That would help."

The faces in the photos blurred as the tears burned in her eyes. "I don't think Peter would want me there."

Shelby snorted. "Think again."

She thought about it the rest of the day—the idea of walking into that courtroom and slipping into the seat beside Peter as if she belonged there. But all she could really think about was what Peter must be thinking. He must think she'd known all along that Kip was facing real jail time. He must think she was willing to stand by and let it happen. Maybe he even thought that she'd urged for it to happen.

Shelby was wrong. Peter would shrink away from her if she sat down beside him in the courtroom. That was what the jury would see. A broken marriage. A family fractured beyond repair.

Chapter Forty-One

Wednesday, end of the day. Only fifteen hours left on Pete's countdown clock. Shelby was standing by for their call; the prosecutor was standing by for hers. Talk it over, she told them, but they hadn't. They hadn't talked at all, about anything. Ever since Pete shot down the surveillance video, Kip was giving him the silent treatment. Once Pete wouldn't have stood for that, but all the old rules were out the window now. When your kid's on trial for homicide, a sullen attitude hardly seems worth correcting.

"Pizza sound good?" Pete called as he headed out that night.

Kip kept on shoveling mulch into a wheelbarrow and didn't answer. The landscapers were gone for the day, but here he was, still at work. Anything to save him from thinking about the plea offer. Anything to save him from talking to his father.

"Okay then," Pete said. "Pizza it is."

He headed down the front lawn, past the newly poured concrete and the yellow tape stretched across the bottom of the driveway. The place looked like a crime scene.

The pizzeria said twenty minutes, and he sat on the bench by the pickup window to wait. A buzz of voices came from the restaurant floor behind him, and sharp cries and irritated demands from the kitchen in front of him, and all around the one-sided conversations of people on their phones. He tuned out all of it. He needed to think, and think hard. The countdown clock was running out. He had only fourteen hours now to make a decision that would determine the rest of his child's life. Take the deal. Roll the dice. Or skip out and head for Canada.

Take the deal. Two years in prison. Roll the dice and go to trial with nothing more than a hired-gun doctor trying to convince the jury that the obvious explanation wasn't the right one. Kip would sit there looking wholesome, his parents behind him would look supportive and proud. Except that Kip would look sullen, Karen would look devastated, and Gary would look resentful at having to be there. Pete would have to look supportive and proud all on his own. He wondered if he could pull it off.

It wasn't enough. Medical testimony that defied common sense and a father who half the time didn't believe his own kid. They were going to lose and Kip would be sentenced to prison and Pete was supposed to stand by and watch it happen. In his whole life he'd never felt so powerless. What kind of man would let this happen to his child?

Door Number Three. Take Kip and run for the border. Find some kind of work that didn't require papers. Construction probably, but he'd settle for line cook in a mining camp if he had to. It wouldn't be the life Kip was meant for, but it sure as hell beat the one he was headed to. Pete started to think through the practicalities, what they needed to pack, where their passports were, currency exchange rates, whether Kevin could wrap up the Miller job on his own. Who he could trust to say good-bye to.

Then he thought of Mia and the geyser-force of the idea shut off like somebody turned a valve. His marriage might be over, but he couldn't leave his little girl, no more than he already had. That meant he'd have to send Kip up there on his own and find some way to sneak money to him across the border. Kip would live like a fugitive for the rest of his life. It might be years before he saw him again.

It was a moment before he realized his phone was ringing. Zack's name was on the screen. "Hey!" he answered, startled and pleased, as he stepped outside to take the call. There'd been some texts and emails back and forth, but this was the first time he'd spoken to either of the twins since the day they were lost at sea.

"Hey, Pete," sounded in two-part harmony; Dylan was on the call, too.

"Where are you? Is everything okay?"

"Bar Harbor. We're in port for a few hours and thought we'd check in," Zack said.

"We know you got that, uh, thing coming up next week," Dylan said. "And we just wanted to say, you know, good luck and everything."

"Thanks," Pete said. "Be nice if you'd say it to Kip."

"Already done. As soon as we hit dry land, we texted him."

Good enough. That was the equivalent of an hour-long face-to-face in their universe. "So how're things up there? Are you having the time of your life?"

"Yeah. The worst time."

"Why? What's wrong?"

"It's been a bad scene, Pete. Dad's drinking too much and fighting with the clients—"

"Then we have to try to smooth things over—"

"These rich people—they're all assholes—"

"And their tips have been lousy!"

"You want to come home? I'll send you the airfare."

"No. Thanks, man—"

"Not that we haven't thought about it—"

"But we decided to tough it out."

"You know why?" Dylan said. "It's funny. We keep hearing Chrissy's voice."

"*You can't just quit!* Remember? She used to say that every time we wanted to quit the team or drop out of chorus or whatever. *You can't just quit!*"

Zack said it with Chrissy's exact intonation, and it made Pete grin to think that it took the memory of their little sister's scolding to motivate two nearly grown men. But she was always one determined little girl. He remembered something else. "That club she started? The antibullying thing? Remember that slogan she came up with?"

They answered him in unison. "*Don't back down. Stand up! Stand up for yourself.*"

They all laughed, but in seconds the laughter trailed off into awkward silence.

"So—you'll be home at the end of the month?"

"Two weeks. We got our cousin's wedding, but we'll hang out after, okay?"

"You bet."

The pizza was boxed and on the counter when he went back inside, and as he drove back to Hollow Road, he thought how much he was going to miss those guys. No child should ever have to have an ex-sibling, and no dad an ex-stepson either. But that was where they were all headed. As bad as a first divorce was, a second divorce had to be even worse. After the first, you were at least still related to the kids you were leaving behind. After the second, there was nothing to tie you together. You were leaving each other for good.

The news was on the radio. Another mass shooting, another lone gunman, this time at a concert hall in Nashville. Pete barely heard it. In thirteen hours they had to call Shelby and tell her yes or no. On Friday he had to wire another fifty grand to the bank, and on Sunday he was supposed to take Mia to Six Flags for the day and he didn't know how he was supposed to manage any of it. How could any man take care of his family in this world? If you couldn't even let them go to a country-western concert, you might as well give up trying.

You can't just quit.

The phrase rang out inside the truck cab as clear as if Chrissy were seated there beside him. *You can't just quit. Don't back down. Stand up for yourself.*

He braked hard and pulled off to the shoulder of the road and sat there a minute with his flashers on and Chrissy's words reverberating in his head. *You can't just quit.*

It was crazy. He couldn't let his eighteen-year-old make this decision on his own but he'd let the words of a fourteen-year-old ghost sway him? But there it was. She was a determined little thing. She could reach him all the way from the grave.

He swung a U-turn and headed back the other way and out to Providence Road and north to Leesburg. Target was still open, and he barreled through the aisles and in twenty minutes filled the cart with almost every item on the college checklist.

It was dark by the time he got back to Hollow House. Kip was there, still at work out front, spreading mulch in the border with a work light strapped to his baseball cap. He did a double-take when his light swept over the heap of bags and boxes in the back. "What's all this?"

"Grab an armful and help me carry them in, would you?"

"Dad—are these *school* supplies?" He swung his head around, and the beam of light swung with it. "What's going on?"

"You're going to trial next week, that's what. And a week after that, you're going to school. So we don't have much time to get ready."

"What are you talking about?"

"I'm talking about saying no to the plea bargain."

"And *lose?*"

"And take our shot. You get up there and tell the jury exactly what happened that night."

His eyes opened wide. "Are you saying—? You believe me?"

Pete nodded. In that moment at least?—yeah, he did. "Who needs corroboration?" He clapped a hand on the boy's shoulder. "You're your own best witness. You can charm the birds out of the trees, and that's what you're going to do at trial. You hear me?"

Kip looked down, and the beam went with him to spill a narrow cone of light on the ground. He wasn't convinced. He didn't think he could do it.

"Come on." Pete squeezed his shoulder. "You can't just quit. Don't back down. Stand up for yourself."

Kip's head came up, his eyes bright with tears. He could hear Chrissy's voice, too. "Yeah," he choked. "I hear you." Then he did something he hadn't done for years, at least not without groans and eye rolls. He hugged his father.

Chapter Forty-Two

The following Saturday Leigh was halfway to the District with a trunk full of designer clothes from Saks when Hunter Beck's voice came on the radio. It was yet another replay of his press conference yesterday pleading for the safe return of his wife and offering a million-dollar reward for any information, *anything at all,* that might help him find her. For twenty-four hours the airwaves had been flooded with this audio clip, and already the full-length video had gone viral online. Leigh had watched it twice herself. As before, Hunter held his press conference on the Dietrichs' front porch, but this time Fred and Carrie stood shoulder to shoulder with him, the three of them united in their love and concern for Jenna. "Hunter's a good man," Carrie said when Leigh spoke to her last night. "It's not his fault he's filthy rich. Well, it is," she amended. "But you know what I mean." Tips were already pouring in from all over the country, she said, so many that Hunter had to hire a call center to deal with them all. Admittedly most of the calls were from hoaxers and crazies, but somewhere in all that chaff, there had to be some wheat. She felt certain that they'd either find Jenna or she'd come home on her own.

"She won't be happy," Leigh warned.

Carrie sighed. "I know it. But we have a grandbaby to think of now."

Hunter's sound clip ended and a jaunty announcer came on with the tip line phone number. He sounded like an adman on cable TV. *Supplies are limited. Call now.* In the middle of the third repetition—*Call 1-800*—Leigh's phone chirped with a calendar alert. It was time for Stephen's radio interview, so she switched over to the NPR station.

The first guest was a professor from Berkeley who'd just completed a study on self-defense and guns in the home. He delivered some alarming statistics. People who kept guns in the home were 90 percent more likely to be killed by guns. They were three times more likely to kill themselves, and more than four times more likely to be shot in an assault than an unarmed person was.

Stephen was introduced next, as the director of the Andrew Kendall Research Center on Gun Violence, the sponsor of the Berkeley research. "What conclusions should we draw from Dr. Gordon's work?" the on-air reporter asked him.

"There's one simple, inescapable conclusion," Stephen said. "If you keep a gun in your home, every single member of your household is more likely to be killed by a gun than your neighbors next door who don't keep a gun. Whether by accident, suicide, or homicide, and no matter if it's Grandpa with a shotgun or a toddler with a handgun."

"But what of the argument that the neighbor without a gun is more likely to be killed by stranger violence than the neighbor who's armed?"

"That argument rests on a fallacy. Unfortunately it's the same fallacy that motivates people to keep guns in the first place. The incidence of home invasion or other stranger violence in the home is minuscule. Fewer than five percent of all violent crimes perpetrated by strangers occur in your home."

"And yet—" The reporter's voice changed. She spoke more softly but with a cloying timbre that made Leigh cringe at what she knew was coming. "—your own son Andrew was killed in your home by a stranger."

Stephen was silent, and Leigh's heart clenched at what he must be feeling. But at the same time it swelled with admiration at what he was putting himself through, the private sacrifices he was making for the sake of public good.

"Don't you ever wonder," the reporter prodded him, "whether a gun in your home might have saved your son's life?"

"No," Stephen said at last. "I don't wonder about that at all."

Leigh gave him a little soundless cheer.

Devra opened the door to her hotel suite wearing a simple sleeveless shift that hung loose on her shrunken frame. She looked so gaunt that Leigh wondered if any of the new clothes she'd brought were going to fit her. The table by the window across the room was spread with the fixings of an elaborate brunch, but the food had barely been touched. The TV was on in the media room, and it sounded like it was tuned to one of the home shopping channels. Spokesmodels hawking cheap trinkets and curios Devra would never want. All she wanted was the echo of their bright chirpy voices.

"Oh, thank you," she said when Leigh presented the boxes and shopping bags, but Devra was listless as she led her into the bedroom to unpack them. She pulled out a peach silk camisole, a black satin nightgown, and when she picked up the silver cocktail dress, she dropped it on the bed with a weak laugh. "What was I thinking? I don't need any of these clothes here."

"Devra, if you're having second thoughts—"

"About the divorce? Never."

"About your living arrangements, then."

With a shrug she wandered back to the living room and stood a moment, gazing out the floor-to-ceiling window. Down below a thousand summer tourists thronged the shoreline of the Tidal Basin and the steps of the Jefferson Memorial. "I confess I do feel a bit lonely sometimes. But Simone is very kind, and you've been wonderful, of course." She pressed her fingers to the glass and watched her ghostly prints appear. "All my life," she said softly, "I've lived behind walls. My father's compound. My husband's palace. The embassy. Even our country home here. When he first showed me the photos of the estate, I thought how wonderful it would be. All that open countryside all around. I imagined taking long walks down the lane or through the woods at the back of the property or just looking out the window at an unimpeded view. But before we spent even our first weekend there, my husband had walls erected around that house, too. There were no long walks. There were no views."

Leigh looked at her sharply. "Are you talking about your weekend home in Virginia?" She leaned forward. "In Hampshire County?"

"Yes. Our *getaway*." Devra let out a bitter laugh. "But I couldn't get away there either."

"This property," Leigh said. "Does it have steel gates and a high brick wall all around it?"

"Like a prison?" Devra didn't turn from the glass. "Just so."

Leigh stayed another hour to drink tea with Devra and sort out the rejects from her Saks order. She left with an armful of garment bags, and on her way out of the hotel, stopped at the front desk in the lobby. The manager was off today, but his assistant took her back to his office to print out the account-to-date. She slipped it in her briefcase and picked up the garment bags and headed for the door.

"Oh, before I forget," he called after her. "One of our room service waiters mentioned that someone asked for your client's suite number last night. He offered him a hundred dollars."

She froze where she was.

"But no harm, no foul," the man said with a smile and a shrug. "He wasn't your client's waiter, and he didn't know who the guy was talking about."

The garment bags slid out of Leigh's arms and puddled on the floor. "Get security," she shouted, already running from the room. "Send them up there. Now!"

Somehow the sheikh had found Devra. Despite all of Leigh's elaborate precautions and cloak-and-dagger maneuvers, he'd found her. She stabbed the call button for the elevator and rushed on when the doors opened. A security guard was already jogging down the corridor when she arrived on the tenth floor, and she stationed him outside the door of the suite while she went in to break the news to Devra.

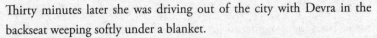

Thirty minutes later she was driving out of the city with Devra in the backseat weeping softly under a blanket.

Later there would be time to track down the room service waiter and get a description of the man who tried to bribe him. For now all she could do was speculate, wildly, about how Devra's location could have been discovered. Leigh hadn't been followed here, she was sure of that. A breach inside the hotel, she thought next. The manager or the concierge could have guessed who Devra was and made an overture to the sheikh. But no, that couldn't be right either, because they would have known her suite number and sold that information to him at the same time. Unless Devra herself was the breach, she couldn't think how she was found out.

Three hours later Devra was booked under a new alias at a golf resort near Charlottesville, with a new hotel manager and concierge sworn to service and secrecy. New security, too: three shifts of bodyguards were scheduled to maintain watch outside her door.

Devra looked around bleakly at her new accommodations. This suite wasn't nearly as large and luxurious as her last one. She went to the window and pushed aside the heavy curtains. The window was only four panes wide, and a parking lot comprised most of the view.

"I'm so sorry," Leigh said.

Devra gazed out at the cars jockeying for spaces in the lot. "This is Virginia, yes?"

"Yes."

"Six months is no longer enough. Here I must be separated for one year before your courts will grant me a divorce."

Leigh came up beside her. In the far distance was the fairway and a cluster of trees that stood like hushed spectators beyond the green. "For no-fault divorce, yes. But you could file immediately on a fault ground."

Devra's bony shoulders sagged. "Such as cruelty."

"Yes."

She pulled the curtains shut and stood a moment, staring at the chintz roses. Then she straightened her spine and turned around. "Do it," she said.

There would be plenty of time later to worry about the requirements for Virginia domicile and the reach of diplomatic immunity. All that mattered now was the petition for divorce. Leigh took out her laptop and drafted it at the tea table in the suite's sitting room. Devra read through it and approved it with a single nod, then Leigh hit a button and it was done— electronically filed with the Hampshire County clerk and officially a matter of public record. But the action wouldn't be joined until the sheikh was served with the petition. She emailed the packet to her process server and also ran off paper copies on the concierge's printer before leaving.

She'd held her anger at a low simmer until then, but it burst into full flame as she started the drive back. By the time she reached St. Alban, it was a white-hot blaze. She burned with anger at His Excellency Faheem bin Jabar, and at Commonwealth's Attorney Boyd Harrison, and at all the faceless tyrants who wielded their power from behind the barricades of their compounds and corner offices while they sent their minions out to do their dirty work. But this tyrant at least would be faceless no more. She knew how to confront him, and now at last, she knew where.

Dusk was falling as she turned onto Hollow Road. She drove past Golden Oldies and the traffic cones blocking the driveway of Hollow House and pulled into the entrance at the Hermitage. As always the gates stood closed. On a brick pillar beside them was a security panel fitted with a speaker and a buzzer, and she leaned out the car window and pressed the buzzer. "It's Leigh Huyett," she shouted. "Let me in."

A flicker of movement caught her eye. A high-mounted camera was rotating her way. She turned her face up and looked straight into the lens. The speaker crackled with the sound of the intercom line opening, but no one spoke.

"You won't get away with this," she said to the camera. "Not anymore. Call your lawyer if you want, but let me in now or I'll call the police. And you won't have immunity here."

The intercom crackled again and shut off.

She sat in the idling car and waited out the silence. The camera was still fixed on her face, but the speaker remained silent. He was pacing in his lair, she imagined, peering at the monitor and barking at Hassan, at Fadi, demanding to know why this barbarian was at his gate. She grew more and more resolute as she waited. She would have it out with the sheikh once and for all. This was America, and he needed to abide by the American rule of law. If he wanted to fight, he needed to do it in court like every other American husband. No more imprisonment, no more witness intimidation, no more espionage.

"This is the end," she said to the camera. "It's over. Do you understand me?"

There was no response. The silence stretched on even longer as the night deepened around her, and a small seed of doubt began to sprout. Could she have made a mistake? Maybe this wasn't the sheikh's country estate. But the compound fit Devra's description exactly, and the proximity explained so much. Lindy Carlson's flower delivery, the prowler sent to watch her from her garden that night. All so easy to accomplish when they were practically neighbors.

She let out a frustrated breath. It was no use. Even if the sheikh was in there, he obviously had no intention of showing himself. The great and powerful Oz would not come out from behind his curtain. She shifted the car into reverse, and that was the moment the gates slid open.

With a start she shifted again and gunned the engine forward before the invisible hand could change its mind. The tires rumbled over the cobblestones into the entry courtyard, and as the gates clanged shut behind her, one of the double front doors of the mansion swung open.

No one came out. The door stood ajar like a spectral invitation.

She hooked her bag over her shoulder and went up the steps. "Hello?" she called in and rapped her knuckles on the door.

No reply. She crossed the threshold. The center hall was the size of a ballroom, two stories tall with a sweeping curved staircase and a black-and-white marble floor like a checkerboard. A crystal chandelier sparkled darkly overhead. No lights were on, and gloom settled like dust in the corners of the cavernous space.

"Hello?" she called again. *Hello hello*, the echo answered. Double doors stood open on either side of the hall, revealing a banquet-size dining room on one side and a drawing room on the other. Both were decorated sumptuously but not in the gilt finishes and heavy silk trappings she saw at the Qatari embassy. These rooms were furnished in classic antebellum style with floral chintzes and Duncan Phyfe case goods. A Virginia plantation in the Jeffersonian model.

No one was in either room, and her annoyance was mounting. Did the sheikh—or Hassan or whoever opened those gates—honestly think he was going to yell boo and scare her away? Or worse? He wasn't on Qatari soil now; he must know he couldn't get away with such strong-arm tactics here. Still—"I've called the police," she yelled. "They're on their way."

A sound came from the back of the house. She followed it past the staircase and through a swinging door to the kitchen. It had the look of an old-time locker room, a long narrow space with plain white wooden cabinets and antique tin hardware. It was a kitchen meant for servants, but where were they? The sheikh's dinner hour was probably approaching. There should have been a cook bustling about to prepare his meal. There should have been a guard outside and a butler at the door.

The sound came again, from behind a door at the far end of kitchen. The hairs rose on the back of her neck. Someone was waiting—breathing—on the other side of that door. Suddenly she was afraid she'd made a mistake of a different kind. If the sheikh didn't respect the rule of law where his wife was concerned, why should he obey it where Leigh was concerned? She should have called in John Stoddard before she attempted this showdown. She would now, she decided, and turned to go.

She stopped as a long shuddering breath sounded from behind that door. "Who's there?" she cried.

No one answered. She walked slowly down the row of cupboards. The door at the end of the room was unlatched, and when she knocked on it, it swung open. Inside was a small windowless space; it might have once been a storeroom or walk-in pantry, but now it served as the security control room. Six video monitors glowed through the dim light, and hunched on a stool watching them was Stephen's wife. Claire Kendall.

Leigh teetered back. "Mrs. Kendall?"

The woman let out another long shaky breath. "He warned me about you. He said you were too clever. That if you ever met me, you would figure out the rest."

"This is—this is your home?"

"My sister's. She lives in England." Her fingers were on the keyboard, and with each dispirited tap of a key, the images on the security monitors flickered and changed. "She invited me to live here after Andy died. She had that wall built and those cameras installed. She said I'd feel safe here. But I don't. I don't think I ever will."

Leigh's eyes adjusted slowly to the gloom. A narrow cot was pushed against one wall, and a table and chair against another. It looked like Claire Kendall was living in this single room.

"He told me to keep away from you, he said I'd give it away, but he was the one, wasn't he? He was never a good liar. I knew someone would hear the truth in his voice one day. And you heard it today, didn't you?"

Leigh's fingers tingled with cold as the realization began to creep through her veins. Claire was talking about Stephen's radio interview. His comments about home invasion and self-defense.

"You wouldn't understand. A strong, independent woman like you. You've probably never been afraid of anything in your life. But I was alone so much after the children were gone. All day and so many nights, too, when he was off on one of his crusades. And you don't know the kind of people he worked with. Thieves and addicts and prostitutes and drug dealers. The kind of people who kill each other over pocket change. He brought that into our lives and then he dragged Andy into it, too. What was I supposed to do, alone in the house with those elements threatening to follow them home?"

Leigh felt sick as she spoke the words. "So you got a gun."

Claire didn't look at her as she slowly nodded. "We had one of our quarrels about it that very night. That's why I was sleeping in the downstairs guest room. You have no idea how terrifying it is to wake in a strange bed in a strange room and have absolutely no idea where you are or what that sound is outside your door."

"It was Andy."

She started to nod again. Her head bowed, but it was as if she didn't have the strength to lift it again to complete the nod. Her chin dropped to her chest.

"It was Stephen's idea to get rid of the gun." Leigh felt numb as she said it. "To tell the police it was a burglary."

The images blipped on the security monitors like a fast-forward montage. Green and grainy shots of Leigh's car in the courtyard. Hollow House up on the hill. The tractor road on the other side of the estate. The entrance by the gates. "Where are the police?" Claire cried as silent tears streamed down her face. She tapped furiously on the keyboard. "Why aren't they here yet?"

"I didn't actually call them. You need to consult with counsel first." Leigh pulled a pen and notepad from her bag and scribbled out a name. "Here." She held out the page. "Here's a Maryland lawyer you should call. He can advise you and liaise with the police there."

Claire didn't reach for it. Both her hands were fixed to the keyboard, her eyes darting from one screen to the next. Leigh placed the paper gently on the counter beside her.

"There!" Claire hit a key and froze the images. "There he is!"

"Who?" Leigh leaned over her shoulder and scanned all six monitors. A figure appeared on one of them, a grainy image of a man. He had something in his hands. A rifle, she thought for a heart-stopping second until she blinked and the image came into focus. It was a broom. It was Kip, sweeping the front walk of Hollow House.

"That poor poor boy."

Leigh backed away. "Is there anyone I can call for you, Mrs. Kendall?"

The woman didn't answer. She was staring at the screen, moaning. "That poor, beautiful boy."

Stephen gave her too much credit. He thought she'd figured it out, and maybe she would have, once, before these last cobwebbed months dulled her faculties. As it was, all she did was stumble on the truth. She was so blind to the facts. Imagining that the Hermitage was Sheikh bin Jabar's country estate when she should have remembered that on the day she first met Stephen, he wasn't driving past the Hermitage—he was driving *out of* the Hermitage. Imagining that when Claire Kendall recognized her as the mother of that sweet girl and that beautiful boy, it was only because Stephen had told her about them or she had seen something on the news. It never occurred to her that she'd actually *seen* them, had watched them for months on the security monitors every time they visited Peter's building site.

Or maybe she never put it together because she didn't want to believe it. Even now she tried to talk herself out of it. In her line of work she dealt in hard facts. She didn't rely on the whispers of intuition. Claire never precisely confessed to anything other than her fearfulness. And Stephen's hesitancy at the final question in his radio interview—*Don't you ever wonder whether a gun in your home might have saved your son's life?*—hardly constituted a confession either.

She went online and reread the newspaper accounts of Andy's death and Stephen's speeches on gun violence and the long-form articles about the foundation. The facts all fit, but they fit with Stephen's proffered explanation, too.

This was none of her business, she told herself. If Stephen were her client, she might have an ethical obligation to pursue the matter, but her duty as an officer of the court didn't require her to report crimes committed by nonclients. If there even was a crime to report.

Chapter Forty-Three

The Saab was parked in front of his cottage on Sunday. She pulled in behind it and sat there as dark clouds bunched up in the sky. It was late afternoon on a muggy August day. A quick tumult of a storm would clear the air and relieve all this pressure. Any moment now Stephen would step out the side door with glasses of iced tea in each hand and some words of gentle reassurance.

But after five minutes, he still didn't appear. She got out and walked around the pebble path to the Snuggery door. She could hear strains of music coming from inside. The notes of a single violin fluttered up the scale, higher and higher, in a piercing melody so beautiful it made her heart hurt. The sound seemed to shimmer in the hot sun like iridescent strings stretched so taut they were in peril of snapping. She recognized the piece. *The Lark Ascending.*

He was there in the Snuggery, reclining low in his easy chair with his eyes closed. He didn't stir as she came through the door. He held a snifter in his palm, and an open bottle of Godet sat on a stack of books on the table beside him.

"I always picture Andy when I listen to this," he said after a moment. His eyes were still closed. "It's as if he's ascending, too. Unbound from this earth. Free."

The orchestra joined in to ride the currents below the violin's flight, and the music swelled to fill the jewel box room.

Leigh cleared her throat. "You talked to Claire?"

"She called, yes."

She took another step into the room. "I was thinking about your lecture that night at the university. About the good lie. I was so self-absorbed that I imagined it was all about Kip. That it was Kip's lie that inspired you."

"It was a subject much on my mind."

"Because of your own lie. You've been struggling to justify it."

He didn't answer.

"Did you succeed? In justifying it."

"That's not my call." He opened his eyes and looked at her across the room. "Have you been to the police?"

"That's not my call."

"Ah. You mean to leave it to Claire."

"Or you. One of you will do the right thing."

He studied the swirl of liquid in his glass. "I believe I already did. I took steps to bring some good out of this tragedy. Thousands of lives will be saved thanks to the work of Andy's foundation." He sat up and leaned forward in his chair. "Sit, won't you?" He lifted the bottle to refill his glass. "Help me finish off this cognac."

"Protects someone, hurts no one. That was your calculation, wasn't it?"

"Not mine—"

"That was how you rationalized it."

"I suppose so. Why put her through that? Andy was gone. The harm was already done."

"Other people were hurt, though."

He looked up. "Who?" He seemed genuinely curious.

"The police department. The taxpayers. All the resources wasted on a wild goose chase to find your fabricated burglar. Any innocent suspects who were hauled in and interrogated. And all your neighbors, who had to live in terror that their house would be next."

He shrugged, dismissing the point more than conceding it.

"Then there's the harm to Claire. Her guilt is tearing her apart."

He took a swallow from the snifter. "The guilt would be there in any case. The truth won't alleviate it. All it would do is add shame and scandal." He cocked his head and gave her a contemplative look. "I hope you'll do that calculation before you go to the police. Weigh the help against the harm. Who would benefit from the truth? No one. But who would it hurt? Claire, of course. And what if the foundation collapses?"

The music came softer now, in a lilting cadence that reminded her of a bird soaring and dipping over a rolling landscape. She pulled a business card from her bag and placed it carefully on the blotter on Stephen's desk. "Here's a lawyer you should call. He's probably the second-best criminal defense lawyer in Montgomery County."

He smiled. "Ah. You gave the best to Claire."

"She's facing a homicide charge. You're only facing accessory charges."

"Neither of us is facing anything. To paraphrase Ben Franklin: so long as we hang together, there's no way we'll hang separately."

She knew that was true. The gun would never be recovered, and what other evidence was there? Nothing but her own testimony about the vague ramblings of a grief-stricken mother. "But she'll confess," she said. "She can't bear it much longer."

"Her sister's on her way as we speak. She's taking her back to London with her on the next flight out."

Leigh's mouth tightened. "Out of the jurisdiction."

"Yes. But don't worry. I'll still be here. Or rather, in Chevy Case. Now that I needn't watch over Claire anymore, I've decided to return to my parish."

"And to the pulpit?"

"That depends on you, doesn't it?"

She was silent, and for a moment so was the music. He held up a finger—wait; wait for it—and the orchestra returned in a lush chorus of strings. She felt the wave building, the volume swelling, the crest beginning to break over her head. "Good-bye, Stephen." She turned away.

"What would you have done, Leigh?" he called after her. "Tell me that. If you'd had the chance to turn Chrissy's death into something meaningful."

She didn't look back. "There's no such thing as a meaningful death. Not for a child." Her voice rang hollow in her ears. "It's always senseless."

He let out a heavy sigh. "Peace be with you, Leigh."

The old familiar refrain came to her—*And also with you*—as she opened the door and stepped out into an eddy of hot, humid air.

The wind whipped the treetops as she drove away, and a mile from home the storm broke. The rain pelted down so hard and fast her wipers couldn't keep up. The water gushed over the windshield, and she drove almost blindly the final hundred yards until she reached the driveway. The garage door rose up, and she rolled in, and abruptly the lion's roar of the downpour switched off, replaced by the steady plops of rainwater dripping off the car onto the concrete floor. She had to cross the breezeway to the back door, and the wind gusted so hard that the rain swept in under the roof and splattered her from head to foot before she could dash inside.

She'd stabled the horses that morning, but she went to the window anyway to check that Romeo hadn't somehow managed to break out. She knelt on the window seat and peered through the glass. The sky was charcoal gray, and the sheets of rainwater slapping against the house were nearly opaque. Lakes were already forming across the patio. Soon they'd join into one big ocean.

A crack of lightning flashed in the eastern sky, and she started the automatic count she taught the children when they were small. One-Mississippi, Two-Miss—

The thunder cracked, and there wasn't time for another Mississippi before a second bolt of lightning streaked the sky. The count died in her brain as the after-flash lit up the patio. A man stood on the other side of the glass.

She pinwheeled off the window seat and lunged for the phone. The man was pressed up against the bay window, huddling under the overhang of the roof. She punched in 911, and it wasn't until the instant before the call connected that she realized it wasn't a man at all.

She dropped the phone and yanked the back door open. "Kip!" she shouted out into the storm. "What are you doing? Get in here!"

He came around to the breezeway but no farther. Water streamed from his shoulders, and his hair dripped down over his face.

"My God, you're drenched!" She pulled him inside and ran to the laundry room for some towels. He was still standing on the threshold when she came back, and she flung a towel over his shoulders and pulled him the rest of the way inside. "What are you thinking, out in weather like this?" She shut the door behind him.

"I didn't know it was going to rain when I headed out."

"Headed out—what? On foot?" She scrubbed the towel over his head and shoulders.

He shrugged.

"Where's your dad?"

"Six Flags. With Mia."

"You walked five miles in the rain?" She draped a second towel around him and turned him to the stairs. "Go get out of those clothes and in the shower before you catch your death. Then get into bed. I'll bring you some hot tea."

He didn't move. "I'm only staying a minute." He pulled the towel off his head and wiped at his face. "I just wanted this chance—" Carefully he hung the towel over a chair back. "I mean, this might be my last chance, and I wanted to say, you know, good-bye or thank you or whatever."

He made her feel cold just standing there. She turned to the stove and picked up the kettle.

"I mean, letting me move in here like you did? You didn't have to do that. You could've told Dad to send me back to my mom. So I just wanted you to know that I'm, you know, grateful. I had a good time here. The best."

She swung the kettle to the faucet and turned on the tap, and the water rang against the hollow metal as loudly as the rain outside. "You remember the first time you came here?" she said after a moment.

"Sure. You had a big cookout, and we played badminton."

"We were all in a flurry that morning. I was busy cooking, and Dylan and Zack were out shoveling up the pasture, and Chrissy kept running up and down the stairs trying on different outfits. *How does this look?* she asked each time, and I always said fine, but she still ran back up to try on something else. Finally I said: *Honey, just wear anything. It doesn't matter.* And she said—remember she was only nine, I couldn't believe it—*I only get one chance to make a first impression.*"

Kip sputtered behind her, more a cough than a laugh.

"I said: *What's the big deal, anyway? It's not like you don't already have two brothers.* And she said: *Yes, but they were here for years before me. This one will be mine from the start.*"

"Like I was a new puppy."

"Exactly." Leigh shut off the tap and put the kettle on the burner. "Like she was going to train you or something."

"She kind of did, though. She made me into a nicer guy. I don't know. A better person."

Leigh put a hand over her mouth to hold back the sob.

"I'm sorry."

"No. No, don't be." She wiped at her eyes. "That's the best thing anyone could say."

"No, I mean—I'm sorry about—everything. I know you can never forgive me, but I had to come here and say it anyway. I'm so sorry, Leigh."

I'm sorry. Now she was supposed to say *I forgive you.* It was like a responsive reading from the Book of Common Prayer. The old familiar refrains engraved in her mind. *The Lord be with you—And also with you. Lift up your hearts—We lift them unto the Lord. I'm sorry—I forgive you.*

"It was an accident, Kip. It wasn't your fault."

"It was." Water dripped from his hair as he shook his head. "It was all my fault. I lied."

Leigh turned from the stove. She could feel her heart tremble in her chest. There. He'd said it at last. It was what she'd been waiting for all these months.

He took the towel off his shoulders and draped it over the chair beside the first one. "So. That's what I came to say." He turned for the door. "I'm gonna take off now."

"You can't go back out in this weather."

He looked back at her, wet and cold and utterly exhausted. "I can't stay either."

"At least let me drive you."

He looked at the floor and nodded.

Five miles took twenty minutes through the teeming rain. Neither of them spoke, although in fairness they really couldn't over the pounding of the rain on the roof and the relentless squeaking of the wipers. The creek along Hollow Road overflowed its banks and surged brown and muddy under all the little driveway bridges along the roadside. A car passed them, and it spewed so much water from its wheels that Leigh had to come to a stop before she could see again to drive.

The driveway at Hollow House was blocked off with traffic cones and tape. She stopped on the road. "I'll jump out here," Kip said.

It was a hundred feet up through gushing rain. "Wait," she said before he could open his door. "At least wrap up a little." She reached for the towel he'd spread on his seatback and pulled it over his head to protect him from the worst of the downpour. "There." She drew the two sides together under his chin. "Now be sure to take a hot shower the minute you get inside."

He nodded and reached for the door handle.

"No, wait," she said again.

He turned and peered out at her from under the shroud of the towel.

She needed to speak the words. *I forgive you.* But her throat was too thick. All she could do was reach for him and hug him tight. For a moment he let her, his body shuddering, before he jerked free and ran up the drive through the teeming rain.

The rain rang on the rooftop and roared inside the car, so loud she didn't hear her phone ring either time. But when she got home she saw that two calls had come in. Andrea Briggs and Shelby Randolph. They both wanted the same thing—her testimony—but with two different spins. Necessarily different, because she played two different roles in this drama. Mother of the victim and stepmother of the accused. Andrea wanted her to tell the jury about Chrissy, and Shelby wanted her to tell the jury about Kip.

She sat on the window seat in the kitchen with her phone in her hand and stared at the rain battering against the glass. Her own reflection stared back. Andrea wanted the jury to know what a truly special girl Chrissy was, and Leigh wanted them to know that, too. She wanted the whole world to know. But she couldn't tell the jury anything of Chrissy's story, not when the ending was so wrong.

But Kip's story—that ending wasn't written yet.

She gazed at the screen on the phone, and the missed calls from Andrea and Shelby. Here was her moment of truth. From the start of this ordeal she'd claimed to herself and everyone else that it was only Kip's lie that upset her. Now he'd confessed the truth, and unless she was lying, too, she had to move past it.

Shelby picked up on the first ring. "Leigh?"

She answered. "Yes."

Chapter Forty-Four

She dreamed of Chrissy that night. It was the grown-up dream again and Chrissy was unloading the dishwasher with her back to the room. Her hair was longer than she'd ever worn it, and the bright crimson curls had turned to strawberry-blond waves. She was tall and slender and there was a supple grace to her movements as she stooped to pluck out the plates and rose on tiptoes to stack them on the shelves. One by one the pieces of flatware slid into their grooves in the drawers and the glasses lined up in the cupboard. "There," Chrissy said and closed the dishwasher door. "All done." And she turned around and smiled at Leigh.

There was a hammering in her head. Someone was trying to break in and steal this moment from her, but she wouldn't let them in. Not while her grown-up daughter was smiling at her. She pushed the pause button and held the image there on the screen of her dream. Chrissy smiled with such love in her eyes, and when she woke, Leigh was smiling, too.

But the hammering didn't stop, and she realized that it wasn't in her dream, it was at the front door. She pulled on her robe and ran downstairs and put her eye to the peephole. A man stood on the front steps dressed all in black. He looked directly at the door and spoke loud enough for his voice to carry through it. "Sorry to disturb you, ma'am."

"John?" She clutched the lapels of her robe together and opened the door. "What time is it?"

"Oh-two-hundred. Sorry. It's an emergency or I would never—"

"What? Is it Devra?" But that couldn't be. John didn't yet know about Devra's escape from Washington.

"No, ma'am." He stepped into the light. His jaw was clenched tight. She'd never seen him look so tense. "It's Jenna Beck, and it's urgent."

"Jenna?" That didn't make any sense either. She'd never involved him in Jenna's case.

"She's in labor, and it looks like she's planning to have the baby on her own. She won't open the door for me, but if you could come with me—"

"Wait. I don't understand. How do you know Jenna?"

"Mr. Beck hired me to keep an eye on her."

"Wait. He knows where she is?"

"Yes, ma'am. For a while now."

"But—" Her head was swirling. "That doesn't make any sense. Just this week he offered a reward to find her."

"That was for her benefit. To get her to come in on her own before the baby was born. I think he was afraid of something like this. I called him, but he won't get down here in time, and anyway she won't open the door for him either." He looked at his watch. "Ma'am, we really need to hurry."

"Well, let me call her parents." She turned to the phone on the hall table.

"I tried them first. They're not home, and they're not answering their mobiles either."

"Oh." She reached for the phone again. "I'll call for an ambulance."

"We already tried that. She said she was fine and sent them away."

"Well, maybe she is fine. You might be mistaken."

"I got an operator on-site with eyes on. He's got four kids. He knows what labor looks like. If you could just get dressed and come with me—we really need to get her to the hospital. If anything happens to her or that baby, Mr. Beck will—well, I don't know what he'll do."

She remembered the viral video of Hunter beside the broken body of his first wife. How he howled his anguish to the streets. "Yes. Yes, of course." She waved John into the house and closed the door. "I'll just be two minutes."

She ran upstairs and grabbed some clothes. How far along was Jenna now? She jammed her feet in a pair of loafers and did the math. Close to forty weeks.

John was standing at attention in the front hall, staring at his watch as she ran down the stairs. "My car's out front," he said and yanked the door open.

She grabbed her bag from the hall table. First babies took the longest, but they also presented the most complications. What was Jenna thinking? She locked the door behind her and followed him to his blue minivan in the driveway.

"Where is she?" she asked as he spun back out on the road.

"In an apartment in Arlington." He turned the wheel with one hand and stuck in his earpiece with the other.

"Arlington!" She'd pictured her holed up in a remote cabin in the Blue Ridge, not living in a near suburb of Washington. "How'd you find her?"

"She got sloppy with one of her credit cards. But Mr. Beck didn't want to spook her. He told us not to approach. Just keep her under surveillance in case she got in trouble." He pressed a button on the electronic dog tags around his neck. "Report."

Leigh watched his face go grim as he listened. "She's pacing," he told her.

"How are you seeing her?"

"Her blinds are open. She's on the thirtieth floor. She thinks nobody can see her, but we've got a surveillance post on the rooftop across the street." He listened again to his operator's report. "Every couple minutes she stops and grips onto something like she can't breathe. Does that sounds like labor?"

She bit her lip with a nod.

"And she put a stack of towels beside her bed. And a pair of scissors."

The silly girl actually intended to deliver the baby by herself. Carrie and Fred needed to know about this. Leigh pulled out her phone. They'd answer if they saw her name, wherever they were, and she'd have them meet her in Arlington. She scrolled to Carrie's number and pressed the call button.

There was nothing but silence in her ear. She frowned at the screen. It showed zero signal bars. That was strange. She never had trouble getting cell service on this road. She pressed the call button again, but again it didn't connect. "No service," she shouted to John.

He pointed to his earpiece. He was listening to his man on the ground. "Roger that," he said. "Maintain position. ETA oh two thirty."

"How are you getting through?"

"Secure radio channel," he said.

Of all the times for cell service to go out. She dropped the phone in her bag and grabbed onto the armrests. The familiar landmarks rippled past as John sped over the dark roads.

In only thirty minutes the dark night gave way to bright lights. A drive that took an hour during Leigh's workday commute took half that time at three in the morning and at the speed John was traveling. He exited the highway and drove a few city blocks to swerve into the entry court of a luxury high-rise building. Leigh recognized it at once. There was a lot of buzz about it when it first opened to residents last year. It was a so-called smart building with high-tech amenities and state-of-the-art security, and it included a ground-level shopping mall, and a rooftop pool and fitness center. Not a bad choice for Jenna's hideaway, she had to admit. Restaurants, a pharmacy, even an urgent care center were all just an elevator ride away.

John parked at the glass-fronted entrance, and a man came loping up to stand at attention beside the driver's door. "Status," John grunted, as if they hadn't been talking on the radio only two minutes before. He swung out with his rucksack over his shoulder.

"Entrance and exit secured," the other man said.

Leigh climbed out and came around to join them.

"Ms. Huyett, this is my operator. Charlie."

Like John this man was dressed all in black and had the same hard body and military bearing, though he was a head shorter and probably a decade younger. The father of four and he couldn't have been more than twenty-three. He spared her a brisk nod as he continued his report. "No movement in the unit. Lights off." There was an Appalachian twang in his voice.

"If she's gone to bed, it must mean the contractions stopped," Leigh said. "It could have been false labor."

"We can't take that chance," John said.

He was afraid of his employer, and she didn't blame him. Still, if Jenna was asleep, she hated to disturb her.

The glass-walled lobby was empty. Leigh would have expected a building like this to have a twenty-four-hour doorman, but instead there was an access control panel by the door with some kind of biometric scanner—fingerprints or eyeballs, she couldn't tell which. Beside it was a video intercom system. She stepped up to the camera and raised her fingers to the keypad. "What's her apartment number?"

"No need," John said and opened the door.

She gaped as he strode into the building. "How—?"

"After you, ma'am," Charlie said.

She let out a little laugh as she went through the door ahead of him. It seemed locks really did fall open for a war hero.

The smart building had a smart elevator system. A computerized call station stood between the banks, but one of the elevators was already open and waiting. John led the way aboard, the doors closed, and the car lifted without a single button having been pushed. In fact, there were no buttons to push.

The doors opened again only seconds later. John led the way, down a hushed corridor with carpeting so thick their footsteps were utterly soundless. He stopped and pointed her to the door at the end of the hallway. "You go on ahead. We'll hang back here."

Leigh continued down the corridor. Mounted to the wall beside Jenna's door were her own biometric access screen and video intercom, similar to but a different brand from the ones at the main entrance. Apparently she'd had her own customized extras installed. Leigh pressed the buzzer under the camera and waited a minute and pressed it again.

The intercom opened, and Jenna's groggy voice came through the speaker. "Leigh? What the fuck?"

"Jenna, open the door. Please."

"How'd you find me?"

"I'm here to help, Jenna. Please, let me in."

The intercom cut out. Leigh pressed her ear to the door, and when she heard the shuffle of feet inside, she turned and gave a nod to the two men crouching out of sight down the hall.

A complicated series of beeps sounded from the other side of the door, and three different dead bolts turned before Jenna opened the door with sleepy eyes and a scowl on her face.

"How do you feel?" Leigh said as she stepped inside. The apartment had a double-height ceiling and a wall of city-view windows, a kitchen tucked off to one side, a bedroom straight ahead.

"Pissed off. What are you doing here?" Jenna wore a cotton sleep shirt stretched thin over a nine-month belly. A silver chain hung from her neck with an oversized pendant that rested heavily against the upper shelf of her abdomen.

"How far apart are your contractions?"

"My—what?"

"Jenna, I know you're in labor. We need to get you to the hospital."

"What are you talking—?" The girl's eyes flared as she looked past her. "Oh, my God!" She clutched at the pendant on her chest. "What did you do?"

"Relax. It'll be all right." Leigh was annoyed to feel the two men crowding into the doorway behind her. They should have waited until she called them. "It's okay," she said soothingly. "We're here to help. This is a friend of—" She looked back again and stopped. Both men were right behind her, and they were wearing black ski masks. "What—?"

John shoved her, and she went stumbling into a glass console table as Jenna shrieked and made a dive for a kitchen drawer. She wrenched at it, but before she could get it open, John grabbed her and lifted her off her feet. He clapped a hand over her mouth. "Get the light," he grunted, and the room went dark.

"John, what are you doing?" Leigh cried. "What's going—?" Something slapped over her mouth, and she felt the sticky grip of duct tape against her lips. Her arms were yanked behind her and her wrists bound together with a strip of something that cut hard into her skin. She didn't understand what was happening. There had to be some mistake.

"Lookit here." It was Charlie's voice, snickering from the kitchen. "A little lady gun."

She gagged against the duct tape when she tried to yell, and she could hear Jenna close by, choking on her own screams. One of the men grabbed her arm and dragged her to the door. It was dark in the corridor now, too. She flailed against whoever was holding her and managed to twist free only to crash to her knees on the thick pile rug. He hauled her back on her feet, and she kicked out blindly, connected with nothing, and fell to her knees again.

"Give it up," John muttered. He dragged her after him until she could clamber to her feet again. She didn't understand what was happening. There had to be some mistake. She chanted the words in her brain as the men bore them down the hall and into the elevator.

Her stomach dropped as they descended. The doors opened again, not on the glass-walled lobby, but on a shadowy space that reeked of garbage. Her feet dragged across a tile floor, through a door, and across the rough scrape of a concrete surface. It was dark outside, too, but she could feel the hot swirl of humid air and hear the roar of traffic a few blocks away. This wasn't the main entrance of the building, it was the service alley in the back, and that wasn't John's minivan she was being forced into, it was a black Jeep.

She landed in a facedown sprawl across the backseat. She aimed a mule kick backward, but he grabbed her legs and bound her ankles together with another set of cable ties and slammed the door behind her. Her fists dug into the small of her back as she scrambled to sit up. On the other side of the car, Jenna was struggling furiously against the younger man. She put one foot on the running board and the other on the door panel and locked her knees to brace herself there. He tried to bend her legs, cautiously, clearly trying not to hurt her but getting nowhere. John came around and took over. He lifted her straight up in the air until her feet came free, then tossed her into the car before she could brace herself again. She landed next to Leigh with an outraged sob behind her gag.

There had to be some mistake, Leigh thought as the men went into a huddle beside the car. The refrain played over and over. There had to be some mistake. John was her favorite client. The savior of Al-Bab. Winner of the Silver Star. Devoted father of Bryce. He wouldn't do this. He was John Stoddard, American Hero.

Then she thought of Hunter Beck, American Billionaire. He must have offered John more money than he ever knew existed, and all he had to do was bring the man his own wife. The irresistible force of Hunter Beck met an ultimately movable object in John Stoddard.

Jenna hadn't imagined the prowler outside her window that night in April. Hunter had in fact sent one of his goons to her parents' house, and not just to spy on her either. It was reconnaissance for the ultimate plan to abduct her, a plan she thwarted when she went into hiding. And Leigh realized something more: she hadn't imagined her own prowler either. That was John Stoddard, too, surveilling her in case she could lead him to Jenna's hideaway. To get close to her, he went undercover as a loving parent longing to be reunited with his child, the perfect cover story to win her trust and admiration. He groomed her the way a spy groomed an enemy asset.

Now she understood why Hunter dropped his appeal. It was a smoke screen. It was all a smoke screen, the way he ingratiated himself to Carrie and Fred, his public appeal and million-dollar reward. All designed to lull Leigh into complacency so she'd be the patsy they needed her to be. So she'd play her part in this black op.

Jenna was glaring at her with hot teary eyes, and she was right to blame her. John was driving the car, but it was Leigh who was delivering her to Hunter, all but tied up with a bow. Or rather, with cable ties around her wrists and ankles.

But she could see that Jenna was livid, not frightened, and after a minute Leigh stopped struggling, too. There was no cause for panic. Hunter wouldn't allow any harm to come to Jenna, not before the baby was born, and as for Leigh, she was nothing but a means to an end. A tool.

Sometimes we go in loud, John had said, but sometimes we go in real quiet. He'd been able to penetrate all of the building's electronic defenses, but not Jenna's customized security. For that he needed a special tool. A Trojan horse.

Leigh.

Chapter Forty-Five

The rain ended before midnight, and Pete lay awake for hours listening to the quiet. The triple-glazed windows blocked out all the noises of the night, and the only thing he could hear was the faint hum of the AC in the vast, empty space. That was good, it was the mark of a well-built house—no settling creaks, no pipe groans, no rattles in the ductwork—but it was driving him crazy. He couldn't sleep with all that quiet going on. No sounds came from across the hall either. Kip must be lying awake, too, listening to nothing.

He squinted at the luminous digits on the clock. After two. He got up and padded to the bathroom, and his reflection blinked back wildly as he switched on the lights. He looked like a wild man with his unruly hair and his thick black beard. He looked like a lost man stumbling out of the wilderness.

He spread a towel over the vanity top and got out the scissors and sheared off most of the growth, then took the electric clippers and buzzed them over his face. The clumps of coarse black hair collected like autumn leaves on the towel. Then he lathered up and scraped the rest off with a razor until he was smooth and hairless again. He peered closely in the mirror. He thought he'd see his old self again, but he didn't. His skin was a sickly white where the beard had been, and his cheeks more gaunt than he remembered. And when did he get that hound dog look in his eyes?

Sleep might help, and he ought to try and get some. He went back to his cot and searched on his phone for a white noise app. There were a bunch of them. Relaxation, Soundscape, Ambience, Sleep Miracle. It would take a miracle, he thought. White noise wouldn't do it. What he needed was an app that would shut down his brain altogether. He did a search for *instant coma,* and as the results started to load, an alarm went off.

His head snapped up. It was a high-pitched whistle alternating with a deep-throated clanging like a fire truck. He jumped to his feet. He'd tested all the alarm systems in the house and didn't remember any of them sounding like that. Could it be the CO_2 monitor in the basement? He put on pants and shoes and was halfway down the stairs when he realized the alarm wasn't inside the house. It was coming from outside, and it was loud enough that all the heavy-duty sound insulation couldn't block it.

He ran out the front door. The sound was even more ear-piercing out here. The sky flashed red for a second, and he sniffed the air for smoke, but it only smelled like pine and hay. The red glow came again, and he tracked it to the place next door. Lights were flashing on and off inside the Hermitage walls.

The door slammed behind him, and Kip ran out, shirtless and bare-foot. "What?" he panted. "What is it?"

"Wait here," Pete told him. "Don't move."

He jogged down the front lawn and along the road. A police car was barreling toward him with its light bar whirling. Another one was close on its tail. The first car cut its wheels and spun into the drive of the Hermitage, and when the second followed tight behind, Pete was sure they were both going to crash into the gates. But they disappeared from sight without any bang of smashing metal. The gates must be open.

Another fifty yards along the side of the road and he saw it for himself. The cop cars were inside the courtyard, their headlights angled at a third car parked at the steps of the mansion. A few figures stood silhouetted in the center of the triangle. Three cops standing with their legs spread, their hands at their belts, while a fourth man ranted at them, his arms flapping wildly as he screamed through the clamor of the alarm.

Abruptly the racket ended, and the red beacon stopped flashing, too.

A fourth cop had disabled the alarm on the security control panel. Pete recognized him as he came closer. "Sergeant Hooper?" he called as soon as his ears stopped ringing.

The cop looked up. "Oh, hey. Mr. Conley, right? How's it going?"

Pete bristled a little at the friendly greeting. Like Kip wasn't going on trial today. Though in fairness, maybe the cop didn't know. His name wasn't on the government's witness list. "Some kind of trouble here?" he asked.

"Security system tripped an alarm. You didn't happen to see or hear anything, did you? Other than the obvious?"

He shook his head. "Somebody break in?"

Hooper shrugged. "Fella claims the gate was open and he just drove in, looking to retrieve some property. Place is empty, no harm, no foul. According to him."

Pete leaned around him for a look. The third car in the courtyard was a silver Porsche, and Drew Miller was pacing circles beside it, still ranting but now into his phone. Pete rolled his eyes. "Let me guess. A camera drone."

The cop's left eyebrow went up. "You know this guy?"

"Yeah," Pete muttered. "I'm building his house."

Hooper looked back at Miller, then up the hill at Hollow House. His face said the word his mouth wouldn't. *Asshole.* Pete hid his smirk.

"Hey, nice work there," Hooper said instead. "I've been watching that place go up while I drive patrol. Boy, what I wouldn't give to live in a house like that."

"You and me both." Inside the courtyard Miller was trying to thrust his phone at one of the other cops and yelling something about his lawyer. "You gonna arrest him?"

"Nah. We'll contact the owner through the alarm company and see if they want to press charges. But if the gate was unlocked like he says, it would only be for trespass. Worst case, he'll get a citation in the mail."

Pete shook his head in disgust. Kip would have been locked up if he'd climbed over that wall. What a day to be reminded of the injustices of the justice system.

"You have a good day, Mr. Conley."

"Yeah. You do the same."

Kip was still on the front lawn where Pete had left him, but somehow Yana Miller was with him now. She must have ninjaed her way over here while Pete was talking to Hooper. Now she was up in Kip's face, her hands beating the air to punctuate whatever it was she was saying to him. Belated complaints about his work, Pete guessed, until she placed the flat of her palm on his hairless chest. Kip jerked away and said something with a quick shake of his head, and she turned and flounced away.

"Hey!" Pete yelled, but too late. She ran past him too close to the edge of the drive, and there, sure enough, was the puncture wound of one slender high heel in the uncured concrete. "What was all that?" he said when he caught up with Kip.

"She, uh, she wanted to wish me luck."

"Kind of handsy about it, wasn't she?"

"It's a Russian thing, I guess."

"Let's get back to bed. Big day tomorrow." He winced after he said it. Like it was a soccer match or something. Kip said nothing. He turned and trudged up to the house.

Pete looked back at the heel print in the concrete. He decided he wouldn't bother to fix it. The Millers would just have to live with it.

"Scream all you want," Stoddard said as he reached for the duct tape on Jenna's mouth.

The rising sun poured a pale pink light over the fallow fields that surrounded the dilapidated farmhouse. It was an isolated shack miles down a lonely dirt road with not even the muted glow of a distant porch light to give hope of a neighbor nearby. Rural Virginia was strewn with these old abandoned farms. If they were even still in Virginia. The roads were dark and unfamiliar, and Leigh had lost all her bearings along the way.

"Fuck you," Jenna said as the gag came off, but she didn't scream. She was all defiance now. "My name is Jenna Dietrich," she announced loudly as he cut through the cable ties around her ankles. "My soon-to-be-ex-husband is Hunter Beck and he hired you to kidnap me. I'm nine months pregnant, and you two men kidnapped me from my apartment in Arlington and brought me to this shack down a long dirt road in the middle of nowhere, and you're not going to get away with this. You two men in ski masks," she said as Stoddard handed her over to Charlie. "You tall man in charge and you other man with the hillbilly accent. You are not going to get away with this."

Jenna had two hours—or three? Leigh had lost track of time, too—to plan what to say when her gag came off, and this was what she came up with. A bizarre speech that sounded either like a screed or a voice-over narration in a movie about her life. Stoddard was still snickering at it as he came around to cut through the bindings on Leigh's ankles and haul her out of the car.

He didn't remove her duct-tape gag, not that she would have screamed anyway. She was mute with fury at him. At herself. At what an easy mark she turned out to be. She stared at him through narrowed eyes, and he stared back through the holes in his ski mask. She didn't understand why he still wore the mask. Obviously she knew who he was. It was only Jenna he was concealing himself from, and when Leigh was finally free to call the police, she would identify him by name and every other biographic fact she could muster. So why bother to hide his face from Jenna? Charlie still wore his ski mask, too, even though rivulets of sweat ran down his muscled neck. She couldn't work it out.

A gnarled old sycamore overhung the ramshackle house, and the path to the side door was knobby with twisted tree roots. Weeds choked the skirting of the porch, and the floorboards sagged with rot. The men herded them up the splintered steps and inside. The kitchen had been stripped of all its appliances and most of the copper pipes in its shredded walls. It was a strange place to choose for the rendezvous with Hunter. Leigh would have expected them to meet at a helipad where Hunter would be standing by with a team of obstetric doctors and nurses ready to whisk Jenna off to a private suite at New York–Presbyterian. But she supposed Hunter chose this place to avoid the paparazzi and other prying eyes. There'd be no one but Leigh to witness the handoff at a derelict farmhouse in the middle of nowhere.

Stoddard opened a door in the wall beside the grimy outline of where a refrigerator once stood. "In you go."

He herded them into a tiny windowless room, an old pantry, Leigh guessed, though there was nothing in it now but cracked-lathe walls and peeling linoleum on the floor. There was no light in the room either, and it went dark as soon as the door closed behind them. It smelled of mice and mildew.

"You're fired," Jenna said to Leigh. "I hope you know that."

Metal squeaked against metal as locks slid shut on the door, one at the bottom, one at the top. "Maintain position," Stoddard said on the other side of the door. "I'm gonna recon the perimeter."

"Roger that."

Slivers of light cut around the edges of the door, enough for Leigh to make out Jenna's bulky silhouette as she bent one knee, then the other, and awkwardly lowered herself to the floor. "I told you. Didn't I tell you?" Jenna grunted as she landed. "But nobody ever listens to me."

Leigh tried to make a noise of apology behind her gag. It came out like a whimper.

"Oh, give it a rest," the girl said. "It's not like we're in any real danger here. In fact, I've been doing some thinking. This little stunt of his ought to be good for another fifty million or so on my settlement, don't you think? Not that you'll be handling it."

Leigh's eyes were adjusting to the dim light. She could see Jenna sitting with her back against the wall and her legs spread wide. She could see the sullen scowl on her pretty young face. She tried again to make a noise of regret.

"Listen"—the girl lowered her voice—"help's on the way."

Leigh looked at her with the question. *What?*

"Remember my panic button?" Jenna pointed her chin at the hump of her belly. "When you all barged in, I pushed the button. It automatically dialed nine-one-one and started recording and GPS tracking."

Leigh peered through the dark, and when she saw the glint of the silver pendant moving up and down with each of Jenna's breaths, she let out her own breath against the duct tape. The 911 operator was on the line and listening in. That was the reason for Jenna's wacky speech outside. The police were on their way. Stoddard and Charlie would be arrested, and Hunter, too, if they named him, and even if they didn't, one way or the other she'd see to it that he was held accountable for this in the courts.

"It automatically rang my parents, too, so I'm sure they're on their way." With a snort Jenna added, "I even put your cell on the call list, God knows why."

Leigh stared at her. Her phone was in her bag. She didn't know where it was now, but she had it with her in Jenna's apartment, and the phone never made a sound. It would have rung if the panic-button call had been received. The power was on, she was sure of that, because she remembered trying to call Carrie when she first got in Stoddard's car. She remembered that she couldn't get a signal.

Her heart plummeted as she realized why. She couldn't get a signal because the signal was jammed. Stoddard had a cell phone jammer in his car or his rucksack. He made sure she couldn't call Carrie or anyone else on the drive to Arlington, and he made sure Jenna couldn't call for help either.

The panic button didn't work. The police weren't on their way. She lowered herself to the floor beside Jenna. There was nothing to do but wait this out.

Karen and Gary were waiting on the courthouse steps, and Kip gave a dutiful peck to his mother's cheek. "You look nice," she said, running her eyes over his graduation-funeral-trial suit. "You shaved your beard," she said next, to Pete, and Kip shot him a look. He hadn't noticed until that moment. Other things on his mind.

Inside they had to wait in line at a metal detector and place the contents of their pockets on the conveyor belt. The guard held out a bin for them to deposit their phones into. No electronic devices allowed in the courtroom.

Shelby was outside the courtroom door with Frank Nobbin and her paralegal, Britta. Today she wore a navy-blue suit with a white blouse and heels no more than two inches high. Pete almost didn't recognize her.

She looked past him down the corridor and frowned before she turned to give cursory handshakes all around. Gary was so far on his best behavior. "Good to meet you," he said, pumping Shelby's hand. "Heard good things." He must have googled her, Pete thought, and wanted to impress this woman who so impressed him.

Shelby sent another glance down the corridor and whispered something to Frank before she led them through the double doors into the courtroom. It was a stately, old-fashioned room with twenty-foot ceilings and an elevated bench clad in the kind of intricate carved wood paneling nobody knew how to do anymore. A woman was already there, on her feet at one of the lawyer tables on the other side of the rail. Pete recognized her as the harried-looking woman from the bail hearing. Andrea Briggs. She was laying out file folders in an orderly line across the table. She paused briefly to shake Shelby's hand and resumed work. Color-coded file tabs fluttered along the edge of each folder.

Britta got busy doing the same on their side of the courtroom while Shelby pointed the rest of them to their seats. "Kip, up here beside me. Pete, sit here please." She pointed to the first row behind Kip, behind the rail. "And Dr. and Mrs. March, right here." Seating arrangements were followed by a two-minute tutorial on how to conduct themselves. No eye rolling during the Commonwealth's opening, no gasps or guffaws or other outcry. Tears were all right, she said with a glance at Karen, but only if they were silent. They should show love and support for Kip. All other emotions were banished.

An oversize wall clock hung over the jury box, the kind with mechanical gears that made an audible tick-tock with every advancing second. Pete checked it against his watch.

At nine fifteen, the front doors opened and the courtroom functionaries came out. Pete watched them set up at their stations in the shadow of the bench. Six feet in front of him was the rigid plane of Kip's back. He'd never seen him sit up so straight in his life. For the first time he noticed that he'd filled out some over the summer. The fabric of his suit coat stretched taut across his shoulder blades.

The rear doors crashed open, and a different kid in a suit came swaggering down the center aisle with a briefcase swinging at his side. He was thirty, tops, but he wore his hair in the elaborate blow-dried style of a fifty-year-old TV evangelist. Shelby got to her feet, and so did Andrea Briggs, but only long enough to shift over to second-chair position at the government's table. This had to be the trial attorney the Commonwealth put on the case. Seth Rodell.

He shook Shelby's hand, briefly and with no smile. He didn't look at Kip at all. He slammed his briefcase on the table and swept aside all of the carefully ordered and annotated files Briggs had laid out for him. Pete watched her face and saw the resentment flicker over it before her eyes hooded. She had at least ten years on him.

The clock ticked and everyone waited, the lawyers at their tables, the parents in their pews, the functionaries staring straight ahead at nothing, like they were audience volunteers in a hypnotist's show. Five minutes stretched to ten then twenty. Frank Nobbin came in and shook his head at Shelby. She sighed as he took his seat behind her.

At last the bailiff came out. "Be upstanding," he shouted, and as everyone lurched to their feet, the judge's black robes flapped into view and he took the bench.

"Be seated."

He was younger than Pete expected, early forties, a shrewd-looking guy with a narrow nose and chin, wire-rimmed glasses, and a brush of brown hair over a high forehead. "Good morning," he said in a reedy tenor. His gaze swept out over the courtroom and landed at the prosecutor's table. "Mr. Rodell. Ms. Briggs."

"Good morning, Your Honor." Rodell spoke for both of them.

The judge looked to the defense table next. "Ms. Randolph, is it?"

"Good morning, Your Honor." Shelby rose to her feet. "May we approach?"

The three lawyers went up and huddled with the judge, and for a few minutes there were no sounds in the courtroom but the tick-tock of time and the rasp of indecipherable whispers. Pete watched their body language instead. Rodell leaned forward as he spoke, punctuating his remarks with a fist against his palm, Briggs fidgeted and swayed, and Shelby stood tall and erect, a woman so supremely self-confident that nothing that happened here in Podunk, Virginia, could possibly rattle her.

The lawyers returned to their respective corners. The judge eyed Kip at the defense table, then lifted his gaze to the spectator benches. "Which ones are the parents?"

"All of them." Shelby pointed. "This is the defendant's father, Mr. Conley." Pete wondered if he was supposed to stand, then did, awkwardly, and ducked back to his seat when Shelby moved on to Karen and Gary.

"Good morning to all of you." The judge spoke with a stiff cordiality that reminded Pete of the principal at St. Alban High. Your kid's in real trouble, but no reason why we can't be civil about it.

"Let's proceed. Mr. Bailiff, bring the panel in. Counsel, if you'd turn your chairs around. And the rest of you, please clear the courtroom."

He banged the gavel for a ten-minute recess.

Shelby ushered them out to the corridor. "What now?" Pete asked her.

"Now we pick the jury. And you wait." She pointed them to the bench along the wall. "After the jury's seated, you'll be allowed back in."

Gary took off to retrieve his phone from Security to check his messages. Shelby had a quick whispered huddle with Frank Nobbin, who then headed for the exit, too. His frown looked deeper than usual to Pete, and Shelby had an anxious crease in her forehead as she watched him go.

"Anything wrong?" Pete asked her. Besides the obvious.

"Not at all." She turned abruptly and swung through the courtroom doors.

Jenna couldn't stop talking. Her vitriol seemed bottomless. "He's gonna pretend like this was some big grand romantic gesture. You know?"

Leigh couldn't speak and didn't nod, but Jenna wasn't looking to her for encouragement. She wasn't looking at her at all as they sat side by side on the floor in the tiny dark room. "He rescued his silly little wife and made her realize the error of her ways. He'll probably hold a press conference to declare his undying love." She made a noise like *pah!*, full of bitterness and contempt. "Yeah, it's undying love, all right. For *her*.

The undead. That's what I call her. He refuses to let her fucking die already."

The *undead*. That had to mean Hunter's first wife. Leigh leaned her head back against the wall. So that was his infidelity. He was still in love with his dead wife, or so Jenna believed. That explained the message he had asked Carrie to pass on: Jenna was the only one who mattered.

"She looked like me, did you know that? Or I look like her, I guess. It was so obvious. Even our names. Jenna. Gemma. Get it? He said it to me once during sex. Her name. Just like that. *Oh, God, Gemma.* Then he refused to admit it! He said I misheard him. But that's all part of why he picked me to replace her, you know what I mean? He must have thought I was, like, made to order in one of his robot factories."

This was why Jenna fled her marriage. The reason she wouldn't confide to anyone: Hunter was carrying a torch for his dear, departed Gemma. Maybe she thought it was too melodramatic or that no one would believe her. But Leigh would have. She'd seen people do that, let their love for the dead get in the way of their love for the living.

"It was his idea to get pregnant right away. I was like, God, what's the rush? I've barely lived, you know? By the time I figured it out, it was too late. I was already knocked up. He was trying to replace that dead baby the same way he tried to replace Gemma. But I don't come in second to anybody, you know what I'm saying? And neither does my baby."

Leigh was starting to wish they'd left Jenna's mouth duct-taped as they had hers. But they probably didn't want her face to look bruised or swollen when Hunter came to claim her, and if she complained too bitterly about the strong-arm tactics of his henchmen, he might not pay them what he'd promised.

None of that explained why they kept Leigh gagged, though. Stoddard didn't want her to talk, and she didn't understand why. Was he afraid to hear the things she'd say to him if she could? She wondered if he felt some particle of guilt at how he'd lied to her, then wondered if she was giving him too much credit. But he was still the hero of Al-Bab. Surely a man who risked his life to save forty anonymous hostages couldn't be completely devoid of conscience.

"I know I got that prenup," Jenna was saying. "But after something like this? That's gotta go right out the window, don't you think? Not that you'll be handling the divorce. I'm gonna get somebody better than my mom's girlfriend this time."

Leigh gave a weary nod and slumped lower against the wall.

It was another thirty minutes before the heavy stomp of boots sounded on the other side of the door. Stoddard was back from his reconnaissance mission. She heard him say, "All clear. Time to make the call."

"You sure this number's good?" Charlie said.

"Better be, after what it cost."

"So that's my price." Jenna's monologue was still in progress. "A hundred million on top of whatever I'm getting anyway. Plus he signs away his rights to the baby, like forever. He agrees to that, and I'll tell the cops this was all some big publicity stunt or something. He refuses, and I tell the cops the truth. And you back me up either way. Which, I mean, God, is the least you can do." She thought a minute. "The thing is we won't have much time to cut the deal before the cops get here. So you'll have to do the negotiations. But right after that, you're fired."

Leigh tried to tune her out as she strained to listen through the door. She didn't understand Charlie's uncertainty about the phone number. Surely Hunter would have given these men his most direct private line. And what did Stoddard mean, what it *cost*?

"You want the girl on or not?"

"On. He'll want proof." Footsteps scuffed. "Hey, mask on," Stoddard barked.

Proof? Leigh's eyes opened wide in the dark. *Proof of life*—that was a kidnapping term. Her spine snapped straight as it hit her. Those men outside the door—they weren't Hunter's henchmen. He hadn't hired them to bring Jenna home. This was a real kidnapping. Hunter didn't know where Jenna was, he never knew. It was John Stoddard with his amazing intelligence-gathering skills who knew. He'd been planning this operation for months, tracking Jenna to Arlington, keeping her under surveillance while he worked out how to penetrate her security systems, grooming Leigh to serve as his Trojan horse if he couldn't. Now Leigh understood the reason for the ski masks—so Jenna wouldn't see their faces and couldn't identify them to the police. And that was why they kept Leigh gagged—so she wouldn't blurt out Stoddard's name to Jenna before her ransom was paid and she was released.

But what would stop her from naming him afterward? she wondered, and an instant later, she knew.

The younger man's boots approached the pantry door.

"Hold up," Stoddard said. "I gotta shut down the jammer."

She stopped breathing as his steps moved across the linoleum. He was going to throw the switch on the jammer, and she might have five minutes before he turned it on again. It was her only chance. She hurled herself at Jenna.

"Hey!" Jenna yelled, rocking back.

Leigh plunged her face against her chest. She felt the hard chunk of metal hit her cheekbone and moved until it lined up with her mouth.

"What the fuck are you doing?"

There had to be a button, and she felt for it with her tongue. There, a round stone set in the silver. She pressed her tongue hard against it.

"Come on. Get *off* me."

The stone didn't move. She couldn't maintain contact with her tongue. She shifted to her chin, but it wasn't small enough to penetrate the recessed setting of the stone.

"Jesus! Get off me, you freak."

Leigh moved again until the tip of her nose touched the cold metal. She nudged it into the recess and pressed against the stone, and she could hear—no, feel—the call button click.

"What is your *deal*?"

She rolled away and collapsed against the wall, praying that it worked. That the call was going out this very minute, to 911, to Carrie and Fred.

"Jeez Louise," Jenna groused. "Panic much?"

Stoddard's footsteps returned. The bolts slid through the hasps, and Charlie opened the pantry door. Stoddard stood across the room, on his feet with a phone in his hand.

"Let's go," Charlie said.

Jenna glared at him. "Take a look, moron. You think I'm just gonna spring to my feet?"

He helped her stand, gingerly, and shut the door again.

Leigh scrabbled across the floor and pressed her ear to the wood. She could hear the beeping tones of a keypad, followed by a long silence.

"Jeez, he's not even standing by?" Jenna griped. "He's like in a meeting or something?"

"Hello, Mr. Beck." Stoddard's voice sounded different, higher pitched and strangely mechanical. He was speaking through a voice distortion device. "You don't know me, but I got somebody here who wants to say hi to you."

"Wait," Jenna said. Her voice sounded different, too. "What?"

Then she screamed.

Chapter Forty-Six

It was two hours before Shelby came out of the courtroom, and this time she had Kip in tow. They had their jury, she reported. Opening statements would begin right after lunch.

Britta rushed ahead to meet the sandwich delivery man. There was a cafeteria in the basement, but Shelby had arranged for their party to eat privately, in one of the attorney conference rooms. "Where's Dr. March?" she asked as Pete and Karen got up from the bench.

"He had a patient emergency," Karen said.

"Will he be back?"

She flushed. "Probably not?"

Shelby's face took on a pinched expression before she turned away to lead them to their lunchroom. Inside was a small conference table surrounded by half a dozen chairs. They shuffled to their seats. Once Kip would have grabbed the seat at the head of the table and made some quip—*The reason I called you all here today*—but today he took a chair on the side and said nothing.

Britta joined them soon after with sandwiches and salads in Styrofoam clamshells plus a tray of sushi for Shelby. "I'm going to have to eat and run," Shelby said, but even if she were planning to eat and stay, she still would have outpaced the rest of them. Pete managed half a turkey sandwich. Karen nibbled at a salad. Kip didn't eat at all.

Pete asked about jury selection. "What we expected," Shelby said, an answer that told him nothing, since he had no idea what to expect.

A hard knock sounded, and Frank Nobbin stuck his head around the door. He'd been gone for two hours, and his mustache drooped lower than ever. "Excuse me a minute," Shelby said and stepped out into the hall. She closed the door behind her.

Pete looked at Kip, who only shrugged in response. He went out into the hall. Shelby and Frank were standing at the end of the corridor, heads bowed together as they spoke in low voices. Frank's head came up when he spotted Pete, and he turned and walked away while Shelby waited with a look of unhappy resignation.

"What?" he demanded in a whisper. "What's going on?"

"Did you talk to Leigh last night?"

He squinted at her. "No. Why?"

"She said she'd be here today. She said she'd testify for us."

"Really?" For half a second he felt a wash of pleasure. Until the rest of it sank in. "So where is she?"

Shelby spread her hands. "She's not answering her phone, and she's not at her office or at home. But her car's in the garage."

"Well, then she must be in the house."

"Unless somebody else picked her up."

He wasn't following. "Who—?"

She gave a pointed look down the corridor, and he followed it to Andrea Briggs as she entered a different conference room and shut the door firmly after her.

The panic button floated on the crest of Jenna's belly. Its silver casing glinted in the faint light, and over the next half hour it rose and fell with her sobs like the starboard sidelight on a boat at sea. She'd been sobbing uncontrollably from the moment it dawned on her that this wasn't some grand romantic gesture. It wasn't even the highhanded act of an autocratic husband. These men didn't work for Hunter, and if the exchange didn't go smoothly, her life might actually be in danger.

Leigh was in danger regardless, she knew that now. She didn't know if the panic button had worked. But it was the only hope she had, and she clung to it like debris from a shipwreck.

When the door opened again, it was Stoddard who stood there. Even behind the ski mask, she could see his calm, appraising expression as he regarded her, as if she were an item on his to-do list. A necessary task to be completed. He reached for her arm and dragged her to her feet and locked the door on Jenna's shrieks.

He pulled off his ski mask. His hair was wet and matted under it, and beads of sweat sprayed the air when he shook his head. "Go about one klick north-northwest into the woods," he told Charlie. "You'll come to a ravine. Do it there." He passed something to him, and Leigh's knees buckled as she saw what it was. A dull black pistol in a carbon fiber holster.

Charlie took his mask off, too. His gaze shifted between Leigh and Stoddard. "Sarge—"

"We trained for this, soldier. Mission comes first. Collateral damage stays collateral."

The younger man stared at Stoddard's chest, the bulge of his Adam's apple bobbing up and down in his throat.

"Think about your kids," Stoddard said more softly. "Think about their lives now versus when you have millions of dollars to spend on them."

Charlie didn't answer, but after a second, he checked the load in the gun and strapped the holster to his hip.

Stoddard grabbed his rucksack off the floor. "What?" he said at Leigh's glare. "Why's a nice guy like me doing something like this? I'm a national hero, right?" He smirked. "But you know what? Those medals don't come with a cash prize. Or even a decent paycheck."

He went outside, and Charlie nudged Leigh out the door after him. Flies landed on her wrists. The cable ties had cut into her skin, and they were there to lap up her blood.

"But if it's any consolation," Stoddard said as he headed for the Jeep, "this isn't the way I wanted it to go down. If you would have told me the sheikha's suite number, I coulda gone that route instead. Or if I'd had more time to work around the girl's security system— But that million-dollar reward blew a hole in my plans. I had to move now, before some civilian found her."

She stopped and stared at him as the final pieces fell into place. Stoddard was a highly skilled soldier, a tactician trained to recognize opportunities and exploit them. Jenna's split from Hunter was all over the news, and he saw his chance. He invented a child custody case—probably invented the child—to get close to her lawyer, and even though Leigh had no idea where Jenna was, it wasn't a wasted effort, because then she handed him a backup opportunity: kidnap the wife of a wealthy diplomat instead. She even did the legwork for him by infiltrating the embassy and installing Devra in a hotel. If only he hadn't made the mistake of bribing the wrong waiter for her suite number. So back to Plan A. He tracked Jenna to Arlington and used Leigh again to infiltrate the fortress and extract the target. Hunter Beck was by far the richer man, so this was by far the better outcome. The only downside was that now there was a witness to neutralize.

Charlie pushed her along the path past Stoddard, where he stood by the open door of the Jeep. The sun filtered through the leaves of the sycamore and lit up a small patch of white at his throat. It was the Nike logo at the neck of his athletic shirt. She stared at it as Charlie gave her another shove. There in the shadows as Stoddard climbed into the black SUV—that flash of white looked exactly like a priest's collar.

She stopped, so abruptly Charlie slammed into her.

Stoddard started the engine and took off down the dirt road, and Leigh watched him go with the blood congealing on her wrists. The mission came first. That was his guiding principle, and it must have been guiding him the night of the accident, too. The night he stopped at the scene of an accident before he drove on to do recon outside Jenna's bedroom window. His mission was his priority, and he wasn't going to jeopardize it by staying until the police arrived or by coming forward afterward. He left the scene and never looked back.

"Let's go," Charlie said.

She tilted her head up to the sky. It was a clear, piercing blue. The sun wasn't yet overhead—incredibly, it was still morning. Hot, though.

A steamy August day. The kind of day meant for the beach or the pool. So many days like this the children begged her to take them to the beach. She regretted every single day she went to the office instead. She had so many regrets.

"Let's go," he said again.

She stumbled through the weeds. A lifetime of regrets heaped upon regrets, and the greatest of these was Kip. He was telling the truth about the roadside priest, the whole time he was telling the truth. And what did she do but turn him out of his home and call him a liar?

Don't be mad at Kip! It wasn't his fault! The dog ran right out in front of us. There was nothing we could do!

We. Even Chrissy tried to tell her, but she wouldn't hear it.

She wasn't a saint. She did one selfish act. She let Christopher take the blame.

Fourteen people sat in the jury box, twelve plus the two alternates. White, black, and brown. Nine women and four men. Kip's peers, supposedly, but they were all two or three times his age. Meanwhile a dozen spectators had settled into the rows across the aisle, all men, who looked like they were four times Kip's age.

"Who're all the old-timers?" Pete whispered across the rail.

It was Frank Nobbin who turned to answer him. "Professional watchers."

"Huh?"

"This is what they do. Spend their days sitting in on trials."

"Why?"

"Beats daytime TV."

"Be upstanding," the bailiff called.

The judge returned to his perch and made a little canned speech to the jurors. He thanked them for their service and reminded them of their oaths, cautioned them against conversations and contacts outside the courtroom, and pointed out the defendant and his parents. Karen's hands trembled in her lap when the jurors' eyes turned her way. Pete tried to reassure her with his own hand over hers, and she gripped tight to his fingers. The jury probably thought they were husband and wife, and for a minute he couldn't help imagining it. None of this would have happened if they'd stayed married. If they were still a little nuclear family unfractured by divorce. If he hadn't married Leigh and moved Kip into her house. If Chrissy could still be alive in some alternative universe.

The judge delivered a few more well-rehearsed remarks about the purpose and limitations of opening statements and yielded the floor to the Commonwealth.

Seth Rodell leaned back in his chair and gazed at the jurors for a long, dramatic moment before he pushed up from the table. Briggs tried to pass him a stack of note cards, but he brushed her aside and strolled to the jury box with his hands in his pockets. He began by telling the jurors that the Office of Commonwealth's Attorney was charged with the awesome responsibility of investigating crimes against the people and deciding when and how to charge the culprits and bring them to justice. It was his honor and privilege to carry out that duty here today.

"This case is about two people," he said as the jurors sat with impassive faces. "You heard their names during voir dire. Christopher Conley and Christine Porter. You see Christopher there at the defense table. But you don't see Christine. You won't. Thanks to Christopher, no one will see her ever again."

Pete clenched his fists and struggled to keep his own face impassive as Rodell rambled on about privileged suburban youth, their recklessness, their heedlessness for the rights and safety of others, their sense of supreme entitlement. "You've seen them on our roads. In our coffee shops and restaurants. Christopher Conley was one of them, a young man who took the world as his oyster. Reckless, self-involved, utterly heedless of the consequences of his actions."

Karen sniffled softly and dabbed at her eyes with a tissue while Pete gritted his teeth. Rodell was a youth himself, the beneficiary of all his own privileges, and here he was delivering the rant of an old man. *You damn kids get off my lawn.* These couldn't be the words of this kid. They had to be written by, or at least for, his boss in his office upstairs. Boyd Harrison, the man who had set all this in motion and couldn't be bothered to show his face in the courtroom.

"On a rainy Friday night last spring," Rodell went on, "Christopher Conley took a vehicle without the owner's permission, on a suspended driver's license, and drove to a party. An illegal, underage alcohol and drug party right here in our county." Ryan Atwood's party sounded like an orgiastic bacchanalia in his telling, packed with similarly entitled young people who drank alcohol to excess, took drugs, and engaged in sexual acts with random partners. "Christopher Conley drank beer at that party. He drank tequila. He smoked marijuana. Then he got into that vehicle, the one he had no right to drive, and he drove it so recklessly that not three miles later he swerved off the road, across a ditch, and crashed head-on into a tree.

"Which would be bad enough," he said. "But sitting in the passenger seat beside him was a fourteen-year-old girl. Christine Porter. A little girl not even in high school yet. A good girl. Her parents' pride and joy. She wasn't a guest at that illegal party. She never would have gone there on her own. She only went to get Christopher to leave. She was on an errand of mercy. And what did she get for her trouble? Christopher crashed into the tree, and an artery burst in her brain, and there was nothing the doctors could do to save her. Twelve hours later she was dead. A sweet young girl at the very beginning of her life. And now, thanks to the selfishness, the thoughtlessness, the utter recklessness of one entitled, privileged, overindulged young man, that life has ended."

Karen followed Shelby's instructions. She wept silently while up at the defense table, Kip hung his head so low his chin looked welded to his chest.

Rodell allowed those last words to linger before he picked up Andrea's note cards from the table. He previewed the Commonwealth's witnesses and summarized their evidence as if they were housekeeping details, mere footnotes to the main text of his speech. He sat down.

Shelby rose. "The defense waives opening statement."

This was the compromise they'd reached. It was her condition for allowing Kip to testify. She wouldn't be the one to tell the jury that Kip wasn't driving. He'd have to do that himself. If his testimony seemed to go well, if the jury seemed to buy it, then she'd make it the cornerstone of her closing argument. If it didn't, they'd try to reopen plea negotiations. That was the deal.

But the jurors' faces changed as she sat down after speaking only those five words. Wariness crept into their expressions, skepticism, and Pete knew that was the moment they lost.

The sun dimmed when they reached the woods, and the air cooled a few degrees under the ceiling of black-green leaves. Leigh slanted her eyes at Charlie, at his young, muscular body. There was no way he wouldn't catch her if she made a run for it, but she couldn't think of a reason not to try. She was going to die either way. So many times the hapless victim on TV went along willingly to his execution, and so many times she yelled at the screen: *Run! The worst he can do to you is what he's already planning to do!*

The worst Charlie could do was shoot her, which was exactly what he was planning to do.

She took a breath and stumbled hard against him as if she'd tripped, and in the second he took to recover his balance, she rocketed away from him. She ran full-out, her legs pumping and the muscles in her flanks bunching up and stretching out farther than she'd ever stretched them before. She couldn't draw in enough air through her nose alone, and after only fifty yards, her lungs were bursting, but she kept on running. She didn't dare pause to look back, but she could hear his boots crunching over the ground behind her. She could hear his steady breathing, and the sound was coming closer. He was pacing one stride for every two of hers, and when he grabbed her it was as casual as swatting a fly. One arm around her waist, and she was in the air, her feet still churning, the last part of her to give up hope.

"Sorry, ma'am," he said.

He threw her over his shoulder, and she kicked her legs against his chest as hard as she could. "Okay now," he said and clamped an arm around her calves.

The world was upside down. She watched the heels of his boots tramp over the roots and leaves as he made a slow inexorable march deeper and deeper into the forest until at last he bent forward and deposited her in a heap amid the deadfall. Six feet away the ground dropped off steeply. It was the edge of the ravine. He would shoot her here, in a place so remote the shot couldn't be heard, and roll her down there, in a trench so deep her body wouldn't be found for months, maybe years.

A bird shrieked overhead, and she looked up to see a hawk skimming the treetops before it soared out of sight. Like a lark ascending. Unbound from this earth. Free. Stephen pictured his dead son when he heard that music, and if she tried, she might see Chrissy, too. Was it actually possible, she wondered, that they would be reunited in death? Was there really a heaven where they could be together again? The idea was so breathtaking it made her close her eyes against the beauty of it. To be with her child again.

Charlie unsnapped the holster flap on his hip and drew out the gun and took a step back. "On your knees," he said.

She opened her eyes. Between her and the sky was an old oak with wide spreading branches. A climbing tree, the twins would have called it. She closed her eyes and saw them next. Twenty years old now, big strapping men, but still her children. How could she think of leaving them? Even to be with Chrissy. Chrissy wasn't her only child. Dylan and Zack were her children, too, and she couldn't leave them yet. And Peter. Always and everywhere, she'd promised him. She couldn't leave him either, or Kip or Mia. She couldn't leave any of them to be only with Chrissy. But she knew that was what she'd already done. She let her love for Chrissy get in the way of her love for the living. She let her love for Chrissy get in the way of her own living.

"On your knees," he said again.

She stayed where she was. This was something else she used to shout at the hapless victim on TV: *Why are you obeying this guy who's about to kill you? Why are you doing anything he says?*

He circled behind her, and she moved with him, twisting around on the ground, her eyes tracking his. "Stop," he said. "Turn away." But she didn't. He was going to have to watch her face as he killed her. That was her price for this murder.

He saw what she was doing. "Okay. Have it your way." He jammed the heel of his hand against the clip and gripped the gun with both hands and took aim.

His phone rang.

They both jerked at the sound. The electronic burble was so unexpected in the deep forest that it took a second to register what it could be. He kept the gun pointed at her, but he took his left hand off the butt to pull out his phone. She rose up on her knees as he squinted at the screen. "Sarge?"

Stoddard's voice came through so loudly she could hear it, too. "Regroup! Get the girl and get out of there!"

Then she heard something else. It sounded like the descant in a hymn, a higher-pitched countermelody coming in above Stoddard's voice, faint but shrill. It was a siren in the far distance. Charlie's head whipped around in search of it. "What? Where?"

She got one foot under her as Stoddard rattled off a series of numbers—numbers in degrees and minutes; they must be coordinates.

"What about the lady?"

The siren sounded again, and she gathered up both legs and took off.

The gun was already in Charlie's hand. He'd shoot before she cleared ten feet. She could hear him tearing through the brush behind her, and she waited for the shot and kept on running.

The siren screeched closer, and she heard him shouting behind her. Ten feet turned to fifty turned to a hundred. Her legs had to do the work of her arms, too, and she could feel the acid burn of the strain deep down in her muscles.

A shot cracked and a projectile whizzed through the air, and suddenly her flight became effortless. It wasn't a struggle anymore. She was flying higher and faster, her toes barely skimming the ground. She soared through the woods, so weightless and free she could only be dead, she was sure of it—until her foot caught on a root and she landed in a sprawl on a bed of broken twigs.

She lifted her head cautiously. A trickle of blood ran down the side of her face. If she was bleeding she must be alive. She risked a glance back. He wasn't behind her. He wasn't anywhere in sight.

Ahead of her the sirens swelled louder and closer, and from the sky, a new sound: high-pitched choppy whirring. She got up and started running again toward the sound of the sirens. They were racing to the right—was that the direction of the farm? She wasn't sure, but she tacked with them and kept on running until abruptly they went silent. All she could hear now was that whop-whop-whop overhead. The rotors of a helicopter. She followed that sound to the edge of the woods and burst out into the clearing.

The helicopter was circling the field. Beyond it a police car was parked before the front porch of the farmhouse and a second one at the side. The rotors spun dizzily as the helicopter touched down, the back of its skids first, then the front, until it landed with a hard bump in a flurry of whipping weeds.

A door popped open on the helicopter, and Hunter Beck jumped to the ground. He jogged in a crouch until he cleared the range of the blades, then he straightened and ran like wildfire through the stubbled fields to the farmhouse.

Leigh took a few faltering steps after him before she gave up and sat down hard on the ground. Her face and wrists were bleeding, her calves burned from running, and her arms were numb from being wrenched behind her back. But the panic button had worked. It had summoned the police, and they must have contacted Hunter, already in the air on his way to the ransom drop. Stoddard and Charlie couldn't have gotten far. They'd be apprehended soon if they weren't already in the back of those police cars. Jenna was safe, and as for Leigh—she was alive. Incredibly, she was alive. She closed her eyes and let out a long tremulous breath.

An engine started up. She barely heard it above the helicopter roar, and by the time she opened her eyes, one of the police cars was streaking past her with its lights on. The other one followed close behind. She couldn't flag them down, not with her arms pinned behind her, and she couldn't shout either, not with the duct tape over her mouth. She scrambled up on her knees as the cars whipped past her.

Out in the field Hunter lurched to a stop to watch them go. His head swiveled to the empty house, then back to the swirling lights of the police cars as they disappeared into the dust. Then he clapped both hands on top of his head and fell to his knees.

The pilot cut the engine, and the blades beat a slow circuit until they came to a stop, and the only sounds were Hunter Beck's howls echoing across the field and rippling into the woods.

The front door cracked open on the farmhouse. A uniformed officer came out and stood on the porch. He looked at the man in the grass and went back inside.

When the door opened again, Jenna came out with her hands on her belly and a puzzled frown on her face. Hunter was doubled over on the ground with his arms over his head, like he was warding off an air attack. She shuffled to the edge of the porch, taking one ungainly step, then another. "Hunter," she called.

He couldn't hear her through his own anguished cries. She raised her voice. "Hunter. I'm all right."

His head jerked up at the sound of her voice, and at the sight of her, he started to sob, unashamed, in great heaving gulps that racked his shoulders. "Oh, baby," she said as tears started to roll down her cheeks. She crossed the field and dropped to her knees beside him, and they held each other and rocked together in the tall grass.

That was when the officer finally spotted Leigh at the edge of the woods.

"Please," she cried hoarsely, gasping to fill her lungs as he removed the duct tape from her mouth. "I need to be in court."

Chapter Forty-Seven

Over the course of her career Leigh had traveled to court by many different modes of transportation: on foot and by planes, trains, and automobiles. Traveling by helicopter was a first. "Take the chopper," Hunter had said, and the West Virginia State Police—they were in West Virginia, it turned out—called ahead to someone in Arwen to clear the landing, and at three o'clock that afternoon, she touched down in a daisy-strewn meadow a mile outside town where a patrol car was standing by to drive her to the courthouse.

Her ID was in her bag somewhere in parts unknown, so she went through courthouse security like a civilian. Her phone was in her bag, too, so she had nothing to deposit in the bin the guard held out to her. She didn't have anything at all. "Could I borrow a pen and paper?" she asked the man. She wrote out the note where she stood and returned the pen, kept the paper. She hoped to find a deputy to pass it to, but no one was stationed outside the courtroom.

A young woman sat on the corridor bench nearby. She wore a poor-fitting black suit and was reading with her head down. It took a minute for Leigh to recognize her. "Officer Mateo?"

The woman looked up with reflexive suspicion at Leigh in her disheveled clothes with her hair pulled back in an untidy bun. It was a moment before she recognized her, too. "Oh. Mrs. Porter." She put a hand on the back of the bench and levered to her feet. Hugely pregnant now, she wore a long, loose blouse under a suit jacket that couldn't come close to buttoning. "I mean—Mrs. Conley."

"Have you testified yet?"

"I'm up next. Should be any minute now."

Leigh held out the folded slip of paper. "Could you hand this to Andrea Briggs when you go in? Before you take the stand."

Mateo eyed it doubtfully. It was an unusual request and it came from an adverse party.

"Did you get your wish?" Leigh nodded at her abdomen.

"Hmm? Oh!" Mateo let out a little laugh. "No. Turns out it's a boy. But you're happy with what you get, right?"

"You're thrilled with what you get."

The courtroom door cracked open and a deputy stuck his head out and beckoned to Mateo. "Showtime," she said as she turned to follow. At the door Mateo turned back and took the note from Leigh's hand before she went inside.

Leigh waited where she was. Two minutes later Mateo was back. "Looks like you're up next instead," she said as she levered herself back to the bench.

Leigh went through the double doors. Courtrooms like this one had been her playing fields for more than twenty years. She always arrived thoroughly prepared and eager to get going. Today she felt neither of those things. She stood uneasily at the back of the courtroom and waited for her cue.

Andrea Briggs looked back with a smile. She whispered to the man seated beside her at counsel table and he rose to the lectern. "Your Honor, for its next witness, the Commonwealth calls Leigh Huyett."

Peter whipped around in his seat. His beard was gone, Leigh registered as she started down the aisle. She recognized the tie he was wearing— Chrissy had given it to him last Christmas. But she didn't recognize the expression on his face. He stared at her with a look of raw betrayal.

Shelby shot to her feet. "Your Honor, this is an unfair surprise. We had no notice—"

"She's on our witness list," said the man at the lectern.

"But you gave us no indication—"

"Who is she, Mr. Rodell?" the judge interrupted.

"The mother of Christine Porter," Rodell said. "The deceased."

"Well." The judge looked at Shelby. "I don't see how you can be surprised by that. And I certainly think the jury would like to hear from her. Proceed."

Leigh looked straight ahead as she crossed the well of the court to the witness box. She put her left hand on the Bible and raised her right hand and swore to tell the truth, the whole truth, and nothing but the truth. When she sat down and looked out over the courtroom, the perspective was strangely unsettling. A trial lawyer never saw it from this vantage. The whole courtroom seemed off-balance. All the regular watchers and curiosity seekers were clustered in the rows behind Briggs. The only spectators on the other side were Peter and Karen. She couldn't look at Peter. The hurt and hostility were like an open wound on his face. She couldn't look at Kip in front of him either, and he couldn't look at her. His head was down, his eyes on the table.

"Good afternoon, Ms. Huyett," said the man at the lectern.

Leigh glanced at Andrea Briggs, still seated at counsel table. This was supposed to be her case. She felt even more uneasy as she pulled the microphone to her mouth. "Good afternoon."

He was a nice-looking young man with the same brash self-confidence of many of the new lawyers in her firm. Smart young men—always men—who used bluster to cover up the gaps in their experience. He started his examination with the preliminaries. Her name and address. Her marital status and family situation. From the corner of her eye she could see the jurors' interest sharpen as it was established that she was both the mother of the victim and the stepmother of the defendant. They leaned forward in their seats. Now, this might be interesting, their posture seemed to say.

The judge's interest sharpened when Rodell asked her what she did for a living. "Ah, Ms. Huyett," he said. "Now I recognize you. You've appeared in my courtroom before. As counsel, not witness, am I right?"

"Yes, Your Honor."

"Well. I'm sorry to see you again under these circumstances."

"Thank you." She was grateful, not for the condolences, but for the reminder. She was a trial lawyer. She knew how to conduct herself in a courtroom. She had more than twenty years' experience to draw upon to get her through the next thirty minutes. She could do this.

She faltered out of the gate.

"Tell the jury about your daughter Christine."

She froze. "Um, tell what—?"

"Tell the jury what she was like."

She stared at him. "What she—I'm sorry, what?"

Now he faltered. The question was supposed to be a softball and here it was spiking back at him. He leaned an elbow on the lectern and adopted a casual stance. "Just to give the jury a picture of your daughter. The kind of girl she was."

Leigh gripped her hands in her lap and answered in a low, flat voice. Chrissy was a good student. She liked sports. She loved horses.

Rodell waited until it became obvious that he wouldn't coax anything more out of her. He moved on. "Let me call your attention to that night last April when your daughter and stepson were in an accident. Do you recall that night?"

Leigh took a deep breath. This was what she came here to do. She sat up straight. "Of course I do." She turned to the jury and went on without waiting for the next question. "It was our wedding anniversary, and my husband and I went away for a few days to celebrate. We were driving home late that night when I got a call from Chrissy. She told me she was at the St. Alban police station. She said there'd been an accident."

"What happened next?" Rodell relaxed at the lectern. If all he had to do was inject the occasional prompt, his job was suddenly looking a lot easier.

"We drove straight there, and my husband went into the interview room with Kip—Christopher—and I sat in the hall with Chrissy."

He sauntered out from behind the lectern with his hands in his pockets. "Did she tell you what happened?"

"Yes." *It wasn't his fault. There was nothing we could do.* "She told me that a dog ran out in front of them. It was raining and the road was slippery, and there was nothing she could do. The truck went off the road and hit a tree."

A wrinkle creased Rodell's forehead, and across the courtroom, Shelby leaned forward.

Hurts nobody, protects somebody, Leigh thought. The classic definition of a good lie. But was it even a lie, when it was so obviously what Chrissy was trying to tell her that night?

Rodell decided to move on. "Did she tell you what happened next?"

Leigh hesitated. She hadn't committed to it yet, with that single slip of a pronoun. Her next answer would be the decisive one. "Yes," she said after a moment. "She told me she couldn't get the truck out of the mud, and Kip told her to slide over and he'd back it out of there for her."

"Wait—what?" Rodell took his hands from his pockets. He shot a look at Andrea Briggs, who shook her head furiously at him. Across the aisle Kip's eyes opened wide. He spun to his father, but Leigh couldn't look at Peter, not yet. She looked at Shelby instead. Her citrine eyes seemed to laser the question across the well of the court. *What are you doing?*

"She wasn't an experienced driver," Leigh said. "She didn't know how to get out of the mud. So she told me that Kip got behind the wheel to give it a try. Then the police officer arrived."

"You're saying—?" Rodell stopped and grabbed both sides of the lectern as the spectators behind him started to buzz. "Your Honor, this is hearsay. Move to strike and to instruct the jury to disregard."

The judge looked to Shelby, who rose to her feet to respond, but for a moment she only stared at Leigh. She looked baffled. *Come on*, Leigh urged her with her eyes. *You know this.* But Shelby still stood speechless.

"Chrissy was, uh, worked up," Leigh prompted her. "When she blurted that out."

"Move to strike *again*," Rodell cried.

"Excited utterance!" Shelby called out as she finally picked up the cue. "Rule 2:803(2). It's not hearsay because it was a spontaneous statement prompted by a startling event and made by a person with firsthand knowledge." The rest came to her on her own. "Also Rule 2:804(b)(3)(B).

Exception to the hearsay rule when it's an admission against interest. Both apply here. The testimony is admissible."

The judge didn't rule on Rodell's objection. He was looking down at Leigh with a sharp frown. "Let me be clear. Are you saying the girl was driving?"

"That's right." Leigh felt suddenly, extraordinarily calm. "That's what she told me."

The judge threw up a hand to stop her before she could speak further. "Mr. Bailiff. Escort the jurors to the jury room. Counsel remain. Everyone else, clear the courtroom."

Nobody moved. The jurors were waiting for the bailiff to come up the aisle, and the spectators were waiting to see what would happen next after this unexpected twist in the drama. Whispers darted through the crowd like the hiss of steam from an old radiator.

Leigh looked over to the other side of the courtroom. Shelby's head was bent to Kip's, and her paralegal and investigator were in their own huddle at the end of the defense table. Behind them Karen stood up uncertainly, but Peter sat motionless, gazing up at Leigh. She could see the moment when he began to understand, then she could see the moment when he knew for sure what she was doing. The look he gave her was anxious—*Are you sure you want to do this?*—but hopeful, too, that it might actually work. He didn't stir until Karen nudged him to get up and let her out. With a final look back at Leigh, he followed her out of the courtroom.

It was five minutes before the last juror filed through the door at the front of the courtroom and the last spectator pushed through the doors at the rear. No one remained but the prosecutors on one side and Kip and his defense team on the other. And Leigh, still on the stand. The judge glowered at both sides in turn. "Why is this the first I'm hearing this?"

"I'd like to know that, too." Rodell's face was red with outrage.

"It's the linchpin of the defense, Your Honor," Shelby said. "You would have heard it as soon as we put on our case. Christopher will testify that his stepsister was driving the vehicle, and the girl's statement to her mother that night corroborates his testimony."

"The Commonwealth had no notice—"

"The Commonwealth is well aware that we've been blanketing the media with our search for the roadside witness to corroborate the defendant's statement."

Rodell looked at Briggs, who whispered something before he straightened again. "We assumed that was a smoke screen," he said stiffly.

"At your peril," Shelby retorted.

The judge ignored both of them and wheeled his chair to look down directly at Leigh. "Why didn't you tell this to the government earlier?"

"I wish I had," she said. "But they never asked. They never interviewed me. About anything. And I was too deep in my grief—I'm sorry—it just never occurred to me that I needed to go to them."

"A grieving mother should hardly be expected to take the initiative in a police investigation," Shelby said.

"But you knew your stepson was facing these charges—"

Leigh cast her eyes down. "My husband and I have been separated since my daughter died. I wasn't in communication with him or Christopher or Ms. Randolph."

Rodell gave her a hard look. "Your Honor, permission to treat this witness as hostile when her testimony resumes."

The judge leaned back in his chair and fixed a baleful eye on the young prosecutor. "Are you sure you want this trial to resume, Mr. Rodell? You might want to confer with your superiors about the wisdom of that course."

"Your Honor, if you allow me to treat this witness as hostile, I can establish that her testimony is a recent fabrication—"

"This is the victim's *mother*." His eyebrows drew down sharply. "Think about how the jury's going to react if you try to impeach her credibility. Think about where their sympathies will lie. Think hard about all of that, Mr. Rodell." He reached for his gavel. "This court stands in recess until nine thirty tomorrow morning. But feel free to contact chambers earlier. I have another matter I'd like to schedule if my calendar should suddenly clear."

He banged the gavel and left.

The banished spectators swelled back into the courtroom on an excited buzz of speculation, in numbers that seemed to be greater than were in attendance before. They poured down the aisle and milled around in the well of the court, peppering the lawyers with questions about what had just happened and what would happen next. Shelby smiled and batted them aside like pesky flies. Seth Rodell wouldn't answer them at all. He was busy berating Andrea Briggs in a scathing whisper. Andrea looked furious, too, and Leigh couldn't blame her. She hadn't asked for this case, but she'd worked it to the best of her ability, and she didn't deserve to have it blow up on her this way. Collateral damage, Leigh thought. It happened in courtroom wars, too.

She climbed down from the witness box and pushed through the crowd in search of Peter. Before she could reach the aisle, Shelby was there, blocking her path. "You owe me a drink," she declared. "Or maybe a defibrillator. I think my heart stopped at least twice."

"I'm sorry," Leigh said. "I didn't want to put you in the position—"

"Of suborning perjury. I know."

"Of worrying that you might be suborning perjury." Leigh pronounced each word carefully.

Shelby arched an eyebrow. "Okay. We'll go with that." She stepped back and raked her eyes over Leigh. "And by the way what the hell happened to you?"

"Long story."

"Tell me later." She looked past Leigh to the prosecution table. "Let me go work my magic now."

Leigh cut around her past a cluster of people in the aisle, still searching for Peter, but it was Karen who came at her next. "Leigh!" She gave her a quick, tremulous hug. "I'm not sure I know what just happened."

"I guess we'll all find out later."

"I have to go now. But call me, would you? Or tell Kip to?"

"You bet."

Leigh still couldn't see Peter through the crowd clogging the center aisle. He must have remained out in the corridor. She decided to take a detour down the side aisle. She pivoted and pushed through the crowd behind her, and came to an abrupt stop. Peter and Kip had somehow circled around, and there they were in front of her. They stopped, too, and the three of them stood facing one another, suspended in a perfect triangle, until Peter reached out and grabbed her. "God, babe," he whispered, holding her tight. "Are you all right?"

She squeezed him back, but it was Kip she was looking at. "I'm sorry, Kip," she said. "I'm so sorry I didn't believe you."

"That's okay." A smile tugged at the corner of his mouth. "I forgive you."

She reached out and pulled him into the hug, and Peter wrapped his arms around both of them until their triangle contracted to a single point in the middle of the courtroom.

Chapter Forty-Eight

Shelby came to the house that night. The last of the FBI team had left, and they were just sitting down to a late supper when Pete heard her car in the drive. Together they went to the window to watch her approach, and as her face passed under the carriage light, Leigh's breath caught.

"What?"

"It's not good news," Leigh said.

He squeezed her hand. She looked done in. He'd tried to get her to go to bed just as he'd tried to get her to go to the hospital, but she insisted she was fine. Scratches and scrapes. A little Bactine and a homemade ice pack was all she would submit to. She had other priorities now. First the manhunt for her kidnappers. Now this.

She pushed aside the sandwich fixings to clear a place at the table, and Shelby took the fourth chair. It was after nine, she'd been running at full throttle for fifteen hours and still looked as cool and crisp as the iceberg lettuce on the plate in front of her.

"I waive it," Kip said.

That caught her off guard. "Jeopardy?"

"Confidentiality. Isn't that what you were gonna ask? So Leigh can be here."

"They want him to waive jeopardy?" Leigh looked stricken. "It's without prejudice?"

Shelby gave a brisk nod to Kip then a slower one to Leigh.

"Wait," Pete said. "Back up."

"Here's the deal," she said. "The government's willing to dismiss all charges, but without prejudice. Meaning they can refile under certain circumstances."

"What about double jeopardy?" Pete asked at the same time Leigh said, "What circumstances?"

She answered Pete first. "He'd have to waive it." Then Leigh. "Only one circumstance, actually. Upon discovery of any new evidence that your testimony today was perjured."

A soft moan escaped Leigh's lips, but Kip was unperturbed. "What new evidence? It's not like Father G.I. Joe's gonna come in and testify that Chrissy wasn't driving."

"They mean me," Leigh said in a small voice. "They're betting I'll recant."

Pete looked at Shelby. "Is that it?"

Reluctantly she nodded. "Harrison came right out and said it. *She'll change her story when her marriage collapses.*"

"Fuck him," Pete said, and Kip shot him a startled look that quickly morphed into a grin.

"I recommend against this deal," Shelby said. "Call their bluff. The judge all but sky-wrote his signal that they should drop the case entirely. We've got them on the ropes now. We go back in there tomorrow. Let Rodell finish his examination of Leigh."

"As a hostile witness this time," Kip said. "That means cross-examination."

"Right."

"Like what Garcia did to me."

"Well, not exactly—"

"No," he said. "Take the deal."

"Kip, no." Leigh reached across the table to cover his hand with hers. "It's all right. I'm happy to go back on the stand."

"There's no statute of limitations for manslaughter," Shelby told him. "You'll have this hanging over your head the rest of your life."

He looked straight at Leigh as he answered. "I'm not worried. Take the deal."

"Kip—"

"I'm the client, right?" He looked to Pete. "It's my decision."

Pete hesitated. Was this only his teenaged brain at work? Zero impulse control, inability to foresee consequences, poor decision making. Already he was back to his wise-assery. *Father G.I. Joe.* And yet. At that moment, gazing across the table at this kid of his, he couldn't help thinking that Kip's judgment was the wisest, most mature of them all.

"That's right," he said.

With a satisfied nod, Kip reached for a slice of bread and started to assemble his sandwich. The subject was closed.

But one question remained open for Leigh, and after dinner while Peter walked Shelby to her car, she stopped Kip on the staircase to ask it. "Something I don't understand." It had been nagging at her since the moment she recognized Stoddard as the roadside priest, but only now did it seem safe to ask. "Why did you tell me you lied when we all know now that you didn't?"

He looked down at her, his face blank.

"When you came here on Sunday," she prodded him. "You told me you lied."

"Oh! Not about that. I didn't lie about who was driving. I meant I lied to Chrissy."

"What?"

"To get her to keep her mouth shut." He gave a sheepish shrug. "I told her any kid caught driving underage is automatically banned from getting a driver's license for the next ten years. And she fell for it. She wanted to get her license when she turned sixteen like anybody else. It was the only way I could get her to play along with the cops."

She did one selfish act in her young life, Stephen had said. *She stood by and let Christopher take the blame.* Leigh had refused to believe it, not when all Chrissy was facing was a slap on the wrist. But if she had believed this?

Everybody lies, Stephen said. Even Chrissy.

The twins came home that weekend, and for five minutes Saturday morning everyone was there. The whole fam damily, Zack declared. Peter and Kip were in the driveway packing the truck with everything a well-equipped dorm room required. Then Karen and Gary arrived to drop Mia off before they hit the road to Durham, too—at the last minute Kip had invited them to join in the parents' orientation program, and it was decided that Mia would stay here with Leigh while they were gone. Then Dylan and Zack ran out in their rented cutaways—they were serving as groomsmen in their cousin's wedding that afternoon—and they posed for pictures while imparting some wisecracking words of upperclassmen advice to Kip. And finally Ted arrived, late, to drive them to the church, and for five chaotic minutes, nine people swarmed the driveway, each one related to the other by blood or marriage or remarriage.

Ted and the twins left first, then Karen and Gary, and then it was time for Leigh to say good-bye. Peter gave her a long, lingering kiss in the driveway while Shepherd barked circles around them and Kip and Mia clambered over the back of the truck to tighten the bungee cords securing the load.

"I wish I didn't have to go," Peter whispered in her ear. "Not now."

She felt the same. Three days apart was too much after four months. But she shook her head. "This is a big weekend for Kip. You need to be there for him. That's Job One. You and I have the rest of our lives for us."

"I'm gonna hold you to that," he said and kissed her again.

Kip jumped to the ground and swung Mia down after him. "Oh, wait," Leigh called before he got in the cab. "I almost forgot!" She ran in the house and snatched up her old iPod from the hall table. Peter was behind the wheel with the engine running when she got back, but Kip was waiting for her in the driveway. "Here." She thrust the iPod into his hands. "A mixtape for the road."

He looked down at it, and his breath caught.

"No—Kip! This is a happy memory."

"Leigh, I don't know—" He choked up and had to start over again. "I don't know how you can ever forgive me."

"There's nothing to forgive. It wasn't your fault."

He bit his lip. "It was, though. It never would have happened if I hadn't gone out that night."

"Oh, Kip." She put her hand on his arm. "It never would have happened if your dad and I stayed home that week. Or if we never got married, or if I never hired him to build the kitchen. We can play what-ifs till the end of time."

Peter opened the truck door to eject Shepherd, and he threw Leigh a *what's-the-hold-up* look. She raised a finger behind Kip's back. One minute. "Don't do this to yourself," she said. "You're starting college this week. You need to get past this."

He looked up at her, his eyes brimming. "How?"

"You make her proud, that's how." She put her arms around him and whispered the rest. "You study hard and do your best and be the kind of man she'd brag about. The kind she'd cheer for and stand up in the audience and holler *That's my brother*."

He choked a laugh.

She kissed his cheek. "Make us all proud, Kip."

He got in the truck, and she held Mia by the hand and Shep by the collar and waved them off.

They decided to bake cookies. Leigh found one of Chrissy's old aprons and set Mia to work blending butter and sugar. The morning had started out sunny, but now some clouds were blowing in, and she had to switch on the lights in the kitchen. She turned on some music, too, a playlist of Disney songs she hoped Mia would enjoy. Chrissy knew them all by heart, and even after her tastes graduated to Justin Bieber and Miley Cyrus, she still loved those old favorites.

So did Mia, it turned out, and she sang along to the music in her little piping soprano. They got the first batch of cookies in the oven and Leigh was scooping out the second when Mia looked up from the spoon she was licking and said: "I like coming here. I can remember Chrissy better when I'm here. Sometimes at home I forget to remember her."

Leigh's hand froze midscoop. The sea of her grief began to swell, the wind whipped in to billow it, and she could tell it was going to crash hard this time. "You do the next batch, honey," she said thickly. "I need to run upstairs and get Kip's sheets in the wash."

She did run upstairs but only to her own room. She knew the day would come when nobody on earth remembered who Chrissy was, and here it was, starting already. It was up to Leigh to tell the stories that would keep her memory alive, but how could she when she couldn't even talk about her?

People died, but grief never did, Stephen said. It could be buried and forgotten but it was still there, and it could rise up when she least expected it, on a happy day full of happy memories. And here it was.

For the first time she understood exactly what she mourned. Not the Chrissy she knew and loved. She'd already had that Chrissy. It was the Chrissy she was meant to become—that was the one she'd lost.

"Leigh?" Mia called from the bottom of the stairs.

Leigh scrambled to her feet. She couldn't let her see her like this. She locked the bedroom door and went into the bathroom and turned on the shower. She could hear Mia knocking, and Shepherd barking frantically, but she couldn't go out there, not yet.

She curled up on the bathroom floor and when she squeezed her eyes shut, Chrissy's face glimmered into view. It was a familiar image—Chrissy hanging over Romeo's neck as they cleared a jump. She was weightless, suspended in the air with a look of such piercing joy on her face that Leigh nearly gasped to see it again. She was such a good rider, better than Leigh ever was. Next year she would almost certainly have qualified for the junior hunter events at Devon. They would have gotten her a new hacking jacket for the occasion and new riding boots, too. They would have made a big family vacation out of the trip. The boys would all come along, and Mia, too, and they'd all be there, hanging on the rail to cheer her on. Maybe they'd bring that boy from school along, too—David. Chrissy didn't know she liked him yet, but Leigh knew, and by next year Chrissy would know it, too. They'd be going steady by then and David would cheer louder than anybody. Chrissy's face would turn red when she heard his voice in the crowd, but she was secretly thrilled. Leigh could see it in her eyes.

She could see it all then, Chrissy's life unspooling ahead of her through other horse shows and new boyfriends, through high school and on to college and beyond. She'd get a master's degree, probably, then work a few years for Teach for America. Leigh and Peter would worry because her school was in a terrible neighborhood in the District, but Chrissy loved her work and loved her kids and came home every weekend to visit them and to see Romeo. He was too old for competitive riding by then and she'd moved on to other interests, too, but she came out every weekend anyway just to stroke his neck and walk him slowly around the pasture.

The reel played on in Leigh's mind. She saw dreams she never knew she had for her daughter. Career, husband, children. A house and garden. Hobbies and vacations. Touring the Louvre. Skiing the Rockies and sailing the Caribbean. A life rich with friends and adventure and contentment. She saw Chrissy standing at a lectern with a PowerPoint on the screen behind her and a rapt audience in front of her. She saw her bathing her newborn while her husband hovered with his eyes full of wonder. And there she was many years later, her copper curls turned to silver, holding Leigh's liver-spotted hand at the end. She was weeping but she was smiling, too, for the lifetime of love they'd shared.

It was Chrissy's whole life spinning out in some parallel universe. The life she might have lived but better, because Leigh invented it for her, so it was a life without grief or heartache or crippling anger. It was all a fiction, but she was amazed at how much comfort it gave her. None of it had ever happened, but it was pretty to think it had, and maybe that was heaven enough.

She sat up and wiped her eyes, and after a few minutes more she went to the window. The rain was lashing against the glass, and the wind was blowing so wildly that the bird feeder spun on its hook and spewed out its seed like a rotary spreader through the garden. It was a moment before she noticed the tiny figure outside in the storm, struggling to open the pasture gate with one hand while she clung to Romeo's halter with the other.

Romeo had gotten loose again, and Mia—little Mia!—was dragging him back to the pasture. Leigh raced down the back stairs and out the door and sprinted through the pelting raindrops. By the time she reached the barn, Mia was latching the door on Romeo's stall.

The little girl turned around, her clothes soaked through and her hair dripping wet over her face and shoulders. "He was out on the road, Leigh," she cried. "I called you and called you, but you didn't hear, so I had to go get him myself."

"Mia—you did this all by yourself?"

Mia blinked up at Romeo's enormous head hanging over the stall door, as if suddenly she couldn't believe it herself. "I did!"

Leigh hustled her inside to a hot bath and made hot chocolate for her to sip while she combed out her hair. Mia chattered excitedly while Leigh worked on the tangles. "He listened to me. I didn't think he would, but he did. I said, *Come along, Romeo*, and I made that noise with my tongue, you know?" She paused to demonstrate a cluck. "And he followed along right after me."

Her hair was dark and long and straight, nothing at all like Chrissy's curls, but the tangles were just as tight, and Leigh pulled the comb through carefully to clear them.

"I think maybe I'm not afraid of horses anymore. Especially not Licorice. 'Cause he's my size, right, Leigh?"

"Right," Leigh said as she pulled the comb through the last tangle.

"You think maybe I'm ready to learn how to ride now?"

"I think you are." She put the comb down and plunged her fingers into the roots of Mia's hair and pulled them through smoothly to the end. When she let go, the child's hair floated weightless through the air until it settled like a cloud on her shoulders.

"Let me tell you about Chrissy when she first learned to ride," she said, and Mia settled back against her knees to listen.

Acknowledgments

I spent my life as a lawyer working in a man's world. It was their playing field, and they set the rules of the game long before I joined the team. So I had to learn to think the way they thought, to speak in sports metaphors, and to tune out the worst of the locker-room language. Which is why it's been such a refreshing change, not to mention pure pleasure, to publish *House on Fire* almost entirely in the company of some extraordinary women.

This story would have met a fiery death if not for Jennifer Weltz, who read more drafts than any agent should have to, and who carefully steered me away from a succession of crashes until I finally came in for landing. I am deeply grateful for her support and guidance. And I am eternally grateful to Jean Naggar, who plucked me out of her slush pile and changed my life forever.

Thanks to my editor, the wondrous wunderkind Sarah Cantin, for her generosity and understanding. If Jennifer reined in the worst of my impulses, Sarah gave me latitude to indulge the better ones. My thanks also to the whole team at Atria Books, including Haley Weaver for nimbly picking up the reins from Sarah; Shelly Perron for carefully (and tactfully) copyediting the manuscript; and Lisa Sciambra for spiritedly introducing this novel to the reading world.

I am also grateful for the work of Dr. Sissela Bok in *Lying: Moral Choice in Public and Private Life* (Pantheon Books, 1978), which informed much of Stephen Kendall's lecture on the Good Lie.

A few good men merit mention. My thanks to James Iacobelli for creating a vibrant jacket illustration, and to Will Rhino for his enthusiastic marketing of this book. And finally, love to my one and only. Always and everywhere.

House on Fire

Bonnie Kistler

This reading group guide for House on Fire *includes discussion questions and ideas for enhancing your book club. The suggested questions are intended to help your reading group find new and interesting angles and topics for your discussion. We hope that these ideas will enrich your conversation and increase your enjoyment of the book.*

Topics & Questions for Discussion

1. The novel's title *House on Fire* echoes the proverb "A liar's house is on fire but no one believes him" (pp. 200–201). What do you think is the significance of this maxim in the book, and why did Bonnie Kistler choose this phrase for the title?

2. Pete seriously contemplates sending Kip to Canada to escape prosecution. Would you consider doing that for your child or another family member?

3. *House on Fire* is told in the alternating voices of Leigh and Pete, and occasionally even Kip. What do the shifting perspectives add to your understanding of the characters? If this story were limited to only one viewpoint, whose would you pick? How would that change the overall story?

4. Compare Pete's and Leigh's parenting styles. Do you think either of them is too strict or too lenient? How is their parenting influenced by their previous marriages? How are they affected by each other's approaches to parenting?

5. Leigh is haunted by visions of Chrissy when she looks at Kip, making it painful for her to be around him. Do you see any pattern as to when Leigh is struck by these visions? What do you think these transformations signify?

6. When Leigh attends Stephen's lecture, he discusses different schools of thought on the ethics of lying. Do you think lying is always wrong, and if not, when is it acceptable? Consider the lies told by Kip, Stephen, and Leigh. Do you believe any of these qualified as a good lie?

7. When Kip is arrested for drunk driving, Shelby tells Leigh, "Try not

to worry . . . Even Hardass Harrison isn't going to throw the book at a nice white boy" (p. 14). What is the role of race and class in *House on Fire*? Where do you see it influencing the plot or how characters respond to different situations?

8. People often insist that one should never speak ill of the dead. Do you agree with this maxim? Why do you think it is so painful to admit that those we have lost were not perfect?

9. Leigh reflects upon the extended mourning rituals of long ago and contrasts them with present-day norms when we're expected to get on with our lives fairly soon. How has mourning been observed in your family, or among your friends? Do you think modern life allows enough time for grieving?

10. Shelby sums up Leigh and Pete's marital problems this way: Leigh's daughter died and her husband left her; Pete's son got arrested and his wife kicked him out. Which of those seems closer to the truth? How would you phrase what happened to capture the fullest sense of their difficulties?

11. Over the course of the novel, there are several instances in which legal logic and its complications are laid bare, such as the parental preference doctrine (p. 183). Did any of the explanations for the reasoning behind these laws and how they can be applied surprise you?

12. While reading, did you believe Kip's claims about the night of the accident? Why, or why not? If Leigh never came to believe Kip's story, would they have been able to move past it? Discuss how that might have played out.

Enhance Your Book Club

1. Take some time during your book club for a short writing exercise. Write from Kip's perspective, five years in the future. How has the loss of his stepsister and the ordeal his family went through subsequently affected his life? What type of man is he now? Does he still have a mischievous or manipulative streak, or is he fulfilling the potential Chrissy saw in him? Share your writing pieces with the group.

2. *House Rules* by Jodi Picoult is another novel that centers on a family whose son has been accused of a crime. Consider reading it as a group and discussing the novel in conjunction with *House on Fire*. Are there parallels in the emotional impact of navigating the legal proceedings for the two families? How do age and ability affect how both other characters and you as a reader view the accused?

3. Leigh's cases may seem extraordinary but they are all based on real-life disputes and reflect the actual state of the law. Do you know anyone who had unusual issues crop up in their divorce? Craft an imaginary divorce case with such issues, and put it to the group: if they could choose, which party would they want to represent? What monetary and custody arrangements would they argue for? Are there other legal or ethical considerations that come into play?